MW01229554

Ready to Cash Out

K.L. HIERS

Proofread by Jennifer Griffin of Marked and Read

Edited by Julie Hanson and Brianna Maxwell

Formatted by Delaney Rain

Cover Art by Morningstar Ashley Designs

Content Warnings

This book contains intense sexual scenes with themes of submission and domination, denial of climaxes, collaring with chains and leashes, and mafia themed violence including kidnapping, murder, and temporary character death.

Don't worry. He's fine.

If any of this material may offend you, please do not read this book.

CHAPTER *One*

TREVANION B. USHER was having a great day.

He'd talked his way out of a speeding ticket, gotten a full refund on a pair of headphones without a receipt, and bought new eyeliner with an expired coupon. His mother had always told him that beauty faded but stupid was forever, so he had aimed high and set out to be beautiful for as long as he could and only let people *think* he was stupid.

The cop had honestly believed that Trev had gotten lost on his way to help orphans learn how to contour and was about to have massive diarrhea, hence the urgent speeds he'd been driving. The clerk at the electronics store had no problem accepting Trev was foolish enough to lose such a valuable receipt and talked down to him the entire time he was ringing up a cash refund. The cashier at the drugstore was stubborn at first, but she became desperate to do anything to make Trev go away when he started crying.

His mother had probably not meant for Trev to use her advice to get away with petty crimes, but hey, Trev did what he had to.

He always had a lie ready in case he got pulled over

because the last thing he needed was cops searching his car since it was usually full of nice things that didn't belong to him. He would happily pretend to be a complete idiot because he still wouldn't be half as stupid as the clerk who gave him a refund on a stolen pair of headphones or the cashier who didn't notice him stealing a new lipstick, mascara, and eyeshadow to go with the eyeliner he was crying over.

Shame was unknown to Trev.

It only got in his way, and he had no use for it. He would use everything at his disposal to get what he wanted, and that sometimes meant putting himself in pretty degrading positions. The payoff to these stunts was always worth it in the end. After all, it kept him out of jail, put money in his pocket, and he thought stolen makeup applied better than if he'd bought it legit.

He wasn't rich by any means, but he had food in the fridge, clean clothes to wear, and he could put gas in his car. He had a job, but it was only part-time running merchandise to different vendors around the city for a local business. The merchandise was the kind that fell off the back of trucks, and Trev let one or two things *fall* into his front seat when it was good enough to sell or trick snotty clerks into giving him full refunds.

Trev used to dream about being a movie star or a singer when he was a kid. His mother had encouraged Trev to go to college and get a good education first. She hadn't wanted him to give up on his dreams, but she'd been a practical woman who'd said he needed a firm foundation to stand on before reaching for the stars.

He dropped out his junior year of high school after she died from a stroke. Her death wrecked him and left him completely alone in the world. His father had died right after he was born in an awful car accident, and Trev had no memory of him. He'd only ever seen him in his mother's photographs. He was a modestly attractive man with a dark olive complexion, black hair, and a fierce smile Trev saw sometimes when he looked in the mirror.

He saw his mother there too, and he was very grateful he favored her more because she had been the most beautiful woman in the entire world in his opinion. She was a gorgeous Black woman with dark amber eyes and warm brown skin. Trev saw her in his sharp cheekbones and full lips, and the rich curl of his dark hair currently dyed hot pink. His skin was lighter than hers, but its warm tones were echoes of his mother's brown skin and not the olive hue of his father's.

Trev's eyes, however, were just like his—a piercing shade of icy blue framed with thick lashes.

Trev knew he was beautiful. He was also very clever, and he could sing too. His mother said she'd had a sister who was a great jazz singer, but she had died a long time ago. Any family his mother talked about seemed to be dead and long gone, and it had just been Trev and his mother versus the universe for as far back as he could remember.

Although losing his mother had devastated him, Trev refused to succumb to depression.

He had a plan, and that plan didn't involve any time for feeling sorry for himself.

What he needed was money.

And lots of it.

Trev had charmed his way into working for an escort service as soon as he'd turned eighteen. He went on private dates, let himself be auctioned off at clubs, and never refused a job. He knew he only had so many years of youthful beauty that he could sell, and he didn't care what it took. His childhood dreams of stardom were impossible to reach, but buying a new house? Getting settled in a real home with a working bathroom and hot water? Finishing high school one day and going to college like his mother had always wanted him to?

That was a dream he could make come true.

He just needed more money.

For years, he'd saved and scraped every penny that he could get his hands on. The escort gig was good while it lasted, but his clients kept complaining that they thought he was stealing from them. Since Trev *was* actually stealing from them, he had to quit to avoid the police getting involved. He had other escort type jobs here and there, usually heavier on the *jobs* bit and less so on the *escorting*, but he was sick of it.

Being fucked professionally wasn't much fun when life was already doing such a grand job of it.

Even so, things weren't always so bad.

Days like today were happening more and more often, and he thought of it as a sign that he was finally headed in the right direction. His current job wasn't entirely legal, but he was in charge of his own schedule and he got to keep his clothes on. His boss respected Trev for his quick thinking and sharp wits, and she never treated him like some dumb pretty boy.

He was even talking to her about getting a full-time position at her store so he wouldn't have to drive around stolen merchandise anymore, and he'd picked up some brochures for GED programs he could take online and be one step closer to his goal.

He missed his mother every day, and he still talked to her when he was home by himself. He hoped she was proud of him, that she saw how hard he was trying, and he maybe hoped more than a little bit that she wasn't paying too much attention to the amount of his boxed wine and poppers consumption or how often he hit up hookup apps.

Trev was only human, and he was so damn lonely.

He had zero interest in dating, but he did have certain physical needs he liked having met on a regular basis. He preferred to hit 'em and quit 'em and move on to the next. The men he met were usually fine with that, though there were always a handful of the wannabe hero types who wanted to take care of him and save him from his woeful life in the slums.

Ugh, as if he was a fragile little puppy made of glass who was totally helpless and begging for a big strong man to save him.

Fucking *vomit*.

Trevanion B. Usher did not need any damn saving, and he certainly did not need anyone to take care of him. Being beautiful did not make him weak. Being young did not mean he was defenseless. He found the very idea insulting, and it was absolutely infuriating. The exact second a man said he wanted to be his daddy or take him home to make sure he was looked after was the same second Trev was done.

He'd kicked out a guy midstroke before.

Trev figured he'd try to settle down eventually, but he already knew his standards were set incredibly high. He wanted a man who would be his partner, someone who would respect him and treat him as an equal. Yes, he wanted to be adored and romanced on the regular too, but he wanted it to be because his man truly loved him, not because he saw Trev as some poor little flower who had to be shielded from the world.

Trev was many things.

Delicate was not one of them.

With the shopping bag from the drugstore in one hand and an iced coffee purchased with the headphone's refund money in the other, Trev strolled triumphantly down the hallway toward his apartment.

Today really had been a great day.

Though his building was a dump, Trev still thought of it as home. He'd moved here after his mother died, and it was one of the few places in the world he felt safe. The hallways smelled of piss and mildew, and he didn't trust the moody elevator not to kill him, but it was the only building in Perry City with rent under a grand and apartments that had solid wooden doors and thick iron bars over the windows.

With the amount of cash he kept here, he wanted to be damn sure it was safe, and not to mention protect his most valuable asset—himself. Perry City wasn't exactly peak civilization. The crime rate was high, the police were corrupt, and the mafia ran everything. News stories of people getting their homes and cars broken into were a regular feature, so Trev left his car doors unlocked to save the assholes the trouble and hope they wouldn't bust his windows.

His apartment, however, was on the third floor, had three deadbolts, and required two keys to get into.

He wasn't taking any chances with his home.

As Trev came off the stairwell beside the dreaded elevator, he could see someone was standing by his door.

Great.

His landlord.

Camille Bransby was propped against his doorway, the fog of smoke from her cigarette filling the hall. She was a thin veil of pale white skin on a skeleton, probably a hundred years old, and she bared her big fake white teeth at Trev in a leering smile. "Hey T. How's tricks?"

"Everything is fine, Mrs. B," Trev replied sweetly. "Thank you so much for asking. How are you?"

"Swell. Just swell." Camille flicked her cigarette ashes on the floor. It wasn't as if the smoke detectors actually worked, so there was no fear of her setting them off. "The hell are you wearing?"

"Clothing, Mrs. B," he replied, making sure to put an extra swing in his hips as he strolled up to her.

Trev was wearing a magenta hoodie he'd cut into a crop top, black denim shorts, and fishnets with a scuffed up pair of Doc Marten boots. His makeup was light, only foundation with black eyeliner and a hint of pink eyeshadow—the same pink eyeshadow he'd stolen from the drugstore today that matched his pink hair.

"And what are you wearing?" Trev gestured to Camille's ever-present quilted purple bathrobe. "Is that your bedspread?"

"Very funny. That's hilarious. It's so funny I forgot to laugh." She snorted. "Listen, I got a little job offer for you."

"A job?" Trev batted his eyes. "What kind of job? Doing your nails? Maybe a makeover? Oh, do you want me to teach you how to put false lashes on? I promise I won't glue your eyes shut."

"Cut the shit, smart ass. This is serious."

Trev let his charming facade drop, asking flatly, "What is it and how much does it pay?"

"A friend of a friend needs some quality entertainment," she replied, "and it pays six months rent."

Trev sipped his coffee to hide how his jaw dropped. Six months of rent was insane. He could save enough to possibly start looking at houses by the end of the year. That was too good of a deal to pass up.

It was too good of a deal period.

"Catch?" he pressed.

"Catch? Catch what?"

"What's the catch?"

"There's not a catch. You just go do your thing, and I credit you six months rent."

"Where and which thing exactly?"

"You know which damn thing."

"Where?"

"Down at the Cannery," she said. "You know it, yeah?"

"Yup."

The Cannery was the sort of place where guests could purchase intimate company for the evening. In special and very desirable cases, guests would even bid on the right to enjoy said company. People wore suits and ties, the security was tight, and it was all around a pretty fancy spot.

Trev hated it.

As an entertainer who was usually placed in an auction, he knew from experience that he could only keep a small percentage of the winning bid. It also meant he would have zero control over who he would be *entertaining* because it was decided by whoever had the biggest wallet. In Trev's experience, the more money a man had, the nastier they tended to be. It was one of the many reasons Trev had quit the escort service, and he was suspicious of Camille's job offer immediately.

This didn't make any sense.

Why would Camille be willing to give up six months worth of rent to help out her friend of a friend?

"Who do you know down there?" Trev asked. "Hmm?"

"What's it to you?"

"Just doesn't seem like your kinda place. Are you friends with Bob?"

"Yeah, sure." Camille nodded earnestly. "It's for Bob."

"Trick question," Trev sneered. "There is no one named *Bob* at the Cannery. Let's try this again." He slurped the last of his coffee noisily. "Who do you know down at the Cannery?"

"Smart little shit."

"Guilty."

"All right, look." Camille sighed. "I can't tell you who it is, but I can tell you they're in trouble with the Luchesis, okay?"

Trev flinched.

That was the mafia family who ran Perry City.

"They wanna make some important member of the family real happy, and they described his type." Camille gestured to Trev. "You're it. They told me that you used to do your thing down there, wished you still did 'cause you were so good, blah blah blah, and what do you know? He's telling me all this, and you live right here in my building."

Trev narrowed his eyes. He didn't trust a coincidence, not with this much money on the line, and he said immediately, "Six months. In writing. And that had better include sewage and trash too."

"You got it." Camille flashed a toothy smile. "I'll even notarize it for you."

"You're serious." Trev frowned. "Really?"

"Uh-huh."

"Hmm. Must be some friend for you to care so much."

"The best of friends." Camille blew out a puff of smoke. "You'll understand one day when you have some."

Trev laughed politely and then rolled his eyes. "When do—"

"Tonight."

Well, shit.

Apparently Trev had to get himself ready to meet a gangster.

"Bring me the paperwork as soon as you have it," Trev said firmly. "I'm not budging until I see it."

"I won't even wait for the ink to dry," Camille cooed.

"Good." Trev unlocked the door to his apartment. "See ya' later, Mrs. B."

"Later, T. Be right over in just a bit."

Trev quickly stepped inside, scowling as he shut the door behind him. He locked it back and checked each deadbolt twice before he let himself relax.

Well, as much as he could anyway.

Trev's mind was racing at top speed trying to make sense of Camille's strangely generous offer. He finished his coffee and trashed the cup, pausing to greet his mother's photograph on the counter. She had always loved to cook, so keeping her picture in the kitchen made sense.

"Hey, Mama," Trev said. "You won't fucking believe this. Mrs. B. wants me to work at the Cannery tonight to help out some friends of hers and is promising me six months of rent. Six fucking months." He tapped his nails along the counter. "Something isn't right. Right? If something's too good to be true, it usually is."

He sighed, glancing over his tiny studio apartment. It was barely bigger than a matchbox, but it was clean and warm. He had decorated loudly with bright pastels, beaded pillows, thick rugs, and an army of potted plants. There was a big framed poster of the jazz singer his mother had said was his aunt hanging above the couch, a male mannequin he'd painted pink and converted into a lamp after chopping off its head, a flat-top casket stained mint green that served as his coffee table, and other eccentric bits of decor that made the space uniquely his.

While he did consider this place home, he still wanted to get the hell out as soon as he could. He wanted a fresh start where no one would know his name and he could reinvent himself. He wouldn't have to be Trev the pretty boy —he could be Trevanion the accountant.

The manager.

The chef.

The waiter.

Trevanion the *anything* because the possibilities were endless if he could only get out of this damn city.

Allan Electronics, the place Trev worked for, had multiple locations across the state. If his manager let him take on a full-time position, he could eventually transfer to another city and buy his dream house far away from the Cannery and anyone who might recognize him without his clothes on. He could work, go to school, and finally have the bright future he so longed for.

But for that, he knew he still didn't have enough money.

And getting more money meant taking the job at the Cannery.

This had to be the last time.

"The last time," he said out loud. "It's going to be the last damn time. I don't care who Mrs. B's stupid friend is. I'm just gonna have one last little private party, do my damn thing, and get the fuck out of there."

His mother's smiling photograph gave no reply, and Trev couldn't shake the knot forming in his stomach.

While he was waiting for Camille to return, he kicked off his boots, put away his new makeup, and then kept himself busy trying to find something to wear tonight. He had a vast wardrobe of all things slinky and seductive, and he was debating between a tiny lace thong or a sequined jockstrap when his phone buzzed.

It was his neighbor, Juicy Cusack.

do u know what time it is?

Trev snorted and typed back.

You literally just texted me. Check your phone, sweetie.

Trev waited calmly for a reply.

oh right thanx

Juicy was the closest thing to a friend Trev had, though Juicy didn't usually remember Trev's name even on his good days. He was pushing every bit of ninety years old—a bachelor with no family to care for him and who probably belonged in a nursing home. There was a nurse who came by twice a week to check on him, but Juicy insisted she was a spy and there were listening devices hidden in her ponytail.

He had a penchant for screaming at things no one else could see and often accused other tenants of being aliens from another planet. He ordered Chinese food every night at precisely eight o'clock after taking his dog out for its evening walk. That might have been the most normal thing about Juicy except he didn't actually own a dog.

Juicy would drag an empty leash behind him and carry poop bags to clean up its invisible messes. When people gave him odd looks, Juicy would bark at them and then apologize profusely for his pet's poor behavior.

Trev thought Juicy was odd but harmless, and he'd

earned Juicy's favor when they first met by asking what his dog's name was.

Juicy had smiled and told him it was Barkimus Winchester III or Barkie for short.

Ever since then, Juicy had taken a liking to Trev, and Trev had the unique honor of being the only person Barkie didn't bark at.

Trev's phone buzzed again, and it was another message from Juicy:

> i may end up with extra sesame chicken 2nite if ur hungry

Trev smiled and texted back that he would be working tonight but thanked him all the same.

It was not unusual for Juicy to claim that he just so happened to accidentally order Trev's favorite Chinese food so he had an excuse to visit. Trev enjoyed hanging out with Juicy, strange as he was, and listening to his wild stories. It was impossible to be sure what was true and what wasn't, and Juicy's tales ranged from being a combat pilot to a Michelin starred chef or even a neurosurgeon who saved a former President.

Trev's phone dinged again.

> fine me and barkie will eat it all

> Barkie is on a diet!

Trev quickly reminded him.

> The vet said he needed to lose weight, remember?

> hes old i can spoil him

Trev chuckled and was getting ready to reply, but Juicy had already sent another text.

be careful tonight they want blood

Trev frowned.

Right.

Because that wasn't foreboding and creepy or anything.

Trev knew Juicy wasn't all home upstairs and had said many other odd things before, but the warning sent a shiver up his spine. He was already having second thoughts about the job tonight and now this.

Maybe he shouldn't—

There was a knock at the door.

Trev hated how he jumped. He groaned as he hurried over to check the peephole and see who it was. When he confirmed it was Camille, he showed her in. He eyed a folder in her hand. "Is that my contract?"

"No, it's the funny papers." Camille scoffed. "What else would it be?" She shoved the folder at him.

Trev opened it to retrieve the paperwork inside. He ignored the dread creeping into the back of his mind and focused on one night of work earning him six full months of rent. He scanned the agreement twice to make sure everything was in order before he signed. "There. Done."

"Thank you." Camille smirked. "My friend will be expecting you. Just tell them you're there for the big party. They'll know what to do."

"That's it? No name?"

"Trust me. They'll know what to do, I said."

He resisted the urge to say that he wouldn't trust her to tell him the correct color of the sky that day, instead batting his eyes and drawling, "Can't wait."

"You have yourself a good time," Camille said as she gathered up the paperwork to scoop back into the folder. "I'll send you a copy later. Be seein' you."

"Bye." Trev followed her to the door so he could lock up behind her. He checked the locks to make sure they were secured and then turned his attention back to his wardrobe. He had a few hours to kill before he needed to leave, and he still had to figure out what to wear. He wanted to make sure he looked extra delicious to ensure a lasting impression.

After all, tonight wasn't going to be an ordinary job.

He had to entertain a gangster.

CHAPTER
Two

THERE WAS no way for Trev to know who Camille's friend was or if one of the lecherous creeps currently drooling over him might be the Luchesi gangster he was supposed to impress.

At least they couldn't touch him yet.

Trev was in a tall plexiglass box with a pole in the middle, slowly walking in lazy turns to show off his body. The box wasn't big enough to do many tricks, but he could drop down into a squat to stick out his ass and give his admirers something to salivate over. It also allowed him to turn his back to them and roll his eyes as hard as he could.

He'd vowed that he would never do this again, and yet, here he was.

He'd painted his face for the gods, keeping his highlights bright but his eyes dark. He wanted his eyes to pop, and he wanted to look alluring, sexy, and a little dangerous.

That would probably please a gangster, right?

The Cannery had a small stage with a short catwalk, and plexiglass cages lined the walls on either side. It was a cramped black abyss of small plush chairs and even smaller tables lit with red neons. There was a curtained doorway beside the bar that led into a hall of private rooms where the real action took place.

The manager had stuck Trev in one of the cages closest to the door, no doubt meant to be a slight as it was not considered a prime spot.

As if that mattered.

There was a small crowd watching him, and he was happy to slowly caress his hands over his body through his black lace panties and matching bralette. His heels were black vinyl, eight inches, and he twirled gracefully around the pole, dragging his stilettos along the edge of the case.

If the manager had put him in the darkest corner with a burlap sack over him, Trev could have still had his pick of any man inside that club.

It wasn't up to him of course, and the red tag hanging on the latch of his cage indicated that his company had already been purchased and he was merely waiting to be claimed. He could practically hear the other dancers gnashing their teeth since the lack of availability didn't deter his flock of admirers.

He saw the same buyers he'd always seen at the Cannery: old men wearing ties, middle-aged guys in polo shirts and khakis, and younger fellows in sports team jerseys and hats trying to look butch. He couldn't imagine any of these pitiful louts were actually gangsters.

Trev would have much rather been at home, eating Chinese with Juicy and his imaginary dog.

Wait.

There.

Three big men in expensive suits tailored to perfection walked in, and everyone cleared a wide path for them. They wore flashy watches and shiny cufflinks, and they exuded raw power and authority with a glance. As one of them adjusted their coat, Trev saw a gun tucked away in a shoulder holster, and he assumed they were all armed.

No weapons were allowed in the Cannery, not *ever*, but they must have made an exception for these men…

Which meant they were definitely gangsters.

Two of the men were nearly identical, maybe brothers, with slick black hair and rough grizzled faces made for radio. The taller of the pair had a neatly trimmed beard while the other was clean shaven. They looked like they knew what blood smelled like, and Trev avoided eye contact when they looked his way.

The third one, however, was a totally different story—he was fine as hell.

He was the tallest of the trio, big and broad, and his shoulders and chest strained the seams of his jacket. He didn't just walk, no, this man *lumbered* like a giant jungle beast. His black hair was thick and curly, and he let it hang loose around his face. His nose had a slight crook to it as if it had been broken, but it only enhanced his rugged appeal.

There was a scar that ran through his left brow and down onto his cheek. It was deep, jagged, like a lightning bolt zigzagging across his face. There was a splash of silver in his dark scruff where the scar ended, and Trev wanted to trace it with his tongue. The man's lashes were so lush that it looked like he had mascara on, and his dark eyes moved over Trev's body, the primal gaze of a predator about to pounce.

Wow.

Trev hoped Mr. Fine was the man he was expected to entertain. He reminded himself he was doing this for six months of rent, but it didn't mean he couldn't enjoy it.

Judging by how Mr. Fine was staring this way, Trev dared

to get his hopes up. Even though the view of his cage was obscured by his other admirers, he made sure to focus his performance to keep Mr. Fine's attention on him.

Mr. Fine turned to the men with him and said something, pointing right at Trev.

The clean-shaven man waved for a bouncer, who then approached to speak with them. There was lots of talking and nodding, and the bouncer gestured to Trev's cage.

Mr. Fine smiled.

Trev smiled back.

Yes.

The bouncer came over to release Trev from the cage, and Trev accepted his hand to step out onto the floor. Trev wiggled his fingers in farewell to the crowd, who parted to let them through, aware of all their hungry eyes moving over his body. He ignored them.

There was only one man whose attention he was concerned with.

Mr. Fine, the very man the bouncer was leading him to. Trev strutted, making sure to hold his head high and swing his hips. He wanted Mr. Fine to take in every gorgeous inch of him, and he was pleased with how his hard expression cracked as he looked Trev over with clear appreciation.

Damn right.

"You know the rules," the bouncer told Mr. Fine firmly. "You and your friend get the room, you do your thing, and no rough stuff. Got it?"

"Understood," Mr. Fine said as he took Trev's hand. He smirked, laying a kiss across Trev's knuckles. "I'll be on my best behavior."

Of course Mr. Fine had a deliciously sexy voice. It was deep and rumbling with heavy bass that Trev couldn't wait to hear groaning out his name. That little kiss was a nice touch too.

"Come on." The bouncer led them through the curtained doorway into the hall and to the suite at the end.

Trev was only slightly impressed. After all, he'd entertained here before, and anyone could rent it if they had enough cash. It was a lush bedroom with a king-sized four-poster bed, a plush chaise, two overstuffed sofas, and a fully stocked bar. A cabinet beside the bar held a variety of toys and supplies, and Trev knew from his previous visits that it was restocked with fresh items daily.

The bouncer opened the door for them, ushering them inside with a polite tip of his head. "You gentlemen have a nice night now."

"Thank you." Mr. Fine shut the door, and he turned to Trev. He was still holding his hand. "My name is Jupiter Prospero. You will refer to me as sir. Do you understand?"

"Yes, sir," Trev replied obediently.

He knew the drill.

This wasn't the first time he'd been with a man who got off on telling him what to do. He knew how to play the willing submissive, and he was actually excited to see what Jupiter was going to do with him. It had been quite some time since he'd been with an aggressive man, and there was something relaxing about falling into a familiar role.

And with any luck, the sex would be worth it.

"What's your name?" Jupiter asked.

"Whatever my sir would like it to be," Trev replied with a bat of his eyes.

"Name." Jupiter tilted his head, regarding Trev as one would a disruptive pet.

All right.

Jupiter didn't like him playing coy.

Switching gears, Trev decided to give an honest answer. "Trevanion. Trev."

Jupiter smiled. "Last name?"

Now it was Trev's turn to give Jupiter a scolding look. Their time together wasn't meant to be a game of twenty questions, and restricting the flow of personal information was critical for his safety. He'd dealt with his share of creeps, weirdos, and would-be stalkers, and his instincts told him to lie.

Then again, Jupiter was a member of the powerful criminal family that ran the city. That presented a new set of risks, and Trev weighed his options. His gut still told him to lie, but his brain reminded him that Jupiter was armed.

"Usher," Trev said at last. He put on a sweet smile and let his eyes fall to Jupiter's lips. He needed to redirect the course of this conversation and fast. "How would you like to begin, sir? I'm yours to—"

"Fix me a drink."

Damn. Too fast?

Jupiter released Trev's hand with a kiss. "Whiskey on the rocks, please."

While that wasn't quite the command Trev was expecting, he did as he was told and headed to the bar. "Of course, sir."

Jupiter sat on the edge of the bed. "Are you from around here, Trev?"

"No." Trev filled a short glass with ice and then grabbed a bottle of whiskey.

"Where?"

"Born in Strassen Springs, moved here when I was a kid."

"Parents?"

"Dead," Trev replied flatly as he poured. He didn't

understand why Jupiter wanted to ask him stupid questions instead of taking off his clothes, but he knew it was in his best interest to play along.

"What happened?" Jupiter pressed.

"Dad, car accident before we moved. Mom, a stroke a few years ago." Trev brought the drink over to Jupiter, standing before him and gazing down at him. For the moment, he could enjoy being taller than Jupiter since he was seated, and he longed to plunge his fingers into Jupiter's dark waves.

Jupiter's brow furrowed as he accepted the glass. "Sorry for your loss."

"Thank you, sir."

"Brothers? Sisters?"

"No sir."

"Just you then?"

"Just me, sir." Trev watched Jupiter sip the whiskey, and he put his hands on his hips.

It was getting harder to play the cute submissive while being interrogated. Something about this felt off, but he couldn't quite place what it was. Jupiter was certainly giving him the right kind of vibes to take him on a trip straight to pound town, but then why was he asking all of these strange questions?

Why did it feel like getting off wasn't Jupiter's goal, that getting something else was?

Information?

But *what*? And why?

Trev didn't have anything to hide. Technically, he wasn't involved with anything that would be of interest to a gangster. What he did for Allan Electronics was laughably small time, and his time as a sex worker was hardly of note.

Be careful tonight.

They want blood.

Juicy's cryptic warning slipped back to the forefront of Trev's mind, but he ignored it. If Jupiter really wanted his blood, he would have skipped this whole song and dance.

Jupiter tugged at the hem of Trev's panties, his thumb swiping down over a dark spot on Trev's upper thigh. "Tattoo?"

"Birthmark," Trev replied.

It was a small splotch that resembled a lopsided heart.

"Cute." Jupiter traced the shape with his thumb.

"Cute, huh?" Trev dared to reach out and drag his fingers through Jupiter's hair the way he'd been dying to. It was softer than he'd thought, and he resisted the urge to give it a cruel tug. Having that particular part of himself called cute annoyed him, and he was becoming impatient.

He didn't want to answer more questions.

He didn't want to screw around.

He wanted to do what he came here to do. He wanted to fuck.

Trev twisted his fingers to tease the barest amount of pressure as he taunted, "I think the word you were looking for is gorgeous."

"Oh?" Jupiter's eyes cut up to meet Trev's, and he smirked. "No doubt about that."

"So." Trev flashed his teeth. "Shall we begin? Or did you have any other questions?" He had to fight not to roll his eyes as he added, "Sir?"

"Kneel."

Thank *fuck*.

"Yes, sir." Trev dropped between Jupiter's spread legs, but he didn't touch yet. He knew Jupiter would probably want to tell him what to do now that they were finally starting, and he couldn't wait. He didn't have to fake being turned on when he looked at Jupiter.

God, he was beautiful.

Trev wanted to lick that damn scar so badly he couldn't stand it, and he wanted to kiss those lush lips and feel them all over his body. He shivered when Jupiter touched his face, and he leaned into his palm with a soft sigh, awaiting Jupiter's next command.

"You're good," Jupiter said, tapping Trev's chin with his thumb. "You wear your mask very well."

Trev flinched.

Jupiter had yet again surprised him.

"I don't know what you mean," he said carefully.

"No?" Jupiter chuckled. "I think it's killing you not to be in charge. You're down to fuck because you're attracted to me, but you hate this, don't you?" He set his glass on the bedside table. "Having to pretend?"

"Don't you?" Trev shot back.

"Excuse me?"

"Gorgeous guy like you paying for it? Please." Trev snorted, the gears in his mind turning fast as he scanned Jupiter's face. "You're only here because there must be something you want that you can't get anywhere else. You want obedience but quality without the headache. Hard to find that on Grindr, but you don't like the bullshit either. The pretending. The *masks*."

"Oh?" Jupiter smiled. "I suppose you think you're what I'm looking for then, huh?"

"I know I am, sir." Trev flicked out his tongue to catch the side of Jupiter's finger. "After all, I'm still here, aren't I?"

"That's true," Jupiter mused. "But let's keep pretending for a moment."

"Why?"

"For my own amusement. Tell me. What if we met in a bar?" Jupiter chuckled. "Do you think we'd still end up somewhere alone together? Would you approach me? Try to charm me into your bed?"

"I don't go to bars but if I did, you'd come to me." Trev didn't think he was being arrogant if it was the truth. He could see how Jupiter looked at him, and he suspected that Jupiter valued honesty. "You wouldn't be able to keep your eyes off me. You'd probably order me a drink, something expensive to impress me. You'd wait for me to drink it and then you'd walk over to introduce yourself."

"What would I say?"

"You'd tell me your name, probably compliment me, and then..." Trev glanced over Jupiter's lips. "Maybe you'd tell me to pick a safe word and see how I reacted so you could take me right there. Or maybe you'd want to talk with me, feel me out to see if I can really give you what you want, enjoy the thrill of the chase."

Jupiter scoffed. "What if I said I'm not much for the chase?"

"You would be for me," Trev challenged.

"Perhaps." Jupiter traced the line of Trev's jaw. "So, what? We'd spend all evening together, drinking, sharing secrets? Would that be enough?"

"Yes, sir. You could have had me from the moment you asked me for a safe word."

"That easy?"

"For the right man, yes." Trev didn't see any point in denying it. "I have needs too. And you look like you'd be the right kind of man to give it to me."

Jupiter chuckled low. "Do I?"

"Big. Strong. No bullshit."

"Is that what your Grindr profile says?"

"Pretty much, sir."

"Let me guess. Sugar baby looking for his big, strong daddy?"

Trev gritted his teeth. "No."

"No?"

Trev held his head high, and any pretenses of flirting fell away as he said firmly, "I don't need a *daddy*. I don't need anyone to take care of me. The only thing I need from a man is a good time for a short while and when we're done, to leave quietly without a fuss."

"Is that why you do this? A little bit of fun without the fuss?"

"Isn't that why you're doing it?" Trev easily deflected. "Have some fun, no strings attached, and we both get what we want?"

"There you go again, so sure that you know what I want."

"You tell me. You're the one who wants to play games, sir."

"Am I?"

"Giving me the third degree when you could be giving me your cock?" Trev arched his brows. "Sounds like a game to me. If this is your idea of foreplay, there's definite room for improvement, sir."

"Just having a bit of fun." Jupiter winked. "That's all."

"Not exactly the sort of fun I imagine you paid for, sir."

"Not quite." Jupiter shrugged. "But perhaps I'm no longer in the mood."

Trev laughed, and he dared to squeeze Jupiter's thigh. "As if you're going to let me go tonight without knowing what it's like to fuck me."

"Wow!" Jupiter laughed. "Your confidence is incredible, baby doll."

"Simply stating facts." Trev leaned in close, looking up at Jupiter through his lashes. "I don't know what you paid, but you don't even care, do you? Because you knew it was going to be worth it the moment you saw me."

"Let's say you're right." Jupiter glanced over Trev's body. "Let's say you are the most beautiful creature I've ever seen…"

Trev already knew he was.

"Do you really think you can give me what I want?" Jupiter's voice dropped to a hypnotic growl. "Can you fulfill my darkest desires? Will you be totally and utterly mine?"

"For tonight, sir, I'm whatever you want me to be."

"Excellent." Jupiter hummed thoughtfully, reaching around to unsnap the hooks of Trev's bralette one-handed.

Trev shrugged his shoulders so that the bralette would fall to the floor. His cock was hard, straining the lace of his tiny thong. He was done with talking. He was dying to get his hands on Jupiter's bulging muscles, especially the one between his legs, but he doubted Jupiter would undress beyond what was necessary to fuck.

Hey, Trev could still dream.

Jupiter touched Trev's chin again. "Stay just as you are, baby doll. You're going to suck me first."

"Yes, sir." Trev's mouth filled with spit from the mere thought of having Jupiter in it, and his heart pounded in a frantic rhythm, nearly as hard and fast as he hoped Jupiter was gonna fuck him.

Jupiter unbuckled his belt, and the drag of his zipper that followed was torturously slow. He clearly knew how much Trev wanted him, and this was a practice in sexual sadism.

But finally, *finally*, they were going to get to the real action. Whatever bullshit Jupiter had tried to weave about resisting Trev and peppering him with weird questions was crumbling in the wake of his clear lust.

Trev had won this game as far as he was concerned, and he couldn't wait to—

There was a knock at the door.

Trev ignored it.

Jupiter stopped just short of pulling out his cock, and he glared at the door.

The knocking turned into impatient banging that rattled the entire frame.

"The fuck?" Jupiter barked.

"It's Emil! Come on!" a gruff male voice barked back. "Let's go!"

"Is it him or not?" another male voice demanded. "You're not supposed to be getting your fucking knob polished in there, all right?"

"Let's go!" the first voice demanded. "Does he have the fucking heart thing or not?"

Trev's blood froze.

The heart thing?

His birthmark.

No, there was no way...

Trev immediately peeled himself away, fumbling on his tall heels. He retreated until his back hit the far wall. "What the actual fuck is going on?"

"Shhh, calm yourself, baby doll." Jupiter zipped his pants back up with a faint scowl. "Let me handle this."

"Handle it, my ass!" Trev snapped.

"I think you meant, handle it, my ass, *sir*."

"Fuck you!"

"Such language," Jupiter tutted.

"Jupe! What's the fucking deal?" The second voice sounded annoyed. "Can we come in or not?"

"You think he's fuckin' him?" the first one asked.

"I mean, I'd fuck him."

"You would, you freak."

Trev decided very quickly that it was in his best interest to get the hell out of there. He didn't know what these men wanted, how they knew about his birthmark, or if this was all some sort of insane setup. Those were all fabulous questions that could be answered *never* as far as he was concerned.

"Your time is officially up, sir," Trev said firmly. "It's been fun, really, but that's my cue to turn into a pumpkin for the night."

"Oh, that's where you're mistaken." Jupiter chuckled as he fixed his belt. "You're not going anywhere."

"Look at that! All those looks and a sense of humor. Love it. Great. So sorry we didn't get to fuck. Bye now." Trev started toward the door, but Jupiter rose from the bed to cut him off. "Move."

"We're not done yet," Jupiter warned. "My family wants to have a little chat with you."

"Sorry, really, but I've had enough chitchat and fucking around without actually being fucked around with for one night." Trev narrowed his eyes, and his lean frame tensed for a fight. Jupiter was between him and the door, and that was a problem. "You paid for me to entertain you for the evening. That's it. Your time went *ding* as soon as your little friends started banging on the fucking door. So, I'm leaving."

"I'm afraid not. I have further need of your company." Jupiter offered his hand. "Play nicely and—"

"Hate to be the one to break the tragic news to you, but tonight was the last fucking time I was ever gonna do this stupid ass bullshit. And wow, it was great to go out with a big bang and all, or not, but I'll be going now." Trev tried to step around Jupiter.

"No." Jupiter grabbed Trev's shoulder.

Trev had nothing on except for his heels, thong, and a growing sneer, but he glared at Jupiter without a shred of hesitation as he snapped, "Take your fucking hand off me or I will fucking kill you."

"Yeah?" Jupiter reached now for Trev's jaw. "How would you do it? Hmm? Tell me."

Fear spiked inside of Trev's very core because there was absolutely no way he could kill Jupiter. Other than the complex moralities involved with taking a life even in self-defense, he was practically fucking naked.

His odds were not great.

Trev hesitated. "You don't want me to spoil the surprise, do you?"

Jupiter smirked. "Please. Try."

"Well... Fuck you!" Trev tried to bolt around Jupiter. "Security! Hey! Code Peach! Fucking Code *Peach*!"

The only reply he heard on the other side of the door was those two men laughing. That couldn't be good. The code phrase was meant to alert the bouncers to come in and end the evening in case of emergencies. Someone was always supposed to be listening to ensure a quick response.

Jupiter grabbed Trev's arm. "They're not coming, baby doll."

Trev immediately went berserk, flailing like a wild animal as he snarled, "Hey! Let the fuck go of me!" He was deeply satisfied when his elbow caught Jupiter's nose, but his victory was short-lived when Jupiter scooped him up like a struggling kitten and then simply tossed him over his shoulder. "The fuck!"

"Settle down," Jupiter scolded, carrying Trev back over toward the bed.

Trev tried to arch up and pull away, but he smacked his head on the ceiling. "Shit!"

"You're going to help us negotiate a little deal with your brother. All I need you to do is—"

"You are fucking insane!" Trev kicked defiantly, wishing he could draw his knee up high enough to nail Jupiter's groin. "Hello! I don't *have* a fucking brother."

"You really don't know, do you?" Jupiter searched Trev's face as if he was actually surprised.

"Know what?" Trev spat.

"Who your brother is."

"Oh, ha ha! You're just hilarious." Trev rolled his eyes. "I already told you! I don't have any brothers or sisters! Only child, remember?"

"That you know of."

"Right." Trev scoffed. "Tell me, genius. Who's this mysterious brother of mine then?"

"Roderick Legrand," Jupiter replied.

"Never heard of him."

"Well, he is known by another name."

"Yeah, and what's that? The fuckin' Easter Bunny?"

"Boss Cold."

CHAPTER *Three*

"WHO?" Trev spat.

"Boss Cold," Jupiter repeated firmly.

The door opened, and the two men who were with Jupiter earlier charged inside.

The clean-shaven one scowled as he snapped, "Hey! We good to go or what?"

"Good." Jupiter still had Trev pinned. "We're just getting to know each other a bit better, that's all."

"Fuck you! You have got the wrong guy." Trev refused to stop struggling. "My mother never had any other kids, you fucking idiot!"

"That may be true, but your father, Boris Legrand, had several. You have a big half brother out there, and he's a dangerous gangster."

Trev tensed.

Boris was his father's name.

He'd thought Boris's last name was Usher. His mother's was Wilson and they never married, but certainly she wouldn't have lied to Trev about something so important.

She would have told him if he had any half-siblings out there.

Unless she had a very good reason not to.

Said half-siblings being gangsters was a solid justification, but that still didn't feel right. Trev's mom had never been afraid to be honest with him about anything, which meant she probably hadn't known about this particular relation.

"Play nice and behave yourself, and you'll even get to meet your family." Jupiter smirked. "Won't that be fun?"

"What the fuck makes you think this guy will even give you what you want for a half brother he probably doesn't know about?" Trev rolled his eyes. "Are you gonna have us go on *Maury* and talk it out or something? Have a big, tearful reunion? This is insane!"

"Boss Cold is very partial to his family, and he's short on blood relatives. That's where you come in."

"That's enough," the bearded man snapped. "You get the thing or not?"

"Nearly." Jupiter reached into his jacket.

Gun.

Jupiter had to be reaching for a gun.

Trev twisted away from Jupiter, adrenaline pumping through every muscle as he finally broke free. He flipped his legs over his head, clumsily tumbling to the other side of the bed. On his feet once more, he scrambled for what to do next.

He was outnumbered, unarmed, and his little stunt had put him in a corner.

Fuck.

Jupiter didn't seem that upset Trev had gotten away from him. He seemed mildly annoyed at best. After all, there was nowhere for Trev to go.

"Be a good boy and come here." Jupiter beckoned Trev over with a finger.

"So you can shoot me?" Trev scoffed. "Fat fuckin' chance, asshole."

Jupiter cleared his throat.

It was then Trev finally looked at what Jupiter had pulled out of his jacket, and it wasn't a weapon.

It was a cotton swab in a sterile packet.

"Sorry, but I'm not into whatever it is you plan to do with that," Trev said sweetly. "How about you bend over and we find a fun place for you to stick it?"

Jupiter chuckled. "Cute."

"Enough," the bearded man snapped again. "Get it already or I will."

"Easy, Sal." Jupiter kept his eyes on Trev. "I'll get it."

"Get what?" Trev demanded.

"We need proof that you're Cold's brother. Just need a little mouth swab, all right?"

Trev eyed the swab. "Ten seconds ago, you were so sure I was. Now you need my spit for some kinda test?"

"We are sure. But Cold will want it." Jupiter smiled. "It won't hurt. Unless you want it to."

Trev didn't like how that sounded like a threat, and he took a deep breath as he again weighed his options.

Limited, not great, and most of them certainly ending in his own demise if he didn't cooperate.

There was only the one door and...

Wait.

The window!

There was a window hidden behind the fancy wallpaper beside the bed. It looked out into the dirty alley behind the club and had been such an unappealing view that the owners had pasted the wallpaper right over it during the last round of renovations.

The club had been flooded when a water pipe broke a few months ago—no, that didn't matter.

All that mattered was now Trev had a way out.

His mind spun rapidly with various scenarios, and he tried to plan his next move. His cell phone and other personal items, including his keys, were in his locker in the club's dressing room. He was going to consider those lost forever because it was too risky to try sneaking out to retrieve them and successfully make a getaway. His main goal had to be getting the hell out of here.

He could buy a new phone later and get the spare set of keys from Camille.

And then strangle her with her own bathrobe sash for setting him up. She had to have known Trev wasn't supposed to come back from doing this little favor for her. It was why she'd been willing to give him such a great deal on his rent, that traitorous bitch—

Plan.

Focus.

He needed a plan.

Trev could play nice for now. As long as he remained in this room, there was a chance for him to escape. He just had to figure out a way to get his captors to leave and hope they didn't know about the old window. Once he was home, he was going to grab all his cash and flee the fucking state. Maybe even the country.

For now, though, he had to keep Jupiter happy.

He could do that.

Trev knew exactly how to make a man happy.

He didn't want to appear too eager and rouse Jupiter's suspicions, so he asked, "Just a swab? That's it?"

"That's it," Jupiter said.

"Well, it won't be the worst thing I've ever had in my mouth." Trev crawled up on the bed, well aware of what a vision he was as he slinked over to be within Jupiter's reach. Even Sal and Emil were staring at him, but he made sure to keep his focus on Jupiter.

"Open." Jupiter tapped Trev's chin.

Trev opened his mouth, and he made sure to flutter his lashes as Jupiter slid the swab in. He wanted it to be a mockery of a blowjob, and he was pleased when Jupiter's lips twitched up in a smile.

"Good boy," Jupiter praised, tucking the swab back into the packet. He handed it to Emil. "Here."

"I'm not touching that." Emil scoffed. "I don't answer to you—"

"But you answer to me," Sal snapped, cuffing the side of Emil's head. "Go on, Emiliano. Run that shit over and put a rush on it. We need the results back yesterday."

Emil scowled as he snatched the swab from Jupiter. "Fine. Whatever."

Sal snorted, watching Emil leave. Once the door shut, he turned his attention to Jupiter. "You wanna keep an eye on our little friend here?"

"I'd be happy to," Jupiter replied. "I'll make sure he's very comfortable."

"I'll let you know when we're ready to move. Just got a few more things to settle. You got it?"

"Yes, sir."

"Hang tight." Sal gave a quick nod and then left.

Two down, one to go.

Trev stretched out on his back and spread his legs as if he was trying to get comfortable. He didn't miss how Jupiter eyed him, but he remained casual as he said, "So. What now?"

"We wait, baby doll."

"For how long?"

"For as long as it takes."

"And then what?"

"You wait some more."

Trev huffed. "So, what—"

"Quiet now," Jupiter warned.

"Yeah, I don't think so." Trev tucked his arms behind his head. "That whole *yes, sir* crap only applied when we were going to have some fun. Now you're my kidnapper, and forgive me if I don't feel as inclined to obey you."

"You'd think you'd be *more* inclined."

Trev popped his tongue. "Yeah, no. I'm good. This is bullshit. You're holding me hostage, you're not going to fuck me, you're—"

"Who said I'm not going to fuck you?" Jupiter's eyes glittered with mischief. "We do have some time to kill."

Trev ran his tongue over his bottom lip, and his stomach fluttered. He knew it was dangerous to poke at a gangster like Jupiter. The chances of getting laid were certainly as high as being whacked, but this was the only hand he had to play.

Jupiter didn't want a perfect little playmate to boss around. Trev could see that now. Jupiter wanted a brat he could bend to his will, a wild thing to tame, and Trev knew exactly how to give it to him.

"Who says I'm going to let you?" Trev challenged.

"Oh, baby doll." Jupiter chuckled. "I know it. You want a real man. Someone who knows how to handle you and give you what you want without having to screw around."

"And what's that?"

"To be put in your place and fucked like a whore and still be taken out to dinner after."

Trev couldn't argue with that, and Jupiter's words created a powerful bloom of heat in his loins. He reached down to squeeze his cock through his panties, taunting, "Sorry, maybe I'm just not in the mood right now."

"Who's pretending now?" Jupiter walked to the foot of the bed.

"Certainly not me." Trev kept stroking himself slowly over the soft lace. "I still have my doubts that you can—"

"Come here." Jupiter pointed to the mattress in front of him.

"Right now?" Trev shivered.

"Right now, *sir*."

"I thought you wanted me to call *you* sir?" Trev grinned. "I can dom if you'd like—"

"*Now*." Jupiter's tone indicated that he was not amused.

Trev had never cared much for being submissive. It simply wasn't in his nature, though he could fake it quite well. He'd never felt any particular joy from being praised and certainly had never longed for anyone to take away his control and dominate him.

Strangely, however, there was a part of him right now that was *excited*.

Jupiter was a criminal. There was no telling what he was truly capable of. The danger had created a new thrill that Trev was having trouble defining, but it pumped adrenaline through his veins until all his muscles felt light, and his cock was rock hard as he crawled down to the foot of the bed.

"Here, sir?" Trev drawled. "Or am I too close? Maybe another inch?"

"You're fine there. You're right where I want you." Jupiter touched Trev's chin again. "I am going to give that beautiful little mouth of yours something more productive to do than talking back to me."

"Yes, sir." Trev's heart thumped away in a frantic rhythm, nearly as feverish as how hard and fast he hoped Jupiter was gonna fuck him later.

Jupiter unbuckled his belt, and the drag of his zipper that followed was torturously slow.

Trev continued to keep his face as neutral as possible, though perhaps he smiled a bit too much when Jupiter finally pulled out his cock.

Big, thick, and beautiful, just like the rest of him.

"Open," Jupiter commanded.

Trev opened his mouth, and he was rewarded with the swipe of the head over his bottom lip.

Finally.

Jupiter rubbed his cock all the way around Trev's mouth, playing over his lips before he began feeding him every girthy inch. "Go on, baby doll. Suck me nice and slow. I wanna make this last."

Trev eagerly took Jupiter into his mouth, swirling his tongue around the shaft as he sucked him. He enjoyed the small gasp Jupiter uttered as he swallowed him down, and he didn't stop until Jupiter's cock had hit the back of his throat.

He bobbed his head, turning at an angle to make sure his tongue slid all the way up and down the shaft. He took his time, swallowing the spit pooling in his cheeks and squeezing the base. He was waiting for Jupiter to grab his hair or fuck his face, but Jupiter appeared content to let Trev do as he pleased for now.

Was he waiting to see what Trev could do?

Was this some sort of test?

Whatever.

Trev savored the weight of Jupiter's cock against his tongue, and he flicked his eyes up to gauge Jupiter's expression.

Jupiter appeared relaxed, though his breathing had certainly picked up.

Trev continued to suck him earnestly, but he was growing impatient. He was pulling out some of his best moves and Jupiter barely acknowledged it. Trev wanted some kind of reaction other than some panting, and he took a quick breath in through his nose before pushing the head of Jupiter's cock down his throat.

"Oh!" Jupiter's eyes fluttered.

Trev continued to deepthroat Jupiter's cock, pushing forward until his nose hit Jupiter's groin. The man's nails immediately dug into Trev's scalp, and Trev would have smiled if he could have. He swallowed around Jupiter's cock so he could feel exactly how far he'd taken him, and then he leisurely withdrew only to promptly suck him down again.

"Christ," Jupiter murmured breathlessly.

There.

That was better.

Jupiter tightened his grip and guided Trev's head to bob on his cock faster and faster. Whatever strict control Jupiter once held was now lost to Trev's tight throat, and Trev took every erratic slam. His mouth flooded with spit and his eyes watered, but he never faltered. He twirled his tongue all around Jupiter's cock to make the most of each thrust, maintaining fierce suction.

Trev could taste the delicious tease of precome, a promise of what would soon follow if he didn't relent. He gasped as Jupiter abruptly pulled out, and he blinked rapidly to focus his vision. To his dismay, Jupiter's expression was...

Blank.

Tepid at best.

Jupiter slid the head of his cock over Trev's bottom lip, playing in the wetness as he took a deep breath to exhale an annoyed sigh. "I seem to recall telling someone that we were going to take this slow."

"Oh?" Trev scowled. "Must have slipped my mind, sir."

"What's wrong, baby doll?"

"Sucking off a rock would be more exciting than sucking you." Trev rolled his eyes, adding as sarcastically as possible, "*Sir.*"

Jupiter smiled. "Were you not enjoying yourself?"

"Were you?" Trev shot back. "Because you could have fooled me."

"Ah." Jupiter smiled. "So, you do concern yourself with wanting your partner to feel good. You want to know that they like what you're doing. You seek validation in sharing mutual passion."

"What?" Trev scoffed.

"That's how you want to be good for me." Jupiter caressed Trev's cheek. "You want to make sure I enjoy your performance thoroughly. It would offend you if I didn't."

Trev opened his mouth to argue, but he shut it when he realized he didn't know what to say.

Jupiter was right, that gorgeous bastard.

Trev did want Jupiter to like what he was doing.

It was a point of pride.

Trev didn't want to simply be another notch in anyone's headboard. He was good at this—no, he was *incredible*, and men had paid handsomely to share his bed. The idea of someone not enjoying their time with him was oddly infuriating, and he hated that Jupiter had somehow managed to zero in on that.

Trev wasn't any ordinary man.

He was gorgeous, he was the best at what he did, and damn it all if he wasn't determined now to prove that to Jupiter and then some.

"What next, sir?" Trev asked, refusing to acknowledge Jupiter's previous assessment.

He would never give him the satisfaction of knowing he was right. Judging by Jupiter's smug expression, he didn't need to, and that only irritated him more.

"Remove your underwear, but please do keep those boots on," Jupiter replied. "I like them."

"Yes, sir." Trev slid his panties down his long legs and kicked them off onto the floor. He spread himself out on his back, letting his legs fall apart to ensure Jupiter got a spectacular view of his body.

Jupiter sighed audibly. "You really are quite magnificent."

"Thank you, sir." Trev rubbed his inner thighs, moving his fingers toward his hole. He didn't touch himself directly, not yet, and instead teased up the line of his taint and cupped his balls.

"Are you ready for me, baby doll?"

"Of course, sir."

Jupiter palmed his cock as he continued to study Trev. His eyes scanned every inch of his flesh, and the tip of his tongue flicked out over his bottom lip, as if he was preparing to dive into a spectacular feast and couldn't quite decide where to start.

Trev remained relaxed, caressing his body in open invitation. He assured himself that he was still in control and that he wanted this as much as Jupiter did.

This wasn't surrender—it was a victory.

He still had every intention of escaping as soon as

possible, but first he had to show Jupiter who was really in charge here. Jupiter's lust for him meant Trev was the one with the true power, and he was submitting to absolutely nothing except his own desires.

Said desires being fucking Jupiter from here to next Sunday and then getting the hell out of this town forever.

"How would you like to please me, baby doll?" Jupiter asked as he lazily stroked his cock. "Do you want to ride me? Be taken from behind? Or—"

"All of it," Trev replied confidently. "I can make you come harder than you've ever imagined in any position. No one can take a cock like I can, and I promise you that you'll be dreaming of being inside my body forever because once you've had me? No one else will ever compare."

Jupiter smiled wickedly. "No one else will ever compare, *sir*."

"Yes, sir." Trev planted his heels into the bed and spread his legs wide.

Jupiter crawled up on the bed, looking every bit like a grizzly bear about to pounce on its prey. He paused only to drop his pants and underwear to his knees and then to grab a bottle of lubricant from the cabinet beside the bed, eyeing Trev hungrily as he slicked himself up.

Trev bit his lip, his cock twitching. He was glad he'd prepped earlier so they could go right to it, and he was dying for Jupiter to fill him. As Jupiter came near, Trev boldly reached for his tie and twisted it around his fingers.

Jupiter grabbed his wrist. "Easy now, baby doll. Don't forget who's in charge here."

"Oh, don't worry. I won't, sir." Trev ignored Jupiter's tight grip and yanked on his tie, crashing their lips together in a fierce kiss.

It was a furious storm of hot swipes of tongue and clicks

of teeth, each of them fighting for dominance. No kiss had ever before felt so much like a battle, and Trev refused to submit even as the tip of Jupiter's cock threatened to breach him.

He was in control.

Him.

Not Jupiter.

Trev groaned when Jupiter pressed in, and the first bite of penetration made him tremble. Jupiter's girth was deliciously thick, and he tipped his head back, relaxing now so it could push farther inside of him.

Jupiter's lips ghosted along Trev's extended throat, his breath hot as he continued to thrust. He didn't stop until he was fully seated inside of Trev, and his grunts were hoarse as he immediately set a brutal pace. He reared back and grabbed the heels of Trev's boots, forcing him to bring his knees to his chest as he pounded into him.

Trev let himself moan, enjoying the quick burn of each ferocious slam. Jupiter's cock was on the right side of being almost too much, and the friction was wickedly hot. He grabbed his thighs to help keep himself in this folded position, his toes curling inside his boots from the incredible fucking.

Jupiter pumped his hips like a machine set on absolutely wrecking Trev's hole, and Trev had to admit that Jupiter was doing a pretty fantastic job. It had been some time since a man could really give it to him like this, and Jupiter's seemingly endless stamina was impressive. He fucked Trev hard enough for their skin to slap together, and each sharp crack of flesh echoed throughout the room, providing a beat for Trev's chorus of desperate cries.

Fuck, it was good.

Trev could have almost been content to lie there and get

fucked into sheer insanity, but he was never one to sit idly by during sex—especially now with his pride on the line. He squeezed down on Jupiter's cock, smirking when he heard him suck in a quick breath, and then he rolled his ass down to meet his frantic slams.

Jupiter uttered a low groan that sounded appreciative, and he adjusted his rhythm to make the most of Trev's feverish grinding.

They were perfectly in sync, as if they'd been doing this for years, taking each other to new heights of savage pleasure. Trev gave everything he had, and he mewled as Jupiter forced him to bend even farther back, dangling his own hard cock right in front of his face.

Jupiter glanced at Trev's dick, watching it bounce as he fucked Trev, and his eyes flicked up to Trev's in a silent questioning.

Trev smirked.

There were certainly many perks to being flexible.

Trev pushed his head forward and licked a luxurious stripe around the head of his own cock.

"*Oh*." Jupiter grinned, and his eyes widened. "You really are a talented boy, aren't you, baby doll?"

"I told you I was the best, sir." Trev lapped across his slit, making sure to keep his gaze locked with Jupiter's as he did so.

Jupiter slammed in hard enough to force Trev's cock into his mouth, and he froze there. "Suck it. Go on. Suck it for me."

Trev easily swallowed down the head of his cock, humming noisily and enjoying the vibrations resonating along his shaft. He didn't suck very hard because it would be far too easy to come, and seeing Jupiter completely entranced by the visual of him sucking himself off made him ache.

Yes.

Trev had Jupiter exactly where he wanted him. He had full control now, he was going to make Jupiter fall apart, and he was—

Jupiter pulled out abruptly, smacking the side of Trev's thigh. "On your knees, baby doll."

Trev gasped as his cock popped out of his mouth, his body stretching back out across the bed. He quickly assumed the ordered position and turned around to offer himself to Jupiter. He made sure to stick his ass up and arch his spine, and he hissed as Jupiter popped his left cheek. "Sir?"

"No more games, baby doll." Jupiter rubbed Trev's cheek to soothe the burn. "You need to get it out of your pretty little head that you're the one calling the shots here."

Trev grunted as Jupiter shoved his cock back in. "When did I say that, sir?" He cried out as Jupiter spanked his other cheek, even harder than before. He bowed his head and fisted the sheets, panting through the new ache. It made him clench around Jupiter's cock, and he felt even bigger, wasting no time in fucking Trev hard and fast.

Jupiter grabbed a hold of Trev's hip and dragged him back into every merciless thrust. "I can see it in your eyes, you smug little vixen."

"I... don't know... what you're talking about!" Trev whimpered as he was given another hard smack, and he dropped onto his elbows. Jupiter was fucking him so hard that he thought he might break, and the intense pressure combined with the new heat flashing over his scalding skin from being spanked overwhelmed his senses.

"Come on now." Jupiter spanked both of Trev's cheeks

and then latched on to his sides to continue his incredible pounding. "You tell yourself you're the best... because if you're not... then you're nothing."

"Fuck you, *sir*!" Trev seethed, finding the strength to lift his head.

No, that wasn't right.

Jupiter had no idea what the fuck he was talking about.

"Mm, and there goes that mouth of yours again." Jupiter grunted as he spanked Trev's ass, delivering three quick smacks in rapid succession.

Trev whimpered and weakly rocked back on Jupiter's cock, trying to seek any new sensation to help distract from his stinging cheeks. The throb created waves of sensation that pounded in his balls and through the head of his cock, and he whined defiantly, "May I have... another... sir?"

Jupiter chuckled low and spanked Trev again.

Trev's head whipped back as he moaned. "God, *yes*!"

Jupiter forced Trev flat against the bed, still fucking him hard as he whispered nastily in his ear, "I wonder if Boss Cold knows his little brother is such a slut for cock."

"I wonder if the Luchesi family knows how much their goon loved watching me suck my own cock." Trev cried as that earned him another spanking, this one to the side of his hip, and he writhed, trying to seek relief from the sting. He'd certainly been spanked before, but no one had ever dared to try and command his entire body like this.

Trev felt small, even vulnerable, but he refused to submit.

Not now.

Not *ever*.

He spread his legs to ease the thundering pressure building inside of him, and he held his head high. He gritted his teeth and let only stunted moans leave his lips, refusing to give Jupiter the privilege of hearing his pleasure.

Jupiter growled, his powerful pace finally stuttering to a dramatic close as he came.

Trev sagged into the bed and panted, offering a soft whimper as Jupiter filled him. His dick longed for attention, and he lazily rubbed his erection into the bed. "Please. Please, I want to come."

"Please, what?" Jupiter asked huskily, dragging his lips along the shell of Trev's ear.

"Please, *sir*."

"What a good boy. Look at that. You can be taught." Jupiter chuckled and reached beneath Trev to grab his cock. He remained buried balls deep inside of Trev as he stroked him, continuing to taunt, "When you come, you'll know it's only because I'm allowing it, baby doll. Because right now... you're mine."

"Sir... yes, sir!" Trev moaned wantonly as he let the sweet wave of bliss finally overtake him, and his cock pulsed until the room spun. He thrust into Jupiter's tight grip until he had nothing left to give, and he shuddered when Jupiter pressed a soft kiss to his shoulder.

"A very good boy." Jupiter sounded like he was smirking.

That beautiful bastard.

After Jupiter pulled out, Trev actually needed a few moments to collect himself. His cheeks were sore, his hole tender, and he was surprisingly sweaty. He managed to roll onto his side to strike a seductive pose and regain his confident smile, asking sweetly, "So, does the good boy get dinner?"

"Dinner?" Jupiter laughed. He'd gotten up from the bed and was cleaning himself up with a towel from the bedside cabinet.

"You did mention dinner, sir," Trev reminded him. "And you don't know how long you're keeping me here."

Jupiter glanced around the room warily.

Trev's heart thumped.

Jupiter was suspicious, but he looked right past the hidden window and to the door as if to verify that was the only way in or out. "Fine." He handed Trev a fresh towel. "But I'm locking you in. Do you understand?"

"Yes, sir." Trev smiled innocently as he wiped himself down.

"Need anything else?"

"If you're taking requests, a bag of frozen peas and a martini. Extra olives." Trev winked. "I promise not to turn into a pumpkin while you're gone."

Jupiter snorted. "I'll be back in ten minutes. Do not get any cute ideas about trying to leave, baby doll. I'd hate to have to punish you."

"Don't threaten me with a good time, sir."

"You're really quite something, Trevanion." Jupiter laughed. He cupped Trev's cheek, musing, "Depending on how this all shakes out, I might just have to keep you for myself."

"Oh? So you won't give me away to the big, bad Boss Cold?" Trev's tone was teasing, but it was a genuine dig for more information. Some men were more chatty after an orgasm, though he doubted Jupiter was one of them.

Jupiter smiled and patted Trev's cheek, saying only, "Behave."

Called it.

Trev gave Jupiter his sweetest smile, stretching out on the bed as Jupiter headed to the door. He stayed in his languid pose even after Jupiter had left, and he waited to hear the door lock and several moments to pass before he sprang to his feet.

Heart pounding in his ears, Trev quickly put his panties back on and then unzipped his boots. He hurried over to the window and used the stiletto heel to slash at the wallpaper. He tore a hole big enough for his fingers to fit in so he could tear it the rest of the way by hand to reveal the window.

"Fuck yes," Trev hissed triumphantly. "Let's fuckin' go, bitch."

He put his boots back on and then hurried to open the window. It was a tight squeeze, but he was able to wiggle through. As soon as his heels hit the pavement outside, he bolted.

It was time for the next phase of his escape plan—getting out of Perry City and praying that he never laid eyes on Jupiter Prospero again.

CHAPTER *Four*

TREV WOULD BE LYING if he said this was the first time he'd fled home almost naked, still full of another man's come, but it was definitely the first time he did so with a legitimate concern for his life.

First of all, fuck Jupiter Prospero.

In a bad way.

A terrible way.

Because he didn't care what that bastard thought about him, and all that mattered was escaping the city as quickly as possible.

Trev cut through the adjacent city park, staying on guard as he hurried to the next block. The park could be rough this time of night and there was always construction being done on the water lines here. The danger of being mugged was nearly as great as falling into a big, poorly marked hole.

He managed to make it out unscathed and then hailed a taxi. The last time he'd driven his own car to the Cannery, it had been broken into. He'd opted to take an Uber to the club instead, but he couldn't use the app with no phone.

The taxi driver cautioned he wouldn't take Trev to any

hourly hotels, and Trev rolled his eyes in reply and gave him his home address.

He wasn't in the mood.

Luckily, the driver wasn't interested in small talk, and the quiet ride gave Trev time to plan.

First, ditch the cab driver.

Trev had a single twenty dollar bill hidden in his boot for emergencies, and he didn't want to part with it. He didn't care if he pissed off the driver. What was the guy going to do? Call the cops?

Considering there would likely be an armed and very unhappy gangster coming after him, Trev would love for the cops to show up—no, wait.

Shit.

Most of the cops were crooked, and even if they weren't, all Jupiter would have to do was show up and say that Trev tried to pick him up for a date of the solicitation kind. It would be his word against Jupiter's, and Trev did not like those odds one bit.

New plan.

First, pay the cab driver with the twenty.

Second, wake Camille up and threaten to strangle her with her bathrobe sash. He wasn't actually going to do it, but she wouldn't know that. There was a chance Camille was already clearing out his apartment since she probably hadn't thought Trev was going to come back. Knowing her, there was a high probability that the locks were already changed. Trev didn't care about anything in that apartment except his cash, and if that was missing, then he was definitely strangling her.

Maybe. Strong maybe on the strangling.

Pay driver, wake up Camille, get money, haul ass.

And go where?

He had no one.

Although his boss was nice enough, there was no way he could go to her with something this insane. Juicy was his only friend, but Trev cared too much about him to get him involved. Plus, he was crazy. Juicy probably wouldn't even understand what Trev was trying to tell him and then threaten to have Barkie bite the gangsters.

What about Boss Cold?

The thought was immediately dismissed.

Yeah, sure. Go running to the gangster who was supposedly his half-brother and didn't even know he existed because that would have such a happy ending. While there was a tiny chance that Cold would really care about him on the basis of blood relation alone, Trev wasn't going to gamble his life on it.

It was more likely Cold would not believe him, not care, or that he would believe him and assume he only wanted money.

No, Trev had to go somewhere else.

He needed to drive south. He would go as far south as he could and never look back. He'd run and run and somehow get over the damn border and keep on running. He was going to be fine.

He was going to survive.

Trev couldn't help but feel a pang of sadness for the loss of his bright future. It was all falling apart right before his eyes, and there was nothing he could do about it.

It was *fine*.

Wherever he ended up, he'd make a new future—an even better one.

Trev hit the sidewalk running, ignoring the cab driver's bitching about his crappy tip. Trev hurried inside and then raced up the stairs, his thighs screaming at him the whole way up. Once he arrived at his floor, he paused to give himself a moment to catch his breath.

He hadn't seen any of his belongings outside, so he hoped that meant Camille hadn't started to clean out his place yet.

Still, Trev wanted to be ready to raise hell if he saw her and doubling over panting from bolting up multiple flights of steps in stilettos wasn't going to be very helpful.

He strutted out into the hall once he wasn't about to keel over, and he was pleased to see it was clear. He hurried to his door, finding that the locks hadn't been touched.

Good.

Maybe Camille had smoked too many cigarettes and landed herself in the hospital again.

Maybe she'd been run over by a bus.

He could hope.

He stalked to Camille's apartment at the end of the hall and knocked furiously.

Nothing.

He knocked harder and even kicked the door.

Still nada.

Great.

Okay. Think, think, think—*Juicy*!

Trev had given Juicy a spare set a while back. He hated to wake him up at this hour, but he didn't have any other choice since Camille wouldn't answer. He hurried over to Juicy's door to knock, but it opened just as he raised his hand.

Juicy was on the other side, an old man with papery white skin and a shock of gray hair that defied gravity. He had Barkie's leash in his hand and blinked at Trev in surprise. "Oh! Trevanion. You're here. I was about to take

Barkie for a walk." He paused. "Are you bringing me my ointment?"

"No, I need my spare keys," Trev replied quickly.

"Why?"

"Because I lost mine."

"Why don't you just go into your apartment and find them? They'll be in the last place you look. Always are."

"Juicy, I need my keys to get inside my apartment. Camille isn't answering and I need to get in, like, now."

"I'd help you, but Barkie really needs to go—"

"Juicy, *please*." Trev usually enjoyed their strange chats, but he didn't have time right now. He turned his gaze to the empty carpet beside Juicy's feet. "Barkie, I'm sorry, but I really need my keys, boy."

Juicy frowned. "Well, if he has an accident, you're cleaning it up."

"Happily."

Juicy padded back inside his apartment, muttering to himself. He returned with the keys. "Now, don't forget to bring these back. They're very important."

"You got it! Thanks, Juicy! Bye, Barkie!" Trev was already at his door, unlocking it as fast as he could. He dashed inside and then locked the door back behind him. It was time for the next part of his plan.

Grab the money and get the fuck out of here.

Trev rushed to his bedroom, throwing on a pair of jean shorts, his pink hoodie, and a pair of combat boots. He grabbed a hot pink butterfly knife from his bedside table to shove down in his boot. He'd worry about cleaning himself up later when he was somewhere safe. The chances that Jupiter and his gangster buddies knew where he lived were extremely high. He got a duffel bag out of his closet, packed some clothes, and then he went for the lockbox that held his money.

Thank fuck it was a combination lock.

He got his spare car key out of a drawer in the kitchen and was headed to the door when the knob jiggled.

Shit.

No, no, no.

Trev looked through the peephole.

Jupiter was here.

Trev dropped his bag and looked around, flinching as Jupiter banged on the door.

New plan.

He had to hide.

He slid the lockbox under the couch, his mind racing. The apartment was not a big place. There were not exactly any good spots to hide where Jupiter wouldn't find him and then drag him right back.

Wait.

The coffin!

Trev opened it and then jumped right in. He slid down, grunting as he lay on top of his DVDs. It was extremely uncomfortable, but he was sure it was definitely not as uncomfortable as being shot would be. He had no idea if this would actually work, and he hoped it wasn't some sort of grim foreshadowing.

He closed the lid, instantly surrounded by darkness. He hated how cramped it was, and it was harder to breathe. He clenched his hands into fists and tried to stay calm. He *had* to stay calm. He could do this. He *had* to fucking do this.

The knocking stopped.

Trev didn't think that was a good sign.

He held his breath, straining to hear what Jupiter was doing.

There were some clicks, a *thump*, and then a gunshot. The door shook. Three more gunshots rang out in rapid succession, and the door crashed open.

Trev bit down on his lip to keep from screaming, his heart leaping into the back of his throat. It was pounding so hard that he was certain Jupiter could hear it, and he froze, terrified to make a single sound that might reveal his location. He didn't even want to breathe.

Jupiter's footsteps signaled his entry, and he stormed off, presumably toward Trev's bedroom.

There was more noise—no doubt it was Jupiter tearing everything apart looking for him.

Trev grimaced when he realized he had left his duffel bag out in the middle of the floor, and no doubt Jupiter would take that as a sign that he hadn't left the apartment yet.

Which meant he was probably going to keep looking for him.

And eventually check the fucking coffin.

Shit.

Trev stopped breathing when Jupiter's footsteps approached, and he regretted hiding inside the coffin. He had nowhere to run if Jupiter opened it, but it wasn't like he'd had any better options.

Where else could he have gone? Under the bed?

Trev's lungs burned as he fought not to inhale except for tiny, gasping breaths that he prayed were inaudible.

Jupiter walked by the coffin, around it, paused, and then...

He left.

Trev still didn't move, straining to listen to confirm that Jupiter was actually gone. Certainly someone would be calling the police because of the gunshots, even here in this crap part of town, and he could just stay here until they arrived. Jupiter probably wouldn't go very far, no doubt waiting around close by so he could snatch Trev up as soon as he saw him.

"Trevanion?" Juicy's voice called out worriedly.

"Shit," Trev hissed.

"Trev? Are you in there?" Juicy called again. "There was a big man here and I think he had a gun. Either that or he had really big jawbreakers."

Trev pushed up the coffin lid. "Juicy, look, it's—"

Juicy was standing at Trev's doorway and screamed. "*Zombie*!"

"I'm not a zombie!" Trev groaned as he climbed out.

"That's exactly what a zombie would say." Juicy shook Barkie's leash at him and barked ferociously. "That's a good boy, Barkie! That's a good boy! Remember your training! Ugo always said two shots! Heart and head! Final shot! In the head!"

"I'm not a fucking zombie, I swear." Trev grunted, rubbing his aching back as he surveyed his trashed apartment. "No head shots, okay? I just needed a place to hide for a second. That guy was here looking for me and I gotta leave for a little while, okay?"

"Leave?" Juicy frowned. "You're coming back, aren't you?"

Trev's heart sank, and he lied. "Of course! It'll just be a few days."

"Oh, okay." Juicy sighed in obvious relief.

Trev grabbed his lockbox and the duffel bag, offering a confident smile. "I'll let you know as soon as I get back, okay?"

"Okay." Juicy smiled warmly. "I was so worried—"

"It's fine, really. But I gotta get going." Trev glanced back at his apartment, and his gaze fell on his kitchen counter. He'd been so focused on the money that he'd forgotten about the only other thing in this dump that really mattered —the photograph of his mother.

He had others stashed away in his lockbox, but this one was his favorite.

"You should let Camille know about the rodent problem," Juicy said.

"Sorry, Mama," Trev whispered to the picture as he shoved it into his duffel bag. He hadn't heard Juicy clearly, asking, "What was that?"

"You need to tell Camille about the rodent problem." Juicy gestured to the mess.

"Right. Yes." Trev patted Juicy's shoulder. "Because this was clearly the work of rats."

"Of course."

"It was a really, really big one." Trev snorted as he poked his head out to look up and down the hallway to make sure the coast was clear. He breezed by Juicy and then ushered him out of the way so he could lock back up.

Right.

Jupiter shot the lock to break in.

Trev growled, adding bitterly, "A big, stupid one named Jupiter."

"Ouch," Jupiter purred. "Name calling? And after everything we've shared together."

Trev froze, slowly turning to see Jupiter walking around the corner at the far end of the hallway.

Well, fuck.

Jupiter smirked. "Hi, baby doll. Miss me?"

"Oh, terribly. I was just about to come see you because I missed you so much." Trev forced a smile, letting the duffel bag drop from his hand. He needed to run, and the lockbox was the most important thing. He'd pay Juicy to mail him the rest of his stuff as soon as he was safely out of the country.

"Are you dating the rat?" Juicy asked from the side of his mouth, trying and failing to be covert.

"No, I am not," Trev replied in the same dramatic whisper. "He says I'm the brother of some fucker named Boss Cold—"

"Oh! I know that guy." Juicy beamed. "He's a—"

"Come on now," Jupiter cut in. "That was a cute little stunt you pulled at the club, but now—"

Trev bolted, snatching Barkie's leash from Juicy. "Sorry! Gotta go!"

Juicy gasped. "Barkie!"

Trev wiggled the leash as he ran down the hall toward the stairs. "There! He's free! Free as a bird!"

"Oh, thank God."

"Dammit! Get back here!" Jupiter shouted.

"Fuck you!" Trev shouted back as he dashed into the stairwell.

"Barkie! Attack!" Juicy screamed, launching into a fierce barking tirade.

Trev prayed Juicy would stay out of harm's way as he slammed the door shut and looped the leash through the handle. He thanked everything that was holy that Juicy had a long leash and he was able to hook the other end to the railing of the stairs. He knew it wouldn't hold long, but hopefully it would be enough time to give him a good head start.

Jupiter tried to open the door, and the leash prevented it from opening more than a few inches. "*Trevanion*. You really do not need to make this so difficult!"

"Bye, sweetie! Miss you already!" Trev shouted, already

halfway down the first set of stairs. He flew as fast as he could, cringing as the door slammed open above him once he hit the ground floor. The leash must have given out, but it didn't matter. He just had to make it out to his car.

He ran outside, clutching the lockbox to his chest. There was a black SUV parked out front that he didn't recognize.

Had to be Jupiter's.

Trev paused to grab the knife out of his boot, flipping it open and stabbing the tire as he hurried by. He twisted it and left it there. "Fuck you, Jupiter."

His lungs felt like they were on fire, but he was almost to his car. The door of the apartment opened behind him, but it didn't matter. He was getting in his car and pulling the key out of his pocket. He could see Jupiter in his rearview mirror, and the bastard must have been really out of shape because he wasn't even running now.

Trev cranked his window down, sticking his hand out the window as he put the key in the ignition. He flipped Jupiter off as he turned the key, ready to burn rubber and...

Nothing.

Trev's stomach twisted, and he tried to turn the key again.

There was no clicking, no clanking, no nothing.

Trev pulled out the key and stared at it to make sure he'd grabbed the right one. It was definitely his spare car key, and he didn't understand why it wasn't working.

What the fuck?

"Car trouble?" Jupiter asked as he approached the open window, smiling smugly. "Don't you hate when that happens?"

Trev glared furiously. "What the fuck did you do to my car?"

"Well, after your little escape, I figured I should make

sure you couldn't leave if you managed to get away from me again." Jupiter chuckled. "Disconnected the battery."

"*Fucker.*"

"What? You didn't think I'd considered that you'd try and give me the slip again?"

"Nope. Definitely didn't give you enough credit. How'd you know this was my car?"

"The same way I know where you live. I even know your shoe size."

"Yeah?"

"Eleven and a half."

"I usually wear a twelve." Trev didn't take his eyes off Jupiter, and he slid his car key into his pants pocket. He kept his hand by his side, subtly reaching over into the seat beside him to look for something he could use as a weapon.

"This has been a lot of fun, baby doll, but now it's time to go." Jupiter glanced back at his SUV. "Looks like we'll be taking your car since you were sweet enough to slash one of my tires."

"I should have slashed them all." Trev smiled sweetly, and his hand closed around—shit, a bottle of glitter body spray.

"You really are quite something," Jupiter said as he crouched beside the car. "I've seen guys twice your size crack under half the pressure."

"It's not the size that counts. It's how you use it." Trev batted his lashes.

"Easy for you to say when you got balls the size of Godzilla's. I really wouldn't mind—"

"Eat shit and die, motherfucker!" Trev snarled as he squirted the body spray right in Jupiter's face.

"The fuck?" Jupiter instantly recoiled, clutching his eyes.

"Bye, bitch!" Trev slid over the seat to escape through the

passenger-side door, snatching the lockbox and running back toward the apartment building. He could probably lose Jupiter on the stairs and then—

Jupiter tackled him to the ground.

"Fuck!" Trev wheezed as the air was knocked out of his lungs and the lockbox went flying. He couldn't believe Jupiter had managed to catch up to him, and he groaned, trying to wiggle out from beneath him. "You... big... bitch!"

"All right. I'm done now." Jupiter growled. "No more running. No more bullshit tricks. We're leaving. Right fucking now."

"You smell amazing," Trev croaked. "Champagne Toast is totally your scent."

"Get the fuck up. We're going." Jupiter dragged Trev up to his feet.

"I need my lockbox." Trev tried to pull away, but Jupiter wouldn't budge. "Hey!"

"What's in it? A bomb? Nunchucks?"

"My fucking dildos." Trev rolled his eyes. "None of your fucking business is what's in it, but I need it. I'm not going anywhere without it."

Jupiter kept his iron grip on Trev's arm. "Give me your key."

"You mean this key?" Trev pulled it out of his pocket.

"Yes, and don't you dare—"

Trev flung it out into the pitch-black street.

Jupiter glared.

Trev stood up as tall as he could and smiled.

Jupiter dragged Trev toward the SUV.

"Hey, hey! My fucking lockbox!" Trev flailed furiously. "I need it!"

"We're fucking leaving. You can either come quietly or I'll put you in the trunk."

Trev glanced at Jupiter's jacket where he knew the gun was. This was not a fight he was going to win, not right now, and he had to be smart. "Let me grab the damn box and I'll behave, okay?"

Jupiter didn't say anything, but he turned back around. He still didn't release Trev, choosing to bend down and grab the box himself. He shoved it at Trev, grunting. "Let's go."

Trev let Jupiter take him to the SUV, and he obediently sat in the passenger seat. He thought about running again, but he was pretty sure Jupiter might shoot him. Perhaps not anywhere lethal, but at least in the leg or something.

Jupiter got behind the wheel, cranking the engine and then peeling out away from the apartment. He made a face at the *thump-thump-thump* of the flat tire.

Trev smiled. "That's going to absolutely ruin your rim."

"Don't worry, baby doll. We're not going far." Jupiter snorted as he pulled his phone out of his pocket. He tapped a few buttons, clearly texting.

"You know that's really dangerous."

Jupiter finished the message. "There. Happy?"

"Overjoyed." Trev smirked as he saw the sparkle of glitter on Jupiter's face when they passed a streetlight. "You should wear glitter more often. Really makes your eyes pop."

"Quiet now."

Trev tried to map out where they were headed, but he couldn't even hazard a guess. It wasn't back to the club, and all he could tell was that Jupiter was taking them out of the city. With as slow as Jupiter was driving because of the flat tire, Trev considered jumping out. He'd get scuffed up for sure, but he could try to run again.

He snuck his hand over to the door handle, keeping his eyes on the road and looking for what could be a potentially safe spot to land. His mind clicked away as he struggled to come up with a better idea than jumping out of a moving vehicle, and he came up with nothing.

Adrenaline flooded his guts and nauseated him, and he took a few quiet breaths to ready himself. This was going to hurt, but probably not as much as whatever Jupiter and his stupid mobster buddies were going to do with him.

Fuck it.

He unbuckled his seat belt and pulled on the handle, heaving all of his weight against the door.

It didn't open.

"Child locks are on." Jupiter didn't even look his way. "Gotta love 'em."

"Shit," Trev mumbled.

"Put your seat belt back on."

"Fuck off." Trev thought about hitting Jupiter with the lockbox, but he didn't have long to think on it.

Jupiter pulled over on a dark side street, and Trev couldn't see enough of the buildings to get his bearings. He thought it might be the storage facility near the highway, but he wasn't sure.

Headlights flashed at them from a vehicle parked a few yards down the street.

"Your chariot awaits." Jupiter got out of the car and then came around to let Trev out. "Best behavior, do you understand?"

"Yes, sir," Trev said sarcastically, though he didn't miss how it made Jupiter smile.

"Good boy." Jupiter took Trev's arm and led him to the other car.

Trev dragged his feet so Jupiter would have to pull him along, and he grimaced when he saw Sal and Emiliano stepping out of another black SUV. "Do gangsters get package deals on big, stupid SUVs? Is that why you all drive them?"

"Sure do." Jupiter snorted. "Family discount."

"Ha," Trev drawled. "You're hilarious."

"What the fuck happened?" Emil demanded as they approached.

"Nothing I couldn't handle," Jupiter replied smoothly. "Mr. Usher was being difficult, but—"

"Wouldn't be too difficult with a broken leg," Sal warned.

"I handled it," Jupiter said with a scowl. "Are we ready or not?"

"Ready," Emil replied. He cut his eyes at Trev and then back to Jupiter. "You're gonna be..." He squinted. "What the fuck is all over your face?"

Jupiter sighed.

"I maced him with glitter body spray," Trev said proudly. "You guys should try some—hey!" He grunted as Jupiter pulled firmly on his arm. "Rude."

Emil glared at Jupiter, holding up his finger as he declared, "You're gonna be his new babysitter, do you understand? I don't want him taking a shit without you there ready to wipe his ass. If he sneezes, I wanna know if his snot was clear or fucking green. I'm not going to tolerate sorry ass bullshit of this fucking level again."

Jupiter bristled, but he nodded. "Understood."

"Ha, you just got your ass chewed," Trev taunted. He laughed until Jupiter tugged on his arm again. "Ow, asshole. That one kinda hurt."

"And you." Emil fixed his furious stare on Trev. "We need you alive, but trust me when I say that *alive* can be a very broad definition."

"Yeah! Alive can mean I maybe cut off some fucking

pieces and you still got a pulse," Sal chimed in. "Alive can mean I peel off your fucking fingernails and—"

"For fuck's sake, he gets it." Emil smacked the side of Sal's head. "Shut the fuck up. Let's fuckin' go." He gestured for them to get into the SUV.

Trev tensed. "Where are we going?"

Jupiter smiled, pulling Trev along. "Your home sweet home until this deal goes through, baby doll. Trust me. You're gonna love it. Just me, you, and a room I promise you won't be able to get out of."

"Oh *goody*."

CHAPTER *Five*

THE DRIVE to the next destination was quiet.

Trev was exhausted from the chase, and he clung to the lockbox. He was stuck in the back seat with Jupiter, and he kept himself as close to the door as possible. It didn't escape his attention how Jupiter stretched his arm over the back of the seat, and the gesture felt oddly protective.

And possessive.

Ugh.

"Where are we going?" Trev asked quietly.

"Somewhere with no windows for you to crawl out of," Jupiter retorted. "Quiet now, baby doll."

Trev could tell from looking out the window that they'd left the city limits, but he wasn't sure where they were headed. He knew the highway they were on and that they were driving north, but that was all he could deduce. He kept an eye on the time, noting that twenty-two minutes passed before they turned off the highway.

Driving at sixty miles per hour figured out to roughly a mile a minute, so they were at least twenty miles out from the city limits.

That would be one hell of a walk, but Trev could always try to hitch a ride too. Maybe he could even steal one of these stupid mafia edition SUVs. He wanted to keep his options open, his mind continuing to spin as they pulled up to a dark building.

It was two stories, brick, and the parking lot was horribly overgrown. The faded sign over the front entrance read Create-A-Critter, and most of the windows were boarded over. It appeared to have been abandoned for quite some time.

"Your penthouse suite is waiting for you, sir," Emil taunted from the front seat, laughing as he got out.

Trev grimaced.

What a fucking tool.

Sal came around to open the back door so Jupiter could exit first. Jupiter offered his hand to assist Trev. He got a firm grip on his arm as soon as Trev's feet hit the pavement as if he expected Trev to make a break for it.

Rightfully so because Trev had already been looking at the surrounding trees, wondering how far he could make it running around in the dark.

Emil led the way to the side entrance of the building. As old as the place was, the keypad was definitely new. Trev tried to see what the code was, but Sal blocked his view.

Not that he could make out much of anything right now because it was pitch fucking black.

The door opened into—surprise—a dark room. Emil flicked on a light switch, revealing it was an old office full of moldy smelling file boxes and assorted plush animals. There was a hallway lined with several wooden doors and a metal pair marked *FACTORY FLOOR* down at the very end.

Jupiter led Trev to one of the doors closest to the factory

doors and then opened it. "Here it is." He smirked. "Your home sweet home."

"Fucking lovely," Trev drawled.

The room was small, reeked of mildew, and the ceiling tiles looked like they could collapse at any second. The floor was clean at least and the bed looked new. There was a mini fridge, a table with two chairs, and...

A length of chain attached directly to the brick, at the end of which was a silver collar with a small padlock.

Trev's stomach twisted.

As Jupiter had said, there were no windows. The only door was the one they'd used to enter, and Trev didn't think he could reach the ceiling tiles even if he stood on the table. Of course, he probably wouldn't be able to reach shit with that collar on.

Great.

Wonderful.

He was going to be chained up in a brick box with no way out.

"You two enjoy your evening," Sal said. "I'll call you tomorrow, all right? Make sure we get you some food and shit to eat."

"Yes, sir." Jupiter tipped his head politely.

"Me and Emil gotta go take a phone call. You get your pet all fixed up." Sal smirked. "We'll be back to check on you before we go."

Trev flinched as the door shut, and he hugged the lockbox to his chest.

Now it was just him and Jupiter.

Maybe he could crack Jupiter in the head with the lockbox.

"Come along, baby doll." Jupiter picked up the collar. "Let's get this over with, huh? And don't even think about hitting me with that damn box and running. Sal and Emil are still right outside."

Well, damn.

"Loving this, aren't you?" Trev hissed, tensing as he allowed Jupiter to snap the collar around his neck. It was heavy, cold, and he hated its weight.

"There." Jupiter checked the fit before closing the padlock. He seemed satisfied and put the key to the padlock in his jacket pocket. "Now you shouldn't be any more trouble."

"Oh, I don't know about that." Trev batted his eyes and gave the chain an experimental tug. "Ever see *Return of the Jedi* before?"

"Many times. Maybe I should get you a little gold bikini to complete the look."

"Have I told you how much I love that glitter on you?" Trev dragged the chain with him to sit on the bed. He set the lockbox down beside him. "Really softens up your features."

"You already know there's nothing soft about me." Jupiter took a seat in one of the rickety chairs. "Now. I suggest you get some sleep. Big day ahead of you."

"Oh?"

Jupiter only smiled. "I can see the wheels turning in that pretty head of yours. I'm not telling you anything."

"Afraid I'm going to run again?"

"The window at the club was clever. How did you know it was there?"

"A leprechaun told me."

Jupiter smiled expectantly.

"Fine." Trev stretched out on his side with a huff. "I used to work there. Before they did some remodeling. That's how I knew."

Jupiter nodded.

"So. You afraid I'm going to run again?"

"Not afraid, but definitely prepared for it." Jupiter crossed his arms. "That's why I'm not telling you anything because I know you'll use the tiniest detail to your advantage. You're smart."

"Aw, thank you." Trev beamed. "You know, I think once I really get to know you, you'll still be, oh yeah, a giant *fucking asshole*."

"Yes, with a job to do."

Trev rolled onto his back, noticing how Jupiter's gaze drifted over his body. "Does that job include fucking me?"

"That was an unexpected perk." Jupiter's eyes paused on Trev's exposed stomach. "But don't worry. It's been a rough night. I'll save your punishment for later."

Trev's loins flooded with a traitorous surge of heat, but he kept his face neutral. "Like I'm ever going to let you touch me again."

"You will." Jupiter chuckled. "You think you're smarter than me and you'll use the only edge you have left. Well, the one you think you have anyway. That I want you."

"I *think* that you want me? Oh please." Trev laughed. He slid his hand up his body to push his hoodie up, moaning wantonly. "Oh, you really are such a talented boy, aren't you, baby doll?" He bit his lip, raising his ass off the bed and humping the air as he continued to mock Jupiter's previous comments. "That's right, *mmm*. Never had anyone suck me like this before, oh my God, *baby*. It's just so good, *mmm*. You're *such* a good boy."

Jupiter's upper lip twitched.

"That was you," Trev said flatly, flopping back against the mattress. "Creaming your glittery little drawers over me."

"You were an adequate partner."

"Adequate?" Trev scowled. "We both know you're full of shit and you're just saying that to piss me off. You might as well stop."

"Why would I do that when it works so easily?" Jupiter chuckled. "You're an open book. I already know you better than you know yourself. Your desire for approval is almost toxic."

"Oh no!" Trev pretended to pout. "That really hurts my feelings coming from the guy whose entire personality screams *daddy issues*." He scoffed. "Let's see. Controlling in bed, probably a perfectionist, you hate being vulnerable, you want to fuck all the time but you never commit so you can't be abandoned again. That about sum it up?"

Jupiter said nothing.

"So, what happened?" Trev pressed. "Daddy leave you all alone? Did he go out for cigarettes and never come back?"

"Do you know what happened to yours?" Jupiter countered.

Trev narrowed his eyes.

"Your brother, Roderick Legrand, killed him."

Trev froze.

No.

That couldn't be true.

Could it?

Why would Boss Cold murder their father?

Why wouldn't Trev's mother have told him any of this? The idea of her lying about Boris's death didn't sit well with Trev, and he hated not knowing what was real or not. He didn't want to believe his mother had been this dishonest, and he sure as hell didn't trust Jupiter to tell him the truth.

Then again, if truth was always more frightening than

fiction, it made sense for Jupiter to be honest if for no other reason than to rattle Trev.

"Bullshit," Trev spat. "Why?"

"You'll have to ask him when you meet him," Jupiter said smugly, clearly pleased he'd upset Trev. "But he sure did. Killed him in cold blood. That brother of yours is a real classy fellow."

"*Half*-brother."

The door opened, and Sal and Emil walked back in. Emil was smiling, but Sal looked grim.

Trev was starting to suspect that was just Sal's face.

"We got it," Sal said. "We're good."

"We're fucking *golden*!" Emil gushed. "We just got the test back! It's fuckin' him."

"Excellent." Jupiter smiled. "And now?"

"We move to the next part of the plan," Sal replied. "Waitin'. Stay put. Need anything?"

"A glass of a nice, dry merlot," Jupiter said wistfully.

Emil laughed. "Fuckin' dumbass. There's some beer in the fridge and it's cold."

"We'll bring you some stuff tomorrow," Sal said. "Our contact for the pipeline will be coming through too."

"Coming here?" Jupiter raised his brow.

"They say he's a real hands-on kinda guy. Wants to see the setup in person. Dunno. We ain't never met this fuck before."

"All right. We'll be here."

"Both of you," Sal said, and it sounded like a warning. "Night."

"Night." Jupiter tipped his head.

"Good night! Sweet dreams!" Trev waved. "I hope you both die in a terrible, fiery death!"

Sal didn't say anything, but Emil gave Trev a nasty glare as they left.

Jupiter stood to lock the door behind them. He tilted his head, popping his neck, then stretched his arms and returned to the chair. He leaned back, crossing his arms and getting comfortable. "Let me know when you're ready for me to turn the light off."

Trev waited a few seconds to make sure Jupiter was perfectly cozy before saying, "Right about now actually would be great. I'm really tired."

Jupiter narrowed his eyes in annoyance, but he got to his feet again.

"Oh, wait!" Trev snapped his fingers. "I just decided I want to stay up a little longer. You can leave it on."

"Cute." Jupiter flicked the switch. "Good night."

The room was pitch black now. There wasn't even any light coming through from under the door.

The chair creaked as Jupiter sat again, and he sighed. His face lit up as he brought out his phone, thumbing over the screen. His expression was hard to read, but Trev got the distinct impression he was being ignored now.

Trev felt around the bed to find the lockbox. He moved it against the far wall so he wouldn't roll over on it. It was already going to be uncomfortable as hell trying to sleep with the collar and chain on.

He shifted around, instantly hating the sound of the chain rattling with a blinding passion. He put his head on the pillows and soon found the tiniest movement made the chain clink.

The only benefit was that the noise made Jupiter look up from his phone and scowl.

Trev waited for Jupiter's gaze to return to his screen

before purposefully moving to rattle the chain. After about the fifth time, Jupiter stopped looking up.

That was fine.

Trev had other petty torments up his sleeve, and he had a new plan.

He had to get the key to his collar out of Jupiter's pocket. To do that, he needed to get Jupiter to come much, much closer. If he was able to seduce Jupiter, Trev felt confident he would leave his clothes on for it like before.

There were countless positions that would give Trev the opportunity to snatch the key. He could hide it in his mouth until Jupiter finally passed out and then he could get the hell out of here.

Jupiter didn't have a car here, so he'd have to follow Trev on foot, and Trev hoped to be long gone by the time Jupiter noticed he was missing again. It wasn't a great plan, but it was the only one he had right now, and he wasn't going to actually sleep here in this dump willingly.

Now, he just had to get Jupiter's attention.

Trev slipped off his boots, deliberately kicking each one off onto the floor. He pointed his toes toward the end of the bed and stretched his arms out, grunting noisily. He wasn't surprised that Jupiter didn't glance up yet, but he was just getting started.

Trev rolled his hips to one side, bringing his knee up to his chest. He then rolled the other way to repeat the movement, the chain clinking away.

"What are you doing?" Jupiter asked, his eyes still fixed to his phone.

"Stretching," Trev replied simply. "Had quite the workout earlier, you know."

"Uh-huh."

Trev raised his feet toward the ceiling, easily folding

himself into a pretzel and exhaling sharply. He held the position for a few moments before uncurling his body. He moved onto his stomach and brought his feet up to touch the back of his head, taking another deep breath.

Jupiter remained unmoved.

Trev wasn't even sure if Jupiter could see anything he was doing with only the glow of the phone to illuminate the room, but there were other senses he could manipulate.

Time to take things up a notch.

He rolled onto his back again and closed his eyes, running his hands over his stomach. He stroked the tips of his fingers around his navel and then dipped down to his hip bones. He needed to take his time and let this build to be particularly convincing.

Trev pressed his hands flat against his skin and slid them upward under his hoodie to thumb his nipples. His heart rate sped up a little, and his face warmed as blood zoomed there and down between his legs. It was hard to focus and actually get turned on, and he searched his brain for his favorite go-to jerk off fantasies.

But all he could think about was Jupiter.

Jupiter's strong hands, his soft lips, and that intoxicating way he had purred *baby doll* in Trev's ear.

Trev shivered, and his skin was instantly awash in white-hot waves of arousal. His body twitched with the memory of Jupiter being deep inside him, and his breath hitched as his nipples stiffened. He continued to tease them until they were both hard, each new stroke sending little zings cascading through his core.

His pulse throbbed through the shaft of his cock as he grew hard, and he both loved and hated how tight these shorts were. He squirmed, thrusting into the air. He squeezed his nipples until he gasped, and he twisted his head back into the pillows.

Trev's breathing was shallow, and he toed at the sheets as his desire spiked.

He pushed his hoodie up as the temperature in the room rose, clawing down his sides to grab his hips. He remembered the press of Jupiter's tight grip, and he clenched, suddenly well aware that Jupiter's come was still inside of him. If he fingered himself, no doubt he'd still find traces of how Jupiter had claimed him.

Christ.

Trev sucked one of his fingers into his mouth and grabbed himself through his shorts. The denim was drawn tight across his cock, and he rubbed along his shaft, his breathing coming faster now in little pants.

"What the fuck are you doing?" Jupiter growled, his voice hoarse.

"Fuckin' busy. Fuck off," Trev replied curtly.

He didn't even bother looking at Jupiter. He knew he was watching, and that certainty made him grope himself more passionately. He pushed two fingers into his mouth, sucking harder as he humped his palm, chasing the tease of friction. He didn't moan outright, instead choosing to stay quiet and keep his attention on his own pleasure.

This was for him,

Not for Jupiter, not for anyone else.

Trev had to believe that.

If Jupiter suspected Trev was trying to lure him in to any kind of trap, it wouldn't work.

Trev lost himself to each pass of his hand, letting the sweet pressure steadily build as he panted. He needed more, and he quickly unbuttoned his shorts to shove them down around his thighs. He popped his fingers into his mouth as he rolled over onto his stomach, quickly smearing spit over his hole. He added more until he was wet enough to push inside.

With a languid sigh, Trev thrust two fingers in and grinded his cock against the bed. He lay as still as he could to keep the chain from rattling, pumping only his hips and hand. The stretch was quick, burned, and he bit his lip as the pleasure ebbed and flowed in steady ripples.

Light blinded him as Jupiter aimed his phone's flashlight right at him, and Trev closed his eyes. "Mm, what?"

"Fuck." Jupiter spoke the word as a growl, and the chair creaked as he approached the bed.

Trev refused to look at Jupiter yet. He focused on his own pleasure, thrusting his fingers as he continued to hump the bed in earnest. Feeling Jupiter's gaze on him was still hot even if he couldn't see it happening, and he let his imagination run wild picturing the lustful way Jupiter was probably devouring him with his eyes right now.

He could hear how Jupiter was panting, the rustle of his clothing as he moved closer, and Trev gasped as the chain was pulled tight.

The collar caught his throat and forced him to lift his head, his eyes fluttering open as he demanded, "What the fuck?"

"Move your hand, baby doll."

"I'm tryin' to come, thanks."

Jupiter pulled the chain again.

Trev whined, surprised how much he liked the new pressure and how it made his breath stutter. He had Jupiter right where he wanted, though he acted very put out as he slowly withdrew his fingers. "What? I'm not allowed to jerk off, *sir*?"

"Not without my permission." Jupiter let the chain relax

but didn't release it. He set his phone on the bed, the light creating fractured shadows as he traced the curve of Trev's ass and then slid a single finger between his cheeks to tease his hole. He pushed in, slick with nothing but Trev's own spit. "Tell me. What were you thinking about?"

"You." Trev pushed back against Jupiter's hand. "How... I can still feel your come inside me... I didn't clean any of it out."

"In too much of a hurry," Jupiter scolded.

"Wanted to keep it," Trev countered, quick enough to sound honest. "I... I wanted to feel you there."

Jupiter growled and thrust his finger in harder.

Definitely the right thing to say.

Trev moaned, but he made an effort to resist letting it out without a fight. He clawed at the sheets and whined, getting caught up in the fantasy of submission. "Please, sir. I want more. Please give me more."

Jupiter let go of the chain. "No."

"But, sir—! Ah!" Trev cried out when Jupiter smacked his ass. He clenched down on Jupiter's fingers, mewling when Jupiter spanked him again. "Please... I'm sorry. I couldn't help it."

"Oh, is that so, baby doll?"

Another slap made Trev's hips buck forward, and he gasped for breath. "Please, s-sir..."

"Since you simply couldn't help yourself, you're going to take your punishment right now," Jupiter taunted, adding another finger.

Trev moaned without reservation as Jupiter moved to spanking his other cheek, and the burn throbbed into his very core. The slam of Jupiter's fingers was a fantastic counterpoint to the pain, and he slipped his hand under his belly to grab his cock.

"Ah ah." Jupiter stilled his fingers and gave Trev a brutal slap. "You're not going to come until I say you can." He pulled his hand away.

Trev felt the bed shift, and he resisted the urge to smirk as he realized Jupiter was climbing up behind him. He could still reach back and make a swipe at Jupiter's jacket pocket from this position. He rocked his hips back and whimpered again, pleading, "Please. Please fuck me. Give me more of your come."

Jupiter spanked him again, warning, "You'll take what you deserve, baby doll. You were very, very bad. You just had to try and escape, didn't you?"

Trev gritted his teeth. "I *did* escape… sir."

Jupiter cracked his hand across both of Trev's cheeks.

"Fuck!" Trev gasped.

"Watch it. No one likes a smart mouth, baby doll."

Trev had a snarky comeback all lined up about exactly what he could do with his mouth, but he kept his teeth together. He cried out when Jupiter gave him another hard spanking, and he melted into the bed. His head was getting light, and there was a strange part of him that wanted to be good.

He wanted to be good for Jupiter.

He really did want to please him, to make him happy and hear him fall apart, to tell him he was the best he'd ever had—no.

Trev had to focus.

This was all part of the game, that was it. He was only fucking with Jupiter so he had a chance to swipe that damn key. He didn't actually care about what Jupiter thought of him, just as long as he played along with Trev's game.

Trev was in control.

Nothing else mattered.

"There." Jupiter palmed Trev's stinging cheeks and squeezed. "Look at that... You can be such a very, very good boy." He massaged the tender skin, pressing a kiss to Trev's tailbone.

Trev shivered, and he twisted his fingers in the sheets. His cock was even harder now, and he turned his head, the chain clinking.

"Easy, baby doll," Jupiter soothed, his voice like velvet as he kissed over one of the welts left behind from his hand. "Just relax now. Stay nice and still for me. You can do that, can't you?"

"Yes, sir," Trev replied.

Jupiter's lips moved along Trev's overheated skin, tracing what might have been the curve of a palm print. His hands slid up to massage Trev's lower back as he shifted his position. "You want to be good, don't you?"

"Yes, sir. So much."

"You still want to please me..." Jupiter's fly unzipped. "Deny it all you want to, but you value my approval."

"Of course I do, sir," Trev pleaded. "I... I want to be good for you, I promise."

"Even now, you're lying to both of us." Jupiter chuckled. "But you did take your punishment so well..."

Trev bit his lip when he heard the telltale rhythmic pump of Jupiter jerking himself off. "Come on, please. Stick it in."

Jupiter chuckled, the sound rough as he stroked faster. He grabbed Trev's ass cheek and squeezed, spreading it wide. "No."

"What?" Trev whimpered.

What the fuck did he mean, *no*?

"You don't deserve to be fucked," Jupiter replied. "You're lucky I'm going to give you my come."

Alarms went off in Trev's brain, and he tried to calculate his next move. He had to keep going with this ridiculous ruse if he wanted to try again, so he swallowed his pride and said, "Y-yes, sir. Thank you, sir."

"You're welcome, baby doll."

Trev put his face in the pillows, listening to the smack of skin until Jupiter came with a low snarl. The first pulse of hot come landed across Trev's hole, and Jupiter pressed the head of his dick in to deliver the rest. Trev moaned hungrily. "Yes, thank you," he said, gasping. "Thank you so much, sir."

Jupiter patted Trev's ass. "Go on. You can come now."

It wasn't hard for Trev to get right back to where he was before. With the added warmth of Jupiter's load inside him, his cock throbbed harder than ever and he humped the bed in earnest. He reached back to finger himself, pushing the spilled come deep inside with a moan.

"Beautiful." Jupiter picked up his phone, and judging by the angle of the flashlight, he was watching Trev pump his fingers in and out of his hole.

"Thank you, sir. Th-thank you!" Trev gritted his teeth, his cheeks burning from the friction and building pressure. He put his entire attention on the head of his dick pressing into the bed, letting the thrill of Jupiter's rapt attention carry him over the edge. He climaxed hard, shuddering as he grinded himself through it.

"Good boy." Jupiter squeezed Trev's hip.

Trev smiled, and his heart thumped unexpectedly.

He tried to dismiss the feeling as soon as it arose, but then Jupiter leaned in to kiss him. The warmth bubbled over and he swore there were actual sparks going off between their lips. A quick slide of Jupiter's tongue made him moan, and every muscle in Trev's body melted into hot, syrupy mush. The kiss was all too brief, but Jupiter had the most beautiful smile when he withdrew.

"Such a very good boy," Jupiter purred.

"Thank you, sir." Trev pulled his fingers free with a little grunt. The odd glow lingered, and he couldn't define it. He didn't need to because it was bullshit.

Fuck.

"Go on and get some sleep now, baby doll." Jupiter returned to his chair and scrolled through his phone. He was still smiling, and he looked especially pleased with himself.

Fuck, fuck, *fuuuck.*

Trev cleaned up as best as he could with the blanket and then kicked it off and out of his way. The sheets beneath were clean at least, and he rolled over to face the wall so Jupiter couldn't see him scowling.

That was a complete and utter failure.

Well...

Not entirely.

Getting off like that was pretty hot, and it would certainly help him later if he had another opportunity to seduce Jupiter.

No, not *opportunity*—a reason.

With a sigh, Trev rolled over and went to sleep.

Jupiter was still a bastard.

This changed nothing.

CHAPTER Six

TREV WOKE UP, bleary eyed and annoyed, and he really needed to piss.

It was dark except for a thin beam of light shining from underneath the door, and he had no idea what time it was. It felt disgustingly early, but he couldn't be sure. He tried to lift his head, and the weight of the collar reminded him that the nightmare he was currently trapped in was very real and not merely a bad dream.

Ugh.

Great.

He rolled over to find that the room was empty, and there was no sign of Jupiter.

Trev jumped to his feet and ran to the door. The chain caught him when he was only two feet from reaching the knob, and he growled in frustration.

Motherfucker.

He hurried back to the bed and climbed up. He braced himself on the edge of the frame and pulled on the chain with his entire weight, trying to wrench it free from the wall. "Come on... you... *fucker*!"

The chain didn't budge.

The door opened.

Trev turned his head, flashing a dazzling smile as Jupiter walked in. "Good morning."

"Morning." Jupiter smirked.

Trev batted his eyes. "Would you believe me if I told you I was stretching?"

"No."

Trev dropped the chain. "Fine." He hopped off the bed. "How about a bathroom break? Is that in my future? Because it's either that or I piss right here."

Jupiter snorted and beckoned Trev over with a finger. "Come here, baby doll."

Trev approached, watching Jupiter pull the key out of his jacket pocket.

Good to know he was still keeping it there.

Jupiter released the padlock and then removed the collar. He rubbed Trev's neck, saying, "Now, you're going to be a good boy and not try anything, aren't you?"

"I won't make a promise I can't keep," Trev said sweetly.

"Come on." Jupiter held the back of Trev's neck, leading him out into the hallway.

Judging by the light coming in from some of the windows, it was early morning.

Ugh, definitely too early to be up.

Jupiter brought Trev to a door two down from the room he was being kept in, and he opened it to reveal a small bathroom.

With no windows, naturally.

"Go on." Jupiter crossed his arms. "I'll be right here."

"You don't want to come hold it for me?"

Jupiter gave Trev a small push. "Now."

"Fine." Trev stalked inside, slamming the door behind

him. He noted there was no way to lock it and sighed. He used the toilet, looking around for anything that might be useful. There was a sink, a bottle of soap, a mirror, some toilet paper, and that was it.

Great.

He finished up, making an effort to wash his hands and freshen up. He scrubbed his face to try and wash off his makeup, longing for his cleansers and moisturizer. He made a face in the mirror when he ended up looking like a raccoon and grabbed some toilet paper to finish cleaning up with.

Trev checked his reflection.

Good enough.

He opened the bathroom door and struck a provocative pose against the frame. "So. Whose dick do I have to suck to get some breakfast, hmm?"

Jupiter snorted, reaching for Trev's arm. "Let me get you chained back up and I'll see what I can do, hmm?"

"Mmm. If you're taking requests, I like pancakes with whipped cream and strawberries."

"Noted."

Jupiter's grip was too firm for Trev to consider making a break for it. He let Jupiter lead him back to the room and put the collar back on, being sure to pay attention to which pocket Jupiter put the key in.

He licked his lips once or twice, just to see how Jupiter's eyes drifted. He also noticed Jupiter was wearing the same suit from last night. "Are you mad at me, sweetie? You didn't come to bed last night."

"I slept in the chair just fine."

"That can't be good for your back. Want a massage?"

"No. Sal and Emil are—"

A door opened somewhere, and Emil called out, "Knock knock! Anybody home?"

Jupiter sighed, and his brow creased—with what? Frustration? Annoyance?

Trev could certainly see how Emil could cause either of those, but that was interesting.

"Emil, watch the fuckin' door," Sal's sterner voice snapped. "Jupiter!"

"Stay here and behave," Jupiter warned Trev.

"So, a rain check on that massage?" Trev teased. "That's fine. I'll be here waiting."

Jupiter rolled his eyes, but his smile had returned before he turned away to leave.

Sal and a man Trev hadn't seen before came up to Jupiter before he made it out of the room. Sal gestured to the man beside him, saying, "Hey, Jupiter. This is our out of town talent. Just gimme a minute and we're gonna go get you guys some food, all right? I gotta walk him through the operation real fast."

The man was tall with thick eyebrows, and his mouth was far too big when he smiled. His gaze immediately settled on Trev, and his weird smile grew impossibly bigger. "Hey, how ya' doin'?"

"I'm currently chained to a wall," Trev drawled. "How the fuck do you think I'm doing, asshole?"

"Oh! Got a mouth on him, don't he?" The man laughed.

"Ignore him," Sal said. "He's just here for a little side project."

"I can dig it." The man eyed Trev and then turned back to Sal. "Needs any help with it? I gots some experience watchin' over *real* valuable property, high-class stuff, just like this. I'd be real happy to offer my services."

Jupiter scowled.

"That won't be necessary," Sal replied, "but thank you. Jupiter is taking care of it until it's time to finish up."

"Aw, I hopes you don't mean, you know, finish up, like—*ugh*." The man stuck out his tongue and drew a line over his throat. "Because that would be just an awful fuckin' waste—"

"I can assure you that—" Sal tried to interrupt him, but his phone rang. "Just a moment. My apologies." He stepped away to answer the phone, and judging by the door opening and shutting, had walked outside.

Which left the man alone here with Trev and Jupiter.

"Hi. Howell Hodges." The man grinned at Trev. He hadn't looked at Jupiter once. "What's your name, babycakes?"

"My name is fuck you in the eye—"

"None of your business," Jupiter smoothly interjected.

Trev hadn't been expecting that, and he blinked at Jupiter in surprise. He quickly recovered, adding, "Yeah, what he said."

"Oh, sorry! Didn't mean to hitta fuckin' nerve." Howell grinned. "Chains? Nice. Yous guys are into that real freaky shit, huh?"

The way Howell was looking at Trev made his skin crawl. He'd definitely felt his share of lustful stares, but there was something about this one that unsettled him to his bones.

It flat out gave Trev the creeps.

"It's business," Jupiter replied, his eyes narrowing, "and as I already said—"

"Yeah, yeah, it's none of mine, right?" Howell stalked the short distance toward Jupiter, his big grin still in place. "Tell ya' what, *bastard*." He flicked Jupiter's tie. "When I wants some of your lip, I'll march my happy ass on over there and pick it off that lil' twink's zipper. Until then, hows 'bout you keep them pretty teeth of yours nice and tight before I makes 'em not so pretty?"

Jupiter remained very still, but his eyes were practically sparking with his rage.

Howell was about the same height as Jupiter, but Jupiter was easily twice his size. He could probably crush Howell with one quick punch, and Trev was really, really wondering why Jupiter hadn't blown up on this asshole yet.

"Understood, sir," Jupiter said with an eerie calm. "I apologize. Please understand that I was given explicit instructions to care for this particular *twink* and to keep him safe from any harm."

"Yeah, I gets it. You was just doin' your job—"

"I'd hate to think what I would have to do if I was suddenly given the impression that you might be a threat."

Trev froze.

That sounded like a warning.

Howell's grin somehow grew even more, and he stepped right into Jupiter's space until they were nose to nose. "Oh? It's like that, huh?"

Jupiter didn't flinch. "It's very much like that."

"Yeah?"

"Yeah."

"Trust me, *bastard*." Howell chuckled, and he roughly adjusted Jupiter's suit jacket, sliding his hands over the lapels. "If I wanna be a fuckin' threat, you'll fuckin' know it. Won't even need a neon sign or nothin'. You'll be able to see this from the fuckin' moon, okay? Astronauts up in fuckin' space pissin' in their lil' space toilets are gonna have a front row view of ya' fixin' to shit yourself when and if I decide to be threatenin'."

Jupiter frowned. He didn't seem afraid, but perhaps a bit confused by the off-kilter rambling.

"The fuck?" Trev whispered.

Who the hell was this guy?

Sal came back then, and he scowled. "Is there a problem here, Mr. Hodges?"

"Nope. No problem." Howell smiled brightly and patted Jupiter's chest. "Just gettin' to know this big guy right here." He smirked at Sal. "Always fun to meet local celebrities, ya' know?"

"I'm sure." Sal grimaced. "Are you ready?"

"Oh, sure. Let's go see this shit." Howell followed Sal back into the hallway.

As soon as they were gone, Jupiter furiously wiped off his jacket as if Howell had left some sort of residue behind. He mumbled something in Italian, and it definitely did not sound kind.

"You okay?" Trev asked.

"Fine," Jupiter replied shortly.

"That guy really must be somebody special to let him walk all over you."

"Don't worry about it."

"Are you really a local celebrity? What are you famous for? Being a giant sack of dicks?"

Jupiter snorted.

"Why did he keep calling you a *bastard*? Really seemed to get under your skin." Trev shrugged. "At least until all the weird space toilet talk. Methinks your daddy issues are starting to show, and you know—"

Jupiter shook his head, leaving the room in a huff.

"Fine! Fuck you!" Trev shouted after him. "I didn't want to talk to you anyway!" He scowled when he heard the side door open and slam shut. "Asshole."

With nothing better to do, Trev lay back down in bed. He stretched out on his side, hoping to look enticing for whenever Jupiter decided to get over himself and come back.

Several minutes passed before he heard another door open, but this sounded like the doors at the other end of the hall that led out to the factory floor. He could hear Howell and Sal talking, and having nothing better to do, he decided to listen in.

"...is cut, okay?" Howell was saying. "Before you even move it. Ya' don't wanna get busted with nothin' that pure, all right? 'Cause then ya' lose it all."

"Understood, sir," Sal said.

"Who's controllin' the pipeline? I wanna know where this shit is comin' from."

"I can assure you it's a legit source."

"I'll decide what the fuck is legit or not. I don't want no fuckin' trouble with anybody either south of the fuckin' border or certain small islands, ya' fuckin' feel me?"

"Of course. Look, we got a federal dog on a leash. He's the source."

Howell laughed. "That's how you motherfuckers managed to float all this, huh? Not bad, not bad. Make sure that leash stays nice and tight though, huh? Don't wanna get bit."

"Never."

"So." Howell cleared his throat. "You wanna tell me more 'bout this lil' side project ya' got goin' on?"

"It's really nothing to concern yourself with," Sal replied. "Just hammering out some old family business."

"And ya' let the bastard be the man on point?" Howell chuckled. "Must not be that important then."

"We're giving him a chance to prove himself."

"Which means he's already fucked up." Howell clicked his tongue. "He's a real piece of shit, huh?"

Sal chuckled. "Trust me, if he wasn't family..."

Trev leaned forward, straining to hear more. He figured Sal must have made a gesture of some kind or perhaps whispered something because there was a pause and then Howell laughed.

"Hey. Do what you gotta do." Howell sounded like he was smiling that big stupid smile of his. "Speak of the devil."

The door opened, no doubt Jupiter returning.

"We're wrappin' up here," Sal said. "Takin' Mr. Hodges out for breakfast. We'll get somethin' to go and bring it back."

"Any requests from you or your lil' pet?" Howell teased.

"Pancakes," Jupiter replied. "With strawberries and whipped cream." He snorted. "Just coffee for me."

"Yous got it." Howell walked by the open doorway, and he flashed Trev a sly smile. "Be seein' ya'."

Trev flipped him off.

Sal was only a few steps behind Howell, and he didn't notice or didn't care. "Keep it quiet here, all right?"

"Yes, sir," Jupiter said, hovering by the doorway as he watched them leave. His expression was tense, but Trev didn't think he'd be in the mood to be offered another massage.

What Trev had overheard Howell and Sal talking about had some potential though. Maybe it would even be enough to unsettle Jupiter so he'd let his guard down and Trev could get his hands on that damn key.

Then again, it might only piss Jupiter off and accomplish nothing.

He had to use this information carefully, and chances

were high that Jupiter already knew what his little mafia friends really thought of him.

"So." Trev clapped his hands. "What now?"

"We wait," Jupiter replied simply.

"Wow. Fucking awesome."

"I'm stepping out." Jupiter grabbed the doorknob. "I trust you won't find any clever ways to escape while I'm gone?"

"Stepping out?" Trev narrowed his eyes. "Stepping out where?"

"Don't worry, baby doll. I'll be right back."

"Right." Trev scowled as the door shut.

He immediately got to his feet, trying again to brace himself on the bed and pull the chain free from the wall. When that didn't work, he hopped down to search the room. There had to be something here he could use.

The fridge was full of cheap beer, and Trev didn't think he could use the tab from a can to pick the padlock. He grabbed the chair and tried whacking it against the wall, hoping to catch where the chain was bolted into the concrete.

All that did was make a bunch of noise, scuff up the wall, and hurt his shoulder.

Fuck.

Trev froze when he heard the side door opening, and he quickly returned the chair. He dashed back into bed to pretend he hadn't been trying to escape again, and he listened intently.

Someone had walked into one of the other rooms, perhaps the bathroom.

There was a pause, the door shut, and then someone went back outside.

Huh.

Trev listened for a bit longer, but he didn't hear anything else of note.

Being kidnapped and held hostage was fucking boring.

He figured he should be grateful that it wasn't more exciting, but he had no idea what to do with himself. He rolled over to hug the lockbox to his chest. What remained of his future was inside here, and he'd be damned if he let anything happen to it.

He dozed for a little while, waking again when Jupiter brought him breakfast.

As promised, it was pancakes with strawberries and whipped cream. He was too hungry to worry about the food being tampered with and dove right in. He did take his time licking cream off his fingers, but Jupiter was back on his phone and ignoring him.

"You know, they say sixty percent of men are losing their eyesight faster because of excessive screen time," Trev said.

"Is that so?" Jupiter didn't look up.

"No, I just made that up so you'd pay attention to me." Trev slurped whipped cream off his fingers. "Come on."

"I'm busy."

"Doing what?"

Jupiter sighed, glancing up at Trev. "What do you want?"

"If you're taking requests, getting the fucking collar off would be top of the list."

"Next."

"How about some dick?"

"Next." Jupiter smiled.

"You're killing all my options here." Trev picked at his food. "I guess you don't have any updates for me. About when I might be getting out of here."

"Not yet. In that much of a hurry to get away from me?"

"What? After all the fun we've had?" Trev snorted. "No way."

"My favorite part was the look on your face when your car wouldn't start."

"Mine was spraying you in the face with glitter body spray."

Jupiter snorted out a laugh. "I think there's still some in my shirt."

"Good. You'll have something to remember me by."

"As if I could ever forget you, baby doll."

Trev hated how his heart thumped when Jupiter smiled at him. They really did seem to have nice chemistry, and the sex had been incredible.

Too bad Jupiter was a giant douche nozzle.

"Look." Jupiter dropped his phone to his lap, giving Trev his full attention. "I can tell you that Boss Cold's men received our message with our offer, plus the results of your DNA test. All right?"

"And?"

"And what?"

Trev wanted to stab Jupiter with his plastic fork. "And what did they say?"

"We'll have an answer soon."

Trev's stomach twisted. "So... Wow. Cold really doesn't give a fuck about me, does he?"

"It wasn't a no," Jupiter said. He almost sounded soothing. "These things take time, baby doll. Cold isn't going to overplay his hand and appear too eager. That's not his style. They call him Cold for a reason."

"It's so very cute you're trying to make me feel better, but what the fuck happens if he doesn't want to make the deal?" Trev pressed. "What happens to me?"

"That's not up to me."

"Right, it's up to your stupid fuckin' boss, right? Sal?" Trev set his fork down. He wasn't hungry now. "You know they talk shit about you, right?"

Jupiter's expression remained passive.

Fuck it.

No time like the present.

"Yeah, while you were doing what the fuck ever, I heard Howell and Sal talking about you. They think you're a joke and a fuckup. They care so little about you they didn't seem to give a fuck if I heard them or not. They were *laughing*. Did you know they think you're a piece of shit? Huh? Or do you just roll over the second they say *hey, bastard*?"

"My relationship with my family is none of your concern," Jupiter said smoothly.

"I'd say it's a big concern since it's you and your stupid family who thought it was great idea to fucking kidnap me. So, what's the deal? Did you get assigned to bitch duty because you're the *bitch*?"

"I know what you're doing, baby doll, and it's not going to work."

"What?"

"Trying to get a rise out of me." Jupiter narrowed his eyes. "Pretty cheap move, to be honest. You must be desperate."

"Maybe I'm just worried about you."

Jupiter laughed. "I doubt it."

"What? I can't be worried about my captor?" Trev batted his eyes. "Maybe I'm developing Stockholm or something. You never know."

"Cute." Jupiter smirked. "Got any other startling revelations to share with me to try and gain my trust? Or are you gonna finish your pancakes and be quiet?"

"Just one," Trev said, popping a strawberry in his mouth.

"Thanks for letting me know you already knew they hate your fucking guts. Are you really a bastard? Or is it because you're a *gay* bastard?"

Jupiter's gaze darkened.

Bingo.

"Struck a nerve, *Daddy*?" Trev smirked.

"Eat your pancakes."

"Wow. I'm so sorry to hear that the mafia isn't a bunch of super open-minded people. Damn." Trev took a big bite of pancake. "Mm, mm. And you still work for them? Really?"

Jupiter headed to the door.

"What?" Trev grinned. "Did I hurt your feelings? Want me to kiss it and make it better?"

Jupiter slammed the door shut behind him.

"Is that a no?" Trev shouted.

After waiting a few minutes, it didn't seem like Jupiter was coming back anytime soon.

Trev hurried to the wall where the chain was attached to a small metal plate. He took his plastic knife and tried loosening the screws that bolted it to the brick.

The knife snapped, and Trev wasn't even sure if the screw had budged at all. He heard footsteps and shoved the broken knife in the pocket of his hoodie. He went back to eating like nothing had happened, and he put on his sweetest smile when Jupiter walked back in.

"Come on," Jupiter said briskly. "Finish eating."

"Why?" Trev frowned. "What's going on?"

"We're moving you. That's all I can tell you."

Trev's frown deepened. "Is it Cold? Did he accept the deal?"

Jupiter narrowed his eyes. "What part of *that's all I can tell you* do you not understand?"

"The *that's*, the *all*, the *I*, the *can*—"

Jupiter snatched Trev's pancakes away.

"Hey!" Trev snapped. "I was still eating that!"

"Later." Jupiter threw the platter on the floor.

Trev gritted his teeth and stood up from the bed, holding his head up defiantly. "Before we go anywhere, I need to use the bathroom."

"Hold it."

"No way!" Trev barked. "I have to piss right fucking now. Do you want me to pee in your car? Because I will. I have a very small bladder and—"

"*Fine.*" Jupiter took the key out of his pocket. "Come here. We're going to make this quick. Emil is coming with a car."

Trev walked up to him, tilting his head back. "Should I be on my knees?"

Jupiter snorted and unlocked the padlock. He grabbed Trev's arm, wordlessly escorting him to the bathroom. "Hurry up."

"Sir, yes, sir." Trev scoffed, waiting for Jupiter to shut the door before using the toilet.

Shit.

Today was not going well.

He'd probably pushed Jupiter too far and his chances of getting close enough to steal that damn key were likely zilch now.

It did make him curious though—why was Jupiter working for people who hated him? Was that normal in organized crime? Trev had no idea, and he told himself he shouldn't really care. He was only interested because of how he could use that and any other information to manipulate Jupiter.

After all, he was running out of time.

If Trev was being moved, that might mean that Boss

Cold had made a decision. God only knew what the Luchesi family had asked for, and Trev sincerely doubted Cold would be willing to make any deal for him.

He didn't know Trev from shit, so why would he?

Would family really mean that much to him?

Trev could be headed to a new location to be disposed of if Cold had refused to bargain for him. This might be the fucking end—a short trip to the quarry, to some sort of landfill, and that would be it.

Shit, shit, shit.

Trev sighed as he went to the sink to wash up.

As far as plans went, this one felt pretty stupid. It might be true that Cold especially valued family, but it still seemed like a strange concept to base an entire plot on. He hoped they were right though.

His entire fate hinged on whether or not some mafia boss wanted to have a reunion with a half-brother he'd never known even existed.

Or if Trev could still manage to escape.

Without that damn key though, he was fucked. There wasn't much he could do with a broken plastic knife, and Jupiter didn't seem to be a big fan of his right now.

Shit, shitty, shit, *shit*.

Trev glanced at the soap bottle, something catching his eye that hadn't been there before. It was tucked underneath the bottle, almost invisible except when he looked directly down through the translucent orange goop.

It was a key.

CHAPTER Seven

A KEY.

It was a *key*.

Trev stared at it for a long moment, honestly in shock and his thoughts zooming at maximum speed. He would have noticed a key if it had been here earlier. He wouldn't have missed that.

Trev tensed.

He'd remembered hearing someone coming back into the building earlier, but who?

Who would have left him a key?

Sal? Emil? That creep, Howell?

And why would anyone risk something so sloppy?

If the key was meant for him, which Trev had to assume it was, there was no way for his generous benefactor to know that he'd be the next one in the bathroom to find it. Jupiter or Sal or anyone else could have found it first.

Still...

It might be the key to the padlock on his collar—wait, no. That couldn't be right. Jupiter had the keys because he'd unlocked Trev's collar to let him come to the bathroom.

So, what was this for?

Jupiter banged on the door.

"Wait a fucking second!" Trev barked.

"Hurry up!" Jupiter shouted back.

Trev shoved the key in his pocket. He'd figure it out later. He checked himself in the mirror to make sure he looked as flawless as possible and then opened the bathroom door. He cocked his hip. "What? Pancake syrup runs right through me. I needed a second."

"Come on." Jupiter held out his hand.

Trev frowned, but he took it.

Jupiter led him toward the side door exit.

"Not going back to our honeymoon suite?" Trev asked, the key burning a hole in his pocket.

"No. No time," Jupiter replied briskly.

"Hey! Fuck you!" Trev dug his heels in. "My lockbox! I'm not leaving without it! You are gonna—"

"Already in the car, baby doll." Jupiter glanced back at him. "I knew you'd ask, so I went ahead and got one of the guys to grab it."

"Thanks." Trev still looked into the room as they walked past to make sure the lockbox was really gone. He also noticed that the chain and collar remained.

If the key did go to the padlock, it was useless now.

There were two men in dark suits waiting outside next to —of course—another black SUV. Jupiter opened the rear passenger door for Trev, ushering him inside.

Trev climbed in, relieved when he saw his lockbox on the floorboard. He grabbed it to put in his lap and then reached over to try the other door.

Locked.

Jupiter snorted as he sat beside Trev. "A for effort."

"Didn't want you to think I was getting used to you or anything," Trev grumbled.

The suited men took the front seats, and the one behind the wheel said, "There's been a change of plans."

"Excuse me?" Jupiter scowled.

"We're headed back to the nest," he said as he drove them to the highway.

"Nest?" Trev raised his brow. "Are we fuckin' birds now?"

Jupiter ignored him, asking the driver, "Why?"

"Sal's orders," he replied. "Take it up with him, Jupe."

"Don't fucking call me that." Jupiter's scowl deepened, and he sat back in the seat. He pulled out his phone.

"I'll call you whatever I want." He and the other man shared a hearty laugh.

Trev filed that away for now and stayed silent. He could tell Jupiter was extremely pissed, and he busied himself looking out the window to figure out where they were headed.

Toward the city, and yet still in the middle of nowhere.

It was a maze of more tiny back roads Trev wasn't familiar with, and he could only imagine what sort of crap fest a place called the *nest* was going to be.

When they rolled up to an actual *mansion*, Trev did his best to not let his surprise show. He didn't know enough about architecture to identify much beyond the big marble columns and fancy fountain, but he could definitely say it was the largest house he'd ever seen in person.

There was an honest to God *butler* waiting for them at the front door with another man in a dark suit.

"You guys buy your suits wholesale at the same place you get your ugly ass cars?" Trev mumbled.

Jupiter silenced him with a glare.

Asshole.

They parked, and then the butler and the other suited man opened the front car doors. The driver handed off the keys to the man in the suit, and the butler came to open Trev's door.

Every muscle tensed and he tightened his grip on the lockbox. Maybe he could make a run for it—

Jupiter's hand slid over the back of Trev's neck and gently squeezed. "Don't even think about it."

Asshole.

The door opened and Trev hopped out, well aware of Jupiter right behind him. He must have looked like he still wanted to run because Jupiter grabbed the back of his neck again. "Mm, *Daddy*."

"Quiet," Jupiter warned, using his grip to steer Trev toward the house.

The front door was opened by—who else—another man in a suit, and Jupiter guided Trev through a large foyer and then directly up a big set of twisting stairs. Everything was white and gold, looked very expensive, and Trev barely had a second to take it all in before Jupiter was shoving him into a lush bedroom.

The furniture was gold, gaudy, and upholstered in purple velvet. The bed was made up with matching purple linens, the floor was covered in thick orange shag rugs, and it was somehow the fanciest and yet also the most hideous room Trev had ever seen.

He immediately noticed the large windows opposite the bed, and he wondered how far of a drop it was to the ground from this floor.

Jupiter squeezed the back of his neck. "You're going to stay here and be good, aren't you, baby doll?"

"Uh-huh. So very good."

"Stay put." Jupiter eyed him. "I mean it."

"What?" Trev batted his eyes. "You don't trust me?"

Jupiter smirked. "No."

"That's a shame. Trust is essential for every relationship, you know."

"I'll keep that in mind." Jupiter headed back through the door.

To Trev's surprise, he didn't close it. Trev peeked out into the hall, finding a new suited man standing guard by the top of the stairs.

The man smiled and made a kissy face.

Trev smiled sweetly and flipped him off. He ducked back into the room and sighed in frustration. He checked the windows, and they were all locked. There were two doors, but one led to a bathroom and the other was a closet.

As nice as it was to entertain the idea of taking a shower later, Trev didn't want to be here that long.

He checked the windows again, eyeing the tall shrubs just outside. He could smash the glass, crawl out on the ledge, and then try to jump into the shrubs and hope he didn't break any bones.

Shit.

He wasn't sure if he was that desperate yet.

Trev ran back to the bathroom. It was bigger than his apartment, with a stone-tiled walk-in shower and a gloriously huge jacuzzi tub. There was a window above the tub, and Trev climbed into the tub so he could peek out.

There was a large tree with branches that were only a few feet away from the window. Although it was also locked, Trev liked his chances of survival from jumping out of this one much better than the others.

Shouting drew Trev's attention back to the open bedroom door. He hurried over, peering out and straining to hear what the commotion was all about.

Fortunately, one of the people yelling was Howell, and Trev could have heard him from the other side of the planet.

"Are you all fuckin' mentally irregular? Hello!" Howell snarled furiously. "Won't it just this mornin' yous was tellin' me how safe and secure your shit was? Watertight? Now what, bitches?"

Someone barked back.

Maybe Emil.

"I know this little *bitch* didn't just try to step up to me!" Howell raged. "Do yous have any idea how many millions of fuckin' dollars we just handed over to the fuckin' pigs? Better be countin' your teeth 'cause yous 'bout to be pickin' 'em up off the floor! Fuck you!"

The shouting continued but moved farther away until Trev couldn't even make out what Howell was saying. He wasn't exactly sure what had happened, but it didn't take a rocket scientist to know the cops were involved and something had gone very wrong for the Luchesi family.

That at least made Trev smile, though it did little to help him with his current predicament.

His sudden relocation may have been because of the cops and not because Boss Cold had arrived at a decision.

Shit.

"Who are you?" a rumbling voice asked.

Trev jumped, whirling around to find an old man walking up from the opposite end of the hallway.

The man was dressed in a thick sweater, sweatpants, and worn slippers. He looked to be in his eighties, and his casual outfit seemed oddly out of place with the fancy house. His dark olive skin was freckled, his hair stark white and neatly trimmed, and his smile was very friendly.

"Trevanion Usher," Trev said slowly.

"It's nice to meet you, young man!" The man reached for

Trev's hand and shook it. "I'm Ugo Luchesi. Are you here for the party?"

"Party?" Trev studied the man's face more carefully and saw a familiar mania that reminded him of Juicy. He patted the man's hand, replying kindly, "No, sir. I'm a friend of Jupiter's. I'm here on, uh, business."

"Ah! Jupiter!" The man's face lit up. "That kid is gonna be the don one day, you know. Lead the whole family—"

"*Zio!*" Jupiter snapped. "Come on now. Why are you out of bed?"

Ugo hissed like a cat.

Trev turned to see Jupiter stalking toward him with Sal and the man who had driven them here in tow.

A woman in scrubs with a big ponytail came tearing around the corner at the end of the hall, clearly out of breath and anxious.

Trev thought she looked familiar, but he couldn't place where he'd seen her before.

She sighed in visible relief. "Mr. Luchesi! There you are!"

"Nurse," Sal said firmly. "Take him back to his room right now."

"Yes, sir," the nurse said, reaching for Ugo's arm. "Come on back with me, sir."

"No!" Ugo scowled and swatted at her. "I'm talking with my new friend! We have to go to the party! You won't take me alive, you ornery old *bitch*!"

The nurse grunted, clearly flustered and becoming more so as Ugo struggled and Sal continued to glare.

"Get him to his room now!" Sal barked.

"I'm so sorry, sir! I'm trying!" the nurse pleaded. "Sir, I—"

"I said *now*!"

The nurse looked as if she was about to burst into tears,

and Ugo was running around her in circles, surprisingly spry for his age.

"Bonsai!" Sal waved at the driver. "Give 'em a hand, would you?"

"Yes, sir." Bonsai stepped into the fray, reaching for Ugo's shoulder. "Come on now, Mr. Luchesi. Why don't you go back with the nice lady? We can—"

Ugo whipped his head around and bit Bonsai's arm.

"Ow! Son of a bitch!" Bonsai screeched.

"Watch ya' fuckin' mouth!" Sal snapped. "That's my grandma, may she rest in peace, that you're talking about!"

"I'm sorry, boss!" Bonsai waved his arm. "He fucking bit me!"

Sal pressed his hands to his temples and muttered something in Italian.

"Zio," Jupiter tried, using a gentle tone and approaching slowly, as if Ugo was a wild animal. "Hey, hey, Zio Ugo. Play nice, okay?"

Ugo bared his teeth and growled.

Jupiter took a step back.

"Hey!" Trev said suddenly. "Mr. Luchesi? You still want to go to the party, right? Your nurse will take you."

Everyone stared at Trev.

"Oh!" Ugo flinched as if a switch had been flipped and appeared to relax. "Is that so?"

The nurse gave Trev a grateful smile, and she offered her arm to Ugo. "Absolutely, sir! Let's go."

"Thank you. I do love a party." Ugo waved farewell as the nurse led him down the hallway, still chatting away excitedly about all the champagne he was going to drink.

"You!" Sal hissed, his eyes burning into Trev. "Don't you ever speak to my father again, do you understand me?"

"Your father?" Trev scoffed. "Come on. I was just trying to help!"

"Shut your fucking mouth, you flaming *whore*."

Trev's temper flared. "Fuck you, *bitch*."

Sal raised his hand.

Trev stood his ground, ready to take the hit. It wouldn't be the first he'd been struck for running his mouth and probably wouldn't be the last.

Jupiter caught Sal's wrist, saying, "No damaging the merchandise, right, sir?"

Trev flinched.

He hadn't been expecting that.

Sal growled and smacked Jupiter across the face. "Fuckin' *disgrace*."

"Hey!" Trev snapped. "Why don't you...!"

Jupiter's stern gaze pleaded for silence.

Trev shut his mouth, but just barely.

Sal's glare found Trev, and he raised his hand again. "I told you to shut your fucking mouth, whore. Nobody was talkin' to you—"

"That's enough." Jupiter put himself in between them. "I'll take him back to my room right now—"

"Oh? Is that how it is?" Sal scowled. "Gonna be a big man in front of your little girlfriend? I swear to almighty *fuck* I don't regret anything as much as I do bringin' you in on this."

"I'm not the one you should be angry with," Jupiter replied calmly. "You should be taking a closer look at Howell—"

"Mind your fucking business," Sal warned, jabbing a finger in Jupiter's chest. "Take your little bitch back to your room and keep him quiet."

"Yes, sir." Jupiter turned around and grabbed Trev's arm, leading him back to the bedroom.

"Hey!" Trev tried to pull away, but he couldn't wiggle out of Jupiter's grip. Maybe he should take some notes from Ugo and bite more often.

Bonsai laughed. "Some things never change, huh? Jupe's still a damn fuckup."

"What? You're just gonna let them say that—" Trev yelped as Jupiter heaved him up over his shoulder to carry him the rest of the way. It was a short distance since they were right outside the bedroom, but Trev's heart pounded a little faster anyway.

That shouldn't have been so hot.

Jupiter shut the door and then set Trev down, ordering, "Go sit down and be quiet."

"Your family really fucking hates you, don't they?" Trev taunted defiantly as he strolled over to the bed.

Jupiter glared.

"So! That old guy." Trev sat down. "Ugo? He's Sal's dad, huh? What is it? Dementia? Alzheimer's?"

Jupiter leaned against the door and crossed his arms.

"Oh! We're back to you not talking to me and me just talking at you. Got it. Love this for us." Trev leaned back on his hands, letting his legs fall apart. "So fun."

Jupiter glanced over him, but still said nothing.

"You didn't have to do that, by the way," Trev said quietly.

"Do what?"

"Defend me."

"Sal was out of line." Jupiter loosened his tie.

"He's a total asshole, no argument there." Trev pursed his lips. "Why'd you do it though? You could have just let him knock me around and you didn't."

Jupiter appeared startled by the question, a look Trev hadn't seen before.

Trev stared at him expectantly.

"Wouldn't look good for us to deliver you to Boss Cold all beat up, now would it?" Jupiter replied.

"That's it?" Trev quirked his brows.

"Should there be another reason?"

"No, I guess not." Trev shrugged. "Just surprised, is all." He looked away. "And thank you."

"You're welcome."

"Not a lot of guys would do that for me," Trev said honestly.

Jupiter met his gaze again. "Sounds like you hang out with a bunch of assholes too."

"Present company included."

Jupiter snorted.

"Seriously." Trev frowned. "It's pretty obvious they don't respect you—"

"Don't," Jupiter cut in.

"Don't what? Call you out on the bullshit?" Trev scoffed and rolled his eyes. "Fine. Keep lying to yourself. It's very cute."

"Says the biggest liar of them all," Jupiter drawled.

"Excuse me?"

"You." Jupiter glared heatedly at him. "You're so fucking *fake*. Do you really think I don't know what you're trying to do? Batting your eyes, acting sweet and trying to get on my good side? I'm not going to let you manipulate me because I'd have to actually give a shit about you first."

Trev swallowed back a bite of anger and used it to fuel a sweet smile as he cooed, "Says the guy who didn't let me get clocked earlier."

"I already told you—"

"Yeah, yeah. Didn't want Boss Cold to get pissed I got roughed up or whatever." Trev bounced off the bed and into a confident strut as he approached Jupiter. "I think you're the one who's fucking fake."

Jupiter laughed. "Oh? Is that so?"

"Uh-huh." Trev held his head high. "You act all big and tough, but you hate how your family treats you like complete dogshit. Are you really some kind of bastard? Or it just good ol' bigotry?"

Jupiter wasn't laughing now.

"*Ding ding*. We have a winner." Trev boldly adjusted Jupiter's lapels. "Who's being fake now? You have to know they hate you for it. Can't imagine what kinda little nicknames they call you behind your back, *Jupe*."

"Don't," Jupiter warned.

"Don't what? Keep calling you out?" Trev remembered the key in his pocket. "I bet they'd even try to set you up and make you look like even more of a fuckup than the one they already think you are for liking dick."

"Baby doll, I'm not in the mood." Jupiter narrowed his eyes. "My relationship with my family is none of your business, and despite what you think, it's perfectly fine."

"Oh? Is that so?"

"Yes."

Trev fished the key out of his pocket. "Then who left me this key?"

Jupiter stared at it in disbelief. "Where the fuck did you get this?"

"Gee, I'm not sure." Trev scratched his head. "It must have slipped my mind."

"No more games, baby doll." Jupiter grabbed Trev's chin to meet his eyes. "Where did you get this?"

Trev had a very smug and snarky response all lined up, but there was an abrupt knock on the door.

Jupiter ignored it, still staring down Trev.

The door opened a few inches, its progress halted by Jupiter's shoulder. Jupiter did not budge, though he did now turn his angry glare to identify whoever had bonked him with the door. "What?"

"It's Howell," Howell said cheerfully.

Trev grunted as Jupiter snatched the key and pushed him back, now standing in between Trev and the door as if to shield him.

Or to prevent him from making a run for it.

"What do you want?" Jupiter said briskly.

"Nothin' from yous, bastard." Howell scoffed, forcing the door open wide enough to slip his thin frame through. "I got somethin' for your lil' guest here."

"Me?" Trev blinked, peeking around Jupiter.

Jupiter gritted his teeth. "You need to leave. We were just—"

"Keep ya' shirt on, ya' beefed out twat." Howell thrust a large paper bag at Trev. "Here."

Jupiter snatched the bag before Trev could accept it. He opened it to dig around its contents and scowled. "The fuck is this?"

"We call that stuff *clothing*," Howell said. "Just s'happened to notice your lil' guest won't dressed real nice and I thought—"

"Thank you. Goodbye now." Jupiter used his larger size to push Howell back through the door.

Trev wrinkled his nose.

He'd literally just met Howell this morning.

It wouldn't be the first time an admirer had become smitten with him, which is what Trev assumed was happening, but it was definitely the first time it had happened while he was being held prisoner.

The *key*.

Trev flinched, hoping his expression didn't register his surprise.

What if Howell had been the one to leave him the key?

Certainly would make sense with the way he was clearly fawning all over Trev, but why risk angering the entire Luchesi family? Did Howell really want to fuck him that badly?

It was weirdly flattering in a way, but still.

Jupiter was too busy trying to cram the last of Howell's body outside into the hall to hopefully have noticed Trev having an epiphany. "Thank you so *much*."

"Seriously! Ya' need any helps at all!" Howell grunted. "Needs me to watch him for a bit, needs me to do anythin' at all—"

"Got it." Jupiter slammed the door shut and then locked it. He growled low in frustration, whirling around on Trev. "You. Speak. Now."

"How about a *please*?" Trev scoffed.

"Baby doll, now. *Please*." Jupiter waved the key. "Where did you get this?"

"I found it, okay?" Trev cocked his hip and crossed his arms. "It was in the bathroom at that fucking dump."

"When?"

"This morning." Trev shrugged. "The last time I went. Which means someone had to have put it there after you and your little buddies went to breakfast." He smirked. "Now do you believe me?"

Jupiter's scowl was difficult to read.

"It could have been anyone," Trev went on. "Sal, Emil, uh—"

"*Howell.*" Jupiter carried the bag over to the bed. He dumped it all out, and it did appear to be clothing. He searched each piece, checking pockets if there were any, and scrutinizing each article.

"What is it?" Trev demanded. "Does it go to the padlock? The fucking one around my neck?"

"Would you have used it if it was?"

"What the fuck do you think?" Trev snorted.

Jupiter dropped the clothing, and he appeared to be thinking.

"Now do you believe me?" Trev demanded. "Look, I clearly don't know everything that's going on, but I know the scent of bullshit very well. And your family? Someone is working against you. Kinda seems like it might be a pretty long list, if I'm being honest." He shrugged casually. "Not that it's any of my business, but..."

"No, it's not." Jupiter eyed Trev for a long moment. "But thank you."

"For?"

Jupiter held up the key. "For showing me this. It's a master key. Very well might have unlocked your chains." He tucked it into his pocket. "I still don't trust you—"

"Well, duh. It's not like I trust you."

"But." Jupiter reached for Trev's hand.

Trev let him take it, and he stared as Jupiter placed a soft kiss on his knuckles.

"Thank you," Jupiter said with surprising sincerity. "Please know that..." His stoic demeanor cracked briefly. "You're not the only one who's trapped."

Trev frowned. "And what does that mean?"

Jupiter turned away from him, gesturing to the clothes on the bed. "If you want to take a shower and change, help yourself."

"Uh, hello?" Trev put his hands on his hips. "What do you mean trapped? Like, is this a metaphorical thing? Like trapped by family obligation or something? Or does someone come around and also chain you to a wall every night?"

"There's towels already in the bathroom, but I'm sure you saw those when you looked around, already trying to find a way to get out of here." Jupiter walked over to a small cabinet, opening the doors to reveal a bar within. He poured himself a drink. "Plenty of hot water, so knock yourself out."

Trev watched Jupiter chug the glass and then immediately pour another. "It's five o'clock somewhere, right?"

Jupiter raised his glass. "*Saluti*."

"Right." Trev didn't think he was going to get any additional information out of Jupiter, but he was clearly rattled by the key.

Trev opted not to share his personal suspicion that it had been Howell, as it seemed like Jupiter was already on that same train of thought. He was curious what Jupiter had meant about being trapped too, but...

No.

That didn't matter.

What mattered was that giving Jupiter the key had hopefully earned Trev some points in his favor and he'd be able to take advantage of that. He needed Jupiter to trust him so he could figure out a way to get the hell out of here. He couldn't count on Boss Cold to save him—and *pffft*, he didn't need him to.

He was Trevanion Usher, and he wasn't done fighting yet.

Trev found a pair of black gym shorts and a white T-shirt in the clothing from Howell. They were the least hideous options and the most likely to fit, and he wondered if they were actually Howell's.

Ew.

Whatever.

Trev toed off his boots and pulled his hoodie over his head. He ignored Jupiter's staring as he undressed, and he left his clothes in a messy heap on the floor beside his boots. He picked up the shorts and T-shirt, boldly strutting into the bathroom. He could hear Jupiter's footsteps following him, but he kept his focus on the task at hand.

He really wanted a shower, but a bath provided much better visuals.

Trev set the clothing on the counter and then bent over to turn on the water in the tub. He didn't make a big show of it, well aware Jupiter was still watching, and he helped himself to some bodywash to use as bubble bath as the tub filled.

He glanced over his shoulder, feigning surprise to see Jupiter in the doorway. "What? You wanna join me?"

Jupiter sipped his drink. "And if I say yes?"

"If. *Pffft.*" Trev laughed as he slipped into the tub. He groaned as he sank down into the bubbly water. "Pour me some vodka first and then get your ass in here."

"Be right there, baby doll."

CHAPTER *Eight*

"HOW DO YOU WANT IT?" Jupiter asked. "Straight?"

"No, gay. But thanks for asking."

"Ha ha." Jupiter chuckled, heading back to the bar.

Trev turned off the water now that the tub was full and then settled into the bubbles. He allowed himself to relax, trying to plan his next move. His best bet to get out of this room still seemed to be the window right above this tub, and he was confident he could break it with his lockbox.

That might make a lot of noise though.

Maybe he could lock the bathroom door and block it with something to buy himself enough time to get through the window.

Hopefully without cutting himself.

Or breaking any bones.

Ugh.

Jupiter returned, offering a glass of vodka to Trev. "Here."

"Thanks." Trev accepted it and took a small sip. "So, are you getting in here with me?"

"I am." Jupiter removed his tie.

"And what are we going to do?" Trev let his smile turn sly.

"We're going to talk," Jupiter said as he set his glass down on the side of the tub so he could take off his jacket.

"Talk?" Trev made a face. "That doesn't sound like very much fun."

"Oh, trust me." Jupiter laughed. "It's going to be very exciting."

Trev enjoyed the vision of Jupiter stripping down, and he looked over his broad, powerful body with unrestrained hunger. He hadn't been able to see much of Jupiter before since he'd kept his clothes on or it had been too dark to appreciate how stunning he was. Jupiter was hot, bulging in all the right places, and Trev wanted to bathe him with his tongue.

He didn't have to pretend to be attracted to Jupiter at least.

That part was easy.

"If you say so, *sir*," Trev teased, pausing to take another sip of vodka. "I think there's much more exciting things I could be doing with my mouth, but hey, you're in charge."

Jupiter touched Trev's shoulder, urging him to move forward. He slid into the tub behind him, spreading his legs so Trev could sit between them and lie back against his chest.

Trev shivered.

This was intimate, and he didn't like how vulnerable he felt, especially when Jupiter wrapped his arm around him. Trev's hand naturally reached up to hold Jupiter's forearm, and his cock twitched.

"So." Trev cleared his throat. "What did you want to talk about?"

"Do you know who Rafaello Luchesi is?" Jupiter asked.

"No, but I'm going to assume he's one of your many other charming relatives."

"He was the don of the Luchesi family at the height of our power. He had three sons... and one bastard."

"You."

"Yes." Jupiter's fingers traced Trev's collarbone. "My mother was one of the maids. I was born just a few years before Rafaello died and he never claimed me. Sal and Emil are my cousins. Their father, Ugo, was Rafaello's brother, but he has not... been doing very well for a long time."

Trev squeezed Jupiter's powerful forearm. "Yeah, I kinda noticed."

"Before Ugo completely lost his mind, he said that one of Rafaello's sons should lead the family. There used to be four of us. Matteo, Cristian, and Luigi. Cold killed them all."

"Except you."

"Except me." Jupiter sighed softly. "I doubt he even knows I exist. The family wouldn't want me to lead anyway. Because I'm a bastard. And yes, because of my... preferences. Some other members of the family created a council and have been leading in Ugo's absence, but Sal and Emil believe they should be in charge."

"Let me guess. Not so much?"

"The council has gotten pretty comfortable running things, but Sal and Emil have been pushing hard for them to dissolve and elect a new don. Of course, they think it should be one of them, but the majority of the council are still loyal to Ugo and if given the choice between choosing Emil or Sal or respecting Ugo's wish..."

"They'd pick the gay bastard?"

"I doubt it, but there's still a chance."

"So, in other words..." Trev pursed his lips. "Sal and

Emil have a big ol' motive to make you look like shit and get rid of you."

"Yes."

"Why are you telling me this? Not that I don't appreciate the quality sharing time with no clothes on..." Trev stroked Jupiter's forearm slowly. "But you've made it very clear you don't trust me."

"Because, ironically, you might be the only one I can trust." Jupiter rested his cheek in Trev's hair. "Neither one of us wants to be here."

"What? Don't want to lead the big scary mob family?"

"No." Jupiter scoffed. "I was happy with what I had. Now everything is much more complicated, and I cannot simply walk away."

"Why don't we walk right out that front door right now then?" Trev said. "Me and you—"

"It's not that easy." Jupiter hugged Trev a little closer. "They're keeping an eye on me too. I can't just leave whenever I want. Not with Sal's goons hanging around watching."

Trev leaned his head back against Jupiter's shoulder and processed the information. It was certainly possible that Jupiter was playing him the same way Trev had intended to play him, but it didn't sound like Jupiter had much to gain by telling him all of this except a slightly more cooperative prisoner.

But maybe...

Maybe it would be easier to escape if they worked together.

Trev rocked his hips back with a smirk. "Sounds like you could use some help making a plan, huh?"

"Perhaps an alliance of sorts." Jupiter's hand dragged down Trev's chest. "It would be beneficial to us both."

"So what?" Trev kept moving, rubbing his ass into Jupiter's groin. "What do you want me to do?"

"Be patient," Jupiter soothed. "When the opportunity arises, I'll make sure we both get out of the city safely. I have to get some money first, and then—"

"I have money," Trev blurted out.

"What?"

Trev fidgeted.

He was putting a lot of faith in Jupiter, perhaps too much.

"I have some money, okay?" Trev said firmly. "Don't worry about that. Just get us the fuck out of here."

"That's what you're hiding in that lockbox, isn't it?" Jupiter's hand traveled down Trev's stomach.

Trev inhaled sharply, and he arched back against Jupiter. "Does it matter what it is?"

"Yes."

"You'll just have to trust that it will get us very, very far away from here."

"Us, hmm?" Jupiter hummed.

Trev blushed, and he replied casually, "As far as you wanna go together. I was thinking of heading to the border and never looking back."

"Maybe." Jupiter's fingers teased down Trev's hip. "I still don't trust you."

"No?"

"Not even for a second."

Trev closed his eyes, his breath hitching as Jupiter stroked the crease of his groin. His cock was already thickening, and he arched into Jupiter's hand, trying to get it where he wanted it. "I g-guess you'll just have to try."

Jupiter denied him and drew his hand back to the curve of Trev's side. "I suppose that depends on you, baby doll."

"What do you mean?" Trev reached up to find Jupiter's cheek, scratching his fingers through his beard. His pulse was climbing steadily, and the teasing was driving him insane.

"Well?"

Trev sagged, grunting in frustration. "What?"

"Are you going to start being real with me? Or are you going to keep playing games?"

"Whatever keeps me alive and gets me the fuck out of here," Trev replied honestly. "I'll do whatever it takes."

"Of that, I have no doubt." Jupiter smoothed his palm across Trev's belly, the tips of his fingers teasing around the base of his cock. "You really are quite something, baby doll."

"Damn right, I am." Trev grabbed Jupiter's wrist and pushed his hand down. He twisted around to press a heated kiss to Jupiter's lips.

Jupiter groaned and grabbed Trev's cheek, kissing him back passionately.

Trev scrambled to turn around and climb into Jupiter's lap, and water splashed out over the side of the tub. He didn't care. He reached between them to get his hand on their cocks, wrapping his fingers around them and giving them a firm tug as they kissed.

He was squeezing too hard, too fast, but the pressure was wonderful and he wanted more. He groaned as Jupiter grabbed the back of his head to lead the kiss, and Trev thrust his tongue into Jupiter's mouth.

Jupiter held Trev at the small of his back, urging him to rock forward.

Trev moved his hips and dropped both of his hands to their cocks. He wrapped his fingers around them and stroked them faster, moaning softly.

This was insane.

This could be a trick, a ploy to make Trev lower his guard so he might make a mistake later.

And yet, it was hard to doubt the passion in Jupiter's lips and the possessiveness in his hand as he palmed Trev's ass cheek.

Jupiter challenged Trev as no one had before, saw through most of his bullshit, and was quite charming when he wanted to be. He was handsome, confident, and...

Oh gross—Trev *liked* him.

Shit, shit, shit.

Trev moved his hands faster, as if he could somehow work off his frustrations via jerking off. It wasn't doing much except making him more horny, and he groaned low, teasing his teeth over Jupiter's bottom lip. "F-fuck."

Jupiter's eyes were so dark they were nearly black, and his voice was hoarse as he whispered, "How about... a little exercise in trust?"

Trev slowed down. "What did you have in mind?"

"Do exactly what I say and I'll make sure you are very, very satisfied."

Trev wanted to refuse, especially since he was already so close, but he couldn't resist the lust in Jupiter's gaze. Although there was no way to possibly know what Jupiter had planned for him, Trev was certain that it would be pleasurable.

"Okay." Trev squeezed their cocks one last time before letting go.

"Okay, *sir*." Jupiter smirked.

Trev resisted the urge to roll his eyes, but he still fixed Jupiter with a very unimpressed stare. "What do you want me to do?"

"Go ahead and get out. I'll help you dry off."

"All right, sir." Trev slid off Jupiter's lap, his hard cock jutting straight out. He stroked himself to ease the throb as he stepped out of the tub, turning so he could admire Jupiter emerging like a bubbly, slick Aquaman.

Jupiter got them towels, and he wrapped one around Trev's waist before pulling him into a deep kiss. He held the side of Trev's face and his hip, again commanding Trev's mouth and setting the pace to a languid crawl and tease of tongues.

Trev went willingly, and he glided his hands over the damp curves of Jupiter's chest. He pushed his hips forward, insistently rubbing his hard cock against Jupiter's. He loved how hot Jupiter's skin felt meeting his own, and the lingering damp from the bath allowed for slick, desperate caresses.

Damn Jupiter Prospero.

Damn him.

Trev *wanted* him.

He wanted to put out the fire burning in his loins, whether by frantic rutting or quick strokes of his hand. He needed an end, he needed *relief*, and his own desires rose up like a storm, clouding all of his senses. He hadn't known that it was possible for another person to have this kind of effect on him, and it was as maddening as it was intoxicating.

"Bedroom," Jupiter rumbled.

His command was a light within the swirling chaos, his hands firm as he directed Trev to the bed. Trev was a little lightheaded, and he was thankful for Jupiter's steadying touch.

The towel fell away when Jupiter picked him up and laid him across the bed, and Trev's stomach dipped from the sudden rush of movement. He scooted back until his head hit the pillows, watching Jupiter crawl up between his legs.

Jupiter's long hair was cold and wet as it brushed over

Trev's thighs, and he smiled up at Trev. "I'm honestly surprised at how easily you agreed."

"To get some dick?"

"To trust me."

"So I can get some dick." Trev pursed his lips and then added, "*Sir.*"

"I'm going to need more than that, baby doll." Jupiter's hair tickled Trev's hips as he kissed Trev's hip. "It's not just your fine little ass on the line here. It's mine too."

"I want to get the fuck out of here." Trev tilted his cock toward Jupiter's face. "Isn't that enough, sir?"

"I need to know that you'll have my back like I plan to have yours so we can both leave in one piece. I have a very good idea of what you're capable of, and while impressive, I'd appreciate a truce until we're free." Jupiter lifted his head. "Can you do that?"

"Yeah, sure."

"Uh-uh." Jupiter flicked out his tongue, teasing over the head of Trev's cock. "Come on, baby doll. Sal and Emil will not hesitate to kill us both if they know we're planning to bail. They want this deal with Cold—"

"And you out of the way," Trev reminded him haughtily. "I'm worth more alive."

"For now. As long as they think Boss Cold still wants to negotiate." Jupiter licked up the side of Trev's cock. "If not..."

Trev didn't need Jupiter to finish that sentence. He already knew what that would mean for him—cement shoes, sleeping with the fishes, whatever it was mobsters said these days. He reached down to slide his fingers through Jupiter's hair. "Fine. I'll trust you... At least until we get out of here safely. But if you fuck me over or I even think for a second that you're planning to, I'm gonna put something a lot worse than glitter body spray in your eye, do you understand me?"

Jupiter smiled. "Yes, baby doll."

"Good. Now—"

Jupiter swallowed down Trev's cock, sucking hard.

"O-oh! Fuck!" Trev groaned and pushed up into Jupiter's mouth, savoring the wet heat surrounding him. Jupiter looked absolutely stunning with his lips wrapped around Trev's cock, and it was easy to be selfish with Jupiter so willingly giving himself over like this. He tightened his hold on Jupiter's hair, thrusting a little harder.

Jupiter allowed it, his eyes burning into Trev's as his fingers made their way up Trev's inner thigh. He squeezed his groin and directed his thumb back behind Trev's balls.

The pressure against Trev's taint drew out a soft moan from his lips, and his heart was pounding nearly as fast as the thoughts spinning in his head. He knew escape had to be his main priority, and he could play nice with Jupiter for a little while to achieve it.

After that...

Trev wasn't sure.

He didn't want to think of a future with Jupiter beyond what was hopefully going to be a few more fantastic orgasms and a way out of here. It was startling to realize it wasn't very hard at all to see himself with Jupiter—a man who challenged him, respected his intelligence and how conniving he could be, and saw potential in him as no one else had before.

Fuck.

Not now.

Trev focused on Jupiter's mouth and the slide of his tongue, and he groaned as Jupiter's thumb pressed against his hole. The pressure was a tease of the penetration Trev longed for, and he tried to tilt his hips down in hopes of gaining it.

Jupiter refused him because of course he did, and he withdrew from Trev's cock with a swipe of tongue over his slit. He directed his attention down to Trev's hole, and he lapped over it with greedy swipes.

Trev reached for his cock so he could jerk off and find some relief, but Jupiter grabbed his wrist. "Mm, what?"

"Trust me." Jupiter squeezed lightly and then let go. He spun a finger around Trev's hole, playing in his spit. He pressed the very tip in, but it was only another tease. "We'll get there."

"Sir… *please.*"

"Please what?"

"I want to come."

"How?"

"*Quickly,*" Trev bit out between clenched teeth. The throb in his balls was incessant, and he was starting to sweat.

"Patience, baby doll." Jupiter pushed his finger in a little deeper, and he licked around it slowly. "Mm, patience."

Trev wanted to tell Jupiter exactly where he could shove his patience, but he tried instead to relax. The press of Jupiter's finger burned, though his pooling spit helped mute the discomfort. Soon it was enough for Jupiter's entire finger to thrust inside of him, though that was also only a whisper of the pleasure he knew Jupiter was capable of with his cock.

That's what he wanted.

He wanted Jupiter to fuck him and stop screwing around.

"Sir, please…" Trev squirmed and used one of his very best sexual moans to hopefully entice Jupiter into action.

"I'm good. I'm ready. Mmm, I need you inside me right now."

"You're not ready until I say you are," Jupiter warned. "You really can't stand it, can you? Not being in control."

Trev's face flashed white-hot, and it was a struggle to swallow back his frustration. He wanted to argue. He could stop this at any damn time he pleased. He didn't have to do a single thing that he didn't want to, and that...

That was the problem.

Trev *did* want this.

His desire for Jupiter was enough to command his compliance, and it was maddening. It fogged his thoughts and made it difficult to focus, and he couldn't deny that Jupiter had found an effective way to force his obedience.

Jupiter smirked at Trev's silence and taunted, "That's what I thought, baby doll."

Trev continued to say nothing, and he slid his hands over his face with a low groan.

"Don't worry. I won't make you wait too long." Jupiter lapped around Trev's hole and then up his taint, his sly chuckle resonating through his tongue. "You are very, very difficult to resist."

"I know," Trev said firmly, trying to regain some of his confidence. "I'm fucking perfect."

"Close enough." Jupiter withdrew his finger and pushed himself up.

Trev watched Jupiter get out of bed, heading back to the bathroom. "What are you doing?"

"Unless you have lube in that lockbox, I need to get my wallet." Jupiter returned with his wallet in hand. He pulled out a small packet of lube with a smirk. "Although, if you happened to have one hidden behind your ear or something, I wouldn't be surprised."

"Well, under normal circumstances..." Trev trailed off with a playful shrug.

"I expect nothing less from you." Jupiter tore the packet open with his teeth as he slid back between Trev's long legs. He leisurely drizzled the lube onto his cock and stroked himself.

Trev wanted to cheer, and he even welcomed Jupiter bowing his head down for a kiss. It was hot as always, but there was a drag in Jupiter's tongue that made Trev suspicious. He tilted into Jupiter's hand as he spread some lube around his hole. "Mmm, come on. You know that's not what I want."

"I know," Jupiter murmured in reply, plunging in two slick fingers. "But right now, this is what you're getting, baby doll. So be a good boy and take it."

Trev sagged into the bed, and he tried to appreciate the meager friction that Jupiter's fingers offered. If he smarted off, Jupiter would do something awful like punish him or whatever, so he was determined to behave. He'd never had to work quite this hard to get laid before, and yes, it was challenging but also...

Exhilarating.

The building tension increased the throb in his loins until he was ready to jump out of bed and hump the damn wall. His eyes burned, his heart pounded, and the agonizing drag of Jupiter's fingers split him somewhere between heaven and hell. It went on for so long that Trev's cock softened, though it still throbbed with his arousal.

Trev found that he was relaxed now, and the surges of adrenaline that usually prompted his muscles to race through this particular act at top speed had drained away. He touched his face, finding it flushed and sweating, and he dragged his other hand across his chest to feel his heart's heavy but slow thud.

The sound of his own breathing was weirdly alien for how steady it was, and the slick press of Jupiter's fingers was wonderfully erotic. His body was soft, easily welcoming each thrust even when Jupiter added a third finger inside of him.

"There," Jupiter rumbled. "There you go, baby doll. So fucking perfect for me."

Yes.

Trev was being so very good now, and it created a new warmth in his chest that bubbled out as he moaned. He loved how Jupiter was looking at him right now, though it was hard to qualify exactly what it was—pride? Desire? Adoration?

Probably all of the above, really.

Because Trev was fucking *perfect.*

Jupiter kissed Trev's stomach as he withdrew his fingers. His hair still tickled from the lingering damp, and he smirked up at Trev. "Look at you... I think you're ready for me now."

"Yes, sir," Trev murmured.

"Good boy." Jupiter kissed Trev's belly. "Tell me, baby doll. How do you want me?"

"What?" Trev didn't think he'd heard Jupiter correctly. He didn't understand why he was being given a choice when Jupiter was supposed to be the one calling the shots.

"You've been so good for me, baby doll. I'm going to let you choose how I fuck you."

Trev's face burned as the possibilities raced through his mind. "I want you to..."

"Yes?"

"I want you to fuck me from behind. Just pound my

fucking brains out." Trev took a deep breath, his body craving some fiercer treatment after everything had been so deliciously slow. "I want to forget everything, okay?" He kept his eyes on Jupiter as he rolled over onto his hands and knees to present himself. "I… I want to trust you."

"Fuck." Jupiter's hands eagerly seized Trev's ass cheeks. "I can do that, baby doll." He teased the head of his cock over Trev's hole and then pressed in, groaning softly. "There we go."

The push of Jupiter's cock was effortless, and Trev gasped at how easily his body swallowed up every inch. Jupiter didn't stop until he'd buried himself completely, and Trev squeezed down just to hear him grunt. "God, yes… Give it to me."

Jupiter rubbed Trev's hip, bowing over him to press a soft kiss to his spine. He then slammed forward, fucking Trev hard and fast, setting a brutal pace.

It was rough, relentless, and exactly what Trev had asked for.

"Yes!" Trev howled, spreading his legs and rocking back to meet Jupiter's slams. He tilted his body until he got the angle that he wanted most, and the resulting pressure made his eyes water. He clawed at the bed, moaning happily.

The feverish slap of their bodies sounded like someone had lit a string of firecrackers, and the bliss left in the wake of Jupiter's powerful thrusts was nearly overwhelming. It was compounded by the contrast of how sweetly Jupiter stroked Trev's body, still kissing his back and shoulders as he fucked him so hard.

"Is this good?" Jupiter growled low. "Is this what you wanted, baby doll?"

Trev groaned loud enough to rattle the windows. "Oh

my God! This! Mm, this right fucking here! Fuck me, it's so good!"

Jupiter growled again, and he seized Trev's hips as he continued to pound into him. "You look so fuckin' beautiful like this. Letting me tear you apart."

Trev braced himself on his forearms to push back on Jupiter's cock. "Yeah, fuck... Come on. Keep talking. Mm, Tell me..."

"Tell you what? How fucking hot you are?" Jupiter murmured. "How I've never met anyone like you...? Mmm, such a little badass... And right now, you're all mine."

"Yours," Trev croaked. "Fuck, I'm all yours."

Jupiter snarled and continued to rail Trev down into the bed, forcing his body flat against the mattress.

It felt *amazing*.

But...

Trev wanted to *see* Jupiter.

This wasn't right.

"Wait, st-stop." Trev grunted. "I just—"

Jupiter stopped.

Immediately.

"Talk to me," Jupiter said urgently. "What's wrong? Did I hurt you?"

"No, no, I'm okay!" Trev swallowed thickly. "This... I changed my mind. I want to see you, okay?" He pulled forward until Jupiter's cock slipped free. He rolled onto his back and spread his legs, saying, "I want to do it like this."

"Whatever you want, baby doll." Jupiter moved on top of Trev. He pressed a soft kiss to his lips, their bodies slotting together as they held one another. "This... is perfect."

"Yeah." Trev's pulse sang with a new thrum of pleasure from the closeness, and he hugged Jupiter's neck tight. "It really fucking is."

Jupiter kissed him as his cock slid back inside, and Trev mewled quietly.

Yes.

This is what he wanted.

Jupiter's weight was grounding and warm, and he loved the closeness, the tender way Jupiter thrust now, and each slide of Jupiter's cock made fireworks light up within Trev's very core. He hitched his legs up on Jupiter's sides to increase the sweet feeling, and then he gasped as Jupiter shrugged them up onto his shoulders. "F-fuck!"

"Talk to me, baby doll." Jupiter mouthed at Trev's jaw. "Is that good?"

"So fuckin' good!" Trev whined, bending his legs until his knees hit his chest. "Mmm, there, just like that." He kissed Jupiter hungrily and grabbed at his hips, urging him to keep up the wonderful pace.

It was slow but deep, hard and steady, and Trev had never known sex could feel this intimate. Jupiter was fucking him like he was the most precious thing in the universe, plunging inside Trev's body until Trev was a blathering, moaning mess.

One of Trev's legs slipped off Jupiter's shoulder, and he spread himself out wide. He was nearly giddy from the wonderful feelings washing over him, and he groaned excitedly. "God, yes… Fuck yeah, get it, baby! F-fuck!"

Jupiter slowed, smothering a groan against Trev's throat.

"Hey, what is it?" Trev tangled his fingers in Jupiter's hair.

"Close," Jupiter warned.

"Me too." Trev nuzzled Jupiter's brow. "God, please. Can I come? Can I please—"

"Yes, *fuck*." Jupiter let loose a deep growl. "Where do you—"

"In me. In me! Give it to me. Right now." Trev slid his hand between them to grab his cock and stroke desperately. "I want it. Mmm, come on. I want it when I come."

Jupiter flashed a sly little grin, and he resumed the rapid rhythm from the previous position.

"Oh, oh *fuck*!" Trev groaned, jerking off quickly to match the frantic pace. "There... Oh fuck, fuck, fuck! C'mon, you motherfucker! Get it! Fuckin' get it!"

Jupiter's reply was a growl, and he grabbed the side of Trev's face to pull him into a deep kiss as he pounded his ass ferociously.

The kick of hot friction was exactly what Trev needed, and he tensed as the incredible pressure built back in his balls and throbbed in the head of his cock. The final release blurred his vision, and he howled as he came. "God, yes! Get it, get it, get it—"

Jupiter smothered Trev's cries with another passionate kiss, and he snarled as his hips bucked erratically.

Trev felt the rush of heat that signaled Jupiter's release, grinding down as Jupiter's cock filled him. He kissed Jupiter, kissed him and kissed him until he was out of breath and whining brokenly. He swore he was still coming even after his cock had nothing left to spill, and he trembled beneath Jupiter with one last urgent moan. "Ho-holy shit."

Jupiter chuckled low. "See what happens when you trust me, baby doll?"

"Hmmph. You mean after you torture and edge the fuck out of me?"

Jupiter grinned. "Same thing."

"Whatever." Trev huffed and tried to feign defiance, but he was smiling. It was difficult to be grumpy when he'd just had a spectacular orgasm...

Or when Jupiter was smiling at him like he'd painted all the stars across the sky.

Trev closed his eyes. "What now?"

"We wait for the right opportunity." Jupiter caressed Trev's hip.

"That's fuckin' stupid." Trev scoffed. "Why don't we try to get out now, huh? Or, hey, even better." He turned his head to look at Jupiter. "Give Sal and Emil something else to worry about?"

"Such as?"

"Why don't we create a very nice, very big distraction?"

"What are you talking about?" Jupiter narrowed his eyes.

"Ugo wanted a party, didn't he?"

"Yeah?"

"Why don't we give him one?"

CHAPTER *Nine*

TRYING to plan a party on such short notice was apparently very easy as a member of the Luchesi family. Jupiter did almost everything on the phone under Ugo's name and then slipped out to *accidentally* give his phone to Ugo. Jupiter later claimed that he had no idea how Ugo had gotten it from him, perhaps during their earlier struggle, and now they were expected to host a party in a few hours.

Emil and Sal were furious, and they got into a screaming match with each other over what to do. Ugo somehow caught wind that he was actually having a party, and Emil refused to back down. Sal finally gave in, but he ordered more security and loudly declared they could use it as a show of strength to help recover from the obvious blow the raid had dealt their reputation.

All of this Jupiter was too happy to tell Trev, and it was nice being on the same side for once.

Jupiter hadn't even threatened to tie Trev up when he left earlier to slip Ugo the phone.

Trev was even more surprised when Jupiter came back holding a garment bag. "Ah, is that for your funeral?"

"Very funny." Jupiter rolled his eyes. "It's for you."

"Me?"

"You're coming to the party with me tonight."

Trev laughed. "Seriously? You're going to have your *hostage* as your date?"

"Yup." Jupiter smirked as he handed him the bag. "You're going to behave, stay by my side at all times, and stay quiet."

"I don't think I can do any of those things."

"Ha ha. You can." Jupiter rolled his eyes. "And you will. You need to be with me so we can leave, remember? Unless you want me to go without you."

"Meanie."

Jupiter grinned.

Trev draped the garment bag over the bed so he could unzip it. "*No.*"

Jupiter scoffed. "What?"

Trev gestured to the suit inside. "No."

"Stop just saying *no*. What's wrong with it?"

"It's ugly." Trev wrinkled his nose. "I'm not wearing that."

Jupiter huffed. "Do you have any idea how hard it was to find something in your size on such short notice? Come on. What's wrong with it?"

"It's black on black. I really am going to look like I'm going to a fucking funeral." Trev groaned loudly.

"This isn't a date," Jupiter grumbled. "It doesn't matter what you wear—"

"Shhh." Trev brought his finger to his lips. "We're both going to pretend you didn't say that." He made a face at the dismal suit. "It's... fine. I'll make it work."

"You'll still look gorgeous."

"Yeah. Duh." Trev snorted. "Of course, I will. So." He dropped his voice down. "What's the plan?"

"We get dressed. We go to the party. Make some excuse to come back up here to grab what we need, and then..." Jupiter gestured vaguely. "We leave."

Trev sat on the bed and crossed his arms. "That's it? We're not, like, trying to study guard rotations, check out video camera feeds? Something like that? So we don't get caught?"

"We're going to have to be very careful."

"Being careful isn't a plan. That's a shit plan." Trev grunted. "Come on. Is there a guard rotation or anything like that we should know about? Like, when do they take piss breaks? There has to be a certain time that'll be easier to slip out—"

Jupiter handed Trev a black box. It was about the size of a shoe box.

"What's that?"

"For your outfit tonight."

Trev frowned as he opened the box, certain it was going to be an ugly pair of shoes. Instead, it was a black leather collar with a long silver chain leash. "Oh, this is gonna be a hard no, Daddy. Nope."

"Emil wants to show off that he's got Cold's little brother on a leash."

"*Literally*? The fuck?"

Jupiter held out the collar. "Sorry. Nonnegotiable. Remember, we gotta play nice."

"You get to drag me around and feel like hot shit," Trev growled. "Being your bitch for the night is not putting me in a *play nice with others* kind of mood."

"I promise I'll make it up to you."

"It better be with your mouth."

"That can certainly be arranged once we're fucking free and clear." Jupiter kissed Trev's forehead.

"We really should talk about a plan."

"We have a plan."

"No, you have a half-assed idea that sounds good in your head." Trev crossed his arms over his chest. "Where is the party going to be? How many exits are there? Guards? Do you have access to the keys for a vehicle in the mobster SUV fleet? Can it be tracked? Weapons, more cash, anything else we can use. Does anyone here owe you a favor or two? Is there anyone else we can trust? Come on. This is all shit we need to know."

"Wow." Jupiter whistled. "Maybe you should be a gangster."

"At least one of us should be."

JUPITER WAS able to get more information about the party's security and confirm that he knew where the keys for some of the fleet were kept. A valet service had been called in for the guests, and most of the mafiamobiles were being moved around to the back of the house where an impromptu parking area was being set up. Only the valets would be working that area, as the majority of the guards would be inside the house.

Armed with this information, Trev formed a plan.

He knew Emil and Sal would want Jupiter to make a few rounds to show off Trev to the guests. Trev would then pretend to get drunk and show his ass spectacularly, prompting Jupiter to take him back upstairs. They would grab Trev's lockbox plus a bag Jupiter would pack for them, head to the kitchen to get the keys out of the case by the back door, bribe the valets with a nice bottle of scotch to go take a break, and then haul ass.

It wasn't a perfect plan by any means, but it was better than nothing.

"What if the valets don't like scotch?" Jupiter asked as he slid the bottle into the bag. "What if they're gin guys?"

"Then I'll suck their dicks." Trev scoffed.

"What? What if they're not gay?"

"Like that matters."

"You don't have to do that." Jupiter frowned. "I'll knock 'em out or something if I have to."

"Jealous?" Trev winked.

"No."

"Oh, you totally are."

"Knocking them out would be quicker. That's all."

"Yeah. Sure." Trev adjusted his shirt and rolled his eyes.

The suit did fit well, though Trev had declined wearing any of Jupiter's ties. He left the top few buttons undone and tried to clean up his boots. The outfit wasn't perfect, but it was at least tolerable now.

"Don't suppose you have any eyeliner?" Trev asked.

"Check the bathroom," Jupiter replied. "One of my cousins stayed here a few weeks ago. She left a ton of crap in there."

"You let your cousin stay in your room?"

"It's not my room," Jupiter said sourly. "It's a guest room, and I'm a guest too, remember?"

"Let me guess." Trev pressed his fingers to his temples as if he was trying to read Jupiter's mind. "You have your own nice bachelor pad with a big screen TV, no art on the walls, plastic silverware, and lots of beer cans everywhere?"

Jupiter grinned. "The beer cans are in the recycling bin. What kind of monster do you think I am?"

"Uh-huh."

"I'm going to get changed. Oh! And I got you something." Jupiter smirked. "It's downstairs though."

"Oh?" Trev narrowed his eyes suspiciously.

"It's in the kitchen actually. Which gives us a nice reason to go down there and take a peek around, make sure the keys are where they're supposed to be."

"In the kitchen?" Trev's stomach grumbled. "Is it food? Please tell me it's food."

"There will be plenty to eat at the party." Jupiter headed to the bathroom with a suit draped over his arm. "Try not to chew on the walls while I'm gone, okay? And don't try to escape either."

"Not making any promises." Trev batted his eyes after Jupiter.

Once Jupiter shut the bathroom door, it was weirdly tempting to make a run for it. He knew he had to stick to the plan and wait, but still. He was putting a lot of trust in Jupiter, and he hoped it didn't bite him in the ass.

If nothing else, Trev wished he had a backup plan.

Kick Jupiter in the nuts and bolt?

Maybe if this was yesterday or when all of this had started, Trev would have considered it more seriously. But now he found himself wanting to see how things played out, to put his trust in Jupiter to the test and let the pieces fall where they may.

Trev didn't usually gamble like this...

Not unless he was sure he'd win.

Jupiter stepped out of the bathroom, dressed in a fresh suit and tie with his hair neatly pulled back. It was black on black like Trev's own, and Jupiter looked absolutely delicious. Trev must have been staring because Jupiter teased, "Not bad, huh?"

Yup.

Fuck.

It was stupid how much he wanted to win big with Jupiter.

"It's all right." Trev shrugged. He picked up the collar. "Care to do the honors?"

"Would love to." Jupiter smirked as he took it and unbuckled it.

Trev shivered as the cool leather touched his skin, and he took a deep breath. The brush of Jupiter's fingers was a tease, and he longed to feel them all over his body. Trev might keep the collar and let Jupiter drag him around a little —fuck, *later*.

They had an escape to pull off.

"There." Jupiter adjusted the collar. "How's that?"

"Fine." Trev touched it.

It was infinitely more comfortable than the other one, and something about it made his breath hitch.

The weight, the texture, the... *something*.

His lashes fluttered when Jupiter attached the leash.

"Still good?" Jupiter frowned. "If it's too much, just tell me to go get you more champagne, okay? Then I'll know to get you out of there—"

"It's okay. Really." Trev flashed one of his well-practiced smiles.

Jupiter didn't look convinced, and Trev hoped he didn't push.

He did not want to explain that the collar was getting him hot right now.

Maybe later.

Much, much later.

"All right." Jupiter grabbed the other end of the leash

and looped some of the excess chain around his hand. "Ready to go?"

"Oh. Yes. Can't wait." Trev curled his upper lip. "This is going to be so much fun."

Jupiter wiggled the leash. "Come on. It won't be that bad. I promise I'll be gentle."

Trev sneered.

As they stepped out into the hallway, Trev took a deep breath.

"Ready?" Jupiter asked, his tone betraying how concerned he was.

"I'm ready," Trev confirmed as he gave Jupiter's arm a squeeze. "Let's go party."

Jupiter led Trev down the hallway, past a massive ballroom that was likely their next destination, and then into the kitchen. It was an impressive space with top-of-the-line appliances, currently occupied by the catering staff and big carts packed full of food.

"And why are we in here?" Trev asked dryly.

He knew part of the reason—to make sure the keys for the fleet were in the little case by the door. A cursory glance confirmed they hadn't been moved, so that at least was good. But Jupiter had said he had something for Trev, though Trev couldn't imagine why whatever it was would be in the kitchen.

Jupiter only smirked, reaching into the fridge. He pulled out a small plastic container, inside of which was a bright pink rose boutonniere. "I had a feeling you were gonna hate the suit, so... Thought maybe you'd enjoy a little splash of color."

Trev smiled. "So, you already knew the suit was hideous in advance."

"I didn't say that. I said I had a feeling that you were gonna hate it."

"Because it's *hideous*."

"Do you want the damn flower or not?"

"Yes, please." Trev batted his eyes and stuck his chest out. "Give it to me, Daddy."

"Oh, I'll give it to you, all right." Jupiter chuckled as he pinned the flower in Trev's lapel. "There."

Trev was actually quite touched, not to mention surprised by Jupiter's thoughtfulness.

The flower really did help offset how much he hated the suit.

Jupiter wound the leash tighter around his hand and then offered his arm to Trev. "Ready, my delicate little flower?"

"Call me that again and I'll jam this flower up your ass," Trev cooed.

"I'll take that as a yes."

Jupiter escorted Trev out of the kitchen and back into the hallway. They entered the ballroom, and it was completely packed.

The turnout for the party was impressive given the incredibly short notice, and everyone was dressed to the nines. Even the catering staff were wearing tuxedos, and Trev was thrown off for a few moments as he tried to adjust to the ritzy environment.

The moment he and Jupiter walked in, all eyes were on them.

As they should be, Trev thought.

Even in this hideous suit, he looked like a million bucks.

This was really no different than all the times he'd worked at the Cannery and had to be shown off to potential buyers. He had spent a long time being put on display and viewed as a piece of meat, although being gawked at by a bunch of men who would probably sooner kill him than fuck him was new.

Emil approached them with a big grin, saying, "Ah, perfect timing. I was just getting ready to make rounds."

"How is Ugo enjoying his party?" Jupiter asked politely.

"Oh, he's having a lovely time." Emil gestured to a table where Ugo was seated with Sal. "He's actually very lucid. It's amazing."

Ugo did indeed seem to be having a nice time, smiling and laughing with some other guests who had approached to greet him.

Trev resisted the urge to make a smartass comment.

He was supposed to be behaving or whatever.

Emil snapped his fingers. "Come on."

Jupiter and Trev followed Emil to the table where Ugo was seated.

Ugo stared at Trev, looking confused, and he asked Emil something but it was in Italian and Trev couldn't understand it. Emil replied, also in Italian, and Trev really wished he knew what they were saying.

He caught Jupiter's eye and shrugged.

Jupiter shook his head.

"This is Roderick Legrand's little brother," Emil said firmly, as if speaking in English was somehow going to clarify things. "Boss Cold's own blood, plucked right from the safety of his home and our prisoner."

Trev resisted the urge to correct him.

"But why?" Ugo pressed. "What is the meaning? What is the reason?"

"We're getting territory back!" Sal exclaimed. "We're getting the warehouse district in Strassen Springs and—"

"No, no, no." Ugo shook his head, appearing agitated. "This was a mistake. Have we not rebuilt? Have we not taken this city? Why keep looking back at the past, eh?"

Emil scowled. "Because Strassen Springs was ours! And it will be again."

Ugo shook his head more passionately, and he yelled in Italian.

Emil yelled back, and then Sal got between them as Ugo rose from the table.

Ugo said something that sounded like a threat, and Emil's face turned bright red.

"What was that?" Trev whispered urgently. "Because Emil's head looks like it's going to pop."

"The price of pride is always blood," Jupiter murmured.

Trev grimaced. "Cheerful."

Sal put a hand on Emil's shoulder, but Emil slapped it away. Emil left the table abruptly, snapping his fingers at Jupiter and Trev. "Come on. Follow me. I want to introduce our little friend to some people who will actually appreciate my fucking efforts."

"Oh goody," Trev mumbled.

Jupiter tugged on the leash and cleared his throat.

Trev bared his teeth in the closest thing he could manage to a smile.

Yes. Behaving.

Right.

Emil was only too proud to pull Trev around from one gangster to another, boasting loudly about how they had Boss Cold's own brother strung up like a little bitch. Trev didn't mind the language—he'd been called much worse, after all—but the way everyone poked, prodded, and grabbed him was driving him insane.

At the club, there were bouncers who handled this kind of thing.

No touching the merchandise was a sacred rule.

Too bad it didn't apply here.

Everyone already knew who he was, so there were no introductions. Several people shoved him, smacked his chest, and a few even spat at him. It was humiliating and *gross*, and Trev was ready to grab the leash from Jupiter and choke out every last one of them.

Emil strutted like a peacock, bragging over and over how they'd snatched Cold's little brother away. He, of course, failed to mention that Cold wasn't quite as concerned as Emil was making him out to be.

Which did still leave a big question unanswered, perhaps *the* question—who had known that Trev was Cold's brother? After all, someone had to have told the Luchesi family, but who?

Trev didn't linger on it for long. He was more concerned with surviving this ridiculous pageant and was at least thankful that Jupiter was keeping a glass of champagne in his hand at all times. The urge to throw said champagne in Emil's face was extraordinary, and he made a mental note to buy a very nice pair of shoes to reward his patience.

Emil eventually left them to tend to Ugo, and Trev chugged his champagne with a hiss.

"Hey, take it easy," Jupiter murmured. "You're only supposed to pretend to get drunk."

"Hey, let's trade places then," Trev shot back haughtily.

"I mean it." Jupiter plucked the empty glass away. "I know this is difficult—"

"Lacing a corset up by yourself is difficult. This is bullshit."

"I'm sorry." Jupiter subtly ran his fingers over the edge of the collar. "I'll make it up to you. Promise."

"Can I kick you in the balls?"

Jupiter snorted. "Seriously?"

Trev smirked.

Whether he trusted Jupiter or not, a swift kick in the nuts would feel extremely vindicating right now.

"It would be a really great start," Trev teased.

"I was thinking more, like, a massage or—"

"Kick in the balls, please." Trev turned to grab another glass of champagne from a passing waiter. When Jupiter tried to take it, Trev twisted out of the way. He couldn't go far because of the leash, but it was enough for him to tip the glass back.

Jupiter scowled. "What are you doing?"

"What? Me? Nothing." Trev smiled sweetly, leaning in close. "Look at everyone."

Jupiter tensed. "What?"

"Look how glassy their eyes are. Have you noticed how much champagne has been flowing?" Trev smirked. "Trust me that I have a lot of experience with what a bunch of old drunk men look like. Everyone here is well on their way to being completely and totally smashed."

"So, what you're saying is..."

"We don't have to actually create a distraction. I don't think they'll even notice that we're gone."

"Are you sure you want to test that?" Jupiter raised his brows.

"Right. So, kick in the balls then?"

"What?"

"Well, I'm supposed to be drunk too, right?" Trev lifted his glass. "You're worried about us not following the plan, so I should still pretend to get wasted and make a scene. I think kicking you in the balls would make a very big scene. Don't you?"

Jupiter tugged on the leash.

"Oh!" Trev gasped. "Now I'm *definitely* doing it." He smiled and grabbed Jupiter's shoulders.

Jupiter grimaced. "Oh no."

"Oh *yes*. You did chain me to a wall."

"Which I am very sorry for."

Trev grinned.

"Have I told you how very handsome you are in that suit?"

"In this ugly suit?"

Jupiter continued to cringe. "Please be gentle."

"Don't worry, Daddy. I'll be gentle." Trev shrugged. "Ish."

"Just do it."

Trev swung his knee into Jupiter's crotch, and yes, perhaps he did it a little harder than he really needed to, but it was so very satisfying to see Jupiter double over. "Fuck you!" he yelled, trying to sound slurred. "You're a fuckin' asshole! And your hair is stupid! And, and your face is fucking stupid too!"

Several of the guests gasped and stared, and two men came up as if to intervene.

"I've got him!" Jupiter threw up his hand to stop their advance. He gritted his teeth as he stood up straight, and then he yanked on the leash. "Come on! I think that's enough for you."

Trev scowled and tried to pull back. He couldn't go far because of the leash, and he shoved Jupiter's chest. "Fuck you! I'm not going anywhere with you!"

"All right. Come here." Jupiter grabbed Trev around his waist.

"Nope, nope! Fuck you!" Trev squirmed frantically. "Somebody help! Help me! Get this fucking nutjob off me!"

The crowd laughed, and some even cheered when Jupiter swung Trev over his shoulder. They clapped as Jupiter carried him out into the hallway, and Trev wanted to scream. He knew that he and Jupiter were only pretending to fight as part of their ruse to escape, but wow.

These gangsters were all a bunch of *assholes*.

Jupiter continued out into the hallway and to the stairs, still carrying Trev.

"You can put me down now," Trev whispered angrily.

"Someone might be watching." Jupiter reached up and smacked his ass. "Come on, we're committing right?" He smacked him again. "Like with hitting me in the balls!"

"Ow! You dick!" Trev growled. "I didn't even hit you that hard!"

"Tell that to my fucking balls!"

Trev rolled his eyes, grunting as Jupiter hauled him over to the stairs. "For fuck's sake. You can put me down now."

"Gonna kick me again?" Jupiter growled.

"I *kneed* you and not even that hard!" Trev snapped. "Will you quit bitching and focus, please?"

Jupiter set Trev down. "I'm not bitching!"

"Said in the bitchiest tone ever. You should be the one on a leash."

Jupiter smacked Trev's ass hard enough to sting. "Let's go."

Trev took the stairs two at a time. Jupiter was on the same page and was only a second behind him. Into Jupiter's room they went to retrieve the lockbox and the bag, and Trev left the leash behind. He kept the collar on. He couldn't say why and chalked it up to madness in the heat of the moment. They hurried back downstairs in equal haste, and

Jupiter went out first into the hallway to make sure the way was clear.

Trev froze, his heart pounding fast.

There was still a chance that a guard might see them and question what they were doing. A guest might see them and ask what was going on. Ugo could come barging through and ask them for a dance.

Anything could fucking happen.

Jupiter came back and grabbed Trev's hand. "Let's go."

Trev let Jupiter take the lead as they jogged down the hallway and around the ballroom, ducking here and there to make sure they weren't seen. Trev thought he heard voices nearby, perhaps the valets, but the kitchen was empty when they finally made it in.

Trev frowned.

This was almost too easy.

Jupiter shrugged at his concerned expression and grabbed a set of keys from the case. He squeezed Trev's hand. "Almost there, baby doll."

Trev could only nod.

They headed outside, racing across a sprawling patio to a crowd of cars. Jupiter hit a button on the keys, and the headlights of a nearby SUV flashed. Another cursory look around revealed no sign of any of the valets.

Trev's stomach *lurched*.

"Jupiter," he whispered. "Something's wrong."

"What do you mean?" Jupiter hissed. "We're almost there."

"Right, but where is everyone? The valets aren't here, none of the guards—"

"Are you really complaining?" Jupiter stopped to stare at him.

"I'm telling you, something is wrong," Trev insisted.

"Look, it's fine," Jupiter argued. "We're gonna get in that fucking car, we're gonna get the fuck out of here, and then we're—"

"I wouldn't do that if I was yous," a familiar voice chirped.

Trev whirled around.

Shit.

It was *Howell.*

CHAPTER *Ten*

"WHAT THE FUCK DO YOU WANT?" Jupiter snapped.

"Just tryin' t'help." Howell held up his hands. "Yous should know they're checking every vehicle that goes in or outta here." He snorted. "They're definitely gonna notice yous trying to sneak out ya' lil' friend there. Everybody is on high alert tonight for this lil' shindig."

"How do you know that?" Trev demanded.

"'Cause duh. Emil personally told me to keep an eye out, and I quote, for anythin' lookin' suspicious." Howell gestured to them. "And yous two are lookin' mighty suspicious."

"How about you just pretend you didn't see us?" Trev tried, offering him a sweet smile.

If Howell really did have a crush on him, maybe he could use that to his advantage.

Trev advanced until he could slide his hand up Howell's shirt and give his tie a playful tug. He pouted his lips and gave Howell his most sultry purr. "Come on, baby. All you have to do is look the other way, okay?"

Howell grinned, but then he shook his head frantically. "Shit! No! Trust me, yous are a very temptin' slice of cake, but I'm workin' here, babe. The best thing to do is both of yous—"

"No," Jupiter said firmly. "You're our new ticket out of here."

"Excuse me?"

"You heard me." Jupiter drew his gun.

Howell did not appear distressed. He gave a slight shake of his head, but Trev wasn't sure why. "Listen to me very, very carefully. If yous get in that car right now, you're not gonna make it outta here."

Trev thought back to the key and the clothes Howell had brought him. Going with his gut, he demanded, "Okay, so what do we do? You want to help us, right?"

"I wanna help *you*," Howell corrected.

"Help me then," Trev pleaded earnestly. "How the fuck do I get out of here right now, huh?"

"If you'd just wait a fuckin' minute—"

"No," Jupiter snapped. "We're leaving right now." He grabbed Howell's neck, slamming the gun up against the side of his head. "Let's go." Without looking at Trev, he tossed him the car keys. "Here."

"Shit! Okay!" Trev scrambled to catch them.

Howell groaned in annoyance. "Oh my fuckin' God, you stupid fucks! Are you—"

Jupiter cracked the butt of his gun against Howell's head again. "Shut up! Get in the fucking car."

A small trickle of blood dripped down Howell's forehead, and he smiled. "Yous are gonna fuckin' regret that."

"Later." Jupiter kept the gun on Howell and forced him into the front passenger seat.

Trev got in behind the wheel and cranked the engine, his fingers trembling from the rush of adrenaline. He waited for Jupiter to climb into the back and get situated, noting that he kept the gun pointed at Howell. "Okay. Okay, now what?"

"Drive," Jupiter said firmly. "Head for the gate."

"What if the guards won't let us through?"

"Be prepared to drive really, really fast."

"Fuck," Trev hissed between his teeth as he pulled out, headed for the driveway. The lights were automatic at least, so he didn't have to worry about finding them, and his heart continued to throb in the back of his throat and nearly choked every breath.

"Yous guys are fuckin' dumb," Howell drawled. "Like, stickin' your dick all up in a cheese grater to blow a load fuckin' *dumb*. If you'd just waited, like, five more minutes, ya' wouldn't have to pull this stupid shit."

"Shut up," Jupiter warned.

"I bet yous used to put forks in light sockets, huh?"

"Shut up."

Trev ignored them as he drove toward the gate at the end of the driveway. The gate was open, but there were two guards standing in the way, doubtlessly armed. They shielded their eyes against the headlights of the SUV, and one beckoned Trev to pull up. The other was reaching under his jacket.

Shit, shit, shit.

"Jupiter?" Trev asked urgently.

"Yous was the kid eatin' glue in class, huh?" Howell continued to taunt. "Probably like smellin' your own farts too. Pull up the covers and Dutch oven yourself on the regular."

"I said, shut up!" Jupiter snapped.

"First time you'd tried to get your fuck on, did ya' try to put it in their belly button? Or did ya' just hump their ass crack?"

"*Jupiter*!" Trev shouted.

They were only a few feet away from the guards now, and Trev had no idea what to do. He could floor it and pray they didn't get shot as they fled, but that seemed like a terrible plan.

The guard was coming up to the window.

"Yous are so fuckin' dumb I bet you'd climb a glass wall just to see what was behind it," Howell kept on, laughing now.

"I will fucking *kill you* if you don't shut the fuck up," Jupiter growled. "Tell these bastards to let us go—"

The guard knocked on Trev's window, and Trev gritted his teeth. "Can you guys *both* shut up?"

Howell cackled. "If yous had double the brains ya' got now, you'd still be a half-wit!"

The guard knocked again, harder this time.

"One sec, sir! The, uh, child locks are on." Trev squirmed miserably. "*Jupiter*, what do I do?"

Jupiter huffed. "Lower the window and—"

"Did yous even get that joke?" Howell grinned back at Jupiter. He didn't seem like he had a care in the world. "Mighta been too much 'cause it had some math in it. Half is a fraction, and—"

Jupiter raised the gun right against the side of Howell's head as he snarled, "I told you to—"

"For fuck's sake!" Trev groaned.

The guard banged on the window, and the other guard drew a gun.

Fuck, fuck, fuck!

Pop.

Trev couldn't immediately identify the sound, but he saw the guard with the gun collapse.

Pop.

A splatter of blood hit the window, and Trev stared in horror as the other guard dropped out of sight.

Shot.

They'd both been *shot.*

Trev gasped. "Holy shit."

"What the fuck?" Jupiter stared. "Who—"

Howell reached back, seizing Jupiter's wrist and giving it a cruel twist.

Jupiter yelled in pain, dropping the gun.

Howell was quick to snatch it up, and he turned in his seat with alarming speed to aim it at Jupiter. "Hey, Trev," he said, his eyes never leaving Jupiter. "Time to drive now."

Someone shouted.

Another voice joined, and they sounded like they were getting closer.

Jupiter turned around, looking through the back window. "Time to drive, Trev!"

"Shit!" Trev hit the gas, taking off through the gate. "Which way?"

"Right!" Jupiter ordered.

"No, fucking left!" Howell barked. "Come on!"

"Fuck!" Trev swerved to the left, overcorrected, and nearly went into the ditch. "Where the fuck are we going?"

"Away from here!" Jupiter shouted.

"At the end of the road, take a fuckin' right," Howell said quickly.

"Why the fuck should I listen to you?" Trev snapped.

"Because I don't wanna fuckin' die with yous two fucks!" Howell rolled his eyes. "We gotta lose these wheels. Fast."

"Why?"

"Because *duh*, they're all tagged." Howell shook his head. "I know where we can scoop up a ride, okay? It's clean."

"How do you know?" Jupiter asked suspiciously.

"Oh my God, 'cause I fuckin' left it there." Howell gestured at the upcoming T-intersection. "Right here and then park next to the big ol' construction barrels."

Trev took the turn as directed, and he saw the barrels Howell was talking about. They were around a big hole in the road, and there was a small sedan parked on the side of the road next to it.

"Park it. Just leave this piece of shit here." Howell nodded at Jupiter. "Yous get out first. Nice and easy."

Jupiter did as he was told while Trev parked the SUV and killed the engine. Trev retrieved the bag and lockbox, pausing as he watched Howell and Jupiter.

Jupiter hovered beside the sedan, and Howell reached into his jacket pocket without taking his eyes off Jupiter. He pulled out a set of keys and held them toward Trev.

"I'm driving again?" Trev huffed.

"Sorry." Howell snorted. "Lil' busy here."

"Right." Trev unlocked the sedan.

In the distance, tires squealed.

"Shit, shit, shit." Howell hissed. "Change of plans."

"What is that?" Trev demanded. "Who is that?"

Jupiter scowled angrily. "Luchesis. They're probably following the tag on the SUV."

"Time to go!" Howell snatched the keys from Trev.

"But... you... What are we doing?" Trev threw up his hands in frustration.

"Yous dumbasses want to live? Then get your asses in the fuckin' car!" Howell shouted as he jumped behind the wheel. "Now!"

Jupiter gritted his teeth. "Fuck. Let's go."

Trev hurried into the car, crawling into the back seat with the lockbox and bag. He stared as Jupiter got in the front seat, snapping, "We're really doing this?"

"I do like living," Jupiter replied.

"Hang onto your butts!" Howell turned the car on and then took off, not waiting for either Trev or Jupiter to even get their seat belts on. He peeled out onto the road, swinging the car around the SUV and driving back the way they came.

"Where the fuck are you going?" Jupiter snapped angrily.

"I got this shit, shuddup!" Howell barked back.

"Uh, guys?" Trev blinked slowly.

Maybe he was seeing things, but it looked like there were two SUVs up ahead, one in each lane and driving right at them.

"Guys?" Trev repeated. "Hello?"

"I sees 'em!" Howell continued forward.

"*Howell—*" Jupiter growled.

Neither of the incoming SUVs changed course, and Trev cringed, certain they were about to collide with one if not both vehicles. At the last possible second, Howell spun the wheel and took them into the ditch. Trev's head smacked the roof as the sedan bounced along through the grass, and Howell hit the gas, taking them back onto the road.

The drivers of the SUVs hit the brakes and got caught up trying to make three point turns without hitting each other to give chase.

Howell hummed as he turned around, smoothly driving by the SUVs as soon as there was an opening.

"Where the fuck are you going?" Jupiter snapped. "You're heading right back to the house!"

"Uh, yeah, because we need to go the other fuckin' way."

Howell snorted. "Road behind us dead-ends into nothin'. We gotta get to the highway and that means drivin' back by the damn house."

Trev scrambled to get buckled in, grimacing as Howell took the next turn hard enough for the tires to squeal. "Jesus fuck! Come on!"

"Hang on!" Howell hit the gas again, zooming by the SUV they'd abandoned. "Those dumbasses ain't gonna let us get away that easy."

"Wait, you're not working for the Luchesis?" Trev demanded.

"What? Fuck those fuckin' fucks!" Howell scoffed. "I tried to fuckin' tell yous that I'm here to help *you*! So just—"

The back window shattered, raining glass over Trev. "Fuck!"

"Fuck me runnin' sideways!" Howell hissed.

"Get down!" Jupiter shouted.

"No shit!" Trev shouted back as he pressed himself against the seat.

"Hey! Big and ugly!" Howell snapped angrily, thrusting the gun at Jupiter. "How's 'bout yous shoot back?"

"Fuck you!" Jupiter growled.

"Fuck you!"

"Fuck *you*!"

"Fuck—"

"Fuck both of you!" Trev snarled. "Someone fucking do *something*!"

Jupiter cursed as he rolled down his window to return fire.

Trev slapped his hands over his ears and gritted his teeth as he pushed himself down into the floorboard. The car swerved again, the gunfire continued, and Trev was certain he was going to puke. He had no idea where they were headed now, but they were definitely headed there in a hurry.

More shots rang out, glass shattered, and Jupiter grunted. "Fuck!"

"Shit, yous hit?" Howell demanded.

"Just fucking *drive*." Jupiter kept firing.

"We'll lose 'em on the highway," Howell said firmly. "Hold on, all right?"

Trev groaned miserably. "Where the fuck are we going?"

"Just stay down," Jupiter said. "Don't worry."

Trev couldn't track the time with his heart pounding in his ears and his head spinning, but he could sense the car picking up speed. They were probably on the highway now, and he hoped the danger had passed.

Howell was clearly working against the Luchesi family. There was no other reason he would have betrayed them and helped Trev and Jupiter escape.

Of course, the big question was why?

Did Howell plan to barter Trev back to Cold himself? What was his motivation for all of this?

Howell eventually pulled off onto an exit, judging by how the car slowed and came to a stop. The car got going again at a much slower speed, though Trev hesitated to move from his spot in the floorboard.

"Riverwood Acres?" Jupiter asked. "Seriously?"

"Yeah, yeah." Howell snorted. "We made it here in one fuckin' piece, didn't we? Who the fuck cares where it is?"

"Is it safe to fucking sit up?" Trev mumbled.

"Yeah, go ahead," Jupiter said.

Trev crawled back into the seat and looked around.

It was a long strip of fancy condos, and Howell parked in front of one with big bushes and a colorful doormat. "Home sweet home!"

Jupiter aimed his gun at Howell.

"Hey!" Howell pouted. "Seriously? After I saved your fuckin' asses? I thought we was past all that shit."

"Guess not." Trev batted his eyes sweetly. "Sorry not sorry."

"We're gonna get out real nice and slow," Jupiter said. "Once we get inside, we're going to have a nice conversation, okay? Real civilized like."

"Fine," Howell grumbled. "Let's go. Yous bleedin' all over my damn seats."

"Shit. Jupiter." Trev had honestly forgotten Jupiter was hurt. "Are you all right?"

"I'm fine." Jupiter flashed him a quick smile. "Let's get inside, okay? You can play doctor on me in a minute."

Trev hurried out of the back seat, pausing to grab the lockbox and Jupiter's bag. He held them close and took a deep breath, glancing around the parking lot.

He half-expected an entire fleet of black SUVs to come rushing in and try to run him over.

Jupiter tucked the gun under his jacket and jerked his head at Howell. "Let's go."

"Sheesh!" Howell scoffed grumpily as he strolled to the door. "Where's the fuckin' gratitude, huh? Where's the fuckin' thank yous at? Did I get us outta there or what?"

"I'm still not sure you didn't have something to do with us almost getting caught," Jupiter challenged as he followed, still scowling.

"What? C'mon!" Howell rolled his eyes and wiggled the keys. "Yous guys really need to learn how to trust somebody. Everythin' I did was to help! C'mon."

"Open the damn door already."

"How 'bout a please?" Howell grinned.

"Now!"

"Fuck, so fuckin' bossy. Yous really need to work on your people skills." Howell mumbled a few more curses as he opened the door "There! Happy?"

"Move." Jupiter pushed Howell inside.

Trev hurried in behind them. He shut the door and locked it.

"What in the actual fuck?" Jupiter scoffed in disgust.

"What?" Trev turned to see why Jupiter was so upset.

The inside of the condo was furnished nicely and clean, but it was impossible to appreciate any of it because there was a man tied to a chair in the middle of the living room. He was gagged with duct tape, but he still shook his head and screamed frantically.

Trev couldn't make it out, but he was certain it was something to the effect of *untie me right fucking now, please*.

"What the hell is this?" Jupiter grimaced as he shoved Howell toward the man. "You're into kidnapping too?"

"Is it really kidnappin' if it's his own house?" Howell laughed.

"You really have no room to talk about kidnapping," Trev muttered to Jupiter.

"Hey, c'mon. He's fine!" Howell waved at the man. "He's still alive, ain't he?"

"Who the fuck is that?" Trev demanded.

"Oh!" Howell laughed. "That's Howell what's his name."

"Huh? *That's* Howell Hodges?" Jupiter snapped. "Then who the fuck are you?"

"A friend." Howell smiled warmly. "Ya' know, ya' ain't been makin' it easy to help yous."

"Me? What the fuck are you talking about?"

"Not you, stupid. Him." Howell smirked at Trev.

"The key." Trev frowned. "*You* left it? That was you?"

“Yeah, it was a long shot, but hey!” Howell shrugged. “It was worth a try.”

“Who the fuck are you?” Jupiter asked again, leveling the gun at Howell’s head. “No more bullshit. No more games! Who the fuck do you work for, huh? And who took out the guys at the gate?”

“All right, all right, sheesh. Keep your fuckin’ panties on, bastard.” Howell snorted. “One question at a time, fuckin’ fuck. I work for Alistair Star, a businessman who’s pretty good friends with a certain somebody’s half-brother.”

“Cold,” Trev realized out loud.

“Yup.” Howell clicked his tongue. “Once he heard you was snatched up, he worked fast to get some solid people down here to help get you out.”

Trev grabbed a dish towel from the kitchen. He could see a tear in the fabric of Jupiter’s jacket on his left shoulder. “Here.”

“Thanks.” Jupiter shrugged his jacket off with a wince, and his sleeve was soaked in blood. He took the towel to press against the wound, but he didn’t take his eyes off Howell.

“We heard about this Howell prick, and hey, wouldn’t you know it?” Howell grinned. “Nobody’s ever actually met this dumb fuck before! It was a cinch to slip on in and just take his fuckin’ place.” He patted the real Howell’s head. “He ain’t been too happy, but fuck ’im.”

Jupiter slowly lowered the gun. “You’ve been posing as Howell to get to Trev?”

“Yeah, duh. Hello? That’s what I just fuckin’ said.” Howell—or whoever he was—scoffed. “Are you listenin’ to a damn word I’m sayin’? Cold and his guys wouldn’t have been able to get here in time. Me and my boy were closer.”

“Your boy?”

"My friend. My buddy. Mr. Pew Pew up on the roof who helped us get away." Howell waved his hand. "He's been stickin' real close just in case any dumb shit went down. And oh look, some real dumb shit went down."

Trev narrowed his eyes. "Cold really sent you to help me?"

"No, I just thought it would be fun to pretend to be a douchebag arms dealer," Howell drawled. "Of course, Cold fuckin' sent us! Wow, yous guys really are fuckin' slow." He shook his finger at Jupiter. "I won't sure 'bout yous. Thought ya' were sidin' up with your family, but you're tryin' to get out too, huh?"

Jupiter glanced at Trev before replying, "Yes."

"Okay, good! I'd hate to kill ya'. Yous seem like a decent guy. For a bastard and all."

Jupiter scowled.

"Cute trick with the party, by the way," Howell teased. "That was yous guys, huh?"

"Yeah, and?" Trev wrinkled his nose. "It worked, didn't it? It gave us a way out."

"If you dumb dumbs had just waited until tomorrow morning, we could have walked right out the front door."

"What are you talking about?" Jupiter asked.

"Uh, hello, duh." Howell put his elbow on the top of the real Howell's head. "The family was gonna scoot out tomorrow to check a new location for their lil' drug operation. Emil, Sal, all of 'em."

"Why didn't you just fucking say that?" Trev groaned.

"Because this big bastard wouldn't shut the fuck up!" Howell gestured at Jupiter. "Besides, how the hell was I supposed to know he was all right? He did chain you to a fuckin' wall."

"Come on." Jupiter scoffed. "One time!"

Trev stared at Jupiter.

"Okay, fine, and the leash thing." Jupiter rolled his eyes. "But that was for the party and not my idea."

"Bleed more quietly, please." Trev huffed and looked to Howell. "Do you have a first aid kit or anything here so we can patch him up?"

"How the fuck should I know?" Howell blinked in surprise. "I don't fuckin' live here. Hey, fuck nuts." Howell tapped the real Howell's head. "Yous got a first aid kit or somethin' here?"

The real Howell screamed angrily.

Howell shrugged. "I think that's a no."

"Well, we need to get Jupiter to stop bleeding everywhere and then we're getting the fuck out of here," Trev said firmly. "The Luchesis saw you leave with us, so it's only a matter of time before they come banging on the door. I, for one, would like to not be here."

"Yeah, yeah." Howell waved his hand. "Don't worry. We got some time, all right? Let me go check the bathroom and see what I can find." He gave the real Howell a friendly pat on the head and then left, heading down an adjacent hallway.

Trev sighed, his shoulders sagging. He was exhausted down to his bones, and he melted when Jupiter wrapped his uninjured arm around him. He let himself relax, bowing his head against Jupiter's chest. "Holy shit, can we do that again, like, never?"

"Which part?" Jupiter teased. "The car chase, me getting shot, or the leash?"

"All of it. Except maybe the leash." Trev managed a tired smile.

Jupiter gave the collar a small tug. "Yeah? Not gonna lie... I did like leading you around."

"I bet you did, Daddy." Trev snorted. "Freak."

Jupiter smiled warmly and kissed Trev's brow. His expression grew serious, and he squeezed Trev a little closer. "Are you all right? You didn't get cut up or anything, did you?"

"No, I'm fine. Promise. Just..." Trev shivered. "Rattled, I guess. Have all of this adrenaline and nowhere to put it."

Jupiter grinned.

"I am not fucking you right now." Trev swatted him.

"Why not?"

"First of all, there's a tied up arms dealer *right there*, we're still on the run from the Luchesis, and oh yeah, you're bleeding on me."

"Ah. So, later?"

"Later."

Howell returned with a small first aid kit. "Ta-dah! There's some gauze and shit in there. Might be enough to fix ya' up."

Jupiter still had the gun in his hand, and he hesitated to put it away.

Howell waved the case. "C'mon. I ain't gonna try to shoot yous right now. We're on the same side, remember? The side where I deliver Trev here to Cold, alive and well."

Trev's heart thumped. "You're taking me to Cold?"

"Uh, yeah." Howell tilted his head. "Am I speakin' English okay? Jesus, that is why I'm here! To get your ass to Strassen Springs."

Jupiter tucked his gun under his jacket to accept the first aid kit. "You're about as clear as fucking mud."

"Choke on a crusty sandpaper fuckin' ball sack."

"What?" Jupiter grunted as he set the first aid kit on the counter so he could take off his shirt. "That doesn't make any fucking sense."

"It'll make plenty of sense when your chin gets all fuckin' raw from the sandpaper!"

"Oh my God."

"Can both of you shut up for two fucking seconds? I can't even hear myself think!" Trev shook his head. "I want to leave the fucking country, okay? I want to get as far away from all of this bullshit as possible."

"And that's fine! Groovy!" Howell flashed two big thumbs-up. "Whatever. But first you're going to see Boss Cold."

Trev thought he heard the door open, but when he turned around to check, he didn't see anyone. He turned his attention back to Howell. "You still haven't told us who you really are," he reminded Howell. "Why the fuck would I go anywhere with you?

"Oh! My apologies." Howell bowed his head politely. "Allow me to introduce myself."

Jupiter grunted and suddenly collapsed, the gauze scattering across the floor.

"Jupiter!" Trev shouted, staring in horror at a handsome man with wild eyes who had just struck Jupiter in the head with the butt of a pearl-handled gun. "What the *fuck*?"

The man smiled.

It was downright chilling.

"That there's my good friend, Erasmus Argento," Howell said with a grin. "Don't worry. He's real friendly once ya' get to know 'im. Never really blinks though, but hey, ya' get used to it after a while. Real crack shot, that one. And oh yeah! My name's Maurice Martine Junior, but yous can just call me Junior."

CHAPTER
Eleven

"WHY THE FUCK did you knock him out?" Trev demanded haughtily. "How the hell are we going to move him now? Do you see how fucking *huge* he is?"

"We're not bringing him with us," Erasmus said coolly. "We're leaving him."

"What? No way." Trev backed away. "The only reason I'm here is because of him! He—"

"Spoiled a perfectly good plan, put your life in danger because of his arrogance, and chained you to a wall." Erasmus quirked his brow.

He still hadn't blinked.

"Fuck you." Trev gave his best syrupy sweet smile. "I'm not going anywhere without him."

Erasmus's upper lip twitched.

"Hey, hey, hey!" Junior, formerly known as Howell, grabbed Erasmus's shoulder. "Easy now. I know how much yous love shootin' people, but let's just get goin', okay? Let the Luchesis worry 'bout him."

Erasmus looked at the real Howell.

"Fine! Okay! Just this once. Have fun." Junior held out

his hand. "Gimme your keys, all right? Let's get the fuck outta here."

Erasmus handed Junior a set of keys.

"C'mon, kid." Junior waved at Trev. "Get your shit. Let's go."

"I already told you I'm not going anywhere without Jupiter." Trev batted his eyes. "And I'm pretty sure my half-brother gave explicit instructions to make sure I wasn't harmed, right? To deliver me in one piece and all that?"

"Your point?"

"Either bring Jupiter or I'm going to make your life very, very difficult."

Erasmus turned to stare at Trev.

"Stop it, creepy," Junior warned Erasmus, waving his hand at him. "We ain't takin' him in the trunk or nothin', all right?" He sighed and addressed Trev, saying firmly, "Look, we gots to come to an understandin' here. He's a Luchesi, okay? He's one of them. We brings him with us, I can promise that Cold will send him back in a body bag."

"But if we leave him here, he's as good as dead anyway!" Trev pointed at Howell. "All that fucker has to do is open his big mouth and tell the Luchesis what happened and that Jupiter was helping me—"

"Oh no, don't worry 'bout that!" Junior patted Trev's back. "We got this handled. Don't we, Razz?"

Erasmus glared at Junior and without looking, he leveled his gun at Howell.

"No, don't yous do it—"

Erasmus fired.

"Ya' crazy dumb fuck!" Junior rubbed his ears. "I'm standin', like, right fuckin' next to yous! You did that on fuckin' purpose!"

Erasmus smiled.

Trev made a face and turned away, his ears ringing and his stomach turning. He really hadn't wanted to see anyone die today or *ever*, and Howell made the third person he'd seen murdered in the last hour.

"Yous were supposed to fuckin' wait until I got the kid outta here!" Junior continued to scold. "Asshole!"

Erasmus shrugged. "Now we can go."

"I'm not going anywhere," Trev warned. "You can both fuck right off."

"Come on! See?" Junior patted Trev's shoulder. "Now your lil' boyfriend can spin whatever dumbass story he wants to! Wasn't that so fuckin' nice of us?"

"How do you even know that will work?" Trev snarled. "What if they don't believe him and still kill him?"

"Sucks to be him?"

"This is *bullshit*."

"Let's get goin', kid." Junior grabbed Trev's arm. "You can scream at us later, but right now we—"

"Fuck you!" Trev snatched up the lockbox and cracked Junior as hard as he could over the head with it.

"Ow! Yous lil' fuckin' bitch!" Junior howled, clutching his head.

Trev turned to swing at Erasmus, but Erasmus was faster.

So much faster.

Erasmus slipped behind Trev like a shadow and slammed his gun against the back of his head.

Shit, shit, shit.

Trev collapsed, the world fading into darkness.

TREV WOKE WITH A GROAN, his head pounding worse than any hangover. He felt the back of his head, gingerly tracing around a sore bump. He was in the back seat of a car, maybe a truck, and Erasmus had fucking knocked him out and…

Jupiter!

Trev bolted up. "Hey! Where the fuck are we?"

"Aw, good mornin', sleepin' beauty," Junior chirped from the front seat. "How was your lil' nap?"

Erasmus was driving and said nothing, though he did stare at Trev through the rearview mirror for a long moment.

Fuckin' creep.

"Fuck you!" Trev growled. "Turn the fuck around! We're going back."

"No can do, kid." Junior shrugged. "We're only, like, an hour away or somethin'. Sit back before I make yous sit back, all right? We don't wanna hafta knock yous out again."

Erasmus smiled, indicating that he clearly didn't mind.

Trev's head hurt too much to argue and he melted into the seat, defeated. He felt around to find the duffel bag and his lockbox, and he briefly considered whacking Junior again.

This sucked.

Short of causing a car accident and then trying to flee on foot, Trev saw no way out of this.

The best thing he could do was let this play out and meet Cold.

Maybe by then, Trev would have thought of what to do next.

Using the duffel as a pillow, Trev tried to relax, but it was hard to rest when his head was pounding and his mind wouldn't let him stop thinking about Jupiter.

Stupid, annoying Jupiter.

Who had an amazing smile, a pretty good sense of humor, a *great* dick, and who they'd left to possibly take the heat from the mafia family he so wanted to escape.

Shit.

Trev hadn't taken the collar off yet, but he couldn't really say why. He should have pulled it off and hurled it out the window the first chance he had. Jupiter was not innocent in any of this, not even close, and yet Trev still wanted to keep it on.

Jupiter had wanted to help him escape.

They were going to run away together.

They...

No, that was stupid.

"Wakey, wakey," Junior sang out. "Eggs and bac-ey!"

Trev realized the truck had stopped moving. He sat up, staring out the windows in shock.

They were at a mansion.

An honest to God mansion that made the Luchesi estate look like a dumpster.

There were more men in suits—of course—but these guys even had *dogs*.

The first blush of the sun was lightening the sky, though Trev didn't have long to admire it before Junior and Erasmus were herding him out of the truck. He scowled as Junior grabbed the lockbox and Erasmus the duffel bag, and then they each grabbed one of Trev's arms to urge him to the door.

"Come on!" Junior grumbled. "I'm fuckin' tired and my goddamn dome hurts 'cause some lil' asshole hit me with a fuckin' box. And oh yeah, next fuckin' time, we're usin' my phone for fuckin' directions. Yours fuckin' sucks moldy ol' fuckin' donkey balls, Razz."

Erasmus grunted.

"Don't yous grunt at me, you moody bitch!" Junior waited for one of the suited men to open the door so they could head inside. "And I fuckin' swear, yous is never having them gas station burritos again. Fuckin' biological warfare—"

"Good mornin'," a deep voice said in greeting.

Trev barely had a moment to admire the polished foyer before he looked up.

And up.

And *up*.

To see a man even larger and more bulging than Jupiter.

He was wearing a ratty T-shirt that said "Bucky's All-U-Can Wings" and gray sweatpants that he filled out very nicely, and he looked like he'd just woken up. His dark eyes met Trev's and his expression froze. He appeared startled as if he'd seen a ghost. "*Fuck.*"

"Right?" Junior cackled. "Didn't believe it myself until I saw 'im."

Trev wrenched his arms free and stood as tall as he could, glaring up at the giant man. "Wow. *Expedition Bigfoot* know you're out here?"

The man laughed. "You're funny."

"Yes, ha ha." Trev rolled his eyes. "Being kidnapped really lets my sense of humor shine."

"Is he here?" A woman's voice called out. "Jules?"

"Come on." The man turned to call down the hallway. "Roe! You gotta see this."

A gorgeous woman came racing up to them, bundled up in a lush silk robe, her heels clicking over the tile floor. She stopped right in front of Trev and stared in shock. Her eyes were the same icy blue as Trev's own, and it was...

Strange.

Like looking in the mirror but not, recognizing parts of himself but there was a stranger mixed in there too.

"Oh. My. God!" The woman screamed and threw her arms around Trev's neck.

"Uh? Hi?" Trev caught her so he wouldn't topple over.

She pulled back, stared at him, and screamed again. "Holy shit, this is fucking wild!"

Trev blinked.

"I'm Rowena Legrand," the woman said quickly. "I'm your sister!"

"Sister?" Trev's heart fluttered. "I..." He laughed. "I have a sister?"

"Look, you'll learn real fast that ol' Boris really got around." Rowena laughed sweetly. "I always said there's a ton of us little Legrands somewhere out there!"

"Legrand?"

"Yeah. Boris Legrand. Our mutual sperm donor."

Trev tensed.

Right. Because it wasn't actually Boris Usher like his mother had told him.

"Trevanion, right?" Rowena asked.

"Trev." Trev smiled wearily.

"God, you're so gorgeous." Rowena squealed. "Boris was a man slut, but damn if he didn't make some fine kids!" She looked at Erasmus and Junior. "Oh! Is that your stuff? Boys, be a dear and put that upstairs for me." She looped her arm with Trev's. "Come on, babe. Time to go meet the rest of the family!"

Trev's heart thumped again.

Rowena's excited energy was infectious and not at all what he expected. He thought this was going to be more brooding gangsters and chains, not a new half-sister who was wearing a kickass pair of Louboutin heels.

"Love your kicks, by the way," Trev noted.

He felt like an absolute trash fire right now and probably looked like one too, suit or no.

"Aw, thanks!" Rowena frowned at him. "Do you need some threads, sweetie? You actually look like you're about Jimmy's size, maybe? Look, let's get you some breakfast, and then you can get a shower and get all cleaned up."

"And Jimmy is?"

"Your brother-in-law," said the giant man who had somehow silently trailed right behind them.

"Holy fuck, you're sneaky." Trev cringed.

"I'm Jules Price," the man said.

"Are you another one of Boris's kids?"

"Nah."

"Might as well be," Rowena chirped. "He grew up with Roddy and me. The *other* big, annoying brother who scared off all my boyfriends."

Trev looked around as they headed to presumably the kitchen, trying to take in the layout as quickly as he could. There were fresh flowers everywhere, the decor crisp and minimal, and he was not the least bit surprised that the kitchen was decked out with the fanciest appliances he had ever seen.

A tall thin man in an apron was humming as he cooked at the stove, and he turned to smile at Trev and the others. His surprise was not as startling as Rowena's or Jules's had been, but Trev noticed it all the same. "Hello," the man said in a thick French accent. "Good morning."

"Jerry. This is Trev!" Rowena shook Trev's shoulders. "Look at him!"

"I see." Jerry tipped his head politely and then looked to Trev. "Eggs, *monsieur*?"

Trev scrubbed his hands over his face. "Wait, wait, wait.

Hold the fuck up." He spun on Rowena. "What is happening here? Where is Boss Cold? What the fuck is actually going on?"

"Breakfast?" Jules frowned.

"Sweetie," Rowena soothed. "Take a big breath. It's okay! You're safe now."

Trev laughed.

Yeah, right.

"Look, babe." Trev snorted sourly. "I love your taste in shoes, but I do not buy this *let's be a happy gangster family* for a fucking second."

"How about you just rent it for breakfast?" Rowena suggested. "Roddy will talk to you and explain any questions that you have, okay? For now, just know that all we want is you safe and fed."

Trev shuddered.

He was surrounded by strangers in a new place and unarmed. He'd never felt more alone, but at least everyone's friendly attitude would allow him some time to figure out what to do next. He fully intended to keep his guard up, but if they wanted a sweet, helpless young man who was so happy to be reunited with the family he never knew he had, he could do that.

The collar at his neck was comforting.

It was also a bitter reminder of how he'd been forced to leave Jupiter behind, and he wondered if he should have fought harder to bring Jupiter with them. Jupiter had certainly been no saint, and Trev decided that this made them even.

For the lying, the chain, and all the rest.

Hopefully, Jupiter would live long enough for Trev to find him and tell him.

"Okay. Breakfast sounds great." Trev smiled sweetly.

That at least wasn't a lie.

Jerry smiled warmly and fixed Trev a plate.

Trev sat down at a table beside a big window to eat. It was scrambled eggs, some sort of sausage, and a few slices of fresh fruit. Rowena had the same and sat down across from him. Jules hovered by the counter, where two more plates were waiting to be claimed.

"Where's Brick?" Rowena asked, her icy eyes flitting to Jules.

"Still sleepin'," Jules rumbled in reply.

Rowena smirked.

Jules rolled his eyes.

"Where's my brother?" Trev asked casually.

"He'll be down after a while." Rowena waved her hand. "Don't worry about it. I'm here to take good care of you, sweetie." She smiled. "So! Ready to tell me your life story?"

Trev batted his eyes. "No."

Rowena scoffed. "What do you mean *no*?"

"We just met!" Trev wagged his fork at her. "What kind of idiot is just going to spill their guts and tell you every dirty detail about themselves?"

Jules laughed as if something was very funny.

Rowena flipped him off and then eyed Trev. "Okay, fine! Later. After margaritas."

"Isn't it a little early?" Trev blinked.

"How about mimosas?" Rowena laughed. "I'm kidding. Mostly. I don't drink much these days, but once upon a time! Oof." She nibbled a piece of sausage. "So, Trev. Hmm. Are you all right? I get if you don't wanna get all personal, but do you need anything?" She wrinkled her nose. "Other than clothes?"

"No. Thank you, but..."

"What?"

Trev hesitated to say anything as this particular request would be rather revealing, but he needed to try. "You guys got me out. What are the chances of getting Jupiter out?"

"Who?" Rowena wrinkled her nose.

Jules scoffed. "Prospero?"

"Yeah." Trev put his fork down. "He tried to help me."

"Oh, the guy who chained you to a wall?" Rowena asked.

"How does *everyone* know about that?" Trev held up his hands. "Never mind. Just... *Ugh*. Yes, he did do that, but he also tried to help me escape. He wants to get away from the Luchesi family too and—"

"That's a question for my brother." She paused. "For *our* brother. I promise, he's really not that scary—"

"I am not scared," Trev cut in firmly.

"Nope!" Junior laughed as he strolled in. "Not this one. This one here has fuckin' balls of steel."

Jules grunted. "Where's Erasmus?"

"How the fuck should I know?" Junior scoffed. "I turn around and he's gone. He's like a fuckin' ghost, okay? He'll pop back up in a second and scare the fuck outta all us."

"Are you boys crashing here?" Rowena asked sweetly. "We got plenty of room."

"Yeah, definitely gonna take yous up on that, Miss Legrand. I'm sure fuckin' tired. Thank you." Junior tipped his head and then smirked at Trev. "Hey. Got all your shit upstairs, okay? You take care of yourself, kid. No hard feelin's 'bout leavin' your lil' boy toy behind, all right?"

Trev smiled icily. "None at all."

"Fuck, that's creepy." Jules laughed.

"What?" Trev cut his eyes to Jules.

"You look just like him when you make that fuckin' face." Jules laughed again.

Him.

Like Cold.

Trev didn't know why that unsettled him.

Everyone here was comparing him to a man he hadn't met, a man who supposedly killed their father. Perhaps Trev should have taken it as a compliment, but it made his blood boil. It only made the full scope of his mother's lies even more obvious.

His father's name, how he'd passed, everything.

If none of that was true, what else had she lied to him about?

And still the most important question of all—why?

Why had she created this fantasy for him about a perfect loving father who had been taken from the world too soon because of a negligent driver? Was that meant for Trev's benefit?

Or her own?

"So!" Rowena eyed Trev's abandoned food. "Ready for that shower?"

"Sure." Trev stood up and made a fuss about tidying up his plate.

Jerry swept over to accept the dishes from him with a courteous smile.

Everything but the knife, of course.

It was only a butter knife but better than nothing.

Trev kept it up his sleeve and followed Rowena upstairs. He knew everyone was watching him as he left, and he had already decided that he didn't trust any of them. Their friendly smiles and kindness could be hiding any number of devious plans, and he refused to believe that they had gone to all this trouble simply because he was related to them. That was insane, and if it was true, then they were idiots.

Why risk so much for a person they'd never met?

For supposedly ruthless gangsters, they seemed like a bunch of chumps.

Rowena led Trev to a large bedroom, gesturing to a door that likely led to the bathroom. "So! Check under the sink and in the tub. There should be some shampoo and stuff. I used to live here, so pretty sure there's at least some bodywash or something."

Trev was already subtly eyeing the windows and the doors. "Uh-huh. Thanks."

"You're not a prisoner here, you know," Rowena said, arching a perfectly manicured brow.

Apparently not subtle enough.

"Hmm?" Trev batted his eyes and tried to feign ignorance.

"Checking the exits? Looking for a way to get out?" Rowena's brow remained quirked. "I already clocked you stealing that butter knife from breakfast, so. Come on. Let's be real for a moment, sweetie."

Trev froze.

Well.

Shit.

Rowena crossed her arms with a heavy sigh. "If you wanna go, you can. We're not going to keep you here. But give Roddy a chance to talk to you, okay? You probably don't trust us. I get it. Probably been through some crazy ass shit, but just know... you're not the only one, okay?"

"The only one what?"

"Who Boris hurt."

Trev narrowed his eyes sharply. "Never met him."

"So?" Rowena cocked her hip. "Trust me. That man has a way of getting to you even from beyond the fuckin' grave."

Trev hesitated to pry because he didn't want Rowena to

know how curious he was, but he couldn't help asking, "Did you know him?"

"Uh-huh." Rowena's smile was strained. "Wish I hadn't. I don't know what your mom told you about him or what you think you might know, but he was not a good man."

Trev bristled, but said nothing.

"Hey." Rowena's expression softened. "I'm sure you have your reasons, okay? If your mom told you he was a saint and his shit didn't stink or whatever, she probably did it to protect you. Give you somethin' nice to think about."

"You're really sure about that, aren't you?"

"I'm sure that your pretty face looks like a cat's ass right now." Rowena smiled like a shark. "Come on. You wouldn't be pissed off unless your mom told you some sweet little story about what a great man he was, right? And here we are, throwing down all the vibes that he wasn't."

"Does it even matter? Cold killed him, didn't he?" Trev bit out the words.

"Yup," Rowena replied without hesitation. "If he hadn't, I would have."

Trev found it hard to believe that Rowena could kill anyone.

Then again...

There was a spark in her eyes that made Trev think maybe she could.

"If you'd met him," Rowena went on, "you probably would have too."

"Pretty bold assumption." Trev frowned. "How do I know you're even telling the truth? What if my mother was right and you're all the ones lying, huh?"

Trev was prepared for Rowena to give him a sob story and try to convince him what a horrible man Boris was. That seemed to be the next logical step in this conversation, and he readied a litany of responses to cut her down because he—

"You don't." Rowena shrugged.

"What?"

"I can't make you trust us. You'll just have to decide for yourself." Rowena wiggled her fingers in a little wave. "Enjoy your shower."

Trev waved back, watching her leave. As soon as the door shut, he hurried over to lock it.

Wait.

He should probably leave it unlocked. Rowena was already suspicious of him, so he should keep it open to show he trusted them. Not that he actually did, of course, but he needed to make them think otherwise. Being on good terms with his new family—*captors*—would be more beneficial in the long run.

Especially if he was going to get back to Jupiter.

Shit.

Trev touched the collar around his neck.

He missed Jupiter, more than he'd been willing to admit before.

Fleeing the country was still Trev's main priority, and now it seemed he had yet another mafia family to escape. This one was definitely kinder and it was nice they didn't seem intent on murdering him, but a gilded cage was still a prison. He didn't trust their intentions were as pure as they made them out to be, and he refused to be used as a pawn again.

Jupiter at least came clean about how he had used Trev and they both had a mutual goal: freedom.

That's what mattered now, Trev decided.

Getting the hell out of here and finding Jupiter.

But first, a shower.

Trev stripped off the suit, got the water going, and scrubbed himself clean. The bodywash and shampoo he found in the shower were a bit too floral for his liking, but he wasn't going to be picky. He took his time, soaking up the hot spray and pressing his brow against the cool tile.

He wanted a few moments to turn off his brain and try to relax, but the train of his thoughts continued to crash through any semblance of peace.

Was Boris really the villain Rowena and the others believed him to be?

Trev's mother had always been so honest with him, so why lie about Boris being a monster?

What was the point?

He reconsidered Rowena's words about his mother wanting to protect him, and he wondered if she was right. Maybe not for the reasons that Rowena thought though.

Maybe for something else...

Trev left the shower to dry off, wishing the shower had washed away some of his scattered thoughts. He wrapped a towel around his waist and poked his head out into the bedroom.

To his surprise, there were a few pairs of pants and a selection of sweaters and shirts on the bed.

Must have been Rowena.

From Jimmy, his brother-in-law or whoever.

Trev picked some black skinny jeans and a light blue sweater he deemed to be the least hideous of the bunch. He didn't have any fresh socks so he opted to go barefoot instead. Not optimal if he wanted to make a break for it later, but he didn't enjoy the idea of wearing his boots without them. He could probably ask Rowena or whoever for some later, but first...

He touched his neck.

The collar.

Trev hurried back into the bathroom to retrieve it. He admonished himself for missing it so soon, but he didn't feel right not wearing it now.

He missed Jupiter so much and—

There was a knock at the door.

Trev grabbed the butter knife he'd stolen earlier and held it behind his back before answering.

Waiting on the other side was a man.

He was tall, broader than Trev and with lighter skin, and his cropped dark hair was more salt than pepper. He was wearing a black pinstripe three-piece suit with white spats.

Who the fuck wore spats? Like, *really*?

Despite his fashion choices, he was effortlessly attractive. The rest of his ensemble was stylish, fit well, and immediately commanded a sense of power and wealth. He'd yet to utter a single word and Trev was already on edge as a result of his proximity alone.

And his eyes...

Like his own and Rowena's, they were icy blue.

Bright, beautiful, and dangerous.

This was Boss Cold.

"Well, hello there, Mr. Usher," Cold said, his voice low with a rumbling purr as he scanned Trev over like a bit of prey he was going to tear apart. "It's so nice to finally meet you."

CHAPTER *Twelve*

"BOSS COLD." Trev snorted. "You give yourself that name?"

"No."

Trev tapped his fingers against the door. "I suppose you want me to thank you, right? Well, thank you. For the very unneeded rescue and making me leave my friend behind." He flashed an icy smile. "I was doing just fine without you."

Cold's expression didn't change.

He didn't even flinch.

He was good.

Trev knew he was better.

"So." Trev batted his eyes. "Anything else?"

"Come with me." Cold's tone was firm and did not leave any room for argument. He was clearly a man who did not take kindly to being disobeyed.

So, naturally, Trev had to defy him.

"Right now?" Trev pretended to check a watch he didn't have. "I'm super busy at the moment. Not sure when—"

"Mr. Usher." Cold did not appear amused.

"That's my name, don't wear it out."

"I'd like to discuss the terms of your release."

Trev snorted. "Am I in prison or something? Thought we were all one big happy family?"

Cold stared expectantly.

He was impossible to read.

That certainly made it harder to manipulate him or figure out what was going through his head, but Trev could still work with this. If nothing else, he knew he was really good at being annoying.

"So, that's a no to the picnic?" Trev asked. "Because I thought it would be really fun for all of us to go play in the yard with the big scary guard dogs. Maybe we'll do a cookout. Grill some burgers. You like burgers, right?"

Still nothing.

"Come on. Everybody likes burgers. Big juicy ones with cheese, lettuce, tomato, onions—"

Cold's upper lip twitched.

Huh.

So, he didn't like onions.

"Fine. No onions." Trev smiled. "I'll remember that. Any other dietary preferences?"

Cold turned and walked away.

"Hey!" Trev scowled.

Cold kept walking.

Trev took a step as if to follow him, but he hesitated.

Was this a trick?

Had he actually pissed off Boss Cold so much that he was walking away from him?

What did Cold even want to talk to him about?

What the *fuck*?

"Hey! Hello!" Trev stalked after Cold with a scowl. "I was talking to you!"

"Were you?" Cold sounded bored. "I thought you were more interested in fucking with me."

"Don't walk away from me."

Cold seemed intent on doing just that, and he strolled downstairs without a care in the world.

"Uh, excuse you!" Trev followed him, fuming. "Where the hell do you think you're going?"

Cold had literally orchestrated an entire plot to get Trev away from the Luchesi family and bring him here, and now he didn't want to talk to him?

Fuck to the no.

Trev hurried to catch up, and he found Cold lounging in a parlor near the front door. There were three big plush chairs and a small table with a vase of fresh lilies.

Cold had taken the chair so his back would be to the wall, and there was a hint of a smile playing over his lips as Trev walked in.

It was then Trev realized he'd been skillfully baited to follow Cold here like a damn puppy.

"Wow." Trev grinned. "You're an asshole."

"Thank you." Cold held out his hand. "Knife, please."

"Left it upstairs."

"Now."

Trev groaned and slid the butter knife out of his sleeve so he could dutifully surrender it. "There. Happy?"

"Ecstatic." Cold dropped the knife onto the table.

"So." Trev plopped down in the other chair. "Is this the part where you ask me lots of stupid questions?"

"On the contrary, this is where you get to ask me lots of stupid questions," Cold retorted. "I can't promise I'll answer them all, but what answers I do give will be honest."

Trev narrowed his eyes.

He was a little grumpy about Cold tricking him into

coming down here, so he decided to go right for the jugular with his first question.

Fuck it.

He didn't have anything to lose.

"Why did you kill our father?"

"Because he was an abusive, violent, cowardly piece of *shit*." Cold's face didn't even twitch. "I beat him until his face was an unrecognizable bloody pulp, threw him down two flights of stairs, and then I shot him fifteen times."

Trev tensed, unable to hide his horror. "Wh-why would you admit to that? Why would—"

"You thought you'd be cute trying to throw me off by asking a question you didn't think I'd want to answer. So, I decided to give you a little more *detail* than I normally share. It's all a matter of public record, as I was arrested, convicted, and then served time for his murder. My only regret about killing him is that I was far too merciful."

Trev scoffed, and his stomach twisted. He thought about his chat with Rowena. "Did he hurt Rowena too?"

"There was no one in his life that he did not hurt if he could."

"I'm sorry. I don't..." Trev hesitated to say more.

"You don't understand why your mother would lie to you?" Cold took the words right out of Trev's mouth. "The easiest answer is usually the right one. She did it to protect you."

Trev leaned forward. "Did you know her?"

"Not well, but I do know she left Strassen in quite the hurry about twenty years ago."

"It was because of me," Trev realized out loud. "I was born here and then we left when I was a kid. Like, four years old or something. She..." He looked at the lilies on the table.

They looked familiar, but he couldn't place why at the moment.

"She wanted to get away from here. From all of *this*. That's why she made up all the stories about our father being some fucking saint and damn aunt Suzanne being a jazz singer and—"

"Suzanne was my mother," Cold cut in gently. "And she was a great singer."

"Really?" Trev's heart lurched. "Wait, what happened to her?"

"She died giving birth to me. So, be thankful you had a mother who loved you enough and was there to spin falsehoods to protect you."

"Were our moms really sisters?"

"No. Good friends with the same terrible taste in men."

"Apparently." Trev snorted. "Do we... Do we have any other family out there?"

"Blood relations?"

"Yeah."

"No. Rowena has some distant relations through her mother, but they're estranged."

Trev huffed out a laugh. "Don't like gangsters?"

"On the contrary," Cold replied. "They're Luchesis."

"Well, fuck." Trev made a face. "Is that, like, a problem...?"

"No." Cold shook his head. "She's made it clear where she stands."

"And you?"

Cold's lips twitched up into a small smile. "The Luchesis are very aware of my feelings toward them."

"You killed a bunch of them, right?" Trev recalled what Jupiter had told him. "Wiped out a whole generation?"

"Allegedly." Cold's smile grew. "Anything else, Mr. Usher?"

"Ew, don't. Just call me Trev." Trev wrinkled his nose. "*Mr. Usher* is old. And creepy."

"Fine. Anything else, *Trev*?"

Trev frowned, scanning over Cold's face as he considered his next question carefully. "What do you want from me?"

"Nothing."

Trev tensed. "Seriously?"

"You've already told me what I want to know."

"But I didn't tell you anything."

"But you did." Cold raised his brow. "You're slow to trust, you think you're clever, and you despise authority."

"Hey, that's my Grindr profile. Also, I love big, hairy tops."

Cold rolled his eyes. "You don't have any allegiance to the Luchesi family, and that's all I care about."

"How do you know?" Trev wagged his eyebrows. "Maybe I'm playing you."

"Because of the questions you asked. The *way* you asked them. Your main concern was for your mother. You're angry that she lied to you. You probably never trusted anyone else and that's why the sense of betrayal haunting you stings so. You're having to reconcile that with how much you loved her, but you still wonder was there anything else she lied about."

Trev did his best to keep his expression calm.

But seriously, who the fuck was this guy?

Cold's pinpoint analysis was even more accurate than any of Jupiter's observations had been, and oh, great, now Trev was thinking about Jupiter.

Which did present another question.

Cold was busy looking smug, and Trev decided to ignore everything he said by asking, "Hey, what about Jupiter?"

"Prospero? Didn't he chain—"

"Chain me to the wall. Yes. We're past that. Moving on." Trev sat on the edge of the chair. "Is there anything you can do to get him out of there?"

"*There* being with the Luchesi family?" Cold made a face.

"You were willing to get me out without even knowing who I was," Trev said firmly. "So, what about him? Can you?"

"*Can I* and *will I* are two very different things." Cold narrowed his eyes. "You were being used as a pawn by the Luchesis to manipulate me. Taking you from right under their noses reminded them of my power and reach."

"Wow. I feel so loved."

"I barely know you. But appearances are important. Letting the Luchesis know that I will not play their silly little games is *important*." Cold arched a brow. "Risking my resources to save your beau? Not very important."

"But he saved me," Trev insisted. "He was *helping* me—"

"To help himself," Cold pointed out. "I know Mr. Prospero is not in a good position and wishes to leave—"

"Yeah! Because they're probably gonna kill him. If he's not already dead." Trev tried not to think about that, but he knew it was a possibility he had to consider.

Cold said nothing.

"Okay. Right. Great talk." Trev stood up. "Consider the terms of my release settled."

"Where are you going?"

"To get my shit, pack up, and head back to fucking Perry City. If you won't help Jupiter, then I will." Trev flashed a sweet smile. "Probably gonna get myself kidnapped again, just so you know!"

"Sit back down," Cold ordered.

"Sorry, *bro*. Gotta go."

"Hey!" There was a loud clacking of heels accompanied by a softer set of footsteps, and Rowena burst into the parlor with a scowl. "What did you do, Roddy? Why is he saying he's leaving?"

There was a beautiful young man with Rowena who didn't appear to be much older than Trev was. He had a youthful face with fair skin, bright eyes, wavy brown hair, and a dazzling smile. That smile faded, however, as he joined Rowena's accusations by snapping, "Rod! We talked about this."

Cold was unmoved, saying, "Before you go, Trev, please allow me to introduce my husband, Jimmy Poe, who loves to eavesdrop with Rowena."

"Hi! Jimmy! Nice to meet you." Jimmy glared daggers at Cold, even as he asked Trev, "You're not really going, are you? You just got here!"

"Afraid so." Trev shook the hand Jimmy held out. "Been a real delight, but I've got to get going. Long walk back to Perry City."

"What?" Jimmy blinked. "You're not serious."

"Let's go then." Rowena held her head high. "Maybe a little road trip is what we need, huh?"

"No," Cold said flatly.

Rowena ignored him. "I'll drive. Maybe we can go get some of your stuff, right? And then we can rescue your man meat."

"No one is going anywhere," Cold argued.

"This could be fun," Jimmy said cheerfully. "I can't

remember the last time I took a road trip anywhere. We can make it there and back in a day, right?"

Rowena slipped her arm through Trev's. "Come on! Let's go get you packed! I just need to call my boyfriend and let him know I'm going out for a bit."

Jimmy took Trev's other arm, and they all headed to the stairs together. "I can take some more time off from the firm. I don't have any active cases right now."

"Not enough innocent people in Strassen, huh?" Rowena teased.

"Definitely not."

Cold hadn't moved from his chair, but still he called after them. "None of you are leaving this house."

"Love you, Roddy! Bye!" Rowena waved.

"Love you so much!" Jimmy cooed sweetly.

"Are we really doing this?" Trev asked when they reached the second floor. "You guys are really going to take me back?"

"Trust us," Rowena said with a wink.

"We know what we're doing," Jimmy added.

Trev was hopelessly lost, but he allowed Jimmy and Rowena to lead him back to his room. "So, should I pack...? Or what?"

"Just wait." Rowena shut the door.

Trev quirked his brows. "Will one of you explain what the fuck is happening right now? Because are we really about to go back to Perry City or not?"

"What?" Jimmy laughed. "No, it's all right. We won't have to."

"Why?"

There was a polite knock at the door.

Jimmy answered it with a sweet smile.

It was Cold. His arms were crossed over his chest and he was scowling. He looked *pissed*.

"Hi, honey," Jimmy chirped fearlessly. "What is it?"

"Something wrong?" asked Rowena with a bat of her eyes.

"I know what you two are up to," Cold warned, "and it's not going to work this time."

"What isn't?"

"Is there a problem?" Jimmy asked.

Cold *growled*.

Well, that was a terrifying sound Trev didn't know a human man could make.

"Just so we're clear, whatever this is?" Trev gestured to Rowena and Jimmy. "It's their thing, okay?"

"There is no need for anyone to go anywhere," Cold snapped. "Trust me that everything will be resolved by this evening. And yes, that includes the predicament with Mr. Prospero."

"What are you talking about?" Trev demanded. "You were about to let me walk out of here."

"Was I?" Cold hummed. "Allowing you to throw a little tantrum is hardly letting you leave the premises, Trev."

"You were going to hold me prisoner?"

"I was going to strongly suggest that you stay."

"That's the same thing!" Trev groaned.

"Well?" Jimmy prompted with his hands on his hips, eyeing Cold. "Come on. We know you already have some great, super intricate plan that you haven't told anyone about except maybe Jules—"

"I know too!" a new voice shouted from the hallway.

"Shut up, Lorre!" Rowena barked.

"—and so why don't we just skip to the part where you show us that you're smarter than everyone and tell us what's really going on?" Jimmy concluded, dramatically crossing his arms over his chest.

Cold sighed, a sound of long and extended suffering as he glared at Jimmy and Rowena. "I am not going to tell you—"

"Trev, start packing."

"Listen to me." Cold gritted his teeth. "I have it under very good authority that Mr. Prospero has left the Luchesi family, all right?"

"Left?" Trev echoed. "What do you mean, left?"

"As in, renounced any and all rights he had as a potential heir and has fled Perry City." Cold made a face. "So, it will do you no good to return there to find him because he is not there."

"But he's alive?"

"Yes."

Trev frowned and had to consciously force his hands down to his sides so he wouldn't be tempted to touch the collar. He wasn't sure what to feel. He should be happy that Jupiter had been able to get away, but he felt strangely hollow.

They were supposed to leave together, but...

No, it was better this way.

Trev would figure this out without him.

"Morning, gents!" A man with a British accent, platinum blond hair, and a bright smile joined Cold at the door. "How are we?" His eyes fell on Trev. "Ah! Mr. Usher. Nice to see you!"

"Who the fuck are you?" Trev drawled.

"Charlie Eastwick," the man said as he offered his hand. He winked. "Friend of the family."

"Right." Trev shook his hand but still made a face. "I'm

going to need you all to start wearing name tags or something."

"All right to speak freely?" Charlie asked Cold, glancing over the others. "It does pertain to Mr. Usher here."

"Then uh, yeah, speak freely. Right now," Trev demanded.

Cold appeared thoughtful for a moment and then said, "Go on."

"I confirmed through my old contacts that the Luchesi family does indeed have federal intel. It's how they knew about the raid and I believe how they were able to locate Mr. Usher," Charlie replied. "Now, I can't say for sure who it is, but I'd put money on Mr. Cham—"

"Wait, wait." Trev held up his hands. "Back up. They used the feds to find me? As in, the FBI?"

"Afraid so, mate." Charlie grimaced. "Apparently your mother was going to enter witness protection but was rejected from the program when the Justice Department declined to prosecute the case she was going to testify for."

"What case?" Cold asked.

"Give me some more time and I might be able to find out."

Trev was nauseated.

His mother had lied to him about Boris and now this?

She had tried to get into witness protection? But why?

"The last address listed in her file was Perry City," Charlie went on. "Can't imagine why she moved there. They were literally in the Luchesi's backyard the whole time."

"Does the name Camille Bransby mean anything?" Trev asked carefully.

"No." Charlie quirked his brows. "Should it?"

"That's my landlord. She's the one who set me up."

"No. She was not," Cold corrected.

Trev stared at Cold and scowled. "No? What about her friend at the Cannery? All that bullshit about six months rent?" He paused expectantly while Cold scowled right back at him. "Yeah, didn't know about that, did you?"

Cold's expression indicated that perhaps he did because he simply looked too damn smug. "It's irrelevant. She did as she was told. All that matters now is that the very thing you wanted to leave to go get is no longer there. So, you might as well stay."

"That's not an answer and you know it," Jimmy argued fearlessly.

"Yeah, that's some bullshit, Roddy," Rowena snapped. "This isn't how we treat family."

"Blood doesn't make him family." Cold's tone was curiously calm, and he glared at the two of them. "If you two are done now, I am actually quite busy."

"So busy that you decided to stomp on up here and tell us a whole bunch of nothing helpful?" Trev asked dryly. "Really?"

"Yeah, and didn't you just say this morning you were staying home today?" Jimmy batted his eyes sweetly.

"I think he did!" Rowena gasped. "Funny how he's magically busy now."

"Right?" Jimmy pretended to look shocked. "Almost as if he's being dishonest."

"Mr. Poe," Cold said firmly, "say goodbye to Rowena and Trev."

"What?" Jimmy visibly shivered. "Right now?"

"Right now." Cold's voice had dropped and had an undeniable purr to it.

Trev quirked his brows. "What's with the *Mr. Poe*? Is that a sex thing?"

"Definitely a sex thing," Rowena whispered loudly.

"Oh." Trev paused. "*Oh! Ew.* He kept calling me Mr. Usher earlier."

"Ew!" Rowena wrinkled her nose.

Cold did not look amused.

"Hey! I'm not going anywhere until you tell us if you're going to help Jupiter." Jimmy stared Cold down. "If you know he left the Luchesis, you have to know where he's going."

"Do I?" Cold asked.

"You always know *everything*."

Charlie smirked. "He's got you there, sir."

Two men crowded at the door beside Charlie. One was tall and lean with a bald head and no eyebrows. He looked like Uncle Fester but creepier. The other was a gorgeous blond with strong cheekbones, tan skin, and long lashes.

"More gangsters?" Trev assumed. "Do you guys get discounts for buying suits in bulk?"

"Ha!" The gorgeous man laughed. "Funny."

"Trev, this is Roger Lorre—" Rowena gestured to the gorgeous man. "—and his husband, Mickey Tamerlane." She waved to Uncle Fester. "More esteemed members of the Gentlemen."

"The who now?" Trev must have missed that.

"The Gentlemen," Rowena repeated. "It's what our lil' family is called."

"I'm sure you'll meet everyone eventually," Jimmy said cheerfully. "Everyone is really nice—"

Cold cleared his throat.

"What?" Jimmy fussed. "They are! Most of the time!" He wagged his finger at Cold. "And hey! You still haven't answered the question."

"I didn't realize you'd asked one." Cold reached out,

cupping the back of Jimmy's neck and urging him out of the room with him. "Come along, Mr. Poe. We can talk about it while we do our *sex thing*."

"That is not... going to work!" Jimmy argued, though his breathless tone said otherwise.

Cold wrapped his arm around Jimmy's shoulders as he led him down the hall. He paused to look back, commanding, "Lorre, Tamerlane. You know what to do. Charlie? Thank you for your assistance."

"Yes, boss." Mickey bowed his head respectfully.

Roger gave a little salute. "You got it."

Trev threw his hands up. "Uh, hello? *Bro*?" He scowled. "This is me. Leaving. Bye bye."

"Dinner will be at six o'clock," Cold called back, already halfway down the hallway now and headed presumably to his bedroom with Jimmy.

"Too bad I won't be here!" Trev shot back.

"Yeah, you will be." Roger leaned against the doorway.

Rowena's icy glare focused on Roger and Mickey. "Oh? Is that so? What did Roddy tell you idiots to do, huh? What's going on?"

Mickey said nothing, arching his smooth brow.

"Charlie?" Rowena snapped. "What about you?"

Charlie flinched and his eyes widened. "You already know what I'm doing! I'm trying to find what case Trev's mother—"

"Ugh! Fine!" Rowena whirled on Mickey and Roger again. "You two! Spill!"

"You know we can't tell you that." Roger grinned.

"Let me guess." Trev was tired of standing and listening to all of this nonsense, so he headed over to the bed to flop down. "If I try to leave, you two will *encourage* me to stay?

Because Cold isn't keeping me prisoner here so much as he's extending my visit without my consent?"

"Only one way to find out," Roger taunted sweetly. "Don't worry. We'll be gentle."

Trev scowled and tried to get his thoughts in order.

So, he was still a prisoner after all.

Great.

At least he wasn't chained to a wall.

Trev didn't like that Cold was clearly withholding information from him, especially about his mother. If he wanted to find out more, maybe opting to stay wouldn't be such a bad idea. It wasn't like he had anywhere else to go right now, and Cold clearly had the reach to track Jupiter. It might be his best bet to find out where he was going and maybe see him again.

Not that Trev cared.

Because it didn't matter.

But… just in case.

"Don't you start," Mickey warned, his voice so quiet that Trev almost didn't hear him.

"Start what?" Roger asked innocently. "I'm just talking."

"Shut up, slut." Mickey smacked Roger's ass viciously.

"Bitch!"

"Is everybody here fucking gay?" Trev blurted out.

"They're pretty much the gay mafia." Rowena giggled. "It's kind of their thing."

"I'd say *queer* mafia is more accurate," Roger teased. "We have a lot of different rainbow flavors. Mickey's gay, but I came out of the cabinet like all the other pans."

"Wow." Trev laughed. "That's actually pretty cool."

"I'm just an ally." Rowena winked. "Boys are my favorite flavor."

"Mine too." Trev winked back. "So, you two are

married." He gestured to Mickey and Roger. "Cold and Jimmy are married. Jules has a boyfriend." He looked to Charlie. "What about you, *Draco*? You got a man?"

"I certainly do," Charlie replied with a warm smile. "Jerry. You may have met him already."

"There's Thirdsies and Pym too!" Rowena waved her hand. "You haven't met them yet, but they are totally a thing."

"Yeah, always looking for a top. That's their *thing*." Roger chuckled.

For some reason, that earned him a glare from Mickey. "Bullshit, Pym fucked you."

"What? Guys can't be fucking vers?" Roger's brow furrowed. "Fuck you."

"Fuck you!"

Rowena sat on the edge of the bed as Roger and Mickey continued to scream at each other, chirping, "Having fun yet?"

"Oh. Yeah. A blast." Trev snorted. "Being held prisoner again, my mother lied to me about even more shit than I thought she did, and oh yeah, *being held prisoner again*."

"You said that twice."

"It bears repeating." Trev hesitated to say more, but Rowena did seem as if she genuinely cared about him, if nothing else because they were related. He could work with that. He'd probably have a much easier time getting information out of her than Cold or any of these other guys.

Mickey had Roger pinned to the floor now as they kept arguing, and Charlie waved a quick farewell before darting back down the hall.

This was apparently not that unusual because Rowena barely blinked.

"So." Trev sighed.

"So." Rowena smiled.

"Is it too early for a drink?"

"In my experience, never."

CHAPTER
Thirteen

TREV LEARNED a lot about Rowena after consuming an entire pitcher of mimosas.

One was that he should have never underestimated how much she could drink.

Another was how much she loved to talk about anything and everything except what Trev actually wanted to know about. She was happy to provide juicy gossip about the Gentlemen's dating drama, dish on celebrities and fashion trends, and share intimate details about her own relationship with a man named Dario Romero, who was apparently quite terrified of Cold.

Trev didn't see what the big deal was.

Cold was highly observant, clearly intelligent, but *dangerous*?

Pffft.

All he seemed interested in was fucking his husband and doing his weird sex thing.

Trev knew he shouldn't underestimate him though.

Cold had been able to plant a mole across the damn state, fool the entire Luchesi family, and oh yeah, had a secret assassin hiding somewhere at the damn Luchesi estate ready to murder at a second's notice.

Maybe Cold really was the monster the Luchesis said he was.

Rowena hummed happily as she shimmied through the kitchen. They'd come back in here to make another pitcher, and Mickey and Roger had followed them. Roger helped Rowena mix while Mickey stayed posed in the doorway, frozen like a statue.

God, he was creepy.

Trev wondered if he was related to Erasmus.

"So, you and Prospero, huh?" Roger asked with a bold grin. "Always heard he played for our team. Good for you."

"Thanks. I think." Trev scoffed.

"He's just jealous." Rowena cackled. "Wanted to have his Romeo and Juliet moment, you know. Fucking the enemy. But without the dying shit at the end."

"What? He's hot." Roger wiggled his left hand. "Married, not blind."

"As if that ring would stop you," Rowena teased.

"You're right. It wouldn't."

While they laughed, Mickey held up a finger as if in warning.

"How did you know what he looked like?" Trev asked. "Is there a mafia dating website? Gaga For Gangsters?"

"Know your enemy," Roger said with a mysterious wink.

"Especially the hot ones?"

"Exactly."

Rowena rolled her eyes, pouring two glasses of the freshly made mimosas. She passed one over to Trev. "Come on, lil' bro. You need to catch up."

"Do I really though?" Trev accepted the glass anyway. "Five o'clock somewhere. Or whatever it is they say."

"So." Rowena hummed. "We can order out for lunch if you'd like since Roddy wants you to stick around."

"Oh, now you're on team *let's keep Trev prisoner*?"

"Nope. I'm on team *my brother is an asshole but he's never been wrong*." Rowena shrugged. "He probably has a good reason for keeping you here. When and if he'll tell us, well, that takes a combination of patience, vigilance, and bitching."

"I've got all three of those, so I should be good." Trev tugged on the sleeves of his sweater.

"You okay?"

"Just getting hot." Trev shrugged. "I'm more of a crop top and booty shorts kinda girl, you know what I mean?"

"Ohhh, I sure do." Rowena grinned and grabbed her glass. She reached for Trev's hand, waving at Roger. "You! Grab the pitcher."

"What do I look like, a waiter?" Roger grumbled.

"Right now you do!" Rowena breezed by Mickey, leading Trev back upstairs.

"Where are we going?" Trev laughed.

"My room!" Rowena turned at the top of the stairs. "Okay, well, technically it's my *old* room since I live with Dario, but whatever. I still visit and have a few clothes here."

"Yeah?"

"Uh-huh. Let's see if we can find a lil' something something that's more your style." Rowena dragged him into a large bedroom that looked like a clothing store had exploded.

There were clothes all over the furniture, some in piles on the floor, and the open closet was completely overflowing. The only area of the room that seemed to be free of clothing was the bed.

No, wait, that's where the shoes were, dozens of boxes peeking out from underneath.

"A *few* clothes?" Trev scoffed. "Really?"

"Oh, pfft, this is nothing." Rowena laughed as she headed to the closet. "You should see what I have at my place with Dario." She thumbed through the racks. "Okay. Let's see."

Trev dodged a flying shirt and then another. "Whoa! Hey! What are you doing?"

"Picking out stuff that might fit you! I've got tons of halter tops, midriff shirts, camis, all that. The only issue is gonna be bottoms."

"What's wrong with bottoms?" Trev joked.

"Not a damn thing!" Rowena laughed. "Except your bottom might be bigger than mine, okay?"

Trev thought about the jeans he'd been gifted. "Got a pair of scissors?"

"Not gonna stab anybody with them, are you?"

"How about you just tell us what you need cut?" Roger snorted. "Trying to make some shorts?"

"Yeah," Trev replied. "Got some jeans in my room I wanna cut up."

"How short?" Roger mused. "Date, clubbing, or prostate exam?"

"How about first date?"

"Do you want to fuck on the first date?"

"Definitely DTF."

Roger grinned. "I got you."

"Seriously?" Mickey rolled his eyes. "You're a tailor now?"

"Fuck you!" Roger sang cheerfully as he walked away.

After Roger was gone, Trev focused on going through the offerings from Rowena. Some of the halter tops were tie-on and would definitely fit, and even some of the camis seemed possible if he didn't want to breathe. She did have some oversized crop top T-shirts and Trev took those too.

Accessories were also a must, and Rowena had several pairs of fishnet stockings that had never even been opened. She let Trev go through her jewelry too, and he wondered how much of it was real or not. He stuck with colorful bangles and gaudy rings, things that were pretty but clearly costume jewelry.

It was too tempting to grab the earrings he recognized as real diamonds or the big sapphire ring. He had always been shameless, and yet...

He didn't want to steal from Rowena.

She had been nothing but kind and gracious, and she was giving him clothes, jewelry, and even promised him whatever makeup he could find in her bathroom. Having already clocked the designer label on much of the clothing, he knew the cosmetics wouldn't be of the drugstore variety.

Trev wasn't sure what to make of this.

Rowena had nothing to gain by being nice to him unless this was something Cold had put her up to.

Same with Jimmy and his own generous albeit hideous gift of clothing and how he'd also stood up to Cold for him.

In Trev's experience, people only did things for him because they wanted something in return. So, what did Rowena and Jimmy want?

They didn't want to fuck him. They didn't want to use him for leverage or as any source of information. They didn't seem to have any need for his money. They didn't really need him for anything, and it only made Trev even more unsettled.

Roger returned with the newly trimmed shorts and then Trev dragged them along with his new wardrobe into

Rowena's bathroom. While he changed, he could hear Mickey and Roger shouting at each other.

"You're still such a fucking whore!" Mickey sneered.

"Me? Are you kidding me?" Roger laughed. "All I did was hand him some shorts."

"I saw how you looked at him."

"Excuse me?"

"Listen here, slut..."

Trev tuned them out and finally settled on a black halter top that showed off his midriff, the jean shorts with fishnets underneath, and his big boots. He asked Rowena for a pair of black socks, of course. He scored eyeliner and mascara from digging around in the drawers, and finally, he felt a bit more like himself when he looked in the mirror.

It was... strange.

He'd spent a lifetime staring at these eyes—they were his, after all—but it was surreal to see them gazing back at him from Rowena or Cold.

Especially Cold.

Rowena's were capable of warmth and joy, even a tenderness that oddly reminded Trev of his mother even though they weren't the two who were related.

Cold's were nothing but ice and more ice.

He had barely blinked when describing the murder of their father, and Trev still hadn't had time to sort out how he felt about that. If what Cold said was true, then he had probably done Trev a favor. Yet, it had robbed Trev of the chance to know Boris for himself.

To see if *anything* his mother had told him might be true.

Or was it all really a lie?

A fairy tale woven for a child who'd wanted to know where his father was?

Trev cursed when his eyes burned.

He dabbed at them, pleased that the makeup hadn't run at least.

It really was some nice stuff.

Trev took a deep breath and then walked out of the bathroom, pausing to strike a pose against the doorway.

"Ah!" Rowena squealed. "Yes!" She grinned and clapped as she jumped to her feet to take in his outfit. "You look *hot*."

"I know." Trev winked as he sashayed forward.

Mickey did not appear impressed.

Roger whistled, which earned him a snarl from Mickey.

"Thank you." Trev did a little spin. "I needed this. Was starting to forget I had an ass."

"And legs too!" Rowena cheered, laughing as she pulled Trev in for a hug.

Trev hugged her back and smiled, not minding the unexpected warmth. Growing up as an only child had been pretty lonely, and maybe it wouldn't have been so bad with a sister like Rowena around.

Would have been nice to have someone to steal clothes from.

"Come on, sweetie." Rowena hooked her arm with Trev's, grabbing the pitcher of mimosas.

"Where are we going?" Trev chuckled. "Off to rob a bank?"

"In these shoes? No! We're gonna go drink some more and watch a movie!" Rowena breezed by Mickey and Roger.

"With our, uh, supervisors?" Trev glanced back at them, noting that the pair did indeed follow them.

"Oh! It's fine. Come on." Rowena scoffed. "Just ignore them. That's what I do."

"Rude," Roger called out.

"Can't hear you! Drinking mimosas!" Rowena sang out

sweetly. She brought Trev downstairs and to a luxurious living room with a giant television, big couches, and a full bar.

Incredibly, there were already two glasses waiting for them on the counter as if someone had been expecting them to bring a pitcher of booze with them.

Rowena hummed as she poured. "So! What movie do you want to watch?"

Trev shrugged. "Whatever. I don't care."

"What about *Mean Girls*?"

"What's that?"

Rowena jerked as if she'd been struck. "You've never seen the epic masterpiece that is *Mean Girls*?"

"No." Trev didn't understand why Rowena appeared faint. "I'm not much of a TV person."

"We're fixing this. Immediately. This is an emergency."

Trev laughed. "Okay."

Voices drew his attention to the doorway. Roger was there, but he didn't see Mickey. He recognized one of the voices as Jimmy, but the other one was new.

Jimmy entered the room, wearing a different set of clothes and his hair ruffled. The man with him was revealed as a tall, bulging man of Korean descent with a dashing smile and biceps bigger than Trev's head.

"Oh! Wow. You look different." Jimmy blinked in surprise when he saw Trev. "But good! Good different. I promise. I'm gonna stop now."

The other man clapped a hand on Jimmy's back. "Open mouth. Insert foot."

"Sorry." Jimmy laughed. "Sometimes my mouth runs faster than my brain."

"We still love you anyway." The man chuckled as he

came over to offer out his hand to Trev. "Hey there! I'm Brick."

"I'm single," Trev replied.

"Sorry, I'm not." Brick grinned.

"That is a crying shame."

"Trev, right?"

"Yeah. But you can call me anything you want."

"He's with Jules," Rowena chimed in. "I admire the effort, but good luck."

"You mean Beefzilla?" Trev wrinkled his nose. "Okay, I'd still try to hit it. At least I'd die doing something I loved."

Brick laughed. "Are you really related to Cold?"

"That's what they tell me. Why?"

"Because you're actually funny."

"Come on!" Rowena waved for them to join them on the couch.

"What are we doing?" Jimmy laughed.

"We are going to day drink and watch *Mean Girls*."

Trev scoffed. "What is this, a mafia wives club meeting?"

"What? No!" Rowena wrinkled her nose. "My sweetie is a good boy." She swatted at Trev's arm. "And Brick and Jules still live in sin, so, technically Brick would be a mafia girlfriend."

"He's not one of the Gentlemen?" Trev asked.

He would believe it as big as Brick was.

And his name was Brick.

Who the hell was named *Brick*?

"Nope. Translator." Brick grinned as he took the other spot on the couch beside Trev. "I sit behind a desk all day, working on a computer."

"Wow. That sounds boring as shit." Trev snorted. "What about you, Jimmy?" He thought he remembered someone mentioning a case. "Are you a lawyer or something?"

"Or something." Jimmy got settled in an oversized plush chair. "I used to work for a big firm here in Strassen, but then I started a nonprofit to help overturn wrongful convictions. Give innocent people who are imprisoned a chance at freedom."

"That's really awesome." Trev smiled.

"What about you, Trev?" Brick asked politely. "What do you do?"

Oh.

Trev was grateful for the mimosa to drown the new feeling trying to crack his confidence.

Insecurity.

Ugh, gross.

Who cared if Brick was a fancy translator or Jimmy was some goody-two-shoes lawyer? He already knew that Rowena ran a club here in the city from their earlier conversation, and Trev was startled by how inadequate he suddenly felt.

"I'm a burlesque dancer," Trev replied with a confident smile.

That sounded better than former escort on the run from the mob.

"Nice!" Brick nodded his approval. "That takes some balls. I could never get up in front of people and dance like that."

"Really?" Trev snorted. "With your body?"

Brick laughed. "Hey, dancing takes a very unique set of skills. Just something about getting up in front of all those people. Not for me."

"That kinda thing gets easier with practice," Jimmy said kindly. "I mean, I have *horrible* anxiety, but I can still get up in court."

"Do you imagine everybody naked?" Trev teased.

"What? No!" Jimmy looked mortified by the thought.

Everyone laughed, and Rowena taunted, "Come on! Like you've never thought about Roddy naked when you're up there on stage singing!"

"Shut up!" Jimmy turned a vivid shade of pink and tried to melt into the chair.

"You sing?" Trev asked, genuinely curious.

Jimmy peeked through his fingers. "Yeah. Uh, sometimes. I used to sing at Rowena's club, but uh, I just do that for special occasions or whatever. Birthdays. Anniversaries. Stuff like that."

"See, you could totally do it!" Trev winked. "If you can sing in front of a crowd, you can absolutely dance. I could show you some moves. Really knock *Roddy's* socks off."

Rowena giggled through a sip of her drink, mashing buttons on the remote to get the movie on. "That would be so *fetch*."

"Like, so *fetch*," Brick echoed in a snobby voice.

"Huh?" Trev was lost.

"Just trust us." Rowena giggled.

"What?" Brick arched his brow. "Wait, have you not seen this?"

Trev wrinkled his nose. "No."

Jimmy gawked. "How have you not seen this movie?"

Mickey scoffed. "Even I've seen it."

"Maybe if you all stop talking about it and we actually put it on, I'll understand what all the damn fuss is about!" Trev clicked his tongue. "*Jesus*, let's go."

Rowena cackled as she hit play. "This is the best day ever."

After a few more drinks, Trev was inclined to agree.

He was actually having *fun*. He hadn't spent this much time with anyone even close to his age before unless it was at work or for sex. In either situation, he only did the bare minimum of socializing and encounters were as brief as possible. Whatever worries he'd had earlier about feeling inadequate or being treated with condescension vanished.

It was nice.

Listening to everyone quoting lines from the movie together was a riot. Trev was an instant fan of the story, though he would have made sure Regina ended up in front of a bus a lot sooner and it would definitely be because he pushed her.

Roger had even come over to sit down with them and join in on the fun.

Mickey did not.

Must not be a fan.

When the movie was over, Jerry swept in with trays of mini burgers and fries. It was exactly what Trev needed to soak up the booze. He couldn't remember when he'd last just hung out with anyone for fun other than his kooky neighbor, Juicy.

God, he was going to miss him.

Barkie too.

Trev stopped drinking after that.

He needed to stay sober and sharp.

He wasn't here to party and have a great time. No matter how honest or genuine Rowena and the others seemed to be, he was still being held here against his will because his half-brother happened to be a gangster who other gangsters hated. He was caught in the middle, a pawn in a game he didn't sign up to play, and he wanted to get the hell out of here.

Whatever Cold was up to, Trev didn't trust it.

He touched his collar.

And yes, he missed that asshole, Jupiter.

Another movie was put on, *To Wong Foo, Thanks For Everything! Julie Newmar*, and Trev had at least seen this one.

He continued to be friendly enough, but his mind was already hard at work trying to figure a new way to escape.

Rowena was too loyal to her brother, so she probably wouldn't help him leave. She could probably be used to dig some more information out for him if he played the family card a bit harder, but from who?

Jimmy?

Jimmy was whipped, loyal to Cold, but he also came off as soft and maybe someone else Trev could play the family card with. Maybe even the relationship card. After all, he was married to a gangster. Trev could use that to talk to him, perhaps get a sympathetic ear about having fallen for a criminal?

Except wait.

Shit.

No.

Trev hadn't fallen for Jupiter.

That was insane.

That was totally stupid and...

Trev sighed.

Maybe he would have one more drink after all.

The movie had ended, and Trev offered to go with Rowena to get some more snacks. He had a bit of a buzz and was hoping to get her chatting. The plan for today seriously couldn't be sitting around, getting drunk, and watching movies. If so, Trev was going to use this time to see what else he could pry out of her.

As they walked down the hallway to get to the kitchen, he heard the front door opening. There were several voices, loud and firm, and...

Trev stopped abruptly and then took a few steps closer so he could hear better.

"Well, well," Jules bellowed with a hearty laugh. "Look what the cat dragged in."

"Will wonders never cease?" Cold taunted. "How nice we finally get to meet."

"I'm here for Trevanion Usher," a man said.

Wait.

Trev knew that voice!

He surged forward, racing down the hallway before Rowena could stop him.

"Jupiter!" Trev didn't quit running until he saw Jupiter—standing there in the foyer, looking tired and exhausted but perfect and warm—and he jumped right into his arms. He knew Jupiter would catch him, he just *knew* it, and he wrapped his arms and legs around him.

He knew he looked like an idiot.

But he didn't care.

"Trev." Jupiter breathed his name out like a prayer and held him tight.

"You're okay," Trev whispered, hating how his eyes burned. He buried his face in Jupiter's shoulder. "Assholes wouldn't let me leave. I wanted to come find you."

"Wow, look at that," Jupiter teased. "You really are sweet on me."

"Shut up."

"Hi!" another voice greeted cheerfully.

Trev lifted his head to see who was talking and he gasped. "*Juicy*?"

Juicy, his neighbor, was here.

"I had to board Barkie," Juicy said with a sigh. "I don't think he'll ever forgive me."

"Yes, he will! Oh my God!" Trev wiggled out of Jupiter's

arms to give Juicy a hug. "What in the world are you doing here?"

"Working on a case! I received a transmission through the fillings in my teeth." Juicy replied with a grin. "You smell nice."

"Thank you." Trev glanced back at Jupiter, hoping he had answers grounded in reality.

"I went over to your place to see if you were there," Jupiter said. "Ran into *Juicy* here, who was packing up a bunch of your stuff. He said he needed to bring it to you as soon as possible. Told me you were going to need it because you were on a dangerous mission."

"How did you know where to find me?"

"Google."

"Don't worry!" Juicy laughed heartily, smacking a hand on Trev's back. "I got us here in one piece." He bowed his head to whisper in Trev's ear, "It's all right. I'm working a case."

"Yeah, you just told me that." Trev blinked. "Uh, okay."

"Pssst. It's for Boss Cold. Did I tell you that already?"

Trev tensed.

There was no way—

"Oh!" Rowena had caught up and she squealed when she saw Jupiter. "That must be Jupiter."

"It is." Trev smirked.

"Been talking about me, huh?" Jupiter teased.

"Don't let it go to your head." Trev scoffed even as he gravitated back toward Jupiter. He really had missed him, and the fluttery feeling he got in his chest when Jupiter smiled at him was ridiculous.

But then he saw how Cold was looking at Jupiter—his eyes full of ice and ready to pierce Jupiter with every single jagged shard.

Trev immediately put himself in front of Jupiter, glaring right back at Cold. "Nope, nope, nope. You are not touching him."

Mickey was suddenly there, standing at the doorway of the parlor with a creepy scowl, and Jules remained posed beside Cold with an equally unfriendly glare.

Jupiter put his hand on Trev's shoulder. "It's all right, baby doll." He addressed Cold now, saying firmly, "Boss Cold, I'm sure by now you've heard that I renounced my family."

"I did," Cold replied calmly. "I'm still curious what makes you think I shouldn't kill you right now?"

"Just say the word, sir!" Juicy said cheerfully.

"Juicy, what the *fuck*?" Trev hissed. "Whose side are you on?"

"Because," Jupiter said, raising his voice to be heard over the bickering, "I have information for you. Information I'd like to trade for Trev."

"Oh my God, I'm not being held prisoner." Trev groaned. "I mean, okay, I sort of am but—"

Jupiter squeezed Trev's shoulder.

"Did you just try to *shush* me?" Trev smacked at Jupiter's hand. "Come on! You don't have to do this!"

"He might," Jules teased, and there was something dark in his eyes that Trev didn't trust at all.

Mickey had his hand on his chest, as if he was about to pull something from under his jacket, and Jules looked ready to pounce and tear Jupiter apart with his bare hands.

For the first time, Trev realized the danger Jupiter was in.

The Luchesi family and the Gentlemen had been sworn enemies for decades, and Jupiter, the bastard heir of Rafaello Luchesi, had strolled willingly right into Cold's very home.

Wow, Jupiter was really fucking stupid.

It would have been romantic but Trev couldn't get over just how stupid it was...

And yet, he probably would have done the same thing.

"You really should be bargaining for protection," Cold drawled. "There is absolutely no reason to let you leave here alive."

"Uh, yeah. There's a lot of fucking reasons," Trev snapped. "You're not touching him. And hey, didn't you hear him? He has information."

Cold regarded Trev with the same disdain of a cat picking at the upholstery of a brand-new sofa. "I sincerely doubt that it is anything useful."

"But it is," Jupiter said firmly. "Life and death, in fact."

"Is that so?"

"The Luchesis are planning a hit," Jupiter replied. "You want the rest, you'll let Trev go."

Cold smirked.

"Well?"

"I'm wondering which hit you're referring to. The one they put out on *me*, thinking they were clever by setting it for the same time as a meeting I have downtown with the mayor? As if I wouldn't hear about it or not plan to have extra security with such a public appointment. Or maybe you mean the one they put out on *you*?"

Jupiter tensed.

"Hmm, no, can't be that one because I don't actually care." Cold hummed. "So, yes, let's go with the first one. Which I already know about, but thanks for trying. The effort is *cute*."

Jupiter stared. "How the *fuck*?"

"You and your family should *really* stop underestimating me. It's bad for your health."

CHAPTER *Fourteen*

"THEN AGAIN..." Cold smirked. "A lot more of you would still be alive."

"Ha ha, very threatening and creepy. Great. Wonderful. Thanks, *bro*." Trev stood as tall as he could. "You're not touching him."

"Oh?"

"He's worth more alive, right?" Trev insisted.

Cold pressed his lips into a thin line. "Potentially."

"Then I'm claiming him as my first official prisoner." Trev grabbed Jupiter's tie. "Look at that. First day in the family and I'm already being so very helpful."

"Be careful," Juicy whispered loudly. "He looks like he might try to make a run for it."

"Roddy." Rowena tapped her foot with a scowl. "You can't kill his boyfriend. That's fucked up. Even for you."

"Not my boyfriend," Trev corrected. "My prisoner."

Although the depth of his affection was already obvious because he hadn't been able to keep his damn hands to himself, Trev reasoned that Cold might appreciate this approach more. If nothing else, to save face in front of the rest of his family. After all, sparing Trev's boyfriend might make him look too soft, but allowing Trev to take custody of a prisoner might be an easier sell.

He just had to determine exactly how valuable Jupiter was to Cold. He had no idea what it would take to be able to walk out of here with him, and Trev doubted that even all the money in his lockbox would be enough to pay for Jupiter's release.

The very fact that Cold hadn't killed Jupiter on sight was a positive sign at least, and Trev had to hope it was a reason that didn't end in Jupiter's eventual death.

Maybe Cold needed information from Jupiter?

Perhaps he wanted to use him as leverage the same way the Luchesi family had used Trev?

Trev's mind spun with all the possibilities, trying to find one that would somehow result in him and Jupiter being able to run off into the sunset and—God, that was stupid. That was the *least* likely outcome, especially given Cold's penchant for murdering *multiple* members of Jupiter's family.

Which he just had to throw right in Jupiter's face.

Okay, wait.

That was a good thing.

Cold wanted Jupiter to be rattled, to be on edge, maybe even afraid—because it would be easier to get whatever it was Cold wanted out of him and certainly Jupiter would have to be alive for whatever that was.

Hopefully.

"Fine," Cold said, snapping Trev out of his mind's whirlwind. "Bring the *prisoner* to the parlor." He eyed Rowena. "Why don't you get Mr. Cusack something to eat?"

"You are not putting me on crazy old man duty!" Rowena warned.

"Jules." Cold nodded his head toward them. "Please escort Rowena to the kitchen with Mr. Cusack."

"My pleasure." Jules reached out his hand to Juicy. "Hey, you like popcorn?"

"Popcorn?" Juicy stared at Jules's hand as if it might bite him. "Is this a trick?"

"I dunno. Might be." Jules shrugged, gently touching Juicy's shoulder and herding him toward the kitchen. "Let's go find out, huh?"

Rowena growled. "This isn't over, Roddy."

Cold waved.

Rowena flipped him off and then stalked after Jules and Juicy.

"You too," Cold said firmly, his icy gaze falling on Trev. "This doesn't concern you."

Trev cackled and then promptly sneered, "Yeah, *fuck you*." He strolled right up to Cold, pushing Jupiter's hands away when he tried to stop him. "You said it yourself! You don't trust me. I'm not family. Blah fucking blah. Message received." He pointed at Jupiter. "He's more fucking family to me right now than you are. We would have been fine without you."

Mickey twitched.

"And fuck you too!" Trev spat.

Mickey smiled and it was extremely unsettling.

"I appreciate your honesty but not your tone," Cold said. "You're free to go whenever you'd like, but Mr. Prospero is staying here."

"You used me as bait," Trev realized out loud. "You *asshole*. You knew Jupiter would come for me."

"I knew the chances of him strolling right to my front door were much greater if you were here, yes. And now that he is, you no longer need to be."

"I'm not going anywhere without him."

"Ah, yes." Cold looked amused. "Because you claimed him as your prisoner."

"Damn skippy."

"It's all right, Trev," Jupiter said. "We'll talk and figure this out."

Cold walked into the parlor, taking the same chair as before. Mickey remained posed at the doorway, his eyes on Jupiter as he followed Cold to take the chair opposite him.

"There's nothing to talk about," Trev bit out as he stomped over to stand beside Jupiter. There was another chair, but he was too wound up to sit. "I have claimed you and boom, that's it. So, we can go."

"If only you had the actual resources to protect your claim." Cold smiled. "I think it's safe to say that Mr. Prospero will be staying here as my guest for the foreseeable future. You, of course, are welcome to remain or free to go if you so choose."

"Not going anywhere without Jupiter," Trev said firmly. "Kinda weird I have to keep saying that."

"I think it's *kind of weird* you believe you have any say in it."

Trev wanted to strangle him.

Maybe this was what having an older sibling was like.

Or maybe it was simply Cold trying to flex his big gangster dick and shut him up. He could easily have any of his guys drag Trev out of here, but he'd allowed Trev to stay. That had to mean *something*, and Trev wasn't going to give up.

"Look." Jupiter cleared his throat. "If you already know about the hit, fine. But I can still help you, Boss Cold."

Cold did not appear interested. "Is that so?"

"The drugs. The pipeline with the FBI. Whatever you want to know."

"So quick to burn your bridges with your family," Cold noted. "You can see why I hesitate to trust you. After all, if it's so easy to throw away your own blood, I am wondering why I should form an alliance with you."

"Well, you've confirmed they want to kill me." Jupiter snorted. "I think that should tell you everything you need to know." He narrowed his eyes. "Besides, I don't imagine blood really means all that much to you."

"No." Cold smiled. "But it still has value."

"You want to ransom me back to my own family?" Jupiter frowned slightly. "Why? You already know they'll just kill me."

"Do you know anything about the park construction in Perry City?"

"Park? What park?"

"The park over by the Cannery?" Trev quirked his brows.

Cold eyed him expectantly.

"It's some big city park in a rough spot of town that they've been trying to spruce up for years." Trev glanced at Jupiter with a smirk. "It's how I knew that the club had been renovated, remember? Water damage from a pipe or something."

"A pipe?" Cold arched his brow.

"Yeah." Trev tried to remember. "They're always digging around and apparently busted a water pipe. Flooded out the whole club I used to work at and a couple of the other buildings." He paused. "The owners were screaming like crazy and oh! That's when that bakery burned down too."

"There was a flood *and* a fire?"

"Yup. The people at the bakery got into a fight with the

crew that were digging. They were in the wrong spot or something, it turned into a big screaming match, and they were so busy arguing that they forgot about something in the oven. Started a huge fire. And the only reason it didn't spread was because of the damn water."

Cold looked thoughtful, but all he said was, "Huh."

Trev tried to study Cold's face as if it would yield more clues, but he felt like he'd given away something for free.

But what?

Shit.

"Why are you asking about the park?" Jupiter frowned. "You think the Luchesis are involved with it somehow?"

"I merely asked a question," Cold said. "Either you know something or you don't."

"Hey, boss!" Roger called out cheerfully as he strolled into the parlor. "Don't mean to interrupt, but I thought you might wanna see this."

Trev frowned and turned around to see what Roger had.

His lockbox!

"What the fuck?" Trev surged forward to grab it, but a firm hand curled around the front of his throat.

It was Mickey.

Jupiter was on his feet in a blink and scowling. "Let go of him."

"Sit back down," Mickey said flatly, squeezing Trev's throat.

Shit, shit, shit.

This was bad.

It was going to turn violent way too fast, and Trev needed to defuse the situation as quickly as possible. Although it was sweet that Jupiter wanted to defend him, he stood absolutely no chance here.

So, Trev did what he did best.

Act like a brat.

"Oh, harder, *Daddy*." Trev rolled his eyes. "Mmm, yeah, come on. Is that all you got?"

Mickey chuckled. It was not a particularly friendly sound. "I'd break you."

Somehow, Trev didn't doubt it.

Still, he couldn't resist taunting back, "Come on, I might be into that shit."

"Hey, hey, everyone keep it in their pants." Roger handed the lockbox to Cold. "That's my line anyway." He grinned at Trev. "*Bitch*."

"Whore," Trev automatically shot back.

"Huh." Mickey hummed. "It's like he knows you."

"Play nice," Cold scolded as if he were speaking to children, flipping the lid open.

"That's mine," Trev snapped, not caring when Mickey squeezed. "What the fuck? It was locked! How did you even get it open?"

Roger snorted. "With my dick."

"I know exactly how much money is in there," Trev warned. "I will know if even a single dollar is missing."

Cold didn't seem interested in the cash. He picked up the stack of photographs first. He flipped through them, his expression blank as he paused on one.

Trev couldn't tell which it was from where he was standing, and he pushed Mickey away. He was aware that Mickey likely only let go because Cold waved at him, but Trev brushed himself off with a huff anyway.

Jupiter finally took his seat but he looked up at Trev worriedly.

Trev flashed him a tense smile, but he was more concerned with what Cold might do with the photographs.

He approached so he could at least see what had captivated Cold so, and he froze.

It was a picture of Trev's mother with the woman he'd thought was his aunt, a beautiful Black woman with a gorgeous afro and...

Lilies.

She had lilies pinned in her hair.

The very same lilies that were all over the house.

"That's your mother," Trev said quietly. He'd almost phrased it as a question, but he was certain by how Cold was staring at the photograph.

"Yes." Cold's voice was strained. "Suzanne."

"We can make a copy, you know." Trev offered a small smile.

This was finally something he could use.

While Cold certainly didn't view Trev as family of any kind, he definitely had a lot of love for his mother.

"There's more." Trev thought of the poster in his apartment. "More pictures. And I actually have a big poster from one of her shows too. It's back at my apartment back in Perry City though. It's yours if you want it."

Cold quietly continued to flip through the rest of the pictures without responding, pausing whenever he found any of Suzanne.

There were more than Trev realized, and Cold was captivated by every image. Even Mickey and Roger appeared interested, as if they too were somehow drawn in by these previously unseen photos. Trev tried to add commentary when he could, noting that Cold always paused to listen.

"That was at the club they worked at," Trev said of one. "My mom said Suzanne always took a few minutes before each show to, like, prepare? And they snagged that pic right before she was about to go on." And then another.

"Oh! Yeah, that one. See that big red thing in the background? It's a hot dog. A giant, hideous hot dog statue they saw here in Strassen somewhere and thought it was funny. My mom actually found one just like it in Perry City and took a picture of it. Maybe it was like a mascot or something."

When they reached the end of the stack, Cold reverently placed them back inside the lockbox and then closed the lid. He handed it to Trev, saying quietly, "I would very much appreciate copies. Thank you."

"No problem." Trev retreated a few steps and hugged the lockbox to his chest.

This had to carry some sort of weight.

The photos, Trev's stories—Cold was clearly affected.

"So." Trev smiled. "Does, uh, this mean my prisoner and I can go?"

"No."

Trev scowled. "Why the fuck not?"

"I am still deciding what to do with him," Cold replied simply. "He doesn't seem to have any vital information—"

"Boss Cold." Jupiter stood, even as the action drew Roger's and Mickey's disdain. "Sir, please. I am confident that I have something of value that would be helpful to you."

"Assuming you know anything I don't already is quite bold," Cold said icily. "Your family is sloppy, weak, and stupid. I have spent literal decades crushing them and this time, same as all the others before it, will end with more of them dead. Whether or not that includes you remains to be seen."

"Doesn't him trying to help me count for anything?" Trev demanded. "Come on."

Cold stared. "He's alive right now, isn't he?"

"Oh, yes, so generous." Trev glowered. "You are just Mother fucking Theresa."

Cold tilted his head, silently considering something for a few moments. His eyes flicked up to Roger and Mickey. "Please see Mr. Prospero to the guest quarters. Make sure he's comfortable. Feel free to be... creative."

Roger grinned. "You got it, boss."

"Hey!" Trev watched helplessly as Roger and Mickey escorted Jupiter away. This wasn't ending at all like he'd hoped except for maybe that Jupiter was still alive, but he didn't have any other cards left to play. He turned back to snap at Cold, but was too startled when he found him standing right behind him instead of sitting. "F-fuck, you're sneaky."

Cold hummed. "You are truly free to leave whenever you'd like, Mr. Usher. I can provide you with a new car, additional cash, and—"

"And Jupiter."

"The car will be much more valuable."

"Nope." Trev popped his tongue. "Jupiter, please."

"He's worth that much to you?"

"Yes. And so is what he did for me. Maybe it's not a big deal to you, but I don't have a great history of people actually showing up when it comes to giving a shit about me." Trev gestured to the room, startling even himself with his honesty and perhaps a side of bitterness. "Not all of us have big, fancy houses and a big ol' mobster family to kiss our ass, okay?"

"Mr. Usher, I—"

"What?" Trev barked, fearless as ever as he let his genuine rage take over. "You gonna try to tell me that you understand what it's like growing up with fucking nothing? That you had to work so fucking hard to get where you are?

Maybe we can even bond over our moms being such great friends?"

"Mr. Usher—"

"Nope. Not done! Because you don't know me. You don't know shit about me! And if you think I'm gonna side with you just because you're throwing your money around and trying to push some fancy crap at me, you've got—"

"*Mr. Usher.*"

"*What*?"

Cold looked over Trev's shoulder. "I thought you might want to know that Mr. Cusack just went by with what looked to be a bag of potatoes and a knife." He clicked his tongue, mocking how Trev had done it earlier. "Might want to go see what that's all about."

"Fuck. Okay! And I will! But first—" Trev held up his finger and gave the lockbox a shake. "You want copies of these absolutely one of a kind photographs?"

"You already know I do. And you said *no problem*."

"I am retracting that. There is a problem." Trev's brain spun. "Tell me why Juicy is here."

"I can't say."

Trev scowled. "Can't say or won't? Because he said he was working a case for you."

Cold just smirked.

The *smirkiest* smirk.

"Hey!" Jules popped in. "Did you guys see where that old geezer went?"

Cold pointed.

"Old fucker is fast," Jules grumbled as he hurried down the hall.

"Me and my little box of photos are gonna go see what Juicy is doing." Trev held up the lockbox. "But me and you are not done yet."

"No, we are not." Cold's lips pressed into a thin line. "Good luck with the potatoes."

Trev snorted and then abruptly left, heading into the hallway to find Jules and Juicy.

Cold was an asshole.

A frustrating, know-it-all, smug asshole.

While Trev could appreciate the family resemblance, it only pissed him off at the moment, as it was not currently doing him any favors. The information about the club and the park had meant something, as did the photographs. Trev reasoned Cold knew that he would never destroy them, so threatening to would carry no weight.

Fine. Whatever. He'd figure out some other way to get him and Jupiter out of here.

He followed the sound of Jules yelling and Juicy screeching back and forth, finding them in a formal den. There wasn't a television in here, but there were several electrical outlets, and Juicy was rubbing potato slices over one of the sockets.

"The fuck!" Jules bellowed. "Listen, old man, I ain't above smackin' you if you don't quit that shit."

"I'm almost done!" Juicy argued. "This is for your protection!"

"Hey, Juicy!" Trev said, keeping his tone light. "Whatcha doin'?"

"Oh! Hello, Trev." Juicy grinned. "I am neutralizing the listening devices that have been hidden inside these outlets." He looked around suspiciously. "They're always listening, you know."

"Yes, they are." Trev nodded and eyed Jules, hoping to prompt him to agree.

"Yeah, them bastards," Jules said with a little frown.

"But you know Boss Cold is a *really* powerful gangster, so

I bet they already potatoed all these sockets." Trev cleared his throat and gave Jules another meaningful look.

"Yup. Sure did." Jules nodded. "Used them Yukon gold ones."

Juicy held the potato as if he might throw it, his eyes narrowed. He perked up suddenly and said, "Oh! Yes. Yukon gold. Those are excellent." He dropped the potato, leaving it with the bag and the knife. "I used to grow those when I lived in Idaho."

"Uh-huh." Trev nodded along. "So, uh, did you ever get that popcorn Jules promised you?"

"Ah, that's right! I forgot about that." Juicy let Trev lead him out of the den. "We were going to watch a movie. I said anything Clint Eastwood. But then Miss Rowena was asking me about where I'm from, what I do for a living, and I realized she might be one of them. And if she's not, she was given those questions to ask me because *they* are listening."

"And that's why you have to rub potatoes everywhere?"

"Yes. Exactly."

Trev took a few turns to find his way back to the living room, wishing Jules would fuck off for two seconds so he could talk to Juicy. He was sure Cold knew Juicy or that Juicy's presence here was not a surprise.

Brick greeted them with a wave. Jimmy had fallen asleep in his chair.

"Hey," Brick said softly. "Was wondering what happened to you guys. You went for snacks and then poof."

"Sorry. Ran into an old friend." Trev patted Juicy's shoulder. "Juicy, this is Brick. Brick, this is Juicy."

"Brick is not a name," Juicy said. "It's a small block of dried clay."

"That it is."

Brick laughed. "It's a nickname. My name is actually Cho, but my last name is Brixton. So, *Brixton*, Brick."

"Plus, my baby boy is built like an absolute brick shithouse." Jules lumbered over to sit with Brick on the couch, and he murmured something that was definitely filthy and not in English.

Brick grinned and replied in the same language. He laughed, adding, "That was very good. Gross, but very good." He noticed Trev looking their way, and he said, "I'm half Korean. Remember how I said I'm a translator? So I speak German."

"Really?" Trev blinked.

"No!" Brick laughed. "Korean." He snuggled into Jules. "I've been teaching Jules. But he only wants to learn how to talk dirty."

"What?" Jules grinned. "That's the fun stuff."

Rowena's heels signaled her impending arrival and she growled as she stalked into the room. "What the fuck? I turn my back for two seconds and that one—" She pointed at Juicy. "—ran off with a bunch of potatoes, while this one—" She pointed at Jules. "—just stands there, staring at me like a dumb puppy, and then bolts!"

"What?" Jules grunted. "I had to go get 'im."

"You left me all alone to finish making all this stupid fucking popcorn for everyone!"

Jules eyed her empty hands. "Well, where is it?"

Rowena smiled sweetly. "Back in the kitchen." She scowled, barking, "Where I left it after running around the house trying to find you!"

Jimmy stirred and blinked drowsily. "Mm, what's going on?"

"Go back to sleep, Jimmy," Rowena cooed. "Jules is going to get us some popcorn."

Jules made a face. "I am?"

Brick playfully swatted his thigh. "You are."

"Okay!" Jimmy yawned and put his head back. "Sounds good."

"They're all very noisy," Juicy said absently as he went to sit down on the couch.

Jules got up with a little growl. "Okay, fine." He poked Juicy's shoulder. "You stay put. I'm gettin' popcorn."

"Oh, awful stuff." Juicy waved his hand dismissively. "Gets all stuck in my teeth. Can't stand it."

Jules twitched.

"Go get the damn popcorn," Rowena grumbled. "Someone is going to eat it."

"Got any decent Chinese places around here?" Trev suggested. "Try that."

"I'll grab a menu," Jules muttered as he left the room.

Juicy had found the remote and was flipping channels, content for the moment to remain as he was. If he heard Trev say anything about Chinese food, he didn't acknowledge it.

"He is a delight," Rowena said, smiling at Juicy fondly. "Insane, but a *delight*." She reached out to squeeze Trev's arm. "You okay, sweetie? How did the talk with Roddy go?"

"Ah, you know." Trev rolled his eyes. "Threats, bargaining, tried to buy me off with a car. Invaded my privacy by having one of his guys break into my lockbox and go through all my shit. I feel like that might be pretty typical."

Rowena's expression softened. "I'm sorry, sweetie. What was he trying to buy you off for?"

"To get me to leave." Trev scoffed. "And I'm not going anywhere without Jupiter."

"Well, hey! He's here now!" Rowena perked up. "I know

you were worried about him. But at least he's here and... Oh." She blinked.

"What?"

"Well, I saw Roger headed upstairs with a bunch of chains..."

"Fuckin' Christ." Trev cringed, glancing back worriedly at Juicy.

"Hey. Go check on him." Rowena patted Trev's shoulder. "I'll keep an eye on our geriatric little friend, okay? And I promise to do a better job than Jules."

Trev hesitated, but he reasoned there wasn't that much more trouble Juicy could get into.

Hopefully.

"Are you sure?" Trev frowned.

"Very sure." Rowena smiled warmly. "Make sure your man piece is all right."

"Thank you." Trev hesitated, but then he pulled Rowena into a hug.

Rowena hugged him back, giving his shoulder a gentle rub. "I got you. Now go on!"

"Going!" Trev pulled back with a smile, surprised to find that he didn't immediately think of how to use Rowena's affection to manipulate his current situation. Well, he was thinking about it now, but she did really seem to actually care about Trev.

That was... strange.

Cold could still go suck on a cement cock, but Rowena was pretty all right.

Trev hurried upstairs, checking the various rooms to figure out where Jupiter was. A lot of the doors were locked, and he didn't see Mickey or Roger. Frustrated, he called out, "Jupiter? Where are you?"

"Hey!" Jupiter shouted back. "In here!"

"Where the fuck is here?" Trev followed the sound of Jupiter's voice until he walked into *another* guest room. "Fuck! How many fucking rooms does this place have?"

"A lot," Jupiter griped from where he was chained to the bed.

Trev stopped short and stared, unable to resist a laugh.

There was a length of chain padlocked around Jupiter's neck. It didn't appear too tight, but it wasn't a proper collar and probably was not comfortable.

Still, Trev grinned. "Well, well... Look at you, Daddy. Love this for you."

"Yeah, yeah. Very funny, right?" Jupiter tugged at the other end of the chain, where it was attached to the headboard with another big padlock. "Roger Lorre lives up to his reputation of being completely fucking insane. Who the hell just has a bunch of chains and locks lying around?"

"Asks the guy who did what now?" Trev arched his brow. "Oh *yeah*. Chained me to a fucking wall."

"You're loving this, aren't you?"

"More than a little bit."

CHAPTER *Fifteen*

"IT'S A GOOD LOOK," Trev continued to taunt. "Very sexy. Is this the part where I offer to buy you a golden bikini? Because I could actually be into that."

Jupiter sighed.

Trev laughed, hurrying over to join Jupiter in bed. "I'm kidding. Mostly."

"Come here, baby doll." Jupiter cupped Trev's cheek to draw him into a kiss.

It was sweet, firm, and Trev melted on the spot. His heart beat faster, his skin warmed, and the unexpected tenderness eased away the remnants of fear still clinging to him. He had been worried about Jupiter, terrified in fact, and he savored every second of this kiss knowing that there had been a very real chance that he wasn't going to have this again.

"Are you okay?" Trev asked when they parted, a bit breathless.

"Are you?" Jupiter frowned.

"I'm fine! I've been watching movies and fucking day drinking. You got shot."

"I'm okay," Jupiter assured him. "Emil's guys found me.

They bought the story at first, but I could tell Sal was suspicious. I got patched up and then got the fuck out of there."

"And you came here."

"Yeah."

"Literally the home of your family's most hated enemy."

"Yup." Jupiter smiled. "Can't help it. This is where you were."

"You're an idiot." Trev kissed him again.

"I was worried about you, baby doll," Jupiter murmured quietly. "Can't run away together if we're not together."

Trev cracked a little smile. "So, that's still the plan, huh?"

"Of course it is."

"What makes you so sure I still want to go with you?"

"Well, you jumping into my arms the second you saw me was a pretty big clue." Jupiter looked smug.

The beautiful bastard.

Trev rolled his eyes, but he still smiled. "Maybe I was just excited to see you. Definitely missed that dick, you know."

Jupiter gave his chain a tug. "Kinda hard to give you any of it right now."

"Ugh, no imagination." Trev's smile faded a little. "Are you really all right? This whole thing is fucked. I've been trying to figure out a way to get the fuck out of here, but so far I've got nothing."

"Unfortunately, it's not up to you or me. We have to wait and see what Cold decides. I really thought telling him about the hit was going to put me in his good graces, but apparently not."

Trev snorted. "That guy could eat coal and shit out diamonds, his ass is wound so tight. He's not going to crack. Our family bonding has mostly been limited to threats, more threats, and oh yeah, he got a big kick out of my old photos. Had some of his mom."

"Really?"

"Yeah." Trev opened up the lockbox to show Jupiter. "Right now, these are the only leverage I have and it's not much."

"Is this your mom?" Jupiter tapped one of the women in the photos.

"Yup. And the other one is Cold's. They were friends. Imagine that."

Jupiter paused on the photo of Trev's mother standing in front of the hot dog statue. "This is at the park."

"What?"

"This statue. It used to be at the Perry City park. The one Cold was asking us about."

Trev studied the background. "Shit. I missed that. Hang on, there's another one where you can see more of it."

The other photograph did indeed show a better view of the park's green grass, winding sidewalks, and a man with dark hair walking his dog and waving. It was blurry and hard to make out much in the way of details, and only part of his mother's shoulder was even in the frame.

Still, Trev had held on to the picture because it was technically one of his mother, and he wouldn't dare let it go. Now he was wondering if there was something else that had grabbed Cold's attention. It couldn't be a coincidence that Cold had asked about the park and Trev just so happened to have photos of it.

"There has to be something here," Trev said, voicing his thoughts out loud. "What could be in that damn park?"

"I have no idea." Jupiter frowned.

"Dead body is always a good guess, right?"

Jupiter laughed softly. "Oh, you think so?"

"I've seen gangster movies! That's what it always is." Trev shook the photo. "There's probably some kind of secret hidden in this picture! Like, I don't know. The trees spell out a word or something that's a code word for a secret chest."

"You've definitely seen too many movies."

"According to Rowena, I haven't seen enough." Trev snorted. "She got all upset because I hadn't seen *Mean Girls*—"

"You haven't seen *Mean Girls*?"

"Shut up. Can we focus?"

"You're the one who brought it up."

Trev gave Jupiter's chains a shake as he crawled into his lap. "Shush now. I'm trying to think. Whatever is in that park, it must be something Cold wants to use against your family. He never did business in Perry City, right?"

"Not that I know of." Jupiter rubbed Trev's hips. "So, whatever is at the park is something my family did—"

"Or something they're trying to hide. Like a body."

Jupiter smirked. "Okay, yes, could be." He looked thoughtful. "Emil and Sal were talking to their FBI snitch about some old case..."

"What?"

"They wouldn't tell me much. Just that they were taking care of it but they needed his help."

"His help to do what?" Trev pressed.

"I don't know, Nancy Drew." Jupiter laughed. "You really are determined to solve the mystery, huh?"

"I don't even know what the mystery is. I just want fucking leverage to get us out of here." Trev slammed his ass down defiantly. "Since you're tied up at the moment, I guess it's up to me now."

"Ha ha." Jupiter bucked his hips up in reply. "Look, it could be as simple as him waiting to see what my family is going to do. He knows about the hit. He probably already knows what's going on with the park—"

"And what? He was just poking at you to see what you'd say?"

"Maybe." Jupiter shrugged. "Cold is very smart. I wouldn't go messing around too much, all right?"

Trev made a face. "What do you expect me to do? Just sit here and wait for him to maybe not kill you?"

Jupiter arched his brow. "You really think you can try to outfox Boss Cold, arguably one of the most clever criminals who's ever lived?"

"Only one way to find out," Trev declared.

"You're very sexy when you're bullshitting, do you know that?"

Trev gave Jupiter's chain a yank. "Who said I'm bullshitting?"

"I am." Jupiter chuckled. "You have no idea what to do right now and you're grasping at straws. You're—"

"About to strangle you with this chain if you don't shut up and make out with me?" Trev batted his lashes. "I've had enough of people digging around my brain, trying to get a damn read on me, and generally pissing me off today. If I want your opinion, I'll fuck it out of you, babe."

"Yeah?" Jupiter gave Trev's ass a firm squeeze. "Is that so?"

"Uh-huh."

"Kinda feel like you want to fuck something out of me right now, baby doll."

Trev shuddered. "Maybe I just want to fuck you..." He slid his fingers over Jupiter's cheek. "I really didn't know if I was going to see you again."

"I missed you too."

"I missed that dick." Trev grinned.

Jupiter snorted dryly. "You really want to fuck right now?"

"Why not?" Trev wiggled his hips. "We got time, don't we? Can't exactly bust you out of here right now since you're chained to a bed."

Jupiter squeezed Trev's ass, his fingers teasing under the edge of his shorts. "I suppose you could show me how creative you can be..."

"Do you happen to have lube with you?" Trev grinned. "Or do I need to go ask my big bro?"

"Do you have my duffel bag?"

"Yeah?" Trev hadn't thought to actually look through it yet though.

"Go on and get it. There's lube in the side pocket." Jupiter smiled softly. "I had definitely pictured us celebrating our escape a little differently than hanging out with your family."

"Just wait here." Trev kissed him. "I can *definitely* take your mind off it."

"I'll be here."

"Right. I mean, where else would you go?" Trev grinned as he crawled off Jupiter's lap.

"Brat."

"Your brat," Trev teased back, swaying his hips as he strolled out of the room. He navigated his way back to the bedroom he was staying in and went for the duffel bag. It was unzipped, no doubt from Roger's earlier snooping, and Trev located a small bottle of lube in the pocket just as Jupiter had said.

He headed back out into the hall, skidding to a stop as Erasmus and Mickey stepped out from where they'd been leaning against the wall on either side of the doorway. "Holy fuck! You are both so fucking *creepy*! Did you both go to fucking creepy sneaky school or something?"

Erasmus didn't blink. Big surprise.

"Boss wanted us to check on you." Mickey sneered. "Make sure you and Mr. Prospero are behaving yourselves."

Trev held up the lube. "I'm about to go fuck his brains out. That okay with you, Mom?"

Erasmus actually laughed.

It was weird.

Trev turned around and marched back toward Jupiter's room. Well aware that Erasmus and Mickey were following him, he started taking off his clothes as soon as he stepped inside the room.

Jupiter blinked. "Uh... You know—"

"That Thing One and Thing Two are right behind me?"

"Yeah."

"I'm aware." Trev threw his shirt on the floor and then kicked his boots off. He turned around and batted his eyes at Erasmus and Mickey. "Did you guys want to watch or can I shut the door? I usually charge for a show, but hey!"

Erasmus tilted his head as if he may have been interested, but Mickey huffed and reached for the doorknob.

"Is that a no?" Trev cooed sweetly.

"It's a *we're gonna be right outside the door, so you better not be trying anything fucking cute*," Mickey warned.

"The only thing I'm trying to do is get all up on some dick."

Mickey shut the door.

Jupiter snorted out a laugh. "Did you really just tell the Shadow that you wanted to get up on some dick?"

"What? Uncle Fester?" Trev grinned as he shimmied his

shorts down along with his underwear and stockings. He was now naked except for the collar.

"Your balls continue to be impressive."

Trev cupped himself and winked. "My everything is impressive, thank you." He crawled up into bed with the bottle of lube.

"That it is, baby doll." Jupiter eyed him hungrily, his gaze settling on the collar. "You're still wearing it."

"Oh?" Trev shrugged casually. "I hadn't really noticed."

"Uh-huh. You really did miss me, didn't you?"

"Shut up."

Jupiter smirked. "So, how exactly are you planning to do this?"

"Duh. Just like this." Trev rolled his eyes. "You just sit right there and let me have at it, all right?"

"It being my dick?"

"Yup." Trev kissed Jupiter, dropping the lube beside him. He didn't need it right this second, and he really had missed Jupiter. His hot kisses, his slick tongue, the way his big hands held him like he owned every inch of him...

Fuck, that was hot.

"Are you gonna suck me, baby doll?" Jupiter asked, tilting his hips forward.

"No." Trev smirked. "You're gonna rim the fuck out of me though."

Jupiter tugged at the chain around his neck. "Can't exactly reach you."

"Oh, don't worry about that." Trev grinned as he turned so he was sitting the other way on Jupiter's lap. He raised himself up into a crouch, bracing himself on his hands as he pushed his ass up right in Jupiter's face.

"Well then." Jupiter grabbed Trev's ass and squeezed. "How can I say no to such an offer?"

"It's an offer you can't refuse, sir." Trev chuckled.

"Cute." Jupiter urged Trev closer, the chain rattling as he leaned in to lap at Trev's taint.

Trev sighed softly and tipped his head forward, savoring the hot swipe of Jupiter's tongue as it moved up to his hole. The slick slide was wonderful, perfectly punctuated with the rough press of Jupiter's fingers kneading his ass cheeks.

He pushed his head down and dropped to his elbows, keeping his legs bent at the right angle to ensure Jupiter could have all that he wanted of him. He could comfortably stay posed like this for hours, and he whined quietly as Jupiter's finger pushed in to make way for his tongue.

"Fuck, that's good," Trev whispered. "Mm, like that. Get me stretched wide fuckin' open for your dick. I want you to just fuckin' slide right in. I can't wait to fucking ride you, Daddy. I'm gonna make you mine, every fuckin' inch of you."

Jupiter growled, the sound loud enough to make Jupiter's lips buzz against Trev's sensitive skin. Trev's dirty talk must have had quite the effect on Jupiter because he abruptly surged forward, roughly grabbing Trev's thighs.

"Hey!" Trev gasped when Jupiter pulled at his legs. "What are you… Oh!"

Jupiter dragged Trev's legs over his shoulders and latched on to his hips, holding him spread and suspended from the bed as he forced his tongue inside his hole.

Trev moaned, his lashes fluttering from the firm push of Jupiter's tongue. "God, yes. There you go. Get that fuckin' tongue in there. God! Fuck! Fuckin' get it!"

The door shifted slightly, as if someone bumped into it, but it did not open.

Trev ignored it, far too busy with grinding back on

Jupiter's face and urging him to thrust faster. "Yeah, that's it... That's it! Right there!"

Jupiter ate Trev out ravenously, and his chains rattled from his intense efforts. He pushed his thumbs in to massage around Trev's rim and slid his tongue in deeper.

Trev groaned, rocking back for more, and he gasped when Jupiter's thumbs pressed right in. He was opening up effortlessly, wet with Jupiter's spit and savoring the stretch. Jupiter definitely seemed to be enjoying himself, and that gave Trev a wonderfully wicked idea.

After all, when would he have another chance to play with Jupiter chained up?

Trev abruptly pulled away, tipping forward so he was on his knees straddling Jupiter's shins. "Mm, that was nice."

"Come on and let me finish," Jupiter urged. "Then you can ride me, baby doll."

"It's all right." Trev reached for the lube. "I'm thinking I'm gonna get myself ready."

"Oh?"

"Uh-huh." Trev peeled the plastic from around the lid and then unscrewed it to deftly remove the seal. "You're going to be a good boy and watch, sir."

Jupiter scoffed. "Am I now?"

Trev smirked when he heard the chains rattle, no doubt Jupiter trying to grab him. As planned, however, Trev had scooted far enough down Jupiter's legs that he was out of his reach. Calmly drizzling lube onto his fingers, Trev teased, "Like I said, be a good boy and watch."

Jupiter growled. "Or, you be a good boy and bring that sweet little ass back up here."

Trev turned his head to look back at Jupiter and smile sweetly. "No."

"Come on, baby doll." Jupiter grunted. "We don't know how much time we have—"

"Oh, don't worry about that." Trev leaned forward, propping himself up on his elbow while he reached back to rub his fingers over his asshole. He smeared the lube around before plunging two right inside with a soft moan. "I'll be sure to get off really fast—"

"No," Jupiter said firmly. "You're not coming until I say so, baby doll."

"Mmm, doesn't seem like there's much you can do about it with your new jewelry, sir," Trev taunted as he fingered himself. This angle was awkward, but he knew it was killing Jupiter to see him fucking his hole like this and not being able to touch him.

He pushed in a third finger, using his other hand to spread his ass cheeks wide.

"Fuck," Jupiter hissed.

"You like that, Daddy?" Trev bowed his head to the bed and arched his back.

"Yeah, I do." Jupiter sounded breathless. "Come on." He pulled down his zipper. "Why don't you sit on back and get this cock in you? Quit messin' around."

"Mmm, no." Trev could hear Jupiter stroking himself slowly, catching snippets of the telltale soft skin on skin sounds in between the wet strokes of his own fingers. He stretched his left hand over to his hole now, dipping in a finger. "I don't think I'm ready yet..."

Jupiter grunted low. "Baby doll. What are you waiting for?"

"Not really sure..." Trev gasped as he twisted his fingers. "I'll let you know in a minute."

"*Trev.*" Jupiter's tone was strained. "You're driving me fuckin' crazy."

"That's the point, sir."

"*Trev...*"

Trev thrust his right hand harder, willing his body to open up so he could slip in more fingers from the left. He was getting so loose and soft, leisurely pumping his fingers in and out while Jupiter shifted beneath him. He could now squeeze in four fingers from each hand, and he knew he had to be gaping now.

He moaned as he pushed his fingers in deep and tugged, trying to pull himself open wider. The discomfort was minimal with how much care he'd used to stretch his hole, but he wanted more. He couldn't get his fingers in far enough to give him the sweet ache that he longed for, and he didn't think he could keep this up another second.

Dragging out this performance would certainly sweeten the ending, but Trev wanted Jupiter's cock and he wanted it now.

He pulled his fingers free and then caressed his hole, sighing. "Fuck, do you see how open I am? How I wrecked my hole for you?"

"Yes," Jupiter said shortly, out of breath. "I see it, baby."

Trev pushed up on his hands, scooting back until his ass hit Jupiter's chest. He sat down in his lap and tilted his hips so Jupiter's cock slotted right between his cheeks. Jupiter immediately grabbed his hips and dug in his fingers as if to keep Trev trapped there, and Trev smirked. "You want it, Daddy?"

"You know I do." Jupiter squeezed Trev's hips.

Trev lifted his ass so he could bring the head of Jupiter's cock to his soft hole. "Aw, is that what you want, Daddy? This right here?"

"Fuckin' *tease*." Jupiter's voice was hoarse, and his cock throbbed in Trev's hand. "Baby doll, *come on...*"

"But I'm having the best time, sir," Trev said sweetly even as he yearned for every inch of that thick length to press inside and completely wreck him.

Jupiter hadn't been the nicest when Trev was chained up, so this would finally square things up between them.

Probably.

Trev pushed the head in, just enough for his body to feel the pressure of being opened once more. It was so much more than his fingers, firm and solid in a way that made him want to slam back and take it all at once. He lifted his hips up so that it slipped out, rubbed it around slowly, and then let it push inside again.

Jupiter grunted noisily.

Trev paid him no mind. He continued to play with Jupiter's cock like it was his own personal toy, fucking it in and out of his hole—but only the first inch or so. The gradual buildup of tension was delicious, and he expected that Jupiter wouldn't be able to tolerate it for long.

It was already driving Trev nuts.

Jupiter grabbed the back of Trev's collar and pulled. "No more games, baby doll." His other hand latched on to Trev's hip, pushing him down just as his hips slammed upward to bury the rest of his cock inside Trev with one smooth thrust.

"Ah! Fuck!" Trev gasped, his hole throbbing to finally be stuffed full. He whined as Jupiter kept a hold of the collar and prevented him from pulling away. Not that he actually wanted to, but he loved the sharp tug against his neck as he struggled. "Oh God… Jupiter."

"Do you like that, baby doll?" Jupiter gave Trev's ass a firm smack.

"Ah… yes." Trev groaned, his back arching when Jupiter pushed his hips forward and yanked on the collar. "God, yes, *sir*."

Jupiter slammed into Trev, fucking him hard and fast. Even with the chains, he was able to get a surprising amount of leverage and pound Trev's ass.

Trev whined, bouncing helplessly on Jupiter's cock. The friction was overwhelming, each thrust pushing against his sensitive inner walls and making him hungry for more. The possessive pull of the collar made Trev feel lightheaded, but it wasn't because his breathing was being constricted in any significant manner.

No, it was the frantic urge to be *owned*.

He wanted to belong to Jupiter in a way he'd never felt before, one that his soul yearned for and simultaneously rallied against. He had never needed anyone and swore that he wouldn't start now, but he couldn't escape how his body craved Jupiter like he was the very air he needed to breathe.

The way he growled so seductively in Trev's ear, the claw of his fingers into Trev's skin, the powerful force behind every slam, and the incredible precision with which he crashed their bodies together to make each collision explode with bliss...

Fuck.

Maybe Trev was already his and he just hadn't realized it until now.

"Turn around." Jupiter let go of the collar. "I want to see you."

Trev's legs were wobbly as he pulled off Jupiter's cock to switch positions. Even though Jupiter had arguably been doing the heavy lifting, Trev's body was wrung out and jittery as if he'd just completed a marathon. He straddled Jupiter's lap and hurried to get his cock back inside of him.

Those few seconds of being empty were a few too many, and he groaned happily as he sank down once more.

God, yes.

Trev sat flush in Jupiter's lap and grinded his hips forward, sliding his hands up Jupiter's chest. "Mm, like this, Daddy? Is this what you wanted?"

"Yes, baby doll." Jupiter hugged Trev close and fanned his hands across his lower back and hips. "You look so beautiful getting fucked. I wanted to see your face when you come on my big cock."

"Yeah?" Trev circled his hips wide and then thrust forward, mewling. "F-fuck, yeah."

"Go on, baby," Jupiter urged. "Go on and get you some, huh?"

Trev was in control now—though he would argue that he'd never lost it—and he put his feet flat on the bend so he could raise up and slam back down. He reached over Jupiter to grab the headboard and fucked himself harder, faster, taking everything that he wanted.

The ache was exquisite, the pressure rich, and the view of Jupiter's face caught in pleasure was divine. Trev loved how he looked at him, as if he was the sexiest thing Juniper had ever seen—which of course he was.

Trev was a fucking god.

He arched his back just to show off his lean figure and take Jupiter's cock at a better angle, alternating between quick drops and slow grinding. The time between switches dwindled as his climax built, and he focused on pushing down as hard as he could and rutting forward to chase down the friction he needed to come.

Jupiter gritted his teeth and grabbed the ring on Trev's collar. "Getting close, aren't you?"

"Uh-huh." Trev shivered. "I need to fucking come, sir."

"And if I told you no?"

Trev's hips stuttered, but he still protested. "I'd tell you to fuck off."

Jupiter's eyes gleamed with mischief. "But you'd still wait, wouldn't you? You still want to relinquish control... Not for the sake of power, but because you like *pleasing* me."

"Not as much as I like pleasing myself," Trev shot back haughtily, his skin burning. He couldn't really be considering not coming. Jupiter was literally powerless to stop him, as he was chained to the damn bed, and yet Trev was still hesitating.

Fucking goddammit.

Jupiter grinned. "It's all right, baby doll... Go ahead." He smacked Trev's ass encouragingly.

"Like I need your permission," Trev grumbled as he got going again. The need to climax was even more urgent now and he grabbed his dick, stroking himself in time with the frantic rock of his hips. Indignation and fury powered his every move, wishing he could fuck that smug look right off Jupiter's stupid smug face.

Jupiter pushed up so Trev could take his cock even deeper. "There, baby doll. There you go. Come on... Wanna see you come for me."

Trev didn't reply, too focused on chasing the last bit of stimulation that he needed to launch himself off that sweet precipice and into orgasm. He found it in the drag of Jupiter's nails across his hip and a particularly hard slam that left his insides throbbing.

It was perfect.

Trev cried out as he came, his cock spilling across his hand as he continued to ride Jupiter. Each pulse sent waves of heat flashing over his skin until he felt like he was glowing, and he squeezed his dick to work himself through each fleeting shudder. "F-fuck! Yes!"

Jupiter growled low, a breathless snarl that signaled his

own end, and he held Trev on his cock as he pressed a scorching kiss to his lips. "Mmm, *baby doll.*"

Trev collapsed against Jupiter's chest, grabbing his long ponytail and twisting it around his fingers as they kissed.

"Wow." Jupiter panted.

"What?"

"You really did miss me."

Trev laughed and kissed him. "I suppose I did." He gracefully slipped out of Jupiter's lap with a groan and then not so gracefully plopped down beside him.

Jupiter fixed his pants but didn't zip them yet. "Well?"

"What?" Trev mumbled

"Are you going to go get a towel or anything?"

"That's your job." Trev smirked.

Jupiter tugged on his chain.

"Ugh. Excuses." Trev rolled out of bed so he could head into the bathroom.

It was clean and well stocked, and Trev grabbed a hand towel from off the rack by the sink. He ran it under the faucet to wipe himself down and then grabbed another for Jupiter. He returned to bed, playfully throwing the towel at Jupiter.

It hit Jupiter's chest. "Hey!"

"Aw, sorry." Trev crawled up beside him with a smile. "I was aiming for your face."

"Very funny." Jupiter cleaned up and then tossed the towel, along with the lube, on the bedside table.

Once Jupiter had zipped his pants, Trev pressed in close so he could rest his head on Jupiter's lap. He was warm and sated, enjoying the closeness and the comfortable silence that followed. He knew he needed to get dressed and return to strategizing their way out of here, but for now, this was nice.

Jupiter ran his hand up and down Trev's back, rubbing lightly.

"Keep that up and I'm going to fall asleep," Trev mumbled.

"Go ahead," Jupiter said. "Not like we have anywhere to be, right?"

"We do. Somewhere with a warm, tropical climate, fuckin' far away from here."

Jupiter chuckled. "Yeah. Is that the plan now?"

"That's always been the plan." Trev smiled softly.

Jupiter didn't say anything else, but he continued to caress Trev's back.

Exhausted and fucked out, Trev soon fell asleep. He dozed until there was a knock at the door. He lifted his head, shouting, "If you want to watch, I'm going to charge you!"

"Are you decent?" Cold's voice drawled.

"Yes," Trev lied.

Cold opened the door, scowled at Trev's bare ass, and immediately shut it again.

Trev snickered, reaching for the sheets to cover himself up with. "Okay, okay! I'm decent now! Promise! Everything is put away!"

"Dinner is in an hour," Cold growled through the door. "Don't be late."

"Was it just me..." Trev wrinkled his nose.

Jupiter made a face. "What?"

"Did that sound more like an order than an invitation?"

"Definitely an order."

CHAPTER Sixteen

TREV GOT DRESSED and cleaned up a bit, though there really wasn't much they could do except for wait.

After all, Jupiter couldn't go anywhere since he was chained to the bed.

It was Rowena who came to get them for dinner, key in hand and dressed in a sleek red satin dress. She had clothing draped over her arm, cheerfully declaring, "Hello, sweeties! It's time for dinner!"

Trev glanced out the open doorway.

There was no way Rowena had come here alone.

Sure enough, he spied Mickey hovering in the hallway.

Erasmus or one of the other creeps was probably not far away.

"I'm guessing this is not an optional invitation," Trev said.

"Aw, come on." Rowena handed Trev the key. "It'll be nice, I promise. I'll make Roddy behave." She smiled warmly. "I'd say things are looking up."

"How do you figure?" Trev unlocked Jupiter's chains.

"Your little boy toy is still alive."

"Touché."

Jupiter rubbed his neck as he slid out of bed, grimacing.

"Here." Rowena handed the clothing to Trev, revealing it was a short black dress. "Thought this would work with your fishnets and boots. You should look real cute."

"Thanks." Trev accepted it with a smile.

"I'll make sure Flopsy and Mopsy give you a few minutes to get ready." Rowena squeezed Trev's shoulder. "I'll be right outside." She left the room, shutting the door behind her.

Jupiter glanced to the windows.

"Armed patrols with *dogs*," Trev said, pretty sure he already knew what Jupiter was thinking. He changed into the dress, shaking his head as he grumbled, "I don't like this either, all right? But Rowena is right."

"About what?" Jupiter managed a little smile. "That you look cute in the dress?"

The dress was short, tight, and had a plunging neckline that showed off Trev's lean chest.

Of course Trev looked good in it.

"Yes; duh, because I would look fine in anything." Trev snorted. "But I was talking about you being alive. If Cold really is the motherfucker they all say he is, he shouldn't give two fucks about murdering you. You don't have any information Cold didn't already have and you're not great leverage except to trade you back to your own family so they can kill you."

"Wow, gee, thanks," Jupiter grumbled. "I feel so much better now."

"How's your shoulder?"

"Still feels like I got shot. I'm fine. Promise."

Trev rubbed Jupiter's chest, smiling as Jupiter wrapped

his arms around him. "You still fuck pretty good for a guy who's been shot."

"Just pretty good?" Jupiter laughed. "I guess I'll have to try again then."

"You should. After dinner?"

Jupiter kissed him. "We'll see."

"That's a yes."

"Oh? Is it?" Jupiter raised his brow. "Still think you're in control, don't you? Even now?"

"I know I am," Trev said firmly.

"You're delusional."

"Well, my delusions have gotten us this far." Trev smirked. "Maybe it's enough to go all the way. Me, you, and the fuck out of here." He kissed Jupiter sweetly, cupping his cheek and scratching at his beard.

Jupiter's smile softened and he squeezed Trev close. "I hope so."

"Come on. Let's go have a nice family dinner, huh?"

"I'd rather talk about this dress some more." Jupiter's hand drifted down to cup Trev's ass through the slinky material.

"Later. I'm hungry."

"So am I."

Trev laughed. "For *food*. You can eat as much as you want of my ass later, all right?"

"Can't wait."

Trev grabbed Jupiter's hand to lead him out of the bedroom.

Mickey was still there, watching Jupiter like a hawk, and Rowena clapped excitedly when she saw Trev in the dress.

"Oh! Yes! I knew it would look good on you," she gushed.

"Thank you." Trev smoothed his hand over the soft material. "I promise I'll wash it or whatever before I—"

"Pffft. Keep it." Rowena shook her head. "I'll see what else I can find until you get your own threads, all right?"

"You do know Juicy filled his entire car with your stuff, right?" Jupiter said.

"*No*." Trev blinked. "You didn't tell me that!"

"Sorry." Jupiter grinned slyly. "We got a little distracted."

"That was just sex. We're talking about my clothing here." Trev poked his chest.

Rowena waved for them to follow her downstairs. "Where is everything? Still out in the car then?"

"As far as I know," Jupiter replied. "Unless Juicy did something with it."

"Where is Juicy?" Trev asked with a grimace. "Kinda feel bad he's probably been running wild without me."

"Oh, he's been fine." Rowena giggled. "Let him have control of the remote and he's been a doll. Erasmus took a real liking to him too."

"Mr. Never Blinks? Really?"

"Don't ask me." Rowena shrugged.

"Him and Junior still here?"

"No, they left a little while ago." Rowena led the way toward the dining room. "Tried to get them to stay for dinner, but Alistair needed them back for something."

"And Alistair is...?"

"Alistair Star," Jupiter supplied.

"Another gangster?" Trev asked.

"No, he's a businessman," Rowena said with another giggle.

Trev didn't get what was so funny, but he decided not to worry about it. He stepped into the dining room just behind Rowena, glancing around the large space.

It was as chic and modern as the rest of the house, and

the table was large enough for at least a dozen people. The centerpiece was a big arrangement of lilies, and the crystal chandelier hanging from the ceiling was absolutely massive.

Cold sat at the head of the table with Jimmy at his right. A man with long wavy hair and light brown skin eagerly pulled out the chair next to Jimmy to help Rowena sit. Brick was beside the young man, with Jules seated opposite Cold at the other end. Roger was at his right, and the last three seats were open.

Cold offered an icy smile, gesturing toward the empty chair beside him. "Trev. If you'd be so kind."

"Yeah. Sure." Trev strolled over to take his seat, nearly falling when Jupiter moved to pull the chair out for him. His face heated up and he sat down quickly, mumbling, "Thanks."

"Of course." Jupiter took the chair beside Trev, reaching under the table to give his knee a gentle squeeze.

Mickey took the last spot between Roger and Jupiter.

Trev eyed the young man, noting he looked as terrified as Trev should have been being the *guest* of a gangster once more. "So, what are you in for?"

The man's big brown eyes snapped to Trev. "What?"

"Are you here as family, a prisoner, or what?"

"This is Dario Romero," Rowena said with a warm smile as her hand slid under the table. "My boyfriend."

Dario squeaked.

"Hi. Nice to meet you." Trev grinned. "I'm Trevanion Usher, new half-brother and pain in Cold's ass."

Dario's gaze whipped to Cold, as if he was scared of the consequences of Trev's words.

Cold looked over his wine glass. "He is not incorrect."

"Whoa." Dario stared at Trev and Cold. "That is..."

"*Creepy* is what I keep hearing," Trev retorted.

"Right. Heh." Dario laughed nervously. "Definitely unnerving."

Jimmy, who was looking much more sober than the last time Trev saw him, piped up and said, "I think it's nice. I never had any brothers or sisters, so I'd love to wake up one day and suddenly have a new sibling!"

"Right?" Rowena grinned. "This is great. And now! Ha! I'm not the youngest anymore."

"Aw, but you'll still always be my baby," Dario cooed.

Cold glared.

"In a respectful way," Dario amended quickly. "Or not at all. Or just—"

Rowena kissed his cheek. "You know he's just doing that to mess with you."

"It's working."

A waiter entered the dining room with a tray of wine, making a loop around the table to serve everyone a glass.

"Where's Jerry?" Brick asked curiously.

"Night off," Jimmy replied with a grin. "Date with Charlie." He gestured to the waiter. "This is Mercutio."

"Hi, Mercutio." Trev wiggled his fingers.

Mercutio smiled politely and left the room once the last glass of wine had been handed out.

Trev eyed the wine with a frown.

It was dark red, almost like blood.

Ugh.

He took a small sip and wow, he thought blood must actually taste better.

"So." Trev set the glass down. "Is this what we're doing now?"

"You mean having dinner?" Cold asked casually.

"I mean, acting like everything is fine and you didn't just have Jupiter chained to a bed," Trev snapped back.

"You're free to leave anytime."

"Not without him."

Jupiter reached for Trev's hand under the table.

Brick looked at Jules, clearly concerned.

Jules shook his head.

"What?" Trev glared. "No one else is going to say anything? We're all just going to act like this is okay?"

No one made a sound.

Well, except for Mickey.

That asshole laughed.

"How long are you planning to keep Jupiter?" Jimmy asked firmly.

"For as long as I need," was Cold's useless reply.

"Look." Jimmy narrowed his eyes. "As much as I love that we have a new member of the family and have really enjoyed getting to know him—" He smiled warmly at Trev before turning a glare back on Cold. "This is fucked up. Even for you."

Cold's expression remained blank.

"If you're not going to let Jupiter and Trev go, why are they even sitting down with us for dinner?" Jimmy demanded. "Why pretend like you care if this is all some screwed up game?"

"I'm with Jimmy," Rowena piped up. "This is bullshit. If you're just gonna whack 'em, it's pretty shitty to let us get attached! It's like giving us a kitten to play with and then taking it back to the shelter!"

Mickey looked thoughtful. "Or taking the kitten and giving it cement shoes."

Rowena stared at him in horror. "What the fuck?"

"What?" Mickey scoffed. "Little tiny kitten-sized cement shoes—"

"Shut the fuck up, you sicko!" Rowena groaned.

"You brought up the fucking kitten!"

"Fuck you, Mickey! Ugh!"

"Come on now…" Cold actually smiled. "I would never hurt a kitten."

"Hey! Focus." Jimmy slammed his wine glass down. "Rod, please. When are you going to let Jupiter go?" He waved at Jupiter. "Hi, by the way. Sorry my husband is an *asshole*."

Jupiter waved back awkwardly.

Cold was quiet for a moment, sipping his wine. "The very fact that I am allowing him to dine with us should speak volumes of my intentions, but since you all can't seem to grasp the obvious…" His fierce gaze locked with Trev's across the table. "After Friday, you will both be free to go." He shot Jimmy a glare. "Happy?"

"Delighted," Jimmy snapped. "Was that really so difficult?"

"Wait, why Friday?" Trev asked.

"That's the day of the hit," Jupiter said quietly. "The meeting with the mayor."

"Yes," Cold confirmed.

"Hey!" Jimmy reached for Cold's arm. "If you already know they're going to try and kill you, why the hell are you still going?"

"I wouldn't go if it wasn't absolutely safe."

"How is going exactly where someone wants to kill you *safe*?"

Dario paled.

Rowena patted his shoulder.

"It's not like he's gonna be alone," Jules said with a little huff. “How ’bout you trust us, huh? Boss knows what he’s doin’.”

“Are we sure about that?” Brick asked quietly from the side of his mouth. “Because I’m kinda inclined to agree with Jimmy.” He blinked. “And also, uh, am I even supposed to be hearing any of this? Isn’t this super private gangster shit?”

Cold just smiled.

“You want us to know,” Trev accused, “but why?”

“We’ll be having a lobster risotto and bone marrow served with a short rib marmalade and brioche to start this evening.” Cold sipped his wine. “Followed by beef Wellington with potato puree, glazed root vegetables, and a red wine demi-glace.”

“I do not understand half of those fucking words, but I know when I’m being hustled.” Trev scowled.

“Dessert will be Mercutio’s own creation, a fudge brownie with salted caramel mousse, banana crémeux, and banana dulce de leche ice cream.”

“You’re driving me fucking *bananas*,” Trev grumbled.

Jupiter squeezed Trev’s hand and then addressed Cold. “Thank you, Boss Cold. That sounds delicious. It’s been ages since I’ve had anything with a demi-glace. I appreciate your kindness and hospitality—”

“Are you for fucking real right now?”

“Thank you.” Jupiter sat up straighter, ignoring Trev as he continued to speak to Cold. “Whatever else I can do to be of assistance and prove my loyalty—”

“Sit. Quietly. And eat.” Cold smirked. “Set an example for my brother.”

“Yeah, no, that’s not happening.” Trev batted his lashes. “And hey.” There was someone missing from the table. “Where is Juicy?”

"Enjoying the company of my personal physician, Doctor Madeline Queen."

"A doctor?" Trev stiffened. "Why did Juicy need a doctor?"

"It's nothing to worry about. He—"

"Like I trust you." Trev stood.

"Trev, please." Jupiter grabbed his arm.

"I will stab you in your bullet wound with a fork." Trev glared back at Cold. "Where is he?"

"Upstairs," Cold replied. "Guest room at the end of the hallway."

"Thanks." Trev waved. "You guys enjoy dinner. I'm going to go check on Juicy."

"Trev." Jupiter tried to pull Trev back down. "Don't be rude."

"Oh, you don't want me to be rude?" Trev narrowed his eyes. "See, I was being polite. If you want me to be rude, I could say I hope you all fucking choke on your fancy ass stupid dinner." He glanced around the table. "Except Rowena. You're cool. And Jimmy. Brick." He lingered on Dario. "You too."

Dario shot him a weak set of finger guns.

Trev didn't wait for any other responses and yanked his arm from Jupiter, stomping out of the dining room.

He didn't expect anyone to follow him, as Mickey and Roger seemed to be assigned to watching over Jupiter, and the others were likely more interested in enjoying their dinner. He knew Jupiter would stay, no doubt wanting to kiss Cold's ass some more.

What the hell was up with that?

Maybe it was some sort of stupid gangster thing.

Whatever it was, Trev didn't like it.

And he sure as hell wasn't going to wait until Friday to get out of here.

He didn't know what Cold was up to, but Trev wanted no part of it. He'd had enough of murder and plotting and gangster bullshit, especially when he was certain he was only being used as a pawn again. It was a game he couldn't get on top of and he saw no clear way to win except to exit as quickly as possible.

But Jupiter...

Shit.

Okay.

Trev had to figure out how to get out of here with Jupiter and—*shit*, Juicy was here too.

Right, got it.

He had to figure out a way to get out of here with Jupiter *and* Juicy and then out of the damn country as fast as they could. He hated that they could be trapped here through Friday, helpless to be strung along by Cold's devious puppeteering. There was no doubt in Trev's mind that Cold thought of them as expendable, which meant he'd be willing to put any of them at risk for his own gain.

Fuck that.

Juicy was his only friend and Jupiter was, well, whatever he was. Even though he was acting like a giant idiot right now, Trev did care about Jupiter and didn't want to see anything happen to him.

If Trev couldn't stop Cold's plans or escape before the shit went down, then he needed to find out what those plans were and do everything he could to keep the people he cared about safe.

With a sigh, Trev trudged upstairs and down the hall to find the guest room. It was exactly where Cold said it would be, and Trev was relieved to see Juicy as soon as he walked in.

Juicy was in bed, bundled up beneath the blankets and sleeping.

There were at least a dozen pill bottles lined up on the bedside table and a petite woman with peroxide blonde hair stood next to the bed, tapping away at her phone. She didn't look up when Trev walked in, but she said, "Ah, you must be Trevanion."

"Trev." Trev sat down on the side of the bed. "You're Doctor Queen?"

"Yes." She kept typing.

"Is he all right?"

"Yes. He's sedated."

"Sedated?" Trev scowled. "What the fuck for?"

"Because he hasn't been on his medication in almost forty-eight hours and was becoming agitated," she said coolly. "He was a danger to himself and others."

"Juicy?" Trev scoffed. "How the hell is he a danger to anyone?"

"Are you family?"

"He's my friend."

Queen finally looked up from her phone. "Friends are not privy to private medical history."

"What about friends whose half-brother is Boss Cold, who probably pays your checks, huh?" Trev rose from the bed and crossed his arms, glaring down at Queen. "If there's something wrong with Juicy, I want to know. Right fucking now."

"No."

"You have five seconds to tell me or—"

"It's all right," Cold said. "You can tell him."

Trev whirled around, surprised to see Cold standing in

the doorway. "Thought you had some bananas cream-wah or whatever to fucking eat?"

"It can wait." Cold looked to Queen and nodded.

Queen shrugged. "Brain cancer with an accompanying dementia disorder. His doctors were able to find a regimen to successfully cross the blood-brain barrier to stabilize him and keep the tumor from growing, but it remains inoperable. Hence his mood swings, the confusion, and violence when he's not medicated."

Trev frowned. "I've never seen him violent. Not ever." He paused. "Sure, he barks at people, but that's about it."

"I don't know what prompted him to leave Perry City, but he is not fit to travel. It's not safe for him or anyone else." Queen put her phone in a large leather satchel and then gathered up the pill bottles to stash them away too.

"What are you doing? Doesn't he need those?"

"A nurse will be coming by to make sure he takes the proper dosages." Queen slung the satchel over her shoulder. "He's not in any condition to manage his own prescriptions and I suspect has not been for some time."

"Abigail?" Cold asked.

"Yes. And my new girl, Lily." Queen headed to the door, brushing by Cold. "You can expect a charge for my usual house call fee and a bonus."

"Oh?"

"Old fucker bit me." Queen sneered and then left.

Trev sat back down on the bed, reaching for Juicy's hand. He chuckled a little, saying lightly, "So, you got some bite to go with that bark? Nice."

Juicy didn't stir, but Trev swore he smiled.

Trev cleared his throat. "You set all of this up for him?"

"I did," Cold replied.

"I guess you want me to thank you or something."

"For you to show gratitude for my kindness? No, never." Cold snorted. "You think it's a trick. Part of my plan somehow."

"I know it is." Trev scoffed.

Cold only smiled. "Take it however you want."

"I'd love to take it right the fuck out of here." Trev grunted. "Me, Jupiter, and Juicy. Far, far away in another country." He held up his hand when Cold started to speak. "No, no. I already know. You need us for your stupid magical plan because somehow us being here is gonna help you not get murdered on Friday."

Cold tilted his head. "If that's what you need to believe, then so be it."

Trev narrowed his eyes.

So, that wasn't it.

Interesting.

Trev didn't know if that was an intentional slip or if Cold was deliberately teasing him, but he didn't take the bait. He turned his attention back to Juicy, saying, "I'm going to sit with him for a while."

"You're aware he's sedated?"

"Are you aware you're an asshole?"

Cold did not look amused, eyeing Trev carefully before he said, "You're really not afraid of me, are you?"

"No more than any other asshole I've met who could probably kill me without blinking twice." Trev snorted out a laugh. "My life hasn't exactly been cotton candy and rainbows. My mom told me once that beauty faded but stupid was forever, so I decided to be beautiful for as long as I could and only let people think I was stupid. I learned how to play their fucking games, figure out what they wanted from me, if they were going to be a threat or not, how to hustle, how to *survive*.

"So, yeah. No. I'm not afraid of you." He stared up at Cold. "I already know you could kill me if you wanted to, probably wouldn't feel that bad about it either, and there's not a lot I could do to stop you. Not that I would go down without a fight, thank you. But since I am still very much alive, I know there must be something you want from me and you can bet your frosty ass that I will hustle and do whatever I gotta do. I've survived a lot of nastier shit than this and I'm going to survive *you*."

Cold smiled again. It was almost fond.

Trev turned his back to Cold as much as he could, refusing to look at him. He was certain Cold would have something cute to say, but Cold was gone when he glanced up at the doorway.

He had no idea if that was good or bad.

He also had no clue what had possessed him to spill his guts like that, but he chalked it up to the lingering frustrations of this impossible situation. He hated feeling helpless, and there was nothing he could do right now to improve his circumstances.

Except wait.

Ugh.

Trev adjusted the blankets around Juicy with a soft sigh and then resigned himself to a nearby chair. He fixed his dress and crossed his legs, trying to get comfortable.

Stupid fancy chair was miserably hard.

He slid off onto the floor, leaning against the side of the chair and sticking his legs out. It made his dress ride up a little, but he didn't care. He felt defeated, angry, and—

"Two trees, three trees, and then around the big wiener," Juicy mumbled.

"What?" Trev blinked.

"Barkie," Juicy replied, his voice heavy and his words

slurring. "That was our route. Two trees, three trees, and the big wiener." His brow furrowed. "Where's... Where's Barkie?" He scowled and suddenly snapped, "Where the *fuck* is Barkie? Where's my motherfucking dog? I will fucking *gut* you from neck to nuts!"

"He's, uh..." Trev jumped up and looked around the room. He'd never heard Juicy raise his voice, much less curse. He grabbed a pillow from the chair to carry over, dropping it down by Juicy's side. "Here. Hey! Hey, hey, he's right here."

Juicy's eyes opened briefly and he stared at Trev without really seeming to see him. He reached down to pat the pillow, instantly relaxing. He smiled and his eyes fluttered shut. "There. There he is. Such a good boy."

Trev watched as Juicy drifted back off. He scoffed, laughing a little in disbelief. "What the actual fuck?"

"Everything okay?" Jupiter asked hesitantly.

Trev looked to the door, his heart skipping a beat when he saw Jupiter standing there holding two plates of food. "Hey! Yeah. Uh." He crossed his arms. "Did Boss Cold let you off your leash to come up here?"

Jupiter nodded at the door. "I still have my escort, if that's what you mean."

Trev didn't see anyone, but he figured it was Mickey. "All done with your ass kissing then?"

"Ass kissing?" Jupiter scoffed, sitting down beside Trev and shoving one of the plates at him. "You mean trying to be polite and show respect—"

"Ass *kissing*."

Jupiter growled. "Fine! What if I was, huh? I don't exactly have a lot of options to play here."

"How much do you know about the hit on Friday?"

"Enough." Jupiter quirked his brows. "Why?"

"Tell me everything you know right now." Trev picked at the beef welly whatever it was. "I'm still going to try and figure out a way to get us out of here. Juicy too."

"You know I can hear you, right?" Mickey called out.

"No one asked you, Uncle Fester!" Trev snapped. He looked to Jupiter. "So. Please. Tell me. Maybe it won't matter, but I can't just sit here, okay? I can only play nice for so long before I just..."

"You need to be in control," Jupiter soothed. "Even when that control is an illusion, you need to know you have some kind of influence over the outcome."

"Illusion, my ass! I am in control. The only damn reason I'm still stuck here is because of you." Trev stabbed at his food. He gasped when Jupiter seized his chin, forcing him to meet his eyes.

Jupiter smiled and kissed him.

Trev briefly considered stabbing Jupiter with the fork, but instead he kissed him back.

"I appreciate you staying for me," Jupiter said quietly. "I know you could run and never look back, and yet you're willing to wait for me."

"Well, yeah." Trev knew he was blushing, and his heart fluttered as the blush spread down his neck. "You did sort of betray your gangster family and come for me."

"That I did." Jupiter smiled.

"And you're starting to finally get really good at sex. That's a solid investment of my time. I don't wanna have to train anyone else."

"Oh, of course." Jupiter grinned, kissing Trev's cheek. "I promise you, we'll get through this."

"And go to the beach."

"The beach? Is that where we're going now? Which one?"

"I don't care. As long as there's sunshine and fucking sand." Trev kissed Jupiter, letting the plate slide out of his lap as he dug his fingers into his long hair.

Jupiter eagerly pulled Trev closer as they kissed and moved his hand over Trev's thigh, slipping underneath his dress.

"Are you guys gonna fuck?" Mickey asked, peeking his head in. "Because you know your little friend is sleeping right there. And that's just weird."

Trev sighed. "So. To be continued?"

Jupiter nodded. "To be continued."

CHAPTER
Seventeen

THE DAYS LEADING up to Friday were miserably dull and unproductive.

Jupiter remained either chained or escorted around the house at all times. While it did make for some fun sex, Trev resented it. It was clearly a show of Cold's power over them, a leash to trap them both even if the chains were only on Jupiter because Cold knew Trev would not leave without him.

Having feelings for someone while also wanting desperately to escape was very inconvenient.

Juicy was back to his usual self thanks to Queen's nurses stopping by throughout the day to give him his meds. Despite having said he boarded Barkie, Barkie was now inexplicably with him and needed to go out for his walks. Juicy took him out around the mansion, often barking at the other patrolling dogs as he dragged the sash from a bathrobe behind him.

He didn't have any interest in returning to Perry City, insisting that he had work to do here. Queen said he needed more time to fully recover before travel anywhere would be an option, and Trev had no choice but to trust her judgment.

He knew there was a chance she was feeding him whatever information Cold wanted her to, but he didn't want to risk it. Juicy's outburst the other day had shocked him, and his concern for his friend was yet another intangible chain holding him here.

Yeah, those pesky feelings were really fucking inconvenient.

Trev divided his time between being with Jupiter and getting to know Rowena and Jimmy better. Brick went back home to North Carolina and Jules was set to follow him next week, no doubt waiting for whatever the hell was going to happen on Friday. Brick didn't seem concerned, but he'd been dating a gangster a lot longer than Trev.

Maybe this kind of crap was normal.

It was Thursday now and Trev had chewed his nails down to nubs, watched *Mean Girls* at least six more times, and hadn't been able to sleep.

Cold had ignored him all week.

Which was fine at first, but it soon became maddening as time ticked down to the meeting. All Trev had been able to deduce was that Cold would be meeting the mayor for lunch at some hoity-toity restaurant in downtown Strassen.

Jupiter's knowledge of the hit was that the assassin would be waiting for Cold inside the restaurant, posing as a member of the waitstaff. They could make their move at any time, which left a huge window for Cold to be attacked.

Trev thought the whole thing was stupid.

Stupid and *dangerous*, and he had no idea why Cold was still going.

Jimmy was also weirdly calm about the whole thing, which made Trev think Jimmy must know something about it. Trev had tried a few times to get Jimmy to open up and share some more information, but Jimmy always skillfully shut him down with a sweet smile and a clever remark that totally changed the subject.

Fucker was pretty good at this mob husband thing.

Trev thought of himself more as a mob fuck buddy because he didn't yet want to put a label on whatever he and Jupiter had together. Yes, the sex was great, but he was very aware that it was much more than that. The unspoken affection hung between them constantly, neither daring to speak of it. Trev's plan was to simply ignore it until they were standing somewhere with sand between their toes.

Maybe then, it would feel real.

Trev looked up when there was a knock at the door.

He'd been hanging out in Jupiter's room, enjoying a light cuddle after a vigorous lunchtime tryst, and neither of them had bothered to put on their clothes.

Jupiter was chained, though Mickey had been kind enough to give him more slack so he had a wider range to move around the bed. He grabbed the blankets to cover himself and made a face, muttering, "I wonder who that could be."

"I dunno." Trev shrugged, not bothering to move. He called out, "Come in!"

There was a pause and Cold asked, "Are you decent?"

"No."

Cold sighed.

Trev snorted and slipped under the covers. "Everything is tucked away now!"

Cold opened the door a small crack, as if checking to make sure Trev was telling the truth. He scowled as he walked in, saying dryly, "If you're available, I'd like to speak with you." His eyes flicked over Jupiter. "Alone."

"Right now?" Trev frowned.

"Yes."

"Yeah, sure. Just give me a second to get dressed."

"I'll be waiting." Cold left just as quickly as he came, shutting the door behind him.

"Huh." Trev slipped out of bed to find his clothes, his DTF shorts and a lavender hoodie crop top Rowena had given him. "Yeah, not fucking weird at all."

"What the fuck is that about?" Jupiter frowned.

"No idea." Trev pulled the hoodie over his head. "I let him borrow those photos yesterday, so maybe he's returning them?"

"Why not just give them to you?"

"No clue." Trev leaned over to give Jupiter a kiss. "I guess I'll find out."

"Be careful." Jupiter frowned. "Don't do anything stupid, okay?"

"Me?" Trev gasped dramatically. "As if." He smirked as he strolled to the door. "You just wait right there for me, all right? Don't go anywhere."

"Ha, very funny."

"Be right back."

"I'll be here, baby doll."

Trev left the room and closed the door, jumping when Mickey was suddenly right beside him. "God, you creepy fucker."

Mickey smiled. "Boss Cold's room is over there." He nodded his head. "Big double doors. Can't miss it."

"Oh. Okay." Trev blinked but headed that way.

In all of his time here, he'd yet to set foot inside Cold's personal rooms. He'd caught a glimpse once or twice saying good night to Jimmy, but this was going to be a first. He wasn't sure what to expect as he opened the doors.

First was a large foyer with a chic sitting area that didn't look much different than the rest of the house.

Beyond that was a den, but it was a complete departure from the modern and luxurious decor. The ratty furniture ranged from a weird shade of orange to a murky brown, and part of the couch was actually being held together with duct tape. A big record player sat in the corner with a ton of vinyl and the walls were covered in personal photographs and posters, including one that was definitely of Suzanne because it looked like the one Trev had back at his apartment.

Cold was sitting on the couch, staring at the cluster of photographs on the wall beneath the poster. There were nine arranged in a circle around a tenth in the middle. There was also a manila envelope on the table.

Trev walked over to the pictures and he smiled when he saw they were the photographs of his mother and Cold's. There was one in the middle that was only of Cold's mother, an old Polaroid. "They turned out great. Look good in here."

"Thank you." Cold tapped the envelope. "These are your originals. What's your price for ten photographs, hmm?"

"Can I take my prisoner and my crazy friend and leave?" Trev asked.

"No."

"Well, then." Trev clapped his hands. "Sorry, but that's my final offer."

"What if I told you that you'll all be free by Saturday evening?"

"What?" Trev narrowed his eyes, stepping toward the couch. "What's the catch?"

"No catch." Cold shrugged. "Oh." He smirked. "Except you will be attending the lunch with me."

"Exsqueeze me?"

"You will be attending the lunch with me."

"The one where someone is coming to kill you?"

"That would be the one."

Trev's mind spun. "What about Jupiter?"

Cold stared blankly.

Trev threw up his hands. "Hello! What about *Jupiter*? What are you doing with him?"

"He'll be safe," Cold replied calmly.

"I'm not going anywhere with you unless you tell me what you're up to. Specifically with my prisoner."

"The prisoner whose bed you've stayed in every night since you've been here?"

"Yeah. To make sure you don't kill him."

Cold smirked. "I think we both know that one, he'd already be dead if I wanted him to be, and two, he is more than a prisoner to you. You can't claim to be using him as leverage because I'm already giving you everything you could possibly want. Ah, except for *him*, of course."

"I really hate you."

"Noted."

"You swear he'll be safe?" Trev scoffed at his own question, muttering, "Like I can even trust you."

"Perhaps this will help." Cold tapped the folder.

"What?" Trev picked it up and was surprised to find it was heavier than it should be if it only contained photographs. He sat at the far end of the couch away from Cold, opening it to first retrieve his photos.

He flipped through them to make sure they were all accounted for and then pulled an old yellowed folder stamped *FBI* full of typewritten pages.

A quick skim of the documents revealed a very familiar name.

His mother's.

"What is this?" Trev demanded.

"Charlie came through with some valuable information," Cold said. "I know why she wanted to go into witness protection."

Trev flipped through the pages, but it was a bunch of legal gibberish. "Why?"

"She witnessed Federico Luchesi kill three men here in Strassen Springs. She went to the police and the detective assigned to the case was on the family's payroll. The Luchesi family had no real love for Feddy, and they did everything they could to make sure your mother would take the stand and put him away."

"Why not just kill him?"

"A promise made to Rafaello Luchesi, the Don at the time. Federico was his favorite cousin and the other members of the family couldn't allow him to know they had any involvement in his incarceration. So, they helped your mother apply for witness protection to make sure she testified."

"Okay." Trev frowned. "So, what the fuck happened?"

"I did." Cold smirked slyly. "The Don was murdered, the family fell out of power, and their influence followed once I took over the city. The case was dropped. Your mother had already moved to Perry City by then, no doubt because the family wanted to keep an eye on her."

"Some fucking witness protection. They literally had her move into their territory."

"At the time, it was truly for her benefit. Federico could have been a viable contender to lead the family after Rafaello's death, and most of his support was in Strassen. Moving her to one of their other strongholds was meant to protect her."

"And no one bothered coming after her or me after the case was dropped? Why risk a loose end like that?"

"An excellent question. You see, most of the senior family members who knew about it died." Cold's smile indicated he was somehow responsible or at least very happy about it. "Enough time passed that no one else cared anymore. Federico was eventually arrested for another crime and then killed in prison. I imagine the only reason it's coming up now is because former special agent Champignon is very eager to punish me."

"What did you do to him? Run over his dog?"

"He failed to convict me some time ago and took it very personally," Cold replied. "In addition to fueling the Luchesi family's meager drug operation, he has likely been searching for anything else at the bureau that he could use against me."

"He finds these files, reads about my mom..." Trev flinched. "Reads about *me*."

"He must have been confident that we were related to put you on the family's radar." Cold shrugged. "That or pathetically desperate."

Trev scrubbed his hands over his face. "So. My mom lied about this, about Boris, about everything, trying to keep me safe from the fucking mob whose fucking town we moved to. I don't get it. Why didn't she just leave Perry City?"

"It could be because the family was still watching her."

Trev snorted. "Yeah? Who?"

"Juicy."

Trev laughed. "What?"

"Juicy Cusack was a hitman who often worked for the Luchesi family," Cold said slowly. "Do you think it was a coincidence he moved in right next door to you?"

"*What*?" Trev laughed again. "You're kidding me, right?"

"You have him in your photographs." Cold nodded at the stack. "I'm surprised you never noticed."

"No way." Trev grabbed the photographs, frantically flipping through them.

The old man at the park...

Trev squinted.

It was hard to be sure, but the man was certainly about the right height and build to be Juicy.

"I don't understand." Trev shook his head. "You're saying Juicy's been following me and my mom for literal decades? Why?"

"As far as I can tell, it was to keep an eye on your mother."

"Why? In case they wanted to kill her?"

"Juicy was loyal to the Don, so it's hard to say. But he knew he had a mission, to watch her, and so he did. Even with his deteriorating mental status, he knew to carry out his mission. Once your mother passed, you remained his only objective."

Trev shivered.

That was either really nice or really creepy.

Maybe both.

"How the fuck do you know this?" Trev demanded. "How did you figure it out?"

"His nurse." Cold raised his brow. "She also works for the Luchesi family, taking care of Ugo Luchesi."

"The... Oh. Holy *shit*." Trev stared. "That's why she looked familiar. I saw her at the Luchesi's place. She's Juicy's nurse too?"

"Yes." Cold nodded. "I've always made it a habit to befriend those at the so-called lowest rung of the ladder. Being able to keep tabs on your enemies is a wise investment, no matter how long it takes to pay off. She kept me abreast of everything going on with the Luchesi family, and I thought it was very interesting that one of her other patients just so happened to be a former hitman."

Trev narrowed his eyes. "So, did you know about me?"

"I did."

"What the *fuck*?"

"I didn't know about our possible relation until the Luchesis dangled you in front of my face. Yes, I knew my mother had a close friend who had a son and had left the city. I knew she was involved with the Luchesis and yes, I knew that Juicy was watching over you. I'd thought it was because of the Luchesi family, which it was."

"Did you know that we were brothers?"

"No. The thought had crossed my mind, knowing our father's promiscuous behavior, but we probably have a lot of siblings out there that we don't know about. I'm not interested in chasing down every single one, thank you."

"Fair." Trev looked at the photograph with Juicy in the background again. "Juicy said he was working for you. Was that more nonsense or what?"

"No." Cold leaned back against the couch. "I called him."

"Called him?" Trev frowned. "Why?"

"To make sure Mr. Prospero got here safely."

"Huh?"

Cold looked annoyed. "Once I heard Jupiter was leaving his family, it was obvious he'd be heading here to find you. Even easier to assume that he'd be visiting your place to collect your things since you two had the not very original plan of running away together. So, I told Juicy he was working for me now and I needed him to escort Mr. Prospero here."

"You are one sneaky fuck."

"Thank you." Cold tilted his head. "I did not expect Mr.

Cusack to forget his medications and lash out as he did, but ah, I will accept responsibility for that."

"You had no way to know that Juicy would do that." Trev scowled as realization struck, and he said, "You had no way to know he would actually do any of the shit you told him to. You clearly knew about his dementia and shit. Why risk it?"

"Because I had nothing to lose," Cold replied simply.

"Right, just putting the people I care about in danger," Trev snapped. "What if the Luchesi fuckers caught up to Jupiter and Juicy? You really think Juicy could have helped fight them off? What would he do? Tell his imaginary dog to bite them?"

"As I said, I had nothing to lose."

"Wow." Trev laughed bitterly. "We're really nothing but pawns to you, huh? Just little pieces for you to move around and fuck with. And since you don't give a shit, you don't care what happens to us."

Cold raised his brow. "And?"

"So, this is why they call you Cold? Because you have so many icicles jammed up your ass?"

"Something like that."

"Fuck you." Trev shoved the photographs back into the folder with the FBI file. "Me, you, lunch tomorrow, and then we're done."

"Saturday is—"

"Saturday I already plan to be fucking gone and as far away from you as possible." Trev glared. "As soon as this stupid lunch bullshit is over, we're gone. Me, Jupiter, and Juicy."

"We'll see."

"Uh-huh. Fuck you very much. Buh-bye." Trev left, his

temper threatening to bubble over. He was so intent on stomping out, he didn't even see Jimmy coming in.

They smacked right into each other, and Jimmy grabbed Trev's shoulders to steady him. "Whoa! Hey! Sorry about that. Are you okay?"

"Fine." Trev flinched and pulled away. "Your husband is a dick."

Jimmy frowned. "What's wrong?"

Trev inhaled sharply.

Jimmy was sweet and not a fitting victim of his venom.

He patted Jimmy's arm. "Look, I'm gonna take all of everything I have going on and go over here, okay? Away from you."

"Whoa, hey now." Jimmy tried to hang on. He turned his head, shouting into the bedroom. "Rod! What the fuck did you do?"

Unsurprisingly, there was no response.

Jimmy pouted. "If you tell me, maybe I can help."

Trev scoffed as he sidestepped out of Jimmy's grasp. "All that matters is that me and mine will be free after tomorrow's little lunch date." He encountered a small drip of guilt. "Cold has made it clear where I stand, so."

Jimmy didn't try to pull Trev back. "Did he? Because sometimes he does this crap thing where he tries to show he cares, but it's, like, in this crazy backwards ass way?"

"Like?"

"Like, marrying me without telling me—"

"What?" Trev shook his head. "Oh my God, who does that? That's so fucked up!"

Jimmy grimaced. "Okay! Better example. That I cannot think of right now." He took a deep breath and gave Trev a big smile. "It may be hard to believe, but Rod does care about you."

Trev crossed his arms. "Uh-huh."

"He wouldn't have introduced us if he was going to do something terrible, okay? His mind is a weird place and I think..." Jimmy tilted his head. "I think the two of you are a lot more alike than you realize."

Trev didn't want to bore Jimmy with a beat by beat recount of what had just happened with Cold, instead saying shortly, "Hard disagree, babe."

Jimmy's big stupid eyes looked sad. "I wish I could tell you to trust me, but I know that's not fair."

"I'd sooner trust you than him."

"Okay, so trust me. Knowing I do trust him. And whatever is going to happen, I know he's thinking of what's best for all of us. And that means you too."

"Wow. That dick must be *good*." Trev quirked his brows. "Because you're sucking on that Kool-Aid hard."

Jimmy laughed a little. "I guess so. But it's because of what I've seen. What I've seen *him* do." He offered his hand. "If you wanna talk about it, I'm free tonight."

Trev took Jimmy's hand to give it a shake, but then he grunted when Jimmy pulled him in for a hug. "Yeah, no, I'm good." He pushed Jimmy away. "How often do you have to stop and spit out Cold's jizz when you talk? Like every other sentence?"

"Ew, that's gross."

"Almost as gross as this conversation." Trev scowled. "He's your man. I get it. You're gonna defend him. But don't waste your breath defending him to *me*, okay? I'm done with his ass and I'm leaving as soon as I fucking can."

"Just..." Jimmy sighed. "Please think about it?"

"Okay. Yup. Thinking." Trev hummed. "Wow! And the answer is still no." He left Jimmy standing there as he stalked back toward Jupiter's room.

"Hey! Trev!" Rowena was coming up the stairs to cut him off.

Trev groaned. "What?"

"What's wrong?" Rowena frowned. "Your face looks like a cat's ass."

"He had a fight with Rod," Jimmy replied from behind him. "He wants to leave after tomorrow."

Trev whirled around to find Jimmy had followed him, and he groaned again, more loudly than before. "Can you both just fuck off? Pretty please?

"What did Roddy do?" Rowena demanded.

"It doesn't matter." Trev forced a smile. "If you want to know so badly, you can go ask him yourself. He's sitting on his ugly couch, being a smug bitch."

"Bitch? Where?" Juicy sounded alarmed. "Barkie hasn't been snipped. Better keep her away from him." He frowned as he approached them, the bathrobe sash he was using as a leash dragging behind him. "Hey! Are we having a meeting? I'm sorry I'm late. No one told me."

"It's fine, Juicy." Trev gritted his teeth. "Everybody is just giving me shit because we're leaving tomorrow."

"Oh! We are?" Juicy frowned. "But we're going to have Chinese tomorrow. And I still haven't found the two trees I was looking for."

"We can get Chinese to go and I will help you look for all the fucking trees you want. Far, far away from here."

Just Trev, his gangster boyfriend, and an old man who used to be a hitman for the mob and was apparently stalking Trev and his mother for years.

Totally fine.

Just fucking fine.

Not that Trev was going to bring any of that up right now.

Rowena pouted. "I'm sorry, Trev. Really. I know Roddy can be a giant dickhole and he's not real good at opening up to people. It's hard for him to trust people."

"No shit," Trev quipped. "Why trust anybody when it's more fun just to screw with them and play them like pawns in his shitty little games? I bet it just leaves his shit throbbing when he gets on that kinda power trip, right? Fuck him."

"Please don't leave," Rowena pleaded. "Come on, Trev. You're family."

"Family?" Trev shook his head and laughed bitterly. "You guys have been nice, really. I appreciate everything you've done for me, but if this is how Roddy treats family? Then I want no fucking part of it."

Rowena and Jimmy both gave him sympathetic looks, like two stupid puppy dogs.

"We can keep in touch, okay?" Trev sighed. "I'll get your numbers before I go. And..." Shit, his phone was still inside a locker at the Cannery. "I will *get* a phone. To put those numbers in."

"Do you even know where you're going?" Rowena asked.

"Heading south and never looking back."

"Oh, Florida is nice," Juicy chimed in. "At least, I think it is." He frowned. "Can Barkie come? I'm not sure how well he'll do on a road trip. We'll have to make stops for him to use the bathroom, you know."

"I'm sure Barkie will do just fine," Trev soothed. "Come on. I'll walk you back to your room."

"There's really nothing else we can do?" Jimmy looked as if he was resisting the urge to tackle Trev with another hug.

"Nope." Trev offered his arm to Juicy so he could lead him down the hall. "We're good, thanks."

"I'm going to go talk to Rod right now," Jimmy said firmly, stomping off with a growl.

"Me fucking too," said Rowena, no doubt stomping off right behind him.

Trev appreciated the thought, but he doubted that Cold was going to be swayed by his sister and husband bitching at him.

Juicy patted Trev's shoulder. "Hey, are you all right?"

"I'm okay." Trev managed a smile. "Just ready to get out of here. How about you?"

"I don't mind so much. It's pretty nice here. Barkie has so much room to play, he's made a bunch of new friends." Juicy hummed thoughtfully. "I'm almost positive there's no bodies buried out there."

"That's nice." Trev opened Juicy's door so Juicy could walk in first. "You know, speaking of bodies, I did want to talk to you about something." He tapped the folder against his chest, watching Juicy as he waddled over to the bed.

Juicy seemed so frail.

It was hard to believe he'd ever been an assassin.

"Cold told me some stuff." Trev reached into the folder to pull out the pictures. "Some really crazy stuff. About you being a hitman for the Luchesi family? And, uh, a bunch of crap about you watching me and my mother?"

Juicy frowned and then he nodded, smiling warmly. "Oh! Of course. You were my mission."

"Mission?"

"To protect you. That's what Ugo wanted."

"Wait, you know Ugo? Ugo Luchesi?"

Juicy smiled again and the cloudiness that usually fogged his gaze cleared. "Of course, I do. He called me to take care of Federico's little problem. Oh, what a mess that was."

Trev stiffened. "What little problem?"

"The bodies."

"The bodies that were never found? Those bodies?"

"It's only natural they never found them! I'm the one who hid them. Drove them straight across to... Hmm." Juicy beamed, but then his smile drooped. "Oh."

"What?"

"I just remembered."

"Remembered what?"

"That I forgot where I put them." Juicy sighed, and his eyes glazed over again. "Can we still go to Florida? Barkie would love to play in the sand."

"Yeah, don't worry. We'll definitely end up somewhere with sand." Trev looked over the photograph of the park. "And hey, don't worry about those bodies." He smirked. "I got a pretty good idea of where they are."

CHAPTER *Eighteen*

TREV STAYED with Juicy until his nurse arrived to give him his meds for the afternoon. He'd tried to get Juicy to open up a bit more about his time as a hitman to confirm his theory, but Juicy only wanted to talk about Barkie. Whatever earlier clarity he had possessed was gone.

But that was all right.

Trev was still very sure he knew where those three bodies were.

Once Juicy was doped up and settled down for a nap, Trev left to go find Jupiter.

Mickey was just walking out of the guest room with Jupiter's chains in his hand.

"Hey." Trev scowled. "What's going on?"

Mickey raised his brow.

"Where's Jupiter?" Trev raised the folder as if he was about to smack Mickey with it.

Mickey did not look impressed.

"Hey, fuck you. Maybe I'll get lucky and you'll get a *really* nasty paper cut."

"Trev!" Jupiter popped up at the door behind Mickey. His chains were gone. "I'm okay."

Trev pushed by Mickey so he could hug Jupiter tight. He slid his hands over Jupiter's neck, rubbing over the marks left from the chains. "What's going on?"

"No idea." Jupiter shrugged. "Mr. Tamerlane isn't exactly chatty."

"I can always put them back on if you'd like," Mickey said with a sweet smile.

"Nope. We're good. Bye bye now." Trev grabbed Jupiter's arm and dragged him inside the room so he could shut the door.

"What did Cold want?"

"Other than to solidify my opinion of him as being an absolute fucking asshole of epic proportions? A lot." Trev ushered Jupiter over to the bed. "Did you know that Juicy Cusack was a hitman for your fucking family?"

"What?" Jupiter scoffed. "Are you serious?"

"Yup. And he's apparently been stalking me and my mom for years 'cause your uncle or somebody told him to." Trev fished out the photograph with Juicy in the background. "Look. That's him."

"Okay, back up, baby doll." Jupiter pinched his brow. "Why would the Luchesi family have a hitman watching you?"

"Because my mom saw Federico Luchesi kill a bunch of people. That's why she was in witness protection. The cops were, like, on the family's payroll and they wanted her to take the stand and put Feddy behind bars or whatever."

"Why wouldn't they just kill him?"

"I asked the same fucking thing. It was because of some promise made to the Don, blah blah blah. Something, something, Cold went on his murder rampage and everybody who knew what was happening was killed. My mom had already moved us to Perry City 'cause your family was gonna, like, keep an eye on her."

"Juicy?"

"That's what Cold said, yeah."

"I've heard about Federico." Jupiter made a face. "The family made arrangements for him to, ahem, have an accident in prison."

"Wow, your family sucks."

"Never denied that."

"Well, listen. Cold is saying all of this bullshit is because of a former FBI douche named Champagne or something. That he was the one who told you guys about me after he read this file and put the pieces together or something."

Jupiter pressed his lips into a thin line. "*Champignon*, yes. I've heard Emil mention him. I didn't know he was an ex-fed, but that makes sense. The drugs the family is trying to move right now? Came from a federal warehouse before it could be destroyed."

"Seriously? Like what? Stuff that got seized in raids or whatever?"

"Exactly. Which is why they need a solid place for distribution. They have to break everything down and repackage it before selling it so no one can tell where it came from. A lot of dealers won't touch anything that was seized, scared that it can be tracked."

"Fascinating, but!" Trev smirked. "Wanna guess what's behind door number three?"

"What? Wait, what happened to doors number one or two?"

"Oh my God, just go with it. Listen, I think I know why everybody is so worked up over that damn park back in Perry City." Trev tapped the photo of Juicy. "Juicy always took Barkie for his walks, right? At least, when he had a real Barkie. And I kept hearing him talking about two trees, three trees, and then around the big wiener. Look."

Jupiter blinked. "What am I looking at?"

"The big wiener is obviously the hot dog statue, right? Look at the trees in the back." Trev tapped the photo. "See this big cluster? It's three trees growing together, right?"

"Okay. Still not following."

"Juicy kept an eye on me and my mom by staying close. Maybe it had to do with his mind going, that it was easier for him to have us there where he could see us." Trev took a deep breath. "He told me that he helped clean up the mess from Federico."

"The bodies," Jupiter realized. "You think his dog walking route was where he buried the bodies?"

"Makes sense, right?" Trev preened. "Juicy probably walked his dog by there all the time to make sure nobody was getting wise to the sudden addition of three corpses fresh from Strassen Springs. Got stuck on the same route and even now, he can't let it go."

"Emil and Sal must suspect they're there," Jupiter said. "I don't know how, but they must. Why else would they care so much about the park?"

"See, that's what I was thinking too." Trev paused. "Cold's definitely suspicious. He was asking about it, so he has to know something is up with the park too. Maybe not that it's potentially full of bodies, but whatever." He paused again. "Okay, which... Why would anyone care about them?"

Jupiter sat down on the edge of the bed. "What do you mean?"

"Federico is already dead, so it's not like the family is worried about him getting arrested for murder. And it sounds like everybody hated his guts or whatever. So."

Trev stared at the photograph as if it would spill more secrets. "Why do they care about the bodies being found now?"

"And how does it tie in with tomorrow's lunch meeting?" Jupiter mused. "If at all."

"Has Cold said anything to you about it?"

"No. You?"

"Yeah, that was the other item on his *I'm a giant asshole* agenda." Trev shoved the photograph back into the folder. "He wants me to come with him on his little lunch date. After that, we can go."

"Wait, wait. He wants you to go with him? To the place he's supposed to be *murdered*?"

"Yeah, but he's going, so—"

Jupiter scowled. "No."

"What?" Trev was so startled that he actually laughed. He scratched at his ear. "I must be hearing things because it sounded like you just tried to tell me no."

"You heard me. No fuckin' way, baby doll."

"Uh, yes way." Trev raised his brow. "If I do it, he's going to let us go. We can finally get the fuck out of here."

"It's way too dangerous," Jupiter argued. "I won't allow it."

Trev laughed again, his temper bubbling up slowly. "Wow, you're *adorable*. Yes, it's kind of hot when you get bossy while we're fucking, but right now? Not so fucking much."

"This is way too dangerous," Jupiter insisted. "Emil and Sal are going to kill Boss Cold tomorrow if he shows up to the restaurant. You understand that, right? Cold is smart, but he's not bulletproof."

"As gross as it sounds to even say out loud, I have to trust that he knows what the fuck he's doing," Trev bit back. "He wouldn't risk his own life. That much is fucking clear. So! It's either this or leave you behind."

"I'm unchained. We could go right now."

"Uh-huh. And the assassin waiting for you outside the door? What about him?"

Jupiter sighed haggardly. "We'll think of something."

"Here." Trev tossed the folder at Jupiter. "Hit him with this. I'm sure that'll work. Good luck."

Jupiter caught it. "I'm serious, Trev. This isn't a game. Before you agreed to anything with Cold, you should have talked to me first."

"Is that so?" Trev planted his hands on hips, batting his lashes as he fought to keep his anger from boiling right over. "Last time I checked, I don't need your fucking permission to do a motherfucking thing. You don't fucking own me, Jupiter. You don't get to tell me what to do. You're not my fucking boyfriend. You're not my fucking anything, you fucking—"

"Then why do you still wear that collar?"

"For the fucking *aesthetic*."

Jupiter set the folder aside as he stood, glaring down at Trev. "I won't allow you to put yourself at risk like this."

"Won't *allow* me?" Trev laughed right in his face. "Fuck you."

Jupiter grabbed the ring of the collar. "I said *no*."

Trev pushed Jupiter's hand away. "If only that meant something to me! What a shame!"

"Trev, I can't let you do this." Jupiter growled.

"Let me? You can't *let* me do this?" Trev growled right back. "You have some serious fucking misconceptions about who I am as a person if you think I would ever *let* anyone control me—"

"Goddammit! This isn't about control!" Jupiter reached

for Trev's shoulders. "This is about you risking your fucking life! It's not worth it, baby doll. Not for this. Not for me."

"Who said I'm doing it for *you*?" Trev shot back furiously. "I don't know what the fuck Cold is planning except that he doesn't give two shits about me, you, or anyone else except for how he can use us. This is the only play I have to get the fuck out of here and to a nice fancy fucking beach, okay? I'm doing this for *me*. I want a fucking happy ending, you arrogant piece of shit, and that means having you with me, okay?"

Jupiter blinked slowly and his mouth opened, but no words came out.

Trev wanted to strangle him.

But also kiss him.

Okay, but he also really wanted to *strangle* him.

Fuck it.

Trev grabbed Jupiter's face and dragged him into a fierce kiss.

There was no future without Jupiter. He knew that now, even though recognizing that terrified him. He was willing to play Cold's games, to do whatever it took to keep this man by his side.

"You *are* worth it," Trev said with a gasp, dragging his fingers through Jupiter's hair.

"But—"

"Shut the fuck up." Trev clamped his hand over Jupiter's mouth. "The risk, the fucking whatever, all of it. You're worth it. To me."

Jupiter hugged Trev's waist tight and he smiled. "And here I thought you were smart."

"I am fucking smart." Trev scowled, but he relaxed as Jupiter toyed with the collar at his neck. "Smarter than you and your stupid family, Cold and his bullshit, and I…" He sagged in Jupiter's embrace.

"What is it, baby doll?"

"There's just something about you that makes me stupid." Trev cradled his cheek. "But still not stupid enough to let you tell me what to do. So." He took a deep breath. "I'm going to do this, okay? Just… shut up and let me do it."

Jupiter's expression softened, and he pressed their foreheads together. "I'm sorry. I know you're a badass motherfucker, but last time I checked? You're not bulletproof either."

"I'll be fine." Trev kissed him. "Now just… shut up and take your clothes off."

Jupiter laughed. "Haven't had enough of me today, huh?"

"I'm pissed off and I want to ride your dick."

"I do believe that is something I can help you with." Jupiter playfully pinned Trev down to the bed.

"I think I liked this better when you were chained up." Trev squirmed beneath Jupiter, leaning in to bite his neck.

"Oh, is that so?" Jupiter chuckled.

"Yeah." Trev grinned. "It was kinda nice being in charge."

"You think you were in charge, huh?" Jupiter's eyes flicked over Trev's body. "Really?"

"I know I was," Trev argued, even as his breathing picked up.

"So, if I tell you to take off your clothes right now?" Jupiter's voice dropped to a low purr. "And get yourself ready for me? What will you do?"

Trev inhaled sharply, a bolt of arousal making his entire body clench. "I will do it, but only because I want to fuck you."

"Right. Because you want to be a good boy and ride my dick, yeah?"

"Yeah. Because I'm fucking horny."

"Because you're fucking horny, *sir*."

"Yeah, yeah, whatever, *sir*. Just give me that dick."

"Well, go on then." Jupiter leaned back, dragging his hands down Trev's chest to his stomach. "Show me how much you want it."

Trev undressed at lightning speed, flinging his clothes off in all directions. He yelped when Jupiter dragged him down into the middle of the bed. "Hey!"

"Roll over, baby doll," Jupiter commanded. "Let me see that perfect ass."

Trev shifted to his hands and knees, arching his back and sticking his ass out. He smiled as Jupiter's hands slid over the curves of his body. "Like what you see, hmm?"

"I sure do." Jupiter palmed Trev's ass cheeks and squeezed. "Now go on. Aren't you supposed to be getting yourself ready for me?"

Trev reached over to grab the lube. "Mm, shouldn't take much."

"I'll be the judge of that, baby doll."

Trev slicked up his fingers, his pulse already throbbing in the head of his dick. As much as he argued against it, he really did enjoy Jupiter taking charge. He loved the push and pull of it, the thrill of the struggle, and the sweet reward of his eventual submission.

It was hotter than it had any right to be, and trusting his pleasure to another person was both terrifying and exhilarating. He'd never relied on anyone else for a damn thing, but...

He wanted to.

He wanted Jupiter to be that person for him, someone

who was going to be there for him and lift him up so he could take on the whole world. As long as Trev had Jupiter at his side, he felt like he could do anything.

And that...

That was special.

Trev slipped a finger inside his hole, sighing softly as he thrust in deep. This was just a tease of what he knew was coming, and he groaned as he pressed in a second finger, greedily fucking himself open.

"Look at you," Jupiter murmured. "Always so fucking greedy for it, aren't you?"

"Yeah?" Trev breathed out slowly. "So what if I am?"

"You like what I do to you? Hmm?" Jupiter spread Trev's ass cheeks wide. "Making you get your little hole ready for me?"

Trev closed his eyes. "Mmm, yeah. I like knowin' that you're watching. That you can't take your, *mmm*, your eyes off me."

"You're so fucking sexy." Jupiter's thumb teased around Trev's asshole.

Trev whined and gasped as Jupiter pushed the tip of his thumb inside. The stretch felt good, and he arched up to urge Jupiter to probe deeper. "Damn right I am."

Jupiter obliged by pushing his thumb farther in and twisting it. He reached between Trev's legs with his other hand to squeeze his balls firmly. "I bet you're already dripping, aren't you?"

Trev thrust his fingers faster. "Maybe."

Jupiter rubbed Trev's balls. "You want me to fuck you now?"

"Yes, *please*."

"Mmm, not yet." Jupiter chuckled, sliding his fingers along the shaft of Trev's cock as he gave another twist of his thumb. "I don't think you're ready yet. Besides, you do look so beautiful like this."

"I look even more beautiful taking your dick," Trev griped.

"Then tell me."

"What?"

"Tell me how much you want it."

Trev gritted his teeth and pushed his fingers in as far as they could go, drawing out a soft gasp. "Please, come on. This isn't enough. My fucking fingers just aren't enough. I want your dick."

Jupiter hummed as if in deep thought. "No."

"Jupiter!" Trev whined, rolling his hips back. "Please. I'm so fucking empty. You know how good I fucking feel. You know I can take whatever you fucking give me. Please fuck me. Right fucking now!"

Jupiter pulled out his thumb and stopped teasing Trev's dick.

"Finally!" Trev sighed in relief.

"Roll over on your back."

"But I wanted to—"

"Roll over on your back," Jupiter repeated sternly.

Trev obeyed with a growl, his hard cock bouncing as he got into position.

Jupiter looked over him with a hungry swipe of his tongue over his top lip. "You really are beautiful. There is certainly no denying that." He traced a finger around the base of Trev's cock. "Even when you're being a brat."

"I am behaving, thank you." Trev spread his legs wide, easily folding himself in half to offer Jupiter a tantalizing view of his ass. He continued to flex until he could tease his tongue over the head of his cock, locking his eyes with Jupiter.

Jupiter growled and pressed closer, grabbing Trev's cock to feed into his mouth. "Go on. Suck."

Trev wrapped his lips around his own dick, sucking gently. He moaned as Jupiter thrust a finger inside of his wet hole, fucking him firmly and forcing his cock to rock deeper into his mouth.

"You are such a talented boy, aren't you?" Jupiter smiled. "You love this, huh? Sucking yourself? Knowing how much it turns me on?"

Trev replied by tilting his hips to push more of his cock inside his mouth and sucking noisily. He groaned when Jupiter continued to finger his hole with rough slams, each one driving his cock closer to the back of his own throat. His toes curled, his muscles tensed, and it would be so easy to come right now.

Jupiter turned his hand, adding a second finger and curling them upward to stroke over Trev's prostate.

"Mmph!" Trev's eyes teared up and he writhed, squeezing down on Jupiter's fingers in hopes of urging him to keep going. The pressure was perfect, the suction hot, and there was always a thrilling element to showing off this particular talent with such a captivated audience. He loved how Jupiter couldn't look away, and he groaned, muffled as it was, to show Jupiter how much he was enjoying himself.

"My sweet little slut," Jupiter taunted, his fingers slowly massaging over that sweet spot. "Just not happy unless you got a dick in you, huh? Even if it's your own?"

Trev moaned louder and bobbed his head, sucking his cock desperately.

"God, look at that." Jupiter pushed his fingers in deep, holding there as he watched Trev intently. "You're getting close, aren't you? You wanna come for me, baby doll? Swallow your come down?"

Trev swirled his tongue around his shaft and moaned frantically.

"Almost there, baby doll? Mmm?" Jupiter curled his fingers again.

"Mmmph!" Trev made a pleading sound, the tension in his loins ready to implode. He ached with the need for release, eager to get himself off, so they could—

"Not yet." Jupiter grabbed Trev's thigh and pulled, yanking his cock out of his mouth.

"Jupiter! The fuck?" Trev growled in frustration.

"I said, not yet." Jupiter gently withdrew his fingers so he could stretch both of Trev's legs out around him. "You wanna be good, don't you?"

"I want to fucking come." Trev got a hold of his cock. "I was right fucking there."

"If you want to, go right ahead." Jupiter smirked, rubbing Trev's thighs. "But then I'm not going to fuck you."

"What?" Trev spat, though his hand stilled.

"You heard me, baby doll." Jupiter bowed his head to kiss Trev's brow. "Be a good boy and wait... and then I'll give you what you want."

Trev wanted to kick him out of bed, and he growled low. "You're serious?"

"Very." Jupiter sat back and removed his clothing. "You're going to wait because you love this. You love doing what I tell you to do and giving up that precious control to me."

"I like your dick," Trev flatly replied.

"And the only way you're getting it is if you do what I tell you to."

"Fucking fine." Trev let go of his cock with a dramatic roll of his eyes, even as his lust threatened to boil right over. "How do you want me, hmm? Because I seem to remember wanting to ride you and now you're playing stupid fucking games."

"You love this."

"My balls sure as fuck don't."

Jupiter chuckled, sliding off the last of his clothing. "Trust me. They will." He picked up the lube to slick up his cock. "We're going to take our time, baby doll. Don't worry. I'll still give you a chance to get on top. But only when I'm ready for you to."

"How about now? Is now good for you?" Trev tucked his arms behind his head. "Because now is really, really good for me."

Jupiter grinned as he pushed between Trev's thighs. "Not yet."

Trev wrapped his legs around Jupiter to draw him in close. He shivered when Jupiter's cock brushed against his hole, and he tried angling his hips to bring him inside. "Jupiter... please."

"You ask so nicely." Jupiter pressed forward, the head of his cock pushing in. "Mmm, there."

Trev sighed, relaxing as Jupiter thrust and filled him in one smooth motion. "There we go. That's what the fuck I'm talking about." He grabbed Jupiter's shoulders and kissed him firmly, squeezing his legs tight.

Jupiter kissed him passionately, fucking him with slow, deep slams.

Trev moaned and dug his nails into Jupiter's back, savoring his dick inside of him. He loved the heat, the weight of being so full, and he crossed his ankles to keep Jupiter at this perfect angle.

Jupiter held him close, fucking into Trev a little harder but maintaining the steady pace. He drove forward, again and again, pounding Trev against the sheets.

Trev took it all with eager grunts and moans, and he wrapped himself around Jupiter as closely as he could. Their lips touched in teasing, quick kisses, and he dragged his nails down Jupiter's spine to grab a firm handful of his ass, trying to encourage him to give him more.

Jupiter's initial response was to slow to a cruel crawl, and he chuckled breathlessly in Trev's ear. "What is it, baby doll?"

"More," Trev said quietly. "Please... Give me more."

"More, huh?" Jupiter trailed a line of kisses down Trev's jaw.

"Please!" Trev bucked his hips down. "Fuck, come on."

Jupiter slipped his arms beneath Trev to lift him. "Come here, baby doll. Like this."

Trev groaned as Jupiter sat up and brought Trev into his lap. He hugged Jupiter's neck as he adjusted to the new position. He slammed his ass down and groaned happily. "Fuck yeah, this is what I'm talking about."

"Go on," Jupiter urged. "Ride this cock."

Trev didn't need to be told twice. Using his hold on Jupiter's neck for extra leverage, he rolled his hips down and fucked himself greedily on Jupiter's dick. He slammed hard and fast, letting the heat build between them until it was ready to boil right over.

Jupiter latched on to Trev's sides, thrusting up into him as he dragged him down to meet each slam. "There you go. There's my good boy. My good fuckin' boy."

Trev moaned excitedly and went faster, chasing the sweet friction as Jupiter's praise fueled his desire. The smack of their skin was loud, their panting breaths hoarse, and Trev gave Jupiter everything he had as they drove each other toward their end.

Yes.

Fuck, yes, this was perfect and wonderful and Trev groaned when Jupiter grabbed his cock. He arched his body back, bracing himself now on his hands so he could grind his ass down for each delicious slam. "Come on... Come on, baby. Make me fuckin' come."

Jupiter kept a firm hold on Trev's cock, thrusting up frantically as he jerked Trev off. "Get it, baby doll. Fuckin' come on my dick. Come on. Get it."

"There, there! I'm fucking coming!" Trev cried out. "F-fuck! I'm coming!" His entire body jerked, every muscle locking up tight before melting into sweet bliss as his climax took over. His cock pulsed across his stomach, and he closed his eyes, sinking into the incredible waves washing over him.

It was hot, shivery, and he went still, grateful for Jupiter's strong arms to keep him upright.

Jupiter hugged him tight, urging Trev to collapse against his chest with his cock still buried deep inside of him. He panted at Trev's neck, and he fanned his hands across Trev's back. "Mm, baby doll."

Trev had been so caught up in his orgasm that he'd barely noticed Jupiter's. He could feel the extra slick slide when Jupiter shifted inside of him, and he moaned softly. "Damn."

"Good?"

"So fucking good." Trev smiled warmly. He groaned in satisfaction and buried his head against Jupiter's shoulder. "Mm, I almost forgot why I was mad at you."

Jupiter chuckled. "Damn. I guess I'll just have to try harder next time." He kissed Trev's hair. "You good, baby doll? Not too much?"

"No, I'm fine. Just snuggle me and be quiet."

Jupiter laughed, shifting them onto their sides so they

could still hold each other even as Jupiter's cock slipped out. Their limbs tangled together as they sought to stay close, and Trev could have easily fallen asleep.

He was warm and sated, and in Jupiter's arms was one of his favorite places to be.

Jupiter cleared his throat. "You know..."

"What?" Trev murmured.

"Even if we really can leave tomorrow, my family will still come after me." Jupiter pulled Trev a little closer. "They have a hit out on me."

Trev touched Jupiter's cheek, scratching at his beard. "That's why we're getting as far away as possible. Me, you, sandy beaches."

"And Juicy?"

Trev chuckled. "Yeah, Juicy too. Which means Barkie."

"The dog? Who isn't real?"

"Just don't say that to him." Trev laughed, trying not to think about Juicy snapping at him the other day. He rubbed Jupiter's chest. "You... You guys are all I have."

"What about Jimmy? Rowena?"

"They're great, but..." Trev was quiet for a moment. "They didn't order extra Chinese food for me. They didn't let me kick them in the balls. They're not... They mean a lot to me, more than they probably should, but they're not..."

"Not what?"

"They're not family." Trev clung to Jupiter. "Didn't think I had any of that left, heh, but... maybe I do and I just didn't realize it."

Jupiter kissed his brow. "Yeah?"

"Yeah." Trev smiled softly. "Do you think Jimmy would let me kick him in the nuts?"

"Hard to say." Jupiter chuckled. "I bet Rowena would."

"She's got the biggest ones here." Trev laughed. "Jimmy

probably would? He's definitely that kinda *will give you the shirt off his back* dude. But he's gonna cry afterward. Rowena would take it and be like, *wow, that's all you got*? She's a fierce bitch."

Jupiter kissed Trev's cheek. "Maybe you have more family than you think."

Trev blushed. "Maybe."

"Try to rest? We still gotta make it through dinner tonight."

"Oh, fuckin' goody."

CHAPTER *Nineteen*

TREV DID his best to prepare himself for what he suspected would be another snooty meal at the table. He hadn't made it to the entrée all week, having opted to leave early because he could only stand Cold's company but for so long.

Tonight would not likely be any different.

In fact, it would almost certainly be worse considering how he and Cold had left things earlier.

Jupiter might have had the magical people skills to kiss ass and keep quiet for days at a time, but Trev...

Trev did not.

As calculating and patient as Trev prided himself to be, he had limits. He could not let any potential benefit of playing nice outweigh how much he'd grown to loathe Cold and this entire situation. Just thinking about it made him sick with rage, and he was close to refusing to come down for dinner entirely.

Jupiter's gentle smile won him over, but Trev warned him that he would not be staying past the appetizers. Jupiter accepted that and when it was time, they headed downstairs with Mickey trailing behind them.

"Are you all right?" Jupiter squeezed Trev's hand.

"I'm fine." Trev forced a fake smile. "Why wouldn't I be?"

"We're almost there," Jupiter soothed. "Tomorrow, right? And then we're—"

"It had *better* be fucking tomorrow or I am going to burn this place to the ground."

Mickey cleared his throat.

"Oh, eat my fucking hole, Fester." Trev groaned. "If I was actually going to set anything on fucking fire, I wouldn't be stupid enough to say it in front of you."

Jupiter squeezed Trev's hand a little tighter. "With some luck, this will probably be our last meal here, okay?"

"Last meal?" Trev hissed. "Oof, not a great choice of words."

"Right. Our final… munch? Hindmost sustenance?"

"Oh my God, stop."

"Closing noms."

Trev laughed. "Okay, that one was funny."

Jupiter smiled triumphantly.

Trev decided to let Jupiter enjoy the levity, however brief it might be, and he paused just outside the dining room to kiss him. "Just for that, I'm gonna ride your dick later."

"Insatiable little thing." Jupiter laughed. "Did you not get enough today?"

"Nope." Trev kissed him again, flinching when something soft hit his head. "The fuck?"

Rowena stood there in a blue shark onesie complete with hood and fin feet, saying, "Come on, fuckers! Go get changed!"

Trev scrambled to make sense of what Rowena had

apparently thrown at him. It was neon rainbow and very fuzzy. "What is this?"

"Your pajamas!" Jimmy poked his head out, revealing he was wearing some sort of blue monster onesie with floppy ears.

"What the hell are you?"

Jimmy pouted. "I'm Stitch."

Trev had no idea what that was, frowning as he held out the lump of fabric. "And I'm what...? A hem?"

"A motherfucking unicorn!" Rowena cheered. "Gorgeous, fabulous, and stabby."

"That sums you up pretty well, baby doll." Jupiter chuckled.

"Here." Rowena threw another blob of fabric at Jupiter. "Meow, bitch."

Jupiter blinked.

"You're a kitty!" Jimmy grinned, but then his face fell. "Sorry if you're not, like, a cat person. There weren't a lot of options in your size."

Trev waved the onesie. "And we have these because?"

"Because this might be your last night with us since somebody said you wanted to leave tomorrow." Rowena crossed her arms. "So, we decided to do something awesome."

Mickey snorted.

Rowena flipped him off. "Roddy is busy, so! He left me and Jimmy in charge of dinner. I gave Jerry the night off and we're gonna order a shit ton of Chinese food, drink margaritas, and watch *Mean Girls* the musical."

As curious as Trev was about a musical rendition of his new favorite movie, he didn't miss that Cold was *busy*.

Busy with what?

"And what is dear Roddy up to?" Trev asked casually.

"Crying in a corner because they didn't have any pajamas that would make him look like a giant turd?"

"Okay, but they actually do have pajamas that look like the poop emoji." Jimmy giggled.

"Oh my God, of course they do."

Rowena shooed Trev and Jupiter back down the hallway. "Go on! Juicy is getting changed too, so put your shit on and come back downstairs."

Trev didn't move. "Where's Cold?"

"Working," Rowena replied casually.

"This late?" Trev asked with feigned concern. "Wow, his boss must be a real dick! Oh wait, he is the boss. And he's a dick."

Jimmy huffed a little. "He's getting everything ready for tomorrow, okay?" His brow furrowed. "And before you ask, no, I don't know what he's doing. Not exactly. I just know that he said he had to take care of some stuff and left with Jules."

"And you're okay with that? With him going off to do God knows what with fucking Bigfoot?"

Jimmy smiled. "Yeah. I am."

"You're nuts."

"You learn to roll with a lot of stuff when you're a mafia husband." Jimmy chuckled. "I trust him."

"I don't." Trev glared at the pajamas.

Rowena squeezed Trev's shoulder. "Hey, it's not something that's gonna happen overnight. Or maybe even ever."

Trev frowned. "You're not going to try and convince me he's perfect and so very trustworthy?"

Jimmy laughed. "Oh, he's far from perfect. Trustworthy, yes. But that took time. And fighting. And then more fighting." He scratched the back of his neck. "Look, what I'm trying to say... uh..."

"What Jimmy is trying to say is that every relationship is different," Rowena cut in gently. "You and Roddy may never get along and that's okay. But I do think once all that crap tomorrow is over, it'll be a lot easier to rent some of this happy gangster family stuff. Maybe even try it on for a while." She smiled. "Or at least come back and visit us, yeah?"

"Yeah. Maybe." Trev frowned.

He honestly didn't know what to say.

Beyond running away to a tropical climate, Trev hadn't thought much about his future. It was strange to consider one with people who genuinely wanted to see him again.

Especially when it wasn't for sex.

It felt like a trick and immediately put Trev on guard, but he couldn't say why.

Jupiter wrapped his arm around Trev's waist. "Thank you, Rowena. Jimmy."

"Yeah, yeah, thanks." Trev waved the pajamas. "We'll go get changed. Be right back."

"Hurry up!" Rowena laughed. "Or we'll start the movie without you!"

"Don't you dare."

Trev managed a little smile, but he was quiet as he and Jupiter headed back upstairs. Mickey was silent as always, though he did sneer a little when Trev shut the bedroom door behind them.

"You okay?" Jupiter asked as they got undressed.

"Huh?"

"You haven't cursed in over a full minute." Jupiter smiled gently. "Either something is wrong or the power of the unicorn onesie has distracted you."

Trev snorted as he zipped up the front of the pajamas. "Can't lie. This is pretty damn comfy."

"So?"

"Just got into my head a little bit. Nothing to worry about."

Jupiter raised a brow. "Said like I have something to worry about."

"It's fine."

"Now I know something's up." Jupiter reached for Trev's hand. "We might not have known each other for that long, but I'd still like to think I know you very well."

"Congratulations on knowing how to hit my prostate in two positions."

"*Three*, and no, not that. I know when you're holding back." Jupiter clicked his tongue. "You and your beautiful brain don't like this, do you?"

"No, we do not. It's stupid. This is all fucking stupid. I'm supposed to blindly follow Cold to his murder lunch tomorrow with no idea what's really happening, but instead of planning or doing any kind of strategizing, I'm going to a *slumber party*."

"We'll figure it out," Jupiter soothed. "I can try to talk to Cold later, see if he's willing to tell me anything."

"Right, 'cause you guys have been bonding so hard over fancy food or whatever." Trev rolled his eyes hard. "Might wanna wipe off your beard. I think you've got some of Cold's jizz drying there. Ah, yup, right there by your mouth."

Jupiter only smiled. "You really don't make it easy to take care of you, baby doll."

"Fuck you. I don't need you to take care of me." Trev scoffed. "I can handle this myself. I'm getting us out of here, aren't I?"

"Yes." Jupiter kissed Trev's forehead. "You are an absolute badass, no argument there, but I can still worry."

"The only thing I need you to worry about is helping me figure out how to pee in this thing. I guess you just unzip it all the way down, right? 'Cause there's no, like, flap or anything."

"And there you go, deflecting because you don't want to admit how much not being in control is upsetting you."

"I *am* in control." Trev gritted his teeth. "I just don't have all the information I want right now to be fully prepared. There's a difference."

"Uh-huh."

"Shut up and put on your jammies."

"Uh-uh. Come here." Jupiter snagged Trev's collar, gently but firmly drawing him into a kiss.

It lingered, sweet and deep, until Trev nearly forgot why he was upset.

"We've come this far," Jupiter said quietly. "We just need to go a little further."

"And then we can go all the way to the fucking beach," Trev murmured.

"You got it, baby doll."

Trev sighed. "Ready?"

"Ready."

Trev had to admit that the hood of his pajamas—complete with ears, mane, and a sparkly horn—was cute. The fit of Jupiter's pajamas was very nice and snug in all the right places, and Trev caught himself staring quite a bit as they headed back downstairs.

Fuck, Jupiter was hot.

Trev was absolutely going to ride his dick in that stupid cat onesie later.

Rowena, Jimmy, and Juicy were waiting for them in the living room with a big pitcher of margaritas ready to go.

Juicy's onesie was a brown dog with spots and big floppy ears, but he had it folded in his lap so he could pet it instead of wearing it.

Mickey leaned against the doorway, watching everyone get settled with another sneer.

Maybe he just always looked like that.

"Don't be jealous," Trev taunted as he got snuggled next to Jupiter. "Maybe if you ask nicely, Rowena will get you your own cool jammies."

"No." Mickey narrowed his eyes. "They're for children."

"Then why do they make them in adult sizes?" Roger demanded as he strolled in wearing a fuzzy red set of footed pajamas with black horns on the hood.

Mickey sighed loudly.

Juicy looked up as Roger grabbed a seat on the end of the couch. "Oh, hello, Satan."

Roger waved. "What's up?"

"We're going to watch a musical rendition of Tina Fey's classic film. I expect it will be riveting."

Rowena waved her phone. "Hey! You guys gotta tell me what you want me to order!"

"Sesame chicken combo!" Juicy declared. "With extra fried rice. And two-and-a-half egg rolls."

Trev mouthed along with Juicy's order, chuckling at Rowena's confused expression. "Just order three egg rolls. I'll eat half of one and he'll get the other half."

"Okie dokie!" Rowena laughed. "Do you want anything else or is that half an egg roll going to be enough?"

"Sesame chicken for me too, please."

"Jupiter?"

"Do they have a menu?" Jupiter asked.

"Why do you need a menu?" Rowena snorted. "It's Chinese. They all literally have the same stuff."

"No, they do not."

"Oh my God, just tell me what you want!"

"Vegetable lo mein."

"Okay, see—"

"With beef and broccoli, boneless spare ribs, and egg drop soup."

"Damn, okay." Rowena chuckled as she typed on her phone. "And I already know Jimmy wants sweet and sour chicken... so there! Order placed. Let's go, hos!" She reached for the remote. "And hitting play... now!"

Trev smiled as Jupiter wrapped his arm around his shoulders, and he tried to let himself relax.

Key word—*tried.*

This was ridiculous.

Pajamas and margaritas the night before Cold was scheduled to be assassinated?

While it spoke volumes of everyone's confidence in Cold's ability to survive, Trev could not bring himself to share it. He knew Cold had to be pretty smart to do all the crazy stuff he did, but Trev still didn't understand the point of literally strolling right into the very place where the Luchesi family planned to kill him.

Just one more reason to get the fuck out of here, Trev decided.

The secrecy bullshit was annoying, and Trev was tired of it. Begrudgingly, he knew Jupiter was right about why he was upset earlier. It was the lack of control that pissed him off and knowing that his fate ultimately hinged on Cold's decisions. The entire situation was awful and Trev hated it.

Jimmy and Rowena only made it worse.

Trev *liked* them.

Jimmy was sweet with an endearingly silly sense of humor, like a guy who never got the chance to be a kid. He could be plenty fiery though, like all the times he'd bucked up at Cold over the past few days without even batting an eye.

Trev wondered what kind of life Jimmy must have had to shape someone so kind and yet still so fierce.

And speaking of fierce, there was no better word to describe Rowena. She was the sister he'd wished he could have had and not only because he would have loved to steal her clothes and makeup. She was loud, brave, fun, and her laugh was one of Trev's favorite sounds.

It was practically a *cackle*.

Trev loved how he and Rowena could have raunchy chats and make Jimmy blush, and then Jimmy would have them rolling moments later with some ridiculous joke. He wasn't worried about his bills, his next meal, or what moves he had left to play.

There was no game here.

Just... friends.

Maybe even family.

That was new.

It made Trev forget why he was trying so hard to get away, and he hated himself for getting distracted by, ugh, the power of friendship or whatever it was.

Of course, thinking about Cold and his gang of fucking assholes killed that feeling immediately. Trev had trouble reconciling how two people he was so fond of could worship such a motherfucker like Cold.

Cold was Jimmy's husband and Rowena's brother, but to Trev?

He was just the guy using him, no different than his dates when he was working as an escort.

Hell, the fucking dates were *nicer*.

At least some of them would give Trev a reach around when they were screwing him. Cold seemed intent on doing everything in his power to make sure Trev hated him entirely and...

Oh.

Trev hissed.

That *motherfucker*.

As if summoned by his thoughts like some sort of warped asshole genie, Cold appeared in the doorway of the living room.

"Good evening," Cold said. "Your food is here."

Jules appeared beside him, carrying several bags of food. "Hey, is there anything in here for me?"

"Hey, baby!" Jimmy hopped up to greet Cold with a kiss.

Rowena stuck out her tongue at Jules. "No! Bring the food here! And everything better be in there!"

Cold touched Jimmy's cheek. "Go eat."

"Okay." Jimmy smiled. "I'll be up after the movie's over."

"Take your time." Cold glanced at Jules and Rowena fighting over one of the bags of food and he chuckled, turning to leave.

"Hey." Trev sat up.

Cold kept going, though it wasn't clear if he was ignoring Trev or he hadn't heard him.

Trev was willing to bet he was being ignored, and he hopped off the couch to go after him.

"Trev?" Jupiter frowned.

"I'll be right back," Trev said quickly, marching out after Cold.

Cold had already reached the stairs by the time Trev

caught up to him, increasing his suspicion that Cold was trying to avoid him. "Hey! Hello!"

"Yes?" Cold paused, turning to eye Trev.

"Too cool to join our pajama party?"

"As a matter of fact, you might find that I'm quite *cold*."

"Oh! Was that a joke?" Trev snorted. "Didn't think you were capable of those."

"Happy to surprise you. Now, if you'll excuse me—"

"No," Trev said firmly.

"Pardon?"

"You said if I'll excuse you and no, I'm not excusing you. I want to talk to you."

Cold looked bored. "About?"

"The fuck do you think?"

"I think it's time for me to go to bed and for you to go eat your dinner." Cold narrowed his eyes. "Big day tomorrow, as I'm sure you're aware."

"Not before I talk to you about what a giant asshole you've been." Trev crossed his arms. "All of this fucking attitude you've been giving me? I think it's because you literally don't know any other way to get close to someone except to piss them off and be a complete bastard and then see if they're willing to stick around for the abuse. Newsflash, *bitch*. I don't like being played with."

"And have you not been playing me?" Cold took a slow step toward Trev. "From the moment you stepped into my home, have you not been trying to figure out a way to escape it? Plotting ways to manipulate me and those closest to me?"

"Like you wouldn't do the same fucking thing."

"That's just it." Cold's eyes glittered. "It's *exactly* what I would do."

Trev crossed his arms and did his best to appear as defiant as he could in a rainbow unicorn onesie. "Yeah, well.

Good for you. You're still an asshole and I get the need to front and be all big and bad. But you can fucking quit that shit now."

"I believe we are more alike than I first anticipated." Cold smirked. "Though I will admit, you are much braver than I was when I was your age."

"Smarter too," Trev quipped without hesitation. "I already figured out your stupid little head game—"

"You mean like the one you're playing with Mr. Prospero?"

"Excuse me?" Trev's face heated up. "I'm not playing fucking anything."

"Is he still your prisoner?"

"He's the guy I'm planning to fuck a lot on a beach far, far away from you until I get bored of his dick."

Cold took another step closer. "Allow me to give you some *brotherly* advice."

"Always wipe front to back?"

Cold's icy eyes flicked over Trev's and his expression softened. "When and if you're fortunate enough to find someone who loves you, not in spite of your faults but in part because of them, hold them tight. And never let go."

Trev's face continued to cook. "Jupiter doesn't love me."

"No?" Cold raised his brow.

"He hasn't said...! We're not, we just...! Oh my God, I hate you for putting this in my brain." Trev groaned. "It's not that serious. It's, it's just *not*. I don't *do* fucking serious." He threw up his hands. "And he chained me to a wall!"

"Actions do speak louder than words." Cold smiled smugly. "Perhaps something to consider."

Trev opened his mouth to argue, but he had nothing to say.

Jupiter had betrayed the Luchesi family and risked his

life by walking right into the home of their sworn enemy. While Trev could rationalize that was to benefit Jupiter since his family members were big assholes, Jupiter had also worn chains of his own with minimal complaint and then sucked up to Cold every night at dinner.

Trev hadn't fully realized why until that moment.

It was for Trev.

Jupiter wanted to be on Cold's good side since Trev was so vehemently set on fighting with Cold at every given opportunity. Jupiter was willing to do anything to make the current situation be as favorable as possible to help Trev.

What was it Jupiter had said?

You really don't make it easy to take care of you, baby doll.

But easy or not, Jupiter still wanted to.

Trev didn't know what to do with that.

He'd always wanted someone who would treat him as an equal and value him beyond his looks, a man who would respect him as a partner and not just a plaything, and hadn't Jupiter proven that? Time and time again?

Trev glared at Cold.

He refused to give him the satisfaction.

Not like Cold needed it anyway, that prick.

Cold nodded back toward the living room. "Go enjoy your movie."

"Go fuck yourself."

Cold laughed, his face instantly lighting up. It was like looking in a mirror—if the mirror added a million years and being a giant prick. "Charming." He headed back toward the stairs. "Good night, Trev."

"Wait, wait! Hey!" Trev jogged after him. "You want some more of my charming personality? How about this? You tell me what the fuck is happening tomorrow or else I take a shit in one of those stupid flower vases. You've got a shit ton of them, so good luck figuring out which one it is."

Cold snorted, dryly replying, "We'll meet the mayor's staff at eleven o'clock. We will have to be searched before entering Il Grifone."

Wow, Trev couldn't believe that threat had actually worked.

He reined in his surprise, asking, "Because it's the mayor, because it's you, or both?"

Cold ignored the query. "Once they've declared that we pose no immediate threat to the mayor, we'll be seated at our table. The mayor will be joining us by eleven fifteen. We'll chat. We'll eat. You will find the value of total and absolute silence—"

"Yeah, sure, Jan."

Cold rolled his eyes.

"And what about the hit? When exactly are people coming to kill you?"

"Leave that to me."

"That is less than fucking helpful."

"You'll just have to trust me."

"Eat my ass, *bro*."

Cold grimaced. "By the time the meal is over, we will both have what we want. That I promise you."

Trev narrowed his eyes. "If you're fucking with me or go back on your word or do anything that hurts my friends, I swear on this fluffy unicorn horn that I will find a way to make you fucking pay."

"I have no doubt that you would *try*." Cold tipped his head. "Valiantly even, but there won't be a need. Just remember. No matter what happens, stay in the restaurant until the meal is over."

Trev flinched. "The fuck is that supposed to mean?"

Cold smiled. "Good night, Trev."

"Hey!" Trev scowled as Cold walked away. "Are you serious? You're just gonna say some weird mysterious ass shit and leave? What the fuck?"

Cold kept going.

"Hello?" Trev seethed. "This is bullshit. Fuck you, damn crunchy griffin ass and your fucking *riddles*!"

"It was the Sphinx who told riddles, not a griffin!" Cold called back cheerfully.

"Fuck you and your damn sphin-sphink, sphincter whatever bitch ass! Oh my God!" Trev wished the horn on his pajamas were real so he could stab Cold with it.

Repeatedly.

He stomped back to the living room and then immediately grabbed a margarita to chug. The brain freeze was a welcome distraction from how irritated he was, and he growled as he plopped down next to Jupiter. His food was waiting for him on the coffee table, but he wasn't that hungry now.

Rowena and Roger were busy yakking about something in the movie and eating. Juicy was nibbling away, totally entranced by the screen while Jimmy appeared to be ready to pass out.

Jupiter wrapped his arm around Trev, drawing him in close. He didn't look away from the TV screen, asking casually, "What happened?"

"Roddy continues to be a fucking delight," Trev grumbled sourly, keeping his voice low as he picked at his food. "That cocky motherfucker. Said this shit about making sure I stay in the restaurant tomorrow until the meal is over and like what? What does that even mean?"

"Did he say anything else?"

"He..."

When and if you're fortunate enough to find someone who loves you, not in spite of your faults but in part because of them, hold them tight.

And never let go.

"Just a bunch of bullshit," Trev said quickly, ducking his head against Jupiter's broad shoulder. His chest felt a little funny when Jupiter kissed his forehead, but that was probably just indigestion. "I thought I'd finally figured him out, at least a little, but I might have been wrong."

"You? Wrong?" Jupiter gasped.

"Fuck off." Trev rolled his eyes.

Jupiter chuckled, cutting himself off with a yawn. "I don't know about you, but I'm about ready for bed." He rubbed his eyes. "Rowena makes a strong fucking drink."

"Is it strong or are you just a *bitch*?" Rowena taunted.

"Definitely a bitch," Roger declared.

Jupiter chuckled. "Just tired, I'm afraid."

Trev glanced over at Jimmy for his input.

Jimmy was curled up in the chair, fast asleep and snoring lightly.

"I think Jimmy wins the *bitch* award for tonight," Trev said affectionately.

"Poor baby." Rowena reached over to lightly pet Jimmy's hair. "Roddy will be back to collect him." She chuckled, glancing over at Trev and Jupiter. "You two wanna head to bed then? Big day tomorrow."

Trev stiffened. "What do you know about tomorrow?"

Rowena shrugged. "Just that you and Roddy are going to lunch with the mayor and gonna stick it to the Luchesis."

"Really? That's it?" Trev frowned. "And you're really okay with that?"

Rowena turned, giving Trev her full attention and a fierce smile. "You're my brother, Trev. So is Roddy. I'm okay because I know it's going to be all right. I know you're new to the family, but you're still family."

"Not to Captain Dick Head."

"Yes, even to Captain Dick Head." Rowena swatted her arm in Trev's direction. "You'll see!"

"Yeah." Trev sighed. "I guess we will."

One way or another.

CHAPTER *Twenty*

TREV WOKE UP WITH A START, his heart pounding and skin prickling with sweat.

He'd had a nightmare, but he couldn't remember what it was about.

He had no recollection of what had been so terrifying, left with only the dregs of lingering adrenaline and an unshakeable sense of dread. He reached for Jupiter, clinging to his bulk for comfort.

Fuck.

Trev couldn't remember the last time he'd had a bad dream.

Even with all the recent insanity of being kidnapped, chained, and seeing people murdered, he hadn't had an incident of bad sleep until now.

Maybe it was nerves.

That was it.

Stupid ass nerves.

Nothing else.

Jupiter stirred, mumbling drowsily, "Good morning."

"Hey. Morning." Trev shifted as Jupiter wrapped an arm

around him, drawing Trev in to nestle his head into the crook of Jupiter's shoulder. Jupiter was warm and firm, and Trev clung to him tightly.

"You okay?" Jupiter grunted.

"Fine," Trev lied, closing his eyes and hoping he could doze back off. He didn't know what time it was, but it definitely felt too early judging by how dark the bedroom was. He tried to get comfortable, wedging himself as close to Jupiter as he could.

Fuck.

Now he had to pee.

Trev grumbled as he headed to the bathroom in nothing but his collar. He tried to keep his eyes closed as he used the toilet, convinced if he stayed sleepy enough that he'd have no problem falling back asleep once he returned to bed.

Yes, this would certainly work.

Once he was done, he crawled back into bed to seek out Jupiter's warmth. He kept his eyes firmly shut, got comfortable, and then...

Well, shit.

Now Trev was wide awake.

"Can't go back to sleep?" Jupiter asked quietly.

"No." Trev grunted. "What time is it?"

"After seven. I think."

"Fucking gross." Trev kicked and rolled over, grumbling even as Jupiter followed to wrap his arms around him.

This was nice.

Jupiter nuzzled Trev's shoulder and settled back down with a yawn.

"Does that mean we're going back to sleep?" Trev asked.

"That's sure as hell what I'm trying to do." Jupiter snorted.

"Ugh." Trev tried again to get his body to relax enough

for sleep to take him again, but his mind was wide awake now and already counting down the hours to the fateful lunch meeting today.

If it was after seven, that meant there was less than four hours to go.

Three hours and what? Fifty minutes? Forty? Less? More?

Trev growled as he sat up.

"Does this mean we're getting up?" Jupiter grumbled.

"Sorry. I can't get my fucking brain to shut up." Trev glanced at the clock on the bedside table.

It was seven sixteen.

Three hours and forty-four minutes.

"I'm going to take a shower." Trev slid out of bed.

Jupiter rubbed at his eyes. "Want some company?"

"I don't care. Whatever." Trev stumbled into the bathroom to remove his collar. He got the shower going as hot as it would go and then stepped in, wishing the water could scald the inside of his head and rinse away his nagging thoughts.

Three hours and forty-one minutes until the meeting.

Or was it forty now?

Thirty-nine?

Shit.

The minutes didn't matter. It wasn't going to be enough time to figure out what to do. The only option left to him was to follow Cold's lead and trust that he would honor his promise to let Trev and his friends go. He hated allowing anyone to have so much power over him, but Trev didn't have a choice.

He had to do this...

Or he'd lose what precious little bit of a family he'd managed to cobble together.

Jupiter, Juicy—and yes, Rowena and Jimmy too. They were all counting on Trev to see this through and do whatever the fuck he was supposed to do to get through this meeting. Trev still didn't understand the purpose of walking right into a fucking trap.

Was Cold trying to outsmart the Luchesi family and lure them into a trap of his own?

How was that supposed to work?

It wasn't like Emil and Sal were going to be hanging around waiting to see it go down.

Right?

Trev rested his head against the cool tile with a loud groan.

"Hey." It was Jupiter. "Whatcha doin' in there?"

"Nothing fun." Trev snorted.

Jupiter stepped into the shower behind him, his big hands sliding over Trev's back. "Talk to me, baby doll."

"Just in my head," Trev replied quietly. "Worried about today."

Jupiter kissed Trev's shoulder. "It's going to be all right. We're going to get through it."

"Glad one of us is so fucking confident."

"It's been a long time since I've had anything to hope for." Jupiter moved his arms around Trev's waist, hugging him gently. "Gave up for a while, you know. That I'd ever be able to get away from my family. Thinking about the future... Fuck, *wanting* a future with someone? I didn't think that would ever happen."

Trev's heart fluttered. "And... now?"

"Now I've got that and more." Jupiter nuzzled Trev's shoulder. "I've never wanted anything so much and I am not going to let a damn thing stand in our way, baby doll. We're getting the fuck out of here. Together."

Trev was glad they were in the shower because it was easy to hide how his eyes teared up. He grabbed Jupiter's forearm and gave it a firm squeeze, breathing in slowly to keep his rising emotions at bay. "Together."

They stood there for a long time, so long that Trev nearly forgot to actually bathe. His hand shook when he reached for the soap and Jupiter was there to help him, his firm touch reassuring. Trev let Jupiter scrub him down and enjoyed the attention, happy to return the favor when Jupiter was done.

He was mindful of the bandage on Jupiter's shoulder where he'd been shot, though he did linger in rubbing soap around it.

Trev wasn't sure why he hadn't thought about it before, but that injury could have been so much worse. Jupiter could have been killed. Hell, *Trev* might have been. They'd both escaped death more times in the last week than Trev was comfortable admitting, and he found himself leaning up to press a needy kiss to Jupiter's lips.

"We'll be okay, baby doll," Jupiter murmured. "I fucking promise you."

Trev wanted to believe that.

They kissed again, and as much as Trev longed for the relief of a passionate release, he couldn't get his body to cooperate. Jupiter seemed to understand and didn't push, and after rinsing off, they both got out of the shower.

Trev was quiet as he dried off, fumbling around on the counter for lotion. He rubbed himself down and smiled when Jupiter took over, massaging it over his back and shoulders. He closed his eyes for a moment before he looked in the mirror, watching Jupiter through the reflection.

Jupiter had a little smile on his face. It helped smooth

the lines of his otherwise worried expression. He glanced up, catching Trev's eye in the mirror. His smile grew.

Trev smiled back. He had no idea what to say, but his heart was light, a warmth bubbling up to the surface that made him blush. He couldn't help but think about what Cold had told him last night. "Jupiter, I—"

There was a firm knock at the bedroom door.

Of fucking course.

Trev strolled out of the bathroom, calling out loudly, "I'm not putting any fucking clothes on, so sorry in advance, but only if you're Rowena!" He opened the door.

Cold was on the other side, one hand firmly planted over his eyes and the other holding out a garment bag. He sighed. "Here."

"What the fuck is this?" Trev demanded.

"Put it on. Then come down for breakfast." Cold sighed again. "You can shut the door now."

"Thanks! I'll think about it!" Trev accepted the garment bag and grinned, not yet shutting the door.

Annoyed, Cold sighed a third time and turned around to stalk away.

Trev snickered as he finally closed the door. He joined Jupiter back in the bathroom, hanging the bag on the back of the door.

"Cold brought that for you?" Jupiter asked.

"Yeah." Trev shrugged. "I guess he doesn't want me to wear a dress. Which is a shame! Because I have that super short black one that..."

Inside the garment bag was a black three-piece suit with magenta pinstriping. The shirt was dark pink, the tie black, and there was a small velvet bag. Inside was a pair of cuff links with glittering pink gems.

He had no idea if they were rubies or what, but there was no doubt they were real.

"Holy shit," Trev whispered.

"Wow." Jupiter smiled warmly. "You're gonna look hot as fuck, baby doll."

"Yeah? Well. I'm not wearing that stupid ass tie though." Trev fiddled with the cuff links and glanced at Jupiter.

"Yes, I will help you put those on." Jupiter kissed Trev's forehead. "Come on. Let's get you ready."

The suit fit perfectly, and Trev opted to keep the top few buttons of his shirt undone. He didn't want to wear the tie anyway and this would allow his collar to show. He had Jupiter put it on for him along with the cuff links, and damn, Trev looked fucking *hot*.

Not that he planned to make dressing like this a habit or anything.

Jupiter's suit was hanging in the closet and freshly dry-cleaned, no doubt Cold's doing as well. While thoughtful, it was a little creepy since it meant someone had to have snuck in and out of the room without either of them knowing it.

Once Jupiter was ready, he and Trev headed downstairs.

It wasn't until they entered the kitchen that Trev realized Mickey wasn't shadowing them.

Cold was seated at the breakfast table with Jimmy beside him. He was reading a newspaper and didn't look up as he commented, "Lose your tie?"

"Yup," Trev replied. "Such a shame. I really liked that tie. No idea what could have happened to it."

"Uh-huh," Cold drawled.

"Good morning!" Jimmy greeted them with a cheerful grin. "You both look great. Love the pink, Trev."

Trev smiled. "Thanks."

Jerry gestured for both Jupiter and Trev to sit, asking

graciously, "What can I get you gentleman to eat, hmm? Eggs? Some bacon, perhaps?"

"I'm good." Trev shook his head. "Just, uh, coffee or something."

"Eggs and bacon sounds great," Jupiter said with a polite smile. "Thank you."

"Right away." Jerry smiled and headed back to the stove.

"Sleep okay?" Jimmy asked.

"Yeah. Great." Trev shrugged. He didn't feel like making small talk, but he roused himself from his thoughts to ask, "You?"

"Yeah, fine." Jimmy smiled softly. "I mean, heh, actually like shit to be honest."

"Yeah?" Trev quirked his brows.

"Anxiety is a bitch. It's okay to be nervous, you know. God knows I always worry about Rod when he has to go to work."

"If only he'd tell you the truth and then maybe you wouldn't worry as much." Trev batted his eyes at Cold.

Jimmy chuckled. "I'd still worry. Trust me."

Trev glanced around the table, noting a few key faces were missing. "Where's Rowena?"

"She left at the ass crack of dawn to meet Dario at the club," Jimmy replied. "Letting some guy in to work on the piano and tune it up or whatever." He smirked. "She's, uh, confident that you guys will be staying for dinner, so she didn't bother saying goodbye."

Trev snorted out a laugh.

Of course.

"And Juicy?" Trev prompted.

"Right here!" Juicy waved as he entered the kitchen, smiling brightly. He was wearing striped pajamas and a robe, but he was barefoot. He'd clearly been doing something outside because his feet were dirty.

Mickey trailed in behind him with a scowl.

"What the hell?" Trev laughed.

Well, that explained where Mickey was.

"I had to take Barkie for his morning walk!" Juicy said as he sat down with a big grin. "That little rascal got off his leash and took me for quite a little adventure!"

Mickey's sour expression indicated that adventure was not the word he would use.

Still, imagining Mickey having to chase Juicy down as Juicy went after his imaginary dog added about ten years to Trev's life and he grinned from ear to ear.

Even Cold had a little smile playing over his lips, as if he too was amused.

Mickey just kept scowling.

"Did you, uh, catch him?" Jimmy asked politely.

"Of course." Juicy stared. "He's right here." He gestured to the empty floor.

"Right. Got it."

Jerry came over to pass a plate of food to Jupiter and coffee for Trev. He smiled at Juicy, saying, "The usual for you and your canine companion, monsieur?"

"Yes, please! Thank you." Juicy beamed, but then his smile dropped as he looked over Trev. "Who's dying today?"

Trev nearly dropped his coffee. "What?"

"I've never seen you in a suit." Juicy frowned. "Are you going to a funeral?"

"No, Juicy. Just going out to lunch." Trev forced a smile. "I promise everything is all right. As soon as we get back, me, you, and Jupiter are going on a trip." He quickly added, "And Barkie too, of course."

"Oh! Splendid." Juicy smiled again.

Jupiter reached under the table to give Trev's thigh a warm squeeze.

Trev smiled and breathed in his coffee, letting the scent soothe him as much as the promise of caffeinated bliss.

Maybe this was going to be all right.

Maybe everything would work out and—

"Someone is still going to die though," Juicy said firmly.

Trev sighed. "Thank you, Juicy."

"Look! You're already dressed for it. So, it shouldn't be a problem."

"Yup. Thanks. Super appreciate that."

"Don't forget. They'll wrap up your leftovers and make it look like a swan."

"Fuckin' *fabulous*."

Now all Trev could think about was tinfoil swans and splattering brains, gangsters busting in with tommy guns and blood dripping from the ceiling in thick streams, but everything was *totally* going to be fine.

Right?

THE RESTAURANT WAS in the historic district of Strassen Springs, the first story of a corner building with big glass windows and checkered awnings. Trev immediately assumed it was an Italian restaurant because it looked like every other Italian place he'd ever seen.

Trev and Cold had ridden here in the back of a limo driven by Jerry. Jules was waiting for them out front and came over to open the door after Jerry pulled up.

Trev must have looked worried because Jules dipped his

head down to say quietly, "Don't worry, boss bro. You got this."

"Thanks," Trev muttered, rolling his eyes at the nickname.

Jules clapped his hand on Trev's shoulder and nearly knocked him over.

Cold led them the short distance over to the restaurant's front door, where two large men in—what else—suits were waiting.

Judging by their ear pieces, Trev assumed they were members of the mayor's security detail.

The shorter of the two men said, "Hello there, gentlemen. If you don't mind, we need to conduct a little search for weapons, all right?"

"Of course." Cold nodded politely.

Trev held up his arms to tuck behind his head at practically the same time Cold did, and he smirked. "Not your first time being frisked, huh?"

"Hardly." Cold snorted.

The security detail was especially thorough, and Trev almost told one of them to buy him dinner next time. He'd made a promise to behave himself or whatever, so he resisted.

He hated this.

He hated the suit, the restaurant, and how his nerves were already fried, though they'd only been here a few minutes.

In that brief time, Trev had counted six men in the security detail, established at least two exits in the restaurant plus a possible third since there was likely a back door, and he spotted three cars with occupants inside who didn't seem like they were getting out anytime soon.

Cold and Trev were left waiting with Jules while the

security detail at the door talked amongst themselves and the others paced around.

Cold didn't look at Trev, but he asked quietly, "What do you see?"

"What?" Trev frowned.

"You've been checking our surroundings. So. What do you see?"

"Six men in the detail, all of them armed. I think there's two ways in and out of the restaurant, probably a third in the back, and a few creeps out on the street sitting in their cars. One in the truck, another in that Ford sedan, and one in casual but seriously ugly clothes in the SUV." Trev shrugged. "Truck and Ford guy are wearing suits, but it looks like they shop at the cheap mafia bitch warehouse, not the fancy mafia bitch one, so, probably cops."

"Not bad." Cold nodded. "There are seven men on the detail. One's in the bathroom. The man in the sedan has adjusted a shoulder holster, so, yes. Probably a cop. The man in the SUV has been listening to something and he keeps checking his ear. Could be another cop in plain clothes."

"Okay, so what about the guy in the truck?"

"He's likely going to be arrested for indecent exposure. He's masturbating."

"What?" Trev looked back, snorting out a laugh when he caught the telltale jerk of the man's elbow. "Jesus Christ."

"Tamerlane is on the roof of the building behind us, but don't bother looking." Cold smirked. "You won't see him. Jerry and Lorre are nearby as well, along with a handful of other... supporters."

Trev did a cursory glance as if he was just looking at the buildings, and he only saw a woman walking her dog and a guy delivering a package.

Maybe the woman with the dog was a ruthless killer.

It made him think of Juicy, and he smiled a little.

One of the men from the security detail approached, saying, "All right, Mr. Legrand. We're ready for you."

"Excellent. Thank you." Cold led the way into the restaurant, Trev trailing behind with Jules.

The inside of the restaurant was very brown with splashes of red in the upholstery and the dingy carpet. There were dozens of framed black-and-white photographs on the walls. It was clean but quite old, and Trev could smell mildew seeping in through the scent of baking bread and a floral deodorizer.

They were shown to a table in the corner. Cold took the seat that would give him the best view of the restaurant and Trev took the next closest one to his left. While he couldn't see as much of the back as Cold could, he could still see the front pretty well.

Where would the attack come from?

If it was one of the staff, then the back.

But what if the staff member tried to come through the front to throw off suspicion?

Did the mayor even know what was going to happen? Did his staff?

Fuck, fuck, fuck, how much of a mess was this?

Cold touched Trev's shoulder. "Remember. No matter what happens, you stay inside the restaurant."

"What?" Trev blinked.

"You heard me. No matter what happens, you stay." Cold pointed at the table. "Right here."

"Yeah, sure."

"Mr. Usher—"

"Got it, bro."

"Trevanion." Cold frowned. "Please."

The urgency of Cold's plea was surprising and Trev shrugged. "Yeah. Okay. I got it."

Jules hovered by the edge of the table. He grunted. "Just trust the boss, all right? This ain't our first rodeo."

"Yeah." Trev snorted. "Exactly how many generations of the Luchesi family have you wiped out again?"

"*Allegedly* wiped out." Jules looked very proud of himself.

Cold sighed.

"So. We're just sitting here waiting for you know what?" Trev asked.

"Yes."

"This is stupid."

"You'll understand. Very soon."

Trev reached up to adjust his collar.

Two members of the security detail took positions against the far wall while the others headed to the front door. A short older man in a suit, with a big white mustache and even pastier skin, was being ushered in, followed closely by a younger man in a sweater vest with big white teeth like Chiclet gum.

Trev hated him on sight.

Sweater Vest came forward, saying politely, "Hi, hi, there. Lawrence Ember, the mayor's personal assistant. He likes to sit in that corner because the light especially this time of day is so much more flattering—"

"No," Cold said flatly.

"Let's try this again." Lawrence feigned a smile. "I'm going to need you to move—"

"I'm going to need you to be quiet now," Cold said softly. "Clearly you didn't hear me the first time. I will not be moving. Do you understand?"

Jules grunted.

Lawrence must have finally realized who exactly he was

trying to order around because he cowered immediately with a sheepish smile. "Right. Of course, sir. It is a lovely spot! I am so very sorry!"

Trev glanced at the photographs on the wall while Lawrence continued to apologize.

They were of people sitting at various places in the restaurant, some of them from many years ago when there apparently were booths instead of tables. A few were more modern shots judging by the clothing and the presence of cell phones, but they were all in black and white.

There was one right beside Cold's head of two old men laughing.

It wasn't a particularly great photo, but it got his attention because it was crooked.

Not by much, just enough to catch his eye.

And annoy him.

Trev had the wildest urge to reach over Cold and fix it.

Of all the dozens and dozens of pictures, the *one* damn crooked one had to be right next to them.

Trev was so transfixed by the photo that he didn't realize the mayor had come over until Cold politely cleared his throat. Trev shot up to his feet, smiling politely at the mayor.

"Mayor Edgar Arnold," the man said, his mustache wagging away as he spoke. "A pleasure to meet you, young man."

"Trevanion Usher," Cold said with a tip of his head. "My younger brother."

Trev wasn't sure why that made him smile, but it did. He shook Edgar's hand. "It's nice to meet you, sir."

"It's always nice to meet more of Mr. Legrand's family." Edgar grinned as he took his seat. "Especially if they're of voting age!"

Trev sat, fiddling with his collar. "I… I don't live here, sir."

"Oh, well, nobody's perfect."

"Trevanion is leaving later today as a matter of fact." Cold sat with a small smile. "He and his partner will be staying at my villa in St. Thomas."

"Wait, what?" Trev stared.

"Surprise." Cold smiled warmly.

"Seriously?" Trev blinked. "You're… You got us a place?"

"You wanted a beach, did you not?" Cold shrugged. "If it's not to your liking, you and Jupiter are welcome to leave. But I thought you might enjoy having accommodations waiting for you."

"What about Juicy?" Trev demanded.

"He's welcome to join you too, of course. Should you accept my invitation, I will make sure he has adequate nursing care onsite."

"Aw, that's so nice." Edgar smiled. "Now, if you don't mind…" He pulled a handkerchief from his pocket to dab sweat off his forehead. "Could we go ahead and order, hmm?"

He was nervous.

Did he know?

"Of course." Lawrence popped up to stand beside the mayor. "I'll get the waiter over here right away."

Trev really did not like that guy.

"Everything here is delicious," Edgar said with a big grin. "I highly recommend the eggplant parm. They make their own garlic bread too, you know!"

"Excellent. Thank you." Cold nodded.

"Oh, but if you like chicken, their chicken alfredo is good too…"

Trev took a few moments to digest Cold's generous offer

while Edgar continued to ramble about the food, wondering if it was a trick of some kind. It was strange for Cold to tell him now with the mayor here, but perhaps he'd waited to make sure Trev would have more motivation to remain quiet and behave himself.

He wouldn't put it past Cold to bribe him.

And a trip to a tropical island in the Caribbean was very persuasive.

The waiter approached them to take their drink orders and pass out the menus, and Trev asked for water. He couldn't think of anything else, his mind occupied as he scanned over the restaurant to look for any sign of trouble.

Jules was relaxed, though his eyes were focused on the back of the restaurant.

Was he looking for the waiter? Or something else?

The majority of the security detail remained clustered near the front door, while a few wandered around looking lost.

Cold was calm as he perused the menu items, seemingly not having a care in the world.

Trev picked at the silverware and fought the urge to grab the knife.

Everything was going to be fine.

It was fine.

It was—

Squealing tires drew Trev's attention to the windows.

A white van barreled down the street and rammed into the truck. The crash was deafening, an alarm instantly sounding.

The security detail tensed and Edgar nearly jumped out of his seat.

Cold didn't even blink.

Neither did Jules.

So this was expected.

Great.

Trev grabbed the knife.

Whatever stupid plan Cold had, Trev hoped it would be over quickly.

Horns honked away as the wreck blocked traffic, and voices shouted frantically. The air had grown tense, and Trev didn't miss how Edgar squirmed in his seat. There was definitely something about to happen.

But what?

What was—

The waiter came toward their table, Cold barely glancing his way.

But the waiter was moving fast, too fast, and Trev stared him down. The hair on the back of his neck stood on end, his blood iced over, and he forgot to breathe.

The waiter was holding a tray out like a shield, but why?

No.

No, no, no.

Jules turned to intercept the waiter, but he was too slow.

The waiter dropped the tray, revealing the gun in his hand.

"No!" Trev lurched forward with the knife.

A gunshot rang out.

Cold's face exploded in a splash of blood.

He fell over.

Someone screamed.

Cold was slumped over the table.

Dead.

CHAPTER Twenty-One

COLD WAS DEAD.

Someone is still going to die though.

No.

No, that couldn't be right.

"Keep your ass right there!" Jules barked as he drew a gun from his jacket.

"What?" Trev's ears were still ringing from the gunshot, and he stared stupidly as Jules ran toward the front door.

The waiter.

The fucking waiter was right here, still armed—

Pfffsh.

Glass shattered as a bullet pierced one of the front windows and the waiter collapsed to the floor in a heap.

Dead.

Great.

He was dead too.

Fucking wonderful.

Lawrence screamed as he dragged Edgar to the back of the restaurant, and the security detail swarmed around them both.

Trev was frozen in his seat.

Cold was *dead*.

That's not how this was supposed to go.

He reached up to touch his cheek, grimacing when he felt something sticky.

Blood.

Trev stood to retreat and make sense of his spinning thoughts. He knew Cold and Jules had told him to stay, but that was before Cold got his brains splattered across the wall.

And the table.

And the chairs.

Jesus fucking *Christ*.

Trev backed away from the table, his heart pounding and his face numb.

Everyone else was so focused on getting Edgar out safely that they'd apparently forgotten about Trev, Jules included.

More gunshots rang out, Trev instinctively ducking as he whipped his head around in search of the source. It seemed to be coming from outside. More people screamed, more shots were fired, and Trev gritted his teeth.

He needed to get the fuck out of here.

He spared Cold a sympathetic glance and then hurried to the back of the restaurant. Whatever was about to go down, he wanted no part of it. His heart ached at the loss of Cold as much as it could, though the sting was sharper when he thought about Rowena and Jimmy finding out.

Shit.

Shit.

Cold had told him to stay at the table, but he could not have meant to hang out with his corpse while people were fucking shooting at each other.

He decided to follow after Edgar and Lawrence since

they had the giant gaggle of security with them. That seemed safer as opposed to waltzing out front where all the *shooting* was going down.

He could leave the restaurant and double back to hitch a ride. Hell, he'd find that guy jacking off in his truck and offer to fucking blow him if he'd take him to Cold's mansion. The only thing that mattered was getting the fuck out of here and back to Jupiter and Juicy.

Trev was fucking done with gangster bullshit for-fucking-ever.

No more murder, no more lies, no more stupid plots that ended in—oh, surprise!—more fucking *murder*.

What the fuck had Cold been thinking?

Some fucking genius.

Trev zipped through the swinging doors into the kitchen, dodging cowering staff members as he hurried toward the rear exit. He didn't see any sign of Edgar or the security detail, but he couldn't have been too far behind them.

He shoved open the door and found himself in an alley. The sound of a car peeling away no doubt signaled Edgar's retreat and Trev groaned in frustration.

Yup.

Time to go bribe the masturbating guy.

He didn't hear any new gunshots, but he still moved cautiously, all of his senses on high alert as adrenaline continued to buzz through his body. He had no way to call for help and nothing to defend himself with other than the stupid knife he'd stolen from the restaurant.

This was great.

Just fucking great.

Trev headed out to the street and around the block toward the front of the restaurant. One of the men from the security detail was on the ground, not moving, and sirens heralded the imminent arrival of emergency services, cops, or both.

Trev didn't want to be around for either, and a quick scan of the area revealed no friendly faces. He had no idea where Jules was, and he saw no sign of Jerry, Lorre, or the limo.

Not even masturbating guy was here.

Trev did notice that the two men he and Cold had potentially identified as cops were gone. He wasn't sure if that made him feel better or worse. He kept walking, suddenly wishing he wasn't wearing a bright fucking pink dress shirt or that he had pink hair.

Kinda made him easy to spot.

Trev had done his best to memorize the route back to Cold's home and quickly set off on foot. It would take hours at this rate, but he wanted to keep moving. He happened to see his reflection in a store window and grimaced.

Fuck, he was still covered in blood.

There was a cafe ahead with a few outdoor tables. He stopped to swipe a cloth napkin and an abandoned glass of what he hoped was water. He doused the napkin and then continued walking, wiping off his face and neck and everywhere else he thought there might be blood.

Shit, shit, shit.

He really needed to change clothes too, but his options were limited. Trying to steal something from one of the nearby shops risked police attention, and he doubted he could convince anyone to give him their clothes. Trading was probably out too.

Especially since his still had blood on them.

He could feel it sticking to his neck in a few places and shuddered.

Ten thousand showers weren't going to be enough to wash this feeling away.

He wished Jupiter was here.

He wanted to jump into his arms and hug him close, to breathe him in and listen to him tell Trev that everything was going to be okay, that everything was going to be all right.

Even if it was a lie.

A green sedan rolled up to the sidewalk and Trev walked faster. He couldn't see who was driving, but he doubted it could be anyone friendly—

"Trev!" someone shouted.

Trev whirled around stupidly when he recognized the voice. "Juicy?"

Juicy was indeed behind the wheel,

He was smiling like an absolute moron.

He was also wearing a hospital gown.

Trev stared.

Juicy waved. "Come on! Let's go!"

"What the fuck are you doing? What the fuck happened?" Trev quickly ran around to jump into the passenger seat. "Wait, *can you drive*?"

"Of course I can drive!" Juicy huffed as he pulled back onto the street with no turn signal. "I've been driving since before you were born!"

"Okay, yes! Got it!" Trev buckled up, grimacing as someone honked their horn behind them. "So, uh, what are you doing here? Why are you in a hospital gown?"

"Oh right!" Juicy nodded. "Jupiter was worried about you."

Trev waited.

Juicy drove.

"And?" Trev prompted. "Jupiter was worried and what?"

"I just told you!" Juicy shook his head.

"Tell me again." Trev was trying to be patient, but he was really not in the mood for Juicy's usual brand of shenanigans.

"Well, we knew Jupiter wouldn't be able to leave because everyone was watching him. So, I faked having a stroke to get myself a little ride to the hospital. Once I was there, I just waited for those stupid doctors to leave and stole a car—"

"You stole a fucking car?"

"Shh, keep your voice down," Juicy warned. "Someone might hear you! But yes, I stole a car and now I'm taking you back to Boss Cold's. I know he won't be pleased, but it had to be done."

Trev scrubbed his hands over his face and groaned. "He's not gonna be pleased about anything. He's fucking dead."

"What?"

"The restaurant. The hit? They fucking got him."

"Oh. Hmm, that can't be right." Juicy seemed confused. "We should go back."

"Excuse me?"

"We should go back! He can't be dead."

"Juicy, I literally wiped his blood off my fucking face." Trev cringed. "Going back to the restaurant is the absolute last fucking thing I want to do right now."

Juicy made a right turn at the next light, insisting, "No, no, no. That's not correct. It simply cannot be—"

"Juicy, listen to me!" Trev grabbed Juicy's shoulder. "He's dead! Jules ran off! The fucking mayor is gone! Everybody is gone! Hello? There's no point—"

"I know what to do!" Juicy argued.

"Goddammit, Juicy!" Trev snapped angrily. "You crazy old bastard! Will you please listen to me? For fucking once?"

Juicy stared at Trev, clearly hurt. "Do… Do you really think I'm crazy?"

"What?" Trev sighed. "No, I'm just—" He froze when he realized Juicy had run a red light and there was a car coming right at them. "Juicy! Look out!" He grabbed the wheel and tried to turn out of the way, but it was too late.

The incoming car slammed into the driver's side with enough force to spin the car around. Trev's world blurred, his stomach heaved, and the seat belt held him tight. It took him several seconds to fully reconcile what had happened and once he had, his concern shifted.

"Juicy!" Trev reached over to grab his shoulder.

"Oh! My. Hmm." Juicy appeared dazed, blood dripping down the side of his face. "That was unexpected."

"Juicy! Your head!" Trev scrambled for something to stem the flow of blood, frantically unbuckling his seat belt so he could take off his jacket. He wadded it up and pressed it to the side of Juicy's head.

"Hey! Ow!" Juicy whined.

"Shut up! You're bleeding!"

"I was *fine* until you slapped me in the head with your coat!"

"Idiot! You're fucking bleeding all over the place!" Trev searched over Juicy's body. "Are you hurt anywhere else?"

"I don't think so." Juicy shrugged. "Hmm. The airbags didn't go off. That's probably not a good sign."

The driver of the car who had struck them was out and hurrying toward them. Several other onlookers were crowding the street to check on the other vehicles involved in the accident. It looked like there had been quite a pileup.

"We need to get out of the car." Trev unbuckled. "Before the cops get here."

"Shouldn't we wait for the authorities to get here?"

"Juicy! No!" Trev checked over himself for any injuries before hopping out of the car with a groan. He was definitely going to be sore later, but for now he was good to move. He had to be.

The accident was drawing too much attention.

People crowded the sidewalk and took pictures and video with their phones, though a select few came over to tend to those in the wrecked vehicles. Trev tried to wave at them and signal he and Juicy were fine, but he wasn't sure how long that would keep any well-meaning Samaritans away.

Trev opened Juicy's door. "Come on, we gotta go."

"Where are we going?" Juicy blinked.

"Anywhere but here." Trev took a deep breath. "We need to get back to Cold's place as soon as we can so we can grab Jupiter and leave, okay? All of this is about to go down in one big giant pile of steaming shit and I do not want to explain a single fucking word of this to the cops!"

"We can't flee the scene of an accident," Juicy scolded.

Trev wanted to shake him. "We're in a stolen car!" he hissed. "Get your ass up!"

"It's not stolen! I bought this car twenty-three years ago! Runs great! Purrs like a kitten!"

"Okay, I didn't want to have to do this." Trev wasn't even sure if it was going to work, but he had to get Juicy out of the damn car. "Come here, boy! Come here!"

Juicy narrowed his eyes. "What are you doing?"

Trev took a few steps back, patting his leg and looking down as if he was talking to a dog. "Hey! Such a good boy! Come here! Come here, Barkie!"

"Hey!" Juicy gasped. "No! Barkie, come here this instant!"

Trev mimed wrapping his arms around the imaginary

dog and scooped him up, tucking him under his arm. He had no idea what kind of dog Barkie was supposed to be, but hopefully he was small enough that Juicy would buy this. "Nope. Me and Barkie are leaving."

"Put my dog down!" Juicy shouted. "Thief! Help! Dog thief!"

"We're gonna go get doggy ice cream, aren't we?" Trev turned to walk away, cradling the imaginary dog and petting his head. "Say bye bye, Juicy!"

"It's a good thing the police are on their way!" Juicy yelled as he came racing after Trev. "I will have them arrest you for dognapping!"

As soon as Juicy caught up, Trev slung his arm around his shoulders and squeezed him close. "Oh, hey! Juicy! Let's take Barkie for a walk, huh?"

"A walk?"

"Yeah! A walk!" Trev passed over the imaginary dog and mimed handing Juicy a leash. "I bet there's plenty of cool places around here for him to pee."

"Oh! All right!" Juicy perked up, taking hold of the imaginary leash and falling into step beside Trev.

Trev could see that Juicy was bleeding from two small cuts on the side of his forehead. "Uh, how's your head?"

"Mm?" Juicy shrugged. "Fine. How's yours?"

"No complaints."

"That's nice. Hmm, I think Barkie wants to go this way."

"You got it." Trev was happy to follow the whims of the imaginary dog as long as said imaginary dog took them far away from the scene of the accident. He heard someone calling after them, but he kept them moving. There was no way they were sticking around to explain any of this to the cops.

Now here Trev was, wearing a bright pink shirt with no

jacket to hide it because his jacket was currently in Juicy's hand balled up on the side of his head. Juicy was in a hospital gown with nothing underneath, shamelessly charging forward as the open back flapped and revealed his bare ass for everyone to see, either not aware of his nudity or simply nor caring.

"Hey, why don't we tie the jacket around your waist?" Trev suggested. "I think your head stopped bleeding." He grunted as Juicy steered them sharply around a corner. "Juicy! Where the hell is Barkie going?"

"To the restaurant!" Juicy swatted at Trev's attempts to help him. "He knows the way and I know what to do now. I've been there before."

"Oh, have you?"

"It's not like it's the first time anybody's ordered a hit there!" Juicy shook his head. "That's why I thought it was so stupid. Like, remaking movies. Why remake *Twister*? Why? A musical reinterpretation is something different entirely, like with the classic film, *Mean Girls*—"

"Hey, Juicy! Focus!" Trev snapped. "What do you mean you thought it was stupid? You never said anything!"

"You didn't ask me."

"Juicy!"

"The restaurant. Il Grifone." Juicy kept waddling ahead, stubborn as ever. "When I was a pilot, I whacked somebody there."

"You mean when you were a hitman?"

"No, I was a pilot!"

Trev skidded to stop when he saw the restaurant at the end of the block. There were dozens of police cars, a fire truck, and countless other cars crowded around it. Men in uniform and in suits were running around like ants as barriers were put up to block off a growing crowd.

"Shit." Trev grabbed Juicy's shoulder and tried to pull him back. "Yeah, no. See all that? See that shit? We want to get very, very far away from that shit!"

"But I told you!" Juicy was annoyed. "That's where we need to be. With the trees. Two trees, three trees, and—"

"Yes, yes! I've heard all about the fucking trees!" Trev hissed, pulling harder on Juicy's arm. "The trees aren't here, Juicy! Those are back in fucking Perry City at the stupid park!"

"No! They're over there! At the restaurant! That's where we need to—"

"I am going to kick the shit out of your fucking dog—"

Juicy gasped. "You wouldn't dare!"

"Juicy—"

"Trev?" Juicy's gaze drifted over Trev's shoulder.

"What? I'm—oh shit!" Trev yelped when big hands grabbed him and the cool barrel of a gun jammed into his temple. He held up his hands, gritting his teeth. "Fuck me."

"Not on your life, you fuckin' whore." It was Emil.

There were two big suited men on either side of him.

Great.

Fabulous.

"What the fuck?" Trev stared. "What the fuck are you doing here?"

"Cleaning up the leftovers." Emil smirked. "We got Cold, we got Cold's little bitch brother, and his..." He stared at Juicy. "This old bitch."

"Old? Who are you calling old?" Juicy raged, swatting feebly at Emil, but one of the suited men grabbed him. "I'll snap your damn neck, you stupid fucks!"

Trev tightened his fists, keeping track of where the knife was in his sleeve. "Just let him go. He doesn't have anything to do with this."

"Oh, no, no." Emil smiled wickedly. "He's just in time to see the big finale. Now that Cold is dead, I am going to take pleasure in killing his brother too." He jerked his head. "We need to get off the street. Now."

Emil grabbed Trev by his collar, dragging him down the sidewalk toward an unfortunately familiar SUV. Trev struggled, but there wasn't much he could do with a gun pressed against his head. He was tempted to scream for help since there were so many cops nearby.

One of them had to notice, right?

At least one person had to come around the corner and see what was happening.

Someone, anyone—driving by, looking out their window, fucking *anything*.

Trev grunted as Emil shoved him into the back seat of the SUV. "Hey! Where's Juicy?"

"The old man is coming too, don't you worry." Emil smirked as he slid in beside Trev.

Trev tried to bolt to the other door, but he ended up with a face full of Juicy as Juicy was wrestled in next to him. "Fuck! Watch it! He has a fucking head injury, you assholes!"

Juicy barked furiously, snarling and swinging his arms. "I will kill all of you! You're all fucking dead! My dog will eat your fucking guts and shit them out, eat them, and *shit you out again*!"

Trev blinked. "Okay. That's a thing you said."

"Oh, I didn't mean you, Trev." Juicy smiled warmly. "You know how much Barkie loves you. I don't think he'd eat you."

Trev sighed haggardly. "Thanks. I appreciate that."

One of the suited men climbed in with Juicy, forcing Juicy and Trev to get sandwiched together in the middle. The other suited man got behind the wheel.

Trev tried to find some possible way to be comfortable, but it was not going to happen with how he was being crushed up against Juicy. "So, uh. Wherever we're going, are we gonna be there soon? Because this fucking sucks—"

"Shut the fuck up." Emil smacked him in the back of his head with the butt of the gun.

"Ow! You fucking piece of shit!" Trev growled angrily and thrashed until another blow made him see stars. He held his head, panting through the pain as he snarled, "You're so... dead. So fucking *dead*!"

"Quiet now." Emil snorted. "Don't worry. We're not going far. Just far enough that the cops won't hear you bitches screaming when we tear you apart."

Trev wasn't sure if Emil was exaggerating or not, but he didn't dare ask for him to clarify.

Had to think.

He had to think.

He had to fucking *think*.

Okay, he had a knife inside his sleeve. That was something, right?

Shit, they were so fucked.

Trev refused to give in to despair, his thoughts flashing back to Cold's head on the table. Cold might have been dumb enough to walk right into a trap, but not Trev.

Trev was smarter.

Braver.

Fucking better.

He had to be or he and Juicy weren't going to make it the fuck out of here.

Trev turned his aching head to look out the window as they drove, quickly trying to map out any store names or street signs that would give him a clue as to where they were headed. Even though he didn't know this area, he could try to memorize those details to aid in his eventual escape or to tell someone else...

Shit, yeah right.

Like anyone was going to come rescue them.

And besides, how would Trev contact them? He didn't have a phone and it wasn't like he knew any of their fucking phone numbers.

He shifted his arm down so the knife was closer to his cuff.

One quick little shake and he'd have the knife in his hand.

New plan.

He was going to stab the fuck out of the driver and then Emil.

Especially Emil, that fucker.

Once the vehicle had stopped, he and Juicy would get out and run. They were still in the city limits, and certainly these fuckers wouldn't try to chase them down and shoot them in broad daylight. Maybe. Possibly.

Trev cringed as the SUV pulled into what looked to be an old garage.

Okay, okay, he had to make his move.

Fuck.

Fuck, shit.

He couldn't get the knife to slide past his cuff.

It was too tight and the knife wouldn't naturally slip by.

If he tried to pull it out, it would be obvious he was trying to do something.

Fuck!

The SUV stopped and the man in the passenger seat got out to close the garage door behind them.

"Let's go." Emil grunted as he got out, his gun still pointed at Trev.

Trev glared fearlessly. "Go on, bitch. Think I'm going to make this easy for you? Fuck you!"

Emil nodded his head toward one of the other men.

They opened the other door to the back seat, going for Juicy.

"Hey, hey!" Trev screamed. "Let him go!"

"Get your bitch ass out," Emil warned, "or I'll make sure he dies real fuckin' slow."

"Ow!" the suited man who had a hold of Juicy cried out.

"What?" Emil demanded.

"Crazy old bat fucking bit me!"

Juicy barked and howled triumphantly. "Get 'em, Barkie! Get 'em!"

Emil grabbed Trev's arm to drag him out, jamming the gun against his head to serve as extra motivation to move quickly. He forced Trev forward into what may have been an old office, empty now except for a desk and some stray papers. It happened so quickly that Trev barely saw anything of the interior of the garage except for at least one door that might have led outside but it was boarded up.

Trev grunted as Emil shoved him into the desk, wheezing as he struggled to catch himself.

Juicy continued to bark furiously, even after the suited man threw him on the floor. "He hasn't had his shots! I hope you get fucking rabies!"

Emil smiled sweetly. "Just you wait. As soon as Sal gets here, it's over for you fucks."

The door slammed shut and locked.

Trev kneeled to help Juicy to his feet, averting his gaze from where the hospital gown had flipped up. "Are you okay?"

"Peachy keen, jelly bean," Juicy replied. "I do have the most dreadful headache though."

Trev looked over Juicy's head. The bleeding appeared to have stopped, but he grimaced when Juicy turned around, flashing his bare ass. He grabbed the jacket off the floor. "Here. Tie this on, okay?"

"Oh, well! If you insist." Juicy shrugged.

Trev leaned against the desk with a groan, quickly taking a closer look at the office.

It was small and eerily reminiscent of the room he'd been chained up in.

No windows and only one door.

Great.

Wonderful.

The door did have a sheet of frosted glass in it, but Trev didn't think smashing it would be a good idea. It would be too loud and would certainly draw way too much attention. Not to mention that Emil or any of those other suited pricks were probably waiting for them on the other side.

Trev searched the walls for any kind of weakness and found nothing. He looked up at the ratty ceiling tiles and waved Juicy over. "Hey! Hey, come here. If we..."

Juicy had tied the sleeves of the jacket around his head like a cape.

"Right." Trev cleared his throat. "If we get up on the desk, do you think you can crawl up through there? I can help give you a boost or pull you up! We might be able to find a way out!"

Juicy stared blankly. "The ceiling won't hold us."

"Come on!" Trev pleaded. "We have to fucking try!"

"No."

"Juicy!" Trev hissed frantically. "I'm not staying here to fucking die!"

"It's not like the movies, kid." Juicy shook his head. "Do you see how rotted out that shit is? We'll collapse back through and hit the damn floor! Probably break your fucking neck!"

"Okay!" Trev threw up his hands angrily. "Do you have any better fucking ideas, huh?"

"Not really, but oh..." Juicy sighed and looked off into the corner with a grimace.

"Oh God. What?" Trev groaned. "What is it now?"

"Barkie just had an accident."

"Of course he fucking did."

CHAPTER
Twenty-Two

IGNORING THE IMAGINARY DOG ACCIDENT, Trev continued to search the room for anything that might help them escape.

The desk was empty except for more paper, a stapler, and a roll of yellowed masking tape.

Yes, good.

Trev could beat Emil in the head with a stapler and shove some of the papers and old tape down his throat. That would work so beautifully. That would be just fucking great.

With a growl, he sat down on the desk and pulled the knife out from his sleeve.

Think, think, think.

The knife was a restaurant steak knife, so he felt it was a slight upgrade to the butter knife he'd previously stolen from Cold's breakfast table.

Cold...

Roderick.

He was gone and Trev was startled by a sudden burst of rage. It wasn't fair. Just when Cold was actually showing him that he wasn't a complete asshole, he had to go and get himself killed.

Rowena and Jimmy were going to be heartbroken.

And what would happen to the others? Jules and Mickey? Would they be all right without their leader? Would the city go down with its criminal king dead in the ground?

Those were someone else's problems, Trev tried to tell himself. It wasn't any of his damn business, and yet he couldn't escape the worries clouding his thoughts. He was more affected by Cold's loss than he first realized, and he didn't know what to do with that.

He hadn't given a shit about losing anyone since his mother.

And now Cold...

Trev felt sick.

His mind drifted to Jupiter now, and he only felt worse. Thinking that he might not be able to see Jupiter again made his stomach turn even harder and his heart ache. They were going to run away together. They were going to have a fucking future together, and it was absolute bullshit to have been given such a wonderful gift, only to have it taken away.

Because Jupiter was a gift, a treasure even, and Trev didn't want to imagine a life without him now.

He touched his collar and his chest tightened.

No.

Fuck this.

He didn't give up when he was chained to a wall. He wasn't going to give up now.

With a grunt, Trev heaved himself up on the desk.

"What are you doing?" Juicy asked. "I don't think there's any spiders up there."

"I'm trying to get us the fuck out of here," Trev said firmly. "I don't weigh as much as you do—"

"Rude!" Juicy gasped.

"I might be able to get through!" Trev insisted. "Just stay here, okay? I'll get the cops, I'll do whatever." He took a deep breath. "But we've got to get the fuck out, okay? I am not fucking dying here. Not fucking today."

Juicy frowned. "You look like you should die on a Monday. Not a Friday."

"Thank you, Juicy." Trev tucked the knife back up his shirt sleeve so he could reach the ceiling tiles and shift one out of the way. The opening was small but Trev was confident he could wiggle through.

Whether or not the ceiling would actually hold him was definitely a concern, but it was better than just sitting here waiting to be murdered.

Trev grabbed the edges of the frame where the tile had been to pull himself up. He grunted from the strain of having to drag himself upward, gasping when he was pushed even higher from below. He looked down to see Juicy there, having climbed on the desk to assist him.

"Up, up, and away!" Juicy said with a grin.

"Thanks, Juicy!" Trev tipped forward, getting his upper body spread across the ceiling and pulling his legs up behind him.

Okay, this wasn't good.

He could already feel the ceiling dipping from his weight, and he looked around quickly, trying to map out the dark space for any place that looked more sturdy. He spied a big wooden beam—some kind of support—and he carefully shifted forward.

The ceiling creaked, and one of the tiles dropped.

Shit, shit, shit.

"I don't think this is safe," Juicy whispered loudly.

"Shut up," Trev hissed back. "Just let me do this!"

"But it's stupid!"

"Shut up!"

Stupid or not, Trev continued to slowly wiggle toward the beam. As far as he could tell, the direction he was currently headed should be taking him to the back of the garage where the door was.

The door that was boarded up...

But maybe he'd be able to pry the boards off. Maybe it wouldn't be as hard to open as he thought. He was strong. He had adrenaline on his side and could definitely snatch off a few old boards with his bare hands before Emil or any of his goons shot him.

Maybe.

Fuck.

He tracked the open space in front of him and tried to weigh his options.

It was either this or going back into the office to die.

He had to fucking try.

He had to—oh no.

The ceiling groaned and gave way, sending Trev right down into the office with a crash.

He hit the desk, the breath knocked out of his lungs. He wheezed, his body immediately racked with pain, and struggled not to scream.

"Keep it down in there!" a man's voice shouted. "Stupid fucks."

Trev didn't have enough air to curse back.

Juicy petted the top of Trev's head. "You are not a spider monkey."

"No shit," Trev croaked.

"Nor a squirrel."

"Yup. Got it."

"Or, hmm, what else climbs really well..." Juicy hummed. "Maybe a sloth."

"Okay, enough!" Trev groaned as he sat up, dusting himself off and glaring up at the ceiling. "Look, at least I was trying! I can't just sit here and do fucking nothing, waiting for those assholes to come in here and blow us away. Which is..."

"What?"

"Why are they waiting?" Trev blinked. "I mean, they could have just shot us both as soon as they brought us here."

Juicy scratched his chin. "I always thought it was strange, but it's just sort of something organized crime enjoys. Witnesses. Taunting. Long, meandering speeches. Ugo was really into that kind of thing."

Trev flinched. "Ugo? Ugo Luchesi?"

He thought Juicy might have said that name before, but he didn't think he'd made the connection until now.

Shit.

"Uh-huh." Juicy reached down to scratch at Barkie's nonexistent head. "He always wanted to come with me on special jobs. He would sometimes even request to shoot them too. They'd already be dead, so it was sort of silly, but he really enjoyed it."

Trev grimaced. "That is fucked up."

Juicy grinned. "He had his ways about him, that's for sure."

Trev sighed heavily. "He's a real treat. Loves parties."

"Oh! You've met him?"

"Yeah." Trev shrugged. "You guys apparently have the same nurse or something. Did you know that?"

"When did I get a nurse?"

"Yup. That's what I thought." Trev glanced at the door with a scowl.

Opening it and just trying to walk out was probably ridiculous.

Okay, but it was worth a try, right?

Trev took the knife from his sleeve as he hopped off the desk. He crept toward the door and then carefully turned the knob, trying not to make a single sound that might draw any attention.

Juicy was right behind him, asking, "What are you doing?"

"Shhhh!" Trev waved at him frantically. "Will you be quiet? I'm trying to get a better look around! Maybe there's another way out of here!"

"There's not. I looked." Juicy blinked slowly. "I saw a door... garage doors. A door that was boarded up. That's it."

"Wait, wait, so did you see two doors or three doors?" Trev let go of the knob, turning to address Juicy. He knew this conversation might ultimately be pointless, but he was willing to try just in case.

"There are..."

"Yeah?"

Juicy grinned. "Five."

"Five. How the fuck do you figure five?"

"The three garage doors for the bay, the one that's boarded up, and this one here to the office!"

"Shit." Trev grimaced.

He already knew that, so that was less than helpful.

Juicy frowned. "Was that not the right answer? Okay! Then there are *six* doors."

"Are you just saying that?"

"No."

Trev scowled but he focused back on the door, slowly

turning the knob. He moved as silently as he could and once the knob could not be twisted more, he opened the door a tiny crack to peek out into the garage.

Three garage doors, the boarded up door, and...

Nothing.

Unless there was one hiding from his line of sight directly to the left or right from this door, there were truly only five doors inside this building, which meant no magical way out of here.

One of the suited men spotted the office door opening. "Hey! Shut the goddamn door before I pump you full of fucking holes!"

Trev grimaced and slammed the door shut.

So much for that.

"I'm sorry." Juicy frowned. "I really thought there might be six."

"No, no, it's okay." Trev offered a small smile. "I understand you're trying to help me. It's... It's really all right." He returned to the desk to plot, his thoughts in shambles.

Fuck.

This...

This really might be it.

"Your mother was really a lovely woman," Juicy said suddenly.

"Excuse me?" Trev quirked his brows.

"Your mother." Juicy smiled. "She knew, I think. That I was watching over you two. She noticed. Of course she did, heh. She was smart. And she knew it wasn't a coincidence that I kept showing up everywhere you were. She was very observant, smart. Clever."

Trev hesitated to say anything that might interrupt Juicy's rambling.

He had said very little to Trev about his mother, and he couldn't imagine another time he might be able to hear any of this. "Yeah? Was she?"

"Oh yes." Juicy nodded. "Mind teasers, brain puzzles, riddles. She had a real knack for them. Whiz at crosswords too. She was always kind to me..." He touched his brow. "Even when my mind started to go. Wherever it goes. Huh. Where does it go?"

"What?"

"Your mind." Juicy stared at him intently. "When it goes, where is it? Where does it end up?"

"Maybe..." Trev smiled. "Maybe it goes to the beach and we'll find it there."

"You really think we're going to make it to the beach?"

"I have to." Trev hit the desk, his frustrations bubbling over. "I have to fucking believe in something. I'm not going to give up. I can't just sit here waiting to get fucking murdered! I was in danger, always at risk. I put myself in stupid fucking situations all the time, I did some of the dumbest shit you can think of, and..."

Somehow I made it.

Why?

How?

"There were so many times I could have died," Trev said quietly. "I was... *arrogant*. I didn't care. I thought I was in control and I was smarter than everyone else was. Which, hey, is true for a lot of people, but... not all of them. I was a fucking idiot. All that mattered to me was the next payout, the next hustle, the next *anything* that would get me away from Perry City."

"And now?" Juicy prompted.

Trev's eyes were hot. "Now..."

Juicy came over to sit beside Trev on the desk, slinging

his arm around Trev's shoulders. "What is it, kid? Talk to me."

Trev stared at a spot on the floor. "Now it's not just about me. There's people I care about and I have so much to lose. You, Jupiter, Rowena, Jimmy..."

"Cold?"

"He's already gone," Trev whispered bitterly. "I think I was just starting to understand him and now he's fucking dead. Because he's like me. *Was* like me. Arrogant, cocky, thought he had everything planned out, that he could control fucking everything. And look where it fucking got him."

"The boss of Strassen Springs?"

"Dead."

"Ah, yes. That too."

"I'm scared that's what is going to happen to me." Trev leaned over to put his head on Juicy's shoulder. "I was so sure I could play this out in some way that would get me what I wanted, and now... Now we're fucking trapped here and there's no goddamn way out. I never got to tell Jupiter how much... I..." He growled angrily. "Fuck, now I just sound like a fucking cliché."

"Never got to tell him what?" Juicy smiled warmly. "You can tell me if you want."

"That I was falling for him," Trev said with a sigh. "That I could see a future for us, a real happily ever after. Get married, adopt dogs, all that shit."

"Aw, you like dogs?"

Trev laughed sadly. "No, I'm a fish person."

"Oh well. Everybody makes mistakes, I suppose." Juicy's eyes gleamed. "I had a sweetheart once. A long time ago."

"Yeah?" Trev smirked. "What was her name?"

"Melba." Juicy's eyes glimmered. "She was perfect. The best smile, an incredible laugh, bright feathers..."

"Feathers?"

"Yes! She loved feathers." Juicy chuckled. "She always wove them into her hair with these little braids. It was beautiful."

"What happened?"

"I... I had to work." Juicy's smile dipped down into a deep crease. "I was a doctor then. I had to make rounds, see patients, I... I was gone for too long. When I finally decided to stop being a doctor, she was already gone."

Trev frowned. "Gone? Like... what? She died?"

"No, you dummy," Juicy scolded. "She married someone else."

"Oh."

"You know I wasn't really a doctor, right?"

"No, yeah, I had my suspicions." Trev bumped their shoulders together.

"I've been so many things. So many lies. So many stories and lives that were all my own for a short while and then faded away so I could take on the next job." Juicy sighed. "And the only thing I regret... is that I didn't get to be Melba's husband. And that's what I wanted to be the most."

"I'm sorry, Juicy."

"Me too, Trev." Juicy nudged Trev. "Maybe you'll still have the chance to be who you want to be."

"Gonna be kinda hard if I'm dead." Trev shook his head, his shoulders sagging. "Maybe in the next life."

"Oh." Juicy blinked slowly and his eyes became strikingly clear. He frowned, reaching out his hand to Trev. "Please. Give me the knife."

"Sure. Wanna stab me in the throat with it? Put me out of my misery?"

"I need you to call for them." Juicy looked over the knife and squeezed the handle tight.

"Call for who?" Trev rolled his eyes.

"The men guarding us. Tell them you're having chest pain."

"Wow, speaking of shit from the movies." Trev rolled his eyes even harder. "Do I look old enough to have a heart attack?"

"Fine. Tell them *I'm* having chest pain," Juicy said firmly. He was oddly focused, his expression stern. "Go ahead."

Trev frowned. "Wait, what are you doing?"

"Getting us out of here so you can be what you want to be in *this* life."

"What the fuck are you going to do?" Trev demanded, his patience thin. "Juicy, come on—"

Juicy grabbed Trev's shoulder and squeezed with surprising strength. "Trev, you're a good kid. You've always been kind to me. Even when I get—" He sighed. "—confused. But I need you to trust me now. That I know what to do, all right?"

Trev tensed.

"Please," Juicy said quietly. "So we can get back to Jupiter, huh? Got a beach to go to, right?"

"Yeah." Trev nodded. "Okay, but if you're wrong and we fucking die, I am so kicking your ass in fucking hell, all right?"

"Deal." Juicy patted Trev's shoulder. "Go on. Now."

Trev headed to the door. He took a deep breath before he pounded on the glass, screaming, "Hey! Hey! Someone come here! Help! Help us!"

There was no answer.

"Hey! Fuckers! Come on!" Trev screamed. "Juicy fell over! He said somethin' about chest pain and just hit the fucking floor! I don't think he's fucking breathing! Come the fuck on, you dickless fucks!"

Juicy silently positioned himself next to the door. When it opened, he would be behind it and out of immediate sight.

A man grunted on the other side of the glass. "What the fuck?"

It wasn't Emil, so probably one of the other big suited idiots.

"Hey! Hey! Please!" Trev smacked the glass frantically. "Please! We need some fucking help in here! Please! Hurry!"

"Yeah, yeah, hang on." The man growled. "Just wait a damn minute."

Trev saw the knob turning and he backed up quickly.

The door opened and the man came in. "Okay! Where the fuck is—"

He didn't even have enough time to finish his sentence.

Juicy was too fast.

With alarming speed, Juicy slammed the door shut with his foot and grabbed the man's head from behind. He twisted it and there was a distinct *crack*, and the man fell to the floor in a heap.

"Holy shit," Trev whispered. "You... You..."

"Come on." Juicy grabbed the man's arm. "Help me move him behind the desk. More will be coming."

"What? Right. Holy shit." Trev grabbed the man's other arm and pulled him behind the desk. "His feet are still sticking out."

Juicy huffed and crouched down, bending the man's legs to keep his feet out of sight. He quickly stood back by the door again, saying quietly, "Come here. Get behind me and don't move."

"You seriously just snapped that guy's neck."

"Yes."

"Like a fucking ninja or something!"

Juicy shushed him.

Footsteps approached, and Trev clicked his teeth together, his heart jumping up into the back of his throat. It was one thing to be told that his sweet old neighbor used to be a hitman, but it was quite another to see him in action as he effortlessly ended a man's life.

Yes, the man worked for the Luchesi family and would have certainly murdered Trev or Juicy given the chance, but still.

Holy shit.

That seemed to be the phrase of the day, and it repeated in Trev's brain over and over on a loop. It wasn't a very productive line of thinking, but it did prevent him from having an absolute fit over the prospect of seeing Juicy murder someone again.

"Hey!" a new man's voice called. "What's going on? Bear? Where are you?"

Bear's taking a little nap nap right now, Trev thought crazily.

The permanent kind.

The new man stormed in, the door swinging open and catching on Juicy's arm. He turned to glare at Juicy. "What are you—"

Juicy grabbed the man's wrist as he raised his gun and stabbed him in the neck.

Trev looked away, but he felt blood spray across his face.

Ugh, that was the second time today.

And it was hot and thick—wait, that...

Trev didn't have enough time to figure out why that felt extra wrong, cringing as he finally opened his eyes to see Juicy taking the man down to the floor and stabbing him again. He turned his gaze back to the ceiling when he realized just how much of Juicy he could see right now. "Is he dead?"

"He's definitely not alive." Juicy stood with a grunt.

Trev peeked open one eye, seeing now Juicy had taken the man's gun. "What now?"

"Now we get the fuck out of here." Juicy pushed Trev back behind the door. "I need you to wait here."

"No!" Trev growled. "You're not leaving me here!"

"There's only one man left unless more have arrived. We need to go while we can and I need to make sure the way is clear."

"What way? The only door I saw is all boarded up!" Trev argued. "Which means using the fucking garage door and that's loud as fuck!"

"All the more reason for you to stay put."

"Suck my fucking dick, Juicy! I'm not—"

A door slammed in the distance with enough force to rattle the entire rickety building.

Which was good because it let them know there was another door, but it was also bad because it might mean that more people were here—Sal?

Why not Godzilla?

Trev scrambled for anything he could use as a weapon. He pulled out one of the drawers from the desk, but then he remembered there was another corpse to loot. He checked over the man's body and found a gun under his jacket.

There.

Better.

He'd never fired a gun but he understood the concept well enough and knew to check to see if the safety was on. He stomped over to Juicy's side, saying firmly, "I'm going with you. We go together or not at all, okay?"

Juicy's eyes appeared heavy, but he nodded. "All right."

Footsteps rapidly approached, at least three or more people, but they stopped just short of the door.

"Well, shit." It was Emil. "I only left for a few fuckin minutes, I swear—"

There was a loud smack, no doubt Sal slapping him.

"You fucking idiot!" Sal shouted. "I can't trust you to fucking watch paint dry, you fucking moron!" He growled in frustration, now addressing Juicy and Trev as he snapped, "You two. Come out, nice and easy. There's nowhere else to go."

Juicy held a finger to his lips.

Trev nodded and said nothing.

"Come on now," Sal said, his patience clearly thinning. "There's a lot more of us than there are of you."

"Not until you've satisfied my list of demands!" Juicy shouted back at him.

"What fucking demands?"

"We want to walk out of here, free and unharmed." Juicy's brow furrowed. "And then we need a car. And dog food. I want the Blue Buffalo kind in the purple bag. None of that cheap shit."

Trev's heart sank.

Whatever clarity Juicy had was leaving him now, and Trev watched in horror as Juicy's hand holding the gun trembled. He quickly reached over to take it from him, biting his lip until he tasted blood.

"What?" Sal scoffed. "You want fucking dog food?"

"Yes!" Juicy snapped angrily, massaging his brow like he was fending off a headache. "I... I need dog food for Barkie. Barkie has got to be hungry by now. I don't know when he ate last."

Sal snorted, his voice dropping as he said, "Kill them both. Old man is off his shit. End this. Now."

"But I thought you wanted to—" Emil started.

"No! You fucking moron!" Sal growled, and there was another smack. "I said I wanted them dead. You could have just brought me corpses and I would have been happy. Now we've lost two men 'cause you thought I needed to *see* them die for some stupid ass fucking reason."

Trev felt the building shift ever so slightly as if the door had opened again, but he didn't hear anything. He was wondering what it was, but he didn't need long to think about it.

Bang, bang, bang.

Three quick shots were followed by three consecutive *thumps*.

"No." Sal gasped sharply. "It fucking can't be."

"How the fucking fuck?" Emil demanded. "How... Fucking *how*?"

"No, no. No fucking way!"

Someone laughed.

A snarky, mean, smug fucking laugh.

It couldn't be...

Trev peeked around the door even as Juicy tried to stop him, his heart freezing in his chest as he stared out at...

Holy fucking shit.

Boss Cold.

Very much not dead and looking especially pleased with himself in a new navy blue suit.

Jules, Lorre, Mickey, and Jupiter were behind him, along with two other men Trev hadn't yet met, one very old and one very young. There was also a redheaded man with glasses and he, like all the rest except Jupiter, was armed.

Cold's gun was big, *really* big, and it had a shiny pearl

grip that caught the light and gleamed, almost as brightly as his teeth as he grinned.

Emil took a step back as Sal screamed, "No! You're dead! You're fucking dead! We saw it! We all fucking saw!" He was shaking. "You're *dead*!"

"I would say I'm surprised you fell for it, but..." Cold chuckled. "I'm really not."

CHAPTER Twenty-Three

"AS ALWAYS, you and the rest of your family remain complete and utter idiots." Cold glanced at the doorway where he saw Trev peeking out. "Ah, Trevanion. Are you all right?"

"Fucking peachy," Trev replied as he flew out of the office to immediately tackle Jupiter. He hugged him tight, burying his face in his chest.

"Trev," Jupiter murmured, wrapping his arms around him and kissing the top of his head. "Why do you have two guns?"

"Buy one, get one free?"

"Let's just... Here." Jupiter gently took the guns away so he could hand them off to Mickey.

Jules was busy disarming Emil and Sal, humming lightly as he did. He whistled at the office. "Hey. Juice. You can come on out now."

Juicy peeked around the corner and then he grinned when he saw Cold. "Ha! I knew you weren't dead."

"Yeah! How the fuck?" Trev demanded. "I saw your head!

I saw…" He tried to remember exactly what he'd seen, but it was only a blur of red. "You were fucking faking it."

"Thirdsies here is very keen on explosions and special effects." Cold nodded to the young man.

"The picture," Trev realized. "The one that was a little off in the corner. That was it, wasn't it? It just popped off and sprayed a bunch of what? Fake blood?"

"Yes. Remotely controlled, of course."

"But the waiter—"

"Really was an assassin."

"And the gun—"

"Personally planted by Valdemar." Cold tipped his head to the old man. "Loaded with blanks. The security detail wouldn't allow anyone to bring a weapon inside the restaurant, so the Luchesi family thought they'd be clever and hide one in the days leading up to the hit."

"So, you found the gun, planted your own loaded with blanks, rigged all that shit up and made sure you'd sit in the corner so you could pretend to be fucking murdered?"

"Yes."

Trev stared.

And he stared.

"Okay." Trev took a deep breath. "But fucking *why*?"

"To make sure these two felt brave enough to stick out their necks," Cold replied, his icy gaze turning on Emil and Sal. "After all, we do have so much to discuss."

Emil only growled while Sal stared furiously.

"And what are you doing here?" Trev gave Jupiter a shake. "I left you at the house!"

"I followed Juicy to the hospital," Jupiter replied. "That, uh, Thirdsies guy came with me and—"

"Juicy!" Trev scolded. "You didn't think to mention that?"

Juicy blinked. "Mention what?"

"Right."

"Anyway." Jupiter chuckled. "We went to the hospital with Juicy and left to go get something to eat. We left Juicy in the room, thinkin' that the old man couldn't get into that much trouble—"

"Big mistake."

"Yeah, I see that now!" Jupiter snorted. "When we came back, he was gone."

"Yes, I was," Juicy said proudly.

"What happened to your head, Juicy?" Jupiter glanced over Trev and Juicy both, his brow wrinkling in concern. "What the hell? Are you guys okay?"

"So, Juicy stole a car and then wrecked it a tiny bit."

Cold scowled. "We'll take care of that." He narrowed his eyes at Juicy. "You. No more driving."

"Oh, all right." Juicy nodded. "I have been trying to cut back. Goes right to my hips."

Cold sighed, a sound of deep and long suffering. "To the business at hand." His icy gaze snapped back to Emil and Sal. "As I said, we have much to discuss."

"I've got fuckin' nothin' to say to you," Sal spat.

"Oh, but I think you do." Cold smiled. "Unless you want your father to spend his golden years rotting away in prison."

"Excuse me?"

"You heard me." Cold tucked his gun away under his jacket. "You will cease any and all operations involving former special agent Champignon or I'll see to it that your father goes to prison."

"For fucking what?" Emil spat. "You ain't got nothin' on our old man."

Sal's grim expression indicated that he wasn't so sure.

"There is potentially going to be a grisly discovery very soon at a little park in Perry City," Cold said. "Three bodies might be found. The three men that Federico Luchesi killed and whose bodies were buried there."

"So?" Emil scoffed. "Feddy killed those fuckers, but—"

"Ugo was with him," Trev realized out loud. "He liked to put in the final shot."

Cold raised his brow in faint surprise, but he nodded. "Yes. Ballistics will confirm that at least one of the bullets in each victim matches a weapon owned by Ugo Luchesi. He was tried but not convicted in several other cases over the years and there are multiple ballistic reports on his personal arsenal."

"Bullshit!" Emil shouted. "That's a load of fuckin' crap!"

"Why else has your family been interfering with the park renovations? You know the bodies are there and that if they're exhumed your father could be implicated in those deaths. It's why the family first tried to buy out the land after that flood. You knew what they might find, but ah, you had the same problem as the rest of us. You didn't know where they were buried."

"Fuck you," Sal said calmly. "No bodies, no fuckin' case. You've got nothin'. I don't care how much fuckin' pull you have. No one's gonna go diggin' up the park on a body hunt."

"Well, then it's a shame because—"

"I know where the bodies are buried!" Trev blurted out. "Juicy told me. The two trees, three trees, whatever. Those are the body locations. He used to walk his dog by them to make sure no one was messing with them and it became part of his routine."

"*Yes.*" Cold's brow furrowed in annoyance. "Mr. Cusack is

the one who brought the bodies to Perry City from Strassen Springs to dispose of them."

"I did?" Juicy blinked. "Huh. Maybe I did."

"No one is gonna believe that crazy old bat," Emil snapped.

"They don't have to believe him," Cold said calmly. "Three dead bodies will be quite convincing on their own. And oh, they will be discovered because the mayor of Strassen Springs has signed a deal to sponsor building a fountain in Perry City's park, just as their mayor has agreed to build one here." He smiled. "I promise you, they will find at least one of the bodies because I have the honor of picking the location for the fountain's installation."

"The meeting with the mayor," Trev said carefully. "That's why you were so set on making it. That's what it was about." He scowled. "The mayor knew, didn't he? That something was going to happen?"

"He knew there was the potential for a little surprise, yes," Cold replied. "But I assure you that we will meet again very soon to finalize all those pesky details."

Sal's grimace deepened. "What the fuck do you want?"

"You will cease all operations involving Mr. Champignon. Your entire family will sever ties with him." Cold smirked. "I don't care what he threatens you with. Trust that whatever it is, I can make it much, much worse."

"You know we have to answer to the council now," Sal said disgustedly. "I can't promise—"

"That's not my problem," Cold cut in. "That's yours."

Emil glared at Sal. "You're really gonna let this motherfucker push us around? Huh?"

"Shut the fuck up." Sal smacked the side of his head.

"Hey! Fuck you!" Emil hit him back. "I'm so tired of your fuckin' shit!"

"Shut up!" Sal barked. "I'm workin' this out."

"Work on my fuckin' dick, you asshole!"

Cold politely cleared his throat.

"What?" Sal growled.

"I wasn't done," Cold said calmly. "In addition to giving Mr. Champignon the metaphorical finger, you will turn over any remaining Luchesi properties here in Strassen Springs to me. Do not even try to deny it. It's how I knew you idiots would come here because you only have but so much real estate. Also, you will lift the hit on Mr. Prospero and cease pursuing him at once."

"What?" Trev gasped.

"That traitorous piece of shit—" Sal started.

"Is now a member of the Gentleman and therefore under my protection," Cold said firmly. "As far as you're concerned, he doesn't exist. Put him completely out of your head. Do you understand?"

"And what the fuck if we say no, huh?" Emil spat angrily. "What if we say to hell with our old man and fuck you right in your stupid fuckin' smug face? So what if he goes to fuckin' jail? Maybe I don't give a shit. Fuck you, bitch ass—"

"Then I'll kill you."

"What?"

"You heard me," Cold said, his voice dropping to a low and dangerous tone. "I will kill you and the rest of your pitiful family. I'll kill your friends, your wives, your mistresses, even your fish. I will completely erase anyone and everyone who could possibly care about you so when you're put in the ground, the only people who will be present are the gravediggers to cover up your casket."

Emil opened his mouth to speak but nothing came out.

"Ha!" Trev cheered. "Fuckin' suck it, you motherfuckers! Hear that? No one there but the assholes throwin' dirt on you and the maggots eating your fuckin' brains! Oh, wait, except you don't have any brains because you're fucking *morons*! Fuck you!"

Cold arched a brow.

"Right. Sorry." Trev grinned and hugged Jupiter tight. "Got a little excited."

Sal made a face. "Fine. Whatever. Jupiter's your fucking problem now and we'll cut the fed loose. Happy?"

"And the properties," Cold said firmly. "Next time your family tries to sneak into my city and purchase real estate, I will not be so kind."

"Understood." Sal nodded. "We'll take care of it."

"I expect you will or we'll be seeing each other again very, very soon."

Sal grabbed Emil and dragged him out of the garage. There was a side door Trev hadn't been able to see before from inside the office, and Sal slammed it shut behind them as they left. The building rattled, dust fell, and it was quiet for a few moments as the tension bled out of the space.

"Wow." Trev clung to Jupiter, though he stared at Cold. "You're a lot fucking smarter than I thought you were."

Cold snorted. "And you're a lot dumber than I thought." He scowled. "What part of *stay at the restaurant* did you not understand?"

"Maybe the part where you pretended to get fucking murdered and your stupid blood splattered all over me?"

"It was important to make it as convincing as possible to anyone watching—"

"Including me?"

"As if you would have been able to act your way through that knowing it wasn't real."

"Fuck you! You don't know!" Trev gasped as Jupiter squeezed him.

Jupiter cleared his throat softly.

Trev grunted. "Okay, fine. Whatever. I get it. And..." He took a deep breath. "Thank you for... you know."

"No, I don't know." Cold smiled sweetly. "For which part? Saving your life, freeing your partner...?"

"All of it." Trev surged forward and hugged Cold tight. "Thank you."

"Oh." Cold stiffened. "You're welcome."

"Don't make this fucking weird. Just hug me back, asshole."

Cold lifted one arm to wrap around Trev, his body slowly but surely relaxing as he gave Trev the world's most awkward hug. "Are we done now?"

"Almost." Trev smiled.

"Ugh."

"Okay, there." Trev let go, grinning. "So. Uh, now what?"

"We go home. I believe Juicy could use medical attention." Cold glanced over at him. "And some clothes."

"It is a bit breezy in here," Juicy remarked.

"Wait, uh." Trev pulled himself away from Cold. "What about the waiter? The crime scene? Hello?" He scoffed. "Aren't we witnesses? And uh, aren't you *dead*?"

"It is very unfortunate that young man decided to take his own life right in front of us. I needed medical attention following such a traumatic experience." Cold shrugged. "Quite a tragedy."

"That's it?"

"What else could there be?"

"You..." Trev's head hurt. "But I heard more shooting. I heard—"

"You heard an off-duty police officer responding to a mugging that happened to coincide with the waiter's tragic suicide."

Trev stared.

"Is there a problem?"

"It's really that easy?" Trev said. "You just... rewrite what happened? Just make it up to whatever fits what you want?"

"Yes." Cold arched his brow. "And?"

"Right. So. That's a whole new level of fucked up, but hey! Gangsters." Trev retreated back to Jupiter's side. "Let's get the fuck out of here."

"Let's," Cold agreed.

"Thank you, Boss Cold," Jupiter said. "I appreciate what you did—"

"I did not do it for you," Cold cut in briskly, already headed to the door. "Save your gratitude for Trevanion."

"Hear that? You need to show me how grateful you are." Trev kissed Jupiter firmly before falling into step behind the others out of the garage, eager to be out of there.

Jerry was waiting just outside with the limo, holding the door open for them with a polite smile.

Cold went in first and the other Gentlemen scattered. Thirdsies, Valdemar, and the redhead left in a big truck. Roger and Mickey vanished in a slick black classic muscle car, and Jules drove off in an El Camino with flames painted on the sides.

Trev climbed into the back of the limo with Jupiter right behind him. He took one of the seats on the side and waited for Jupiter so he could collapse against him. Before he could even blink, he realized they were missing someone. "Where's Juicy?"

"Safe." Cold pushed a button that rolled down the screen separating them from the front seat.

Jerry was behind the wheel and Juicy was riding shotgun, excitedly talking away. Trev couldn't hear what he was saying because there was still a window between them, but judging by how happy Juicy looked, he imagined it was about Barkie.

Then again, it could have been about murdering people too.

There was no telling now.

"I've already called Dr. Queen to come examine him," Cold said. "We'll make sure he's all right. I understand that she was concerned he has not been taking his medication."

"But you've had nurses coming to see him, like, every day?"

"Mr. Cusack is nothing if not resourceful." Cold chuckled as if that was a joke he found very funny. "It's nice to see that he hasn't lost his touch."

"Yeah. Super nice to see him in action. That was just great. Love all this murder. So. What happens to all the bodies back there?" Trev asked quietly. "They gonna be the result of a gas leak or something?"

"Do you really want to know?" Cold asked.

"No, I guess it doesn't matter."

Jupiter kissed Trev's brow and held him tight. "The only thing that matters is right here, baby doll."

Trev's heart skipped a few beats, and he sagged against Jupiter's chest. "Yeah. There were a few seconds there where I thought…" He didn't even want to finish the thought. "I'm just glad it's over. It is fucking over, right?"

"Yes," Cold replied simply. "Emil and Sal will return to Perry City to lick their wounds. They may spin whatever story they'd like to ensure the council's compliance."

"And if they don't?"

"I think I've made it clear that the consequences are severe." Cold smirked. "Unlike the Luchesi family, my assassins don't fail."

Trev mirrored Cold's smug smirk. "Technically, he didn't

fail. If you fucked up and it had been a real gun, you'd be dead."

Jupiter made a small sound. It may have been a snort of laughter that he was trying to hide with a cough. He stared down at Trev with wide eyes and then looked at Cold, no doubt bracing for his reaction.

Cold leaned forward, his face curiously calm. "Well, then it's a very good thing I do not tend to fuck up, isn't it?"

"Yup." Trev clicked his tongue. "Must run in the family."

Cold smiled at that. "Perhaps it does."

Trev smiled too.

Jupiter gave him a gentle squeeze, and somehow that was all Trev needed to be sure that things were really going to be okay. They were both alive, free, and Cold wasn't the full-blooded asshole Trev had thought he was.

"Did you mean what you said?" Trev asked suddenly. "About the trip?"

"Trip?" Jupiter echoed.

"Yes." Cold nodded, leaning back against the seat. "I own a villa that sits right on the beach of Magen's Bay in St. Thomas."

"And that is where?" Trev pressed. "The Caribbean, right?"

"Yes, the Virgin Islands. Trust me that it is a lovely slice of paradise, and you are welcome to stay there for as long as you'd like while you sort out whatever it is you want to do."

"What about Juicy?" Jupiter asked carefully. "Is he coming too?"

"Yup." Trev gestured to Cold. "Cold is gonna get him nursing care or whatever down there with us. Hopefully nurses that will make sure he's taking all the drugs he needs."

"Yes," Cold confirmed with a slight huff. "I'm happy to

make the arrangements. If you still wish to leave this afternoon, I can make flight arrangements for you. You can fly right out of Strassen Springs, if you'd like."

"Just like that?"

"Yes."

"Wow." Trev grinned up at Jupiter. "What do you think?"

"I think that sounds like a wonderful and generous gift," Jupiter said, bowing his head to kiss Trev's brow. "We can go whenever you want, baby doll."

Trev closed his eyes and held Jupiter close. "Fuck yeah."

Things were looking up.

Instead of waiting for the other shoe to drop, Trev found he was surprisingly optimistic about the future. A trip to paradise was a pretty fabulous light to have waiting for him at the end of what had been a pretty damn dark tunnel.

Knowing he'd be going there with Juicy and Jupiter made it sweeter still.

Cold's phone buzzed and he made a face when he looked at the screen.

"Let me guess," Trev said. "Rowena or Jimmy or both saw the news and are freaking the fuck out about you having possibly been murdered for real?"

Cold glared. "You really are quite clever."

"I love that you said that like it's an insult." Trev batted his eyes. "But I'm going to take it as a compliment."

"It can be both." Cold tapped at his phone, still scowling.

Trev watched him aggressively type. "Everything okay?"

"Fine." Cold's pissed off expression said otherwise. He looked up at Trev, his smile strained. "Our sister would like you to stay tonight for dinner. She's taken it upon herself to make arrangements to throw you a party."

Trev laughed. "Seriously?"

"Yes."

"Wow, uh..." Trev glanced up at Jupiter. "What do you think? I mean, you had so much fun at the last party we went to, dragging me around on a leash."

Cold arched a brow, and his expression hardened.

Jupiter smiled, and Trev swore he looked nervous. "That wasn't my idea by the way. Just to be clear."

"Maybe I'll drag you around this time." Trev pulled at Jupiter's tie and purred.

Jupiter chuckled. "If you'd like."

"So." Cold rolled his eyes. "Is that a yes?"

"A big yes," Trev confirmed. "Shit. I don't know if I have anything to wear—"

"Rowena has assured me she took care of that." Cold smirked. "You'll find there is little she doesn't think of. She's very fond of planning events like this."

"She's pretty great." Trev smiled warmly. "So are you, you know. When you're not trying to be the world's biggest—"

"Asshole?"

"I was gonna be nice and downgrade you to *prick*, but hey, asshole still works."

Cold just smiled, reaching into his pocket to pull out a second phone. He handed it to Trev. "Here."

"What is this?" Trev blinked as the phone buzzed in his hand. There was an incoming call.

"We call them smartphones. This one is for you. Rowena mentioned you needed one."

"Ha ha, seriously."

"Answer it. Or Rowena is going to get very upset with you."

Trev swiped his thumb across the screen and then held the phone to his ear. "Hello?"

"Hi, sweetie," Rowena crooned. "How was your nice little

mafia adventure? Good? Great?"

"I don't know about all that, but uh, still here, right?" Trev laughed.

"I'm going to strangle the fuck out of Roddy as soon as he walks in the damn door. Ugh, that motherfucker. You get a pass because you didn't actually know what was going on. Everybody else is on my shit list."

"Not Jupiter, right?" Trev smiled up at Jupiter.

"No, he's okay," Rowena replied. "Oh! And Juicy! That old geezer is at the very top for scaring the *fuck* out of me. Making me think he was dying. What a bitch."

"Yeah, uh." Trev grimaced. "Maybe go easy on him. He's had, uh, a very exciting day."

"Whatever." Rowena popped her tongue. "Now listen, sweetie. Shoe size. Ready go."

"Uh. Twelve?"

"Okay." Rowena hummed thoughtfully. "And would you rather have Chinese, Japanese, or like, a blend of both? Like maybe a buffet with some sushi? Hibachi?"

"What?" Trev frowned. "What are you doing?"

"Oh, you're right." Rowena laughed. "We should just do it all."

"Do what? *What are you doing*?"

"Whatever I want." Rowena made kissy sounds. "Because this means you're staying today—"

"Yeah, but—"

"—so, I can probably get you to stay at least another week!"

Trev scowled. "Roe, girl. No. Me and Jupiter are leaving—"

"Love you! Bye!" Rowena made more kissy sounds.

"Love you too, but—" Trev grunted as Rowena abruptly hung up.

He wasn't sure what was more alarming—Rowena planning what sounded like a very, very big party or how easy it had been to say *love you too.*

Did he really mean that?

Was it just a reflex?

Rowena had treated him like family from the moment they'd first met. Jimmy too. Trev supposed he loved them in a way, the siblings he'd never had. Rowena was ever the big sassy sister and Jimmy a sweet brother with a big heart. Juicy was family too, Trev decided, for all he'd done for Trev over the years, especially the times he had no idea.

Okay, maybe the whole stalking him because Juicy was actually a former hitman was a little creepy, but still.

Juicy did always invite him over for Chinese food.

Plus, his imaginary dog liked him, so that had to count for something.

And Jupiter.

Jupiter was...

Trev wasn't sure how to fully quantify his feelings for Jupiter just yet except that they were strong, and he didn't want to spend another moment away from him.

The things they'd been through together had created a unique bond, forged in a wild mix of passion, chaos, and determination. Trev had never felt like this about anyone, nor had someone prove their affections so intensely. Jupiter had upended his entire life at great personal risk to himself just to be with Trev, and as far as romantic gestures went, that was pretty damn special.

Plus, that dick was fantastic.

The rest of Jupiter was too, and Trev could not imagine having survived this insane adventure with anyone else. Though he wasn't sure what the future held, he was happy knowing that he wouldn't be facing it alone.

He had an incredible partner.

Wonderful friends.

A *family*.

Trev couldn't really ask for more.

Well, he *could* because who wouldn't want a new Ferrari or a Chanel bag, but he was honestly happy with what he had. It was beyond anything he could have ever hoped for and there truly was no price tag on this kind of happiness.

"Everything all right?" Cold asked.

"Yeah, our sister might just be a little bit nuts," Trev replied. "Crazy runs in the family too, huh?"

"It doesn't just run," Cold drawled. "It *gallops*."

"Must be why we get along so well," Jupiter teased Trev lightly. "My crazy plays really well with yours."

"That's not the only thing that plays well together." Trev grinned slyly.

Cold sighed.

"I'm talking about sex," Trev said bluntly, delighted by Cold's obvious discomfort. "Because we have such *great* sex. Like, wow, he tears my ass the fuck up. Thanks for chaining him to the bed, by the way, because wow, new kink unlocked—"

"Trevanion?"

"Yeah?"

"Would you like to walk the rest of the way back?"

"And piss off Rowena because you made me miss my own party?" Trev batted his eyes.

"That is a risk I'm willing to take."

"Behave yourself," Jupiter scolded gently, nudging Trev.

"Why?" Trev asked. "Will I get a prize if I do?"

Jupiter gently grabbed his collar and kissed him.

"Is that it?" Trev teased. "I was expecting a bit more incentive. At least some tongue."

Jupiter leaned in close, his lips brushing Trev's ear as he whispered, "As soon as we're alone, I'm going to fuck you until you can't say anything else but my name, baby doll."

Trev grinned.

Yup.

Priceless.

CHAPTER
Twenty-Four

WHEN ROWENA LEGRAND wanted to throw a party, that bitch threw a party.

After screaming furiously at Cold, she dragged Trev off to get their nails done.

And no, she didn't make them go back into the city to visit a salon but in fact had a manicurist come to the house. She spent a lot of the time fussing about their brother and his big, stupid secret plans, and Trev was happy to nod along.

Why, yes, Cold was an asshole.

But that asshole was their brother and was sending Trev and his boyfriend, plus his crazy friend and his crazy friend's imaginary dog, to a private villa in the Caribbean.

So, maybe Cold wasn't so bad after all.

Once their nails were done, Rowena surprised Trev with a hairstylist who dyed his fading pink hair into a deep magenta.

It was the perfect color to match his new dress—a pink sequined cocktail number with a plunging neckline and short skirt. She had gotten shoes to match—a pair of pink crushed velvet boots with staggering stiletto heels.

Oh, and stockings?

Fishnets, naturally.

The spoils didn't end there.

Rowena had also picked out a collar encrusted with pink diamonds, along with matching chandelier earrings. Trev nearly fainted. Just one of the earrings had to be worth ten times what he had stashed away in his lockbox. He wasn't surprised when Jupiter turned up later in a new suit with a pink tie and glittering cuff links.

There was an entire feast laid out beside the pool, including a hot buffet of Chinese food, a sushi bar, and a hibachi station. The staff were courteous and eager to serve their wares, and Trev could not have imagined a more perfect party.

Yes, most of the guests were criminals—*allegedly*—but hey, that was part of the fun of being part of a mafia family, right?

Rowena kept the party going by personally topping off drinks and shoving food into faces when needed, and she was a sparkling dream of gold in a glimmering gown with a high slit. With a fierce smile and her infectious cackle, she kept the celebration going well into the night.

Jules was there, but he didn't stay long because he had a flight to catch to meet back up with Brick. He promised to catch up with Trev in St. Thomas and gave the weirdly specific advice of not trying to fuck on the master bathroom counter.

From experience?

Probably.

Valdemar gorged himself on sushi until he passed out next to the pool, and Thirdsies, who was apparently his grandson, dedicated most of his time to making out with the redhead, Pym, on a lawn chair.

Roger and Mickey spent most of their time either fighting or making out. Juicy was cleared by Dr. Queen, and after getting patched up, he came down to join the party. Barkie was with him and really liked playing in the pool, according to Juicy.

Jerry and Charlie were there too, and they helped separate Roger and Mickey whenever their arguing got too intense. Thirdsies and Pym didn't have much to contribute other than Pym trying to hide whenever Mickey brought up his name because Roger had apparently slept with him while Mickey was in prison.

Jimmy and Rowena passed out drinks and did their best to keep everyone happy and fed. The way they wrangled everyone reminded Trev of ringmasters at a circus, and it was clear they had done this before.

It was absolute madness, but Trev was actually enjoying himself.

He was happy to stretch out on one of the plush patio chairs with Jupiter at his side. As far as parties went, this was pretty amazing. The food was great, the drinks were strong, and he looked hot as fuck in his new outfit.

As the hours ticked by, Trev wondered where Cold was. He hadn't seen him since they'd gotten home. He scanned the crowd to find Rowena, waving to get her attention. "Hey!"

Rowena had a sway in her hips as she approached. "Hi, sweetie! Everything okay? You get enough to eat?"

"Yeah, and then some." Trev laughed, patting his stomach. "Another bite and I'm pretty sure I'll pop my zipper."

"Aw, are you sure?"

"Yeah, totally. I was just wondering where *Roddy* is at? Is he not coming down for the party?"

"Oh, he's here. He's upstairs." Rowena snorted. "Jimmy said he might come down later, but who the fuck knows."

Trev stood. "I'm gonna go talk to him."

Rowena blinked in surprise. "Seriously? Usually it's best to just let him... you know. *Brood* or whatever he does."

"It won't take long." Trev leaned over to kiss Jupiter.

"Want me to come with you?" Jupiter asked.

"No, it's okay." Trev gave Jupiter's shoulder a squeeze. "I'll be back before you know it. We still gotta pack."

"Pack?" Rowena echoed.

"Yeah, we're leaving tomorrow."

"You mean Monday."

"Uh, no." Trev chuckled. "I agreed to stay for the party, but—"

"Maybe next Monday?" Rowena batted her eyes.

"I'm going to go talk to Cold." Trev wagged his finger at Jupiter. "Do not let her talk you into staying. We have a beach to get to. A beach where I am planning to have a lot of sex with you. But only if we go."

Jupiter's eyes twinkled and he nodded firmly. "You got it, baby doll."

Trev headed inside, and he was not surprised when he glanced back and saw Rowena had swiped his seat to talk to Jupiter.

Whatever.

A few more days might not be so bad.

Trev chuckled to himself as he walked up to Cold's room, expecting to find the door shut so he'd have to knock. He was surprised to find it not only open, but also to hear music playing.

"Cold?" Trev called out as he cautiously walked in.

"In here," Cold replied.

Cold was seated on his ratty couch, looking at the framed photographs on the wall. A record was playing a jazzy cover of a Patsy Cline song, but Trev couldn't remember the name of it. Trev didn't recognize the singer either, but she had a lovely voice.

Trev approached, listening quietly.

Gaze not leaving the photos, Cold nodded toward the record player and said, "My mother."

"Singing? Wow." Trev smiled. "My mom always said she was a great singer."

"She was." Cold took a small sip from his glass. "You're quite talented too."

"*Duh.* But please. Tell me more." Trev sat on the couch next to him.

"You figured out where the bodies were buried, probably days ago. You've been keeping it to yourself, waiting for the right time to play it."

"Yeah. And how long have you known? Since you saw the photographs?"

"Much longer than that." Cold tapped the side of his glass. "I learned many years ago that information is a critical asset to maintaining power. With the right secret, you can bend entire cities to your will without firing a single bullet." He smirked. "Or stabbing someone with a steak knife."

Trev scoffed. "Technically, Juicy did the stabbing. I just provided the knife."

"Still. You took the initiative to arm yourself. You're a survivor, right?" Cold chuckled. "If I recall correctly, you said you were going to survive me."

"Yeah." Trev smiled.

"Do you feel that you have?"

"I don't think you're something I need to survive

anymore." Trev shrugged. "And maybe, heh, just maybe I understand you a little better now. Even the asshole parts."

Cold laughed. "Is that so?"

"You lost a lot. Made you hard. Made you *cold*, no pun intended." Trev shrugged. "You put up walls so nobody can get through. You were right when you said we were a lot alike. But I had my mom. At least for a little while. You only had Boris, who as far as I can tell was actually an absolute fucking monster, so..."

Cold tilted his head, staying quiet while Trev gathered his thoughts.

"I'll never know why my mom decided to keep everything from me. Yeah, I can say it was because she wanted to protect me and keep me out of trouble. She loved me. And I could just as easily say the same thing about you and your mafia shenanigans. You did what you did to protect yourself, but you were also looking out for me. And Juicy. And even Jupiter.

"You didn't have to do all that. Getting the Luchesi fuckers to back off or taking care of Juicy the way you have. You did that because you know they're important to me. Could have done without the murder and the lying and all that extra bullshit. You have a really weird fucking love language, but... thank you."

Cold smiled softly. "You're welcome."

"Are we gonna hug again?"

Cold made a face. "I'd prefer that we didn't."

Trev laughed. "Fine. I didn't want to hug you anyway."

Cold tipped his glass back, emptying it. "I'm sure Rowena would be happy to accept any and all physical affections on my behalf."

"I'm sure she's going to chain both me and Jupiter to the fucking bed so we can never leave."

"That is entirely possible." Cold nodded. "She's very fond of you."

"How about I leave Monday? That'll give us the weekend to hang out and celebrate not being murdered or pretend murdered or any kind of murdered."

"As you wish." Cold rose to turn off the record player. "I'll make the arrangements."

"Thank you. We've come quite a ways from me stealing your silverware and trying to escape, huh?"

"That we have." Cold picked up his empty glass to refill it.

"So." Trev fidgeted. "What's gonna happen with Champignon? You think he's gonna be pissed you just cut him off from his Luchesi buddies?"

"Mm, we haven't come *that* far," Cold scolded lightly.

"What? No discussing your top secret mafia plans?"

"No."

"Maybe I could help." Trev grinned. "I am pretty smart, you know."

"That you are, but you don't really want to be involved. You have your heart set on a future with a sandy beach, as I recall." Cold took a small sip of his drink. "Plus, you still have a prisoner to attend to. Or has he been upgraded from prisoner yet?"

Trev smiled warmly. "Yeah, I'm working on that. Never been real great at relationships, but I am going to try. He deserves that, you know? He's worth it."

Cold nodded. "I understand."

"Was it like that for you and Jimmy?"

"In the sense that yes, it made me want to make an effort that I hadn't before." Cold glanced down at his glass. "I didn't have relationships. I had transactions. Simple, brief, efficient. Jimmy..." He smiled. "Well, there was nothing *simple* about him, and I found myself not wanting our time together to end. That was when I knew."

"That you loved him?"

"And that it was possible for someone like him to care about someone like me." Cold raised his glass. "As you've so eloquently stated on multiple occasions, I am quite the asshole."

"No fuckin' shit."

Cold snorted. "And as always, your vocabulary is a *delight*."

"Thanks. I *am* a delight." Trev grinned as he stood up. "Are you going to come down for the party?"

"No." Cold stepped back toward the couch. "But please. Go. Enjoy yourself. And let me know when you'd like to leave."

"That depends on our sister." Trev laughed. "If she had it her way, we might never leave."

"Our sister," Cold repeated. "Hmmph."

"Sounds funny, doesn't it?"

"Indeed." Cold smiled, that rare smile that relaxed his face and softened every line. "But I'm starting not to mind it so much."

"Are you sure we're not gonna hug again?"

Cold's smile dropped. "Please no."

Trev chuckled and offered out his hand. "How about a nice, friendly handshake?"

Cold rolled his eyes, but he shook Trev's hand. "Have a good night, Trev."

"You too, Rod." Trev left with a warm smile and a spring in his step.

The conversation had gone better than he thought, and it paved over some of the friction lingering between them. He did truly feel as if he understood Cold better now, though that didn't do much to help Cold's lacking personality.

Cold was still an asshole.

But he was Trev's brother.

And he really didn't mind the asshole part as much now.

Trev strolled toward the stairs, but he paused when he saw Jupiter coming up them. "Hey!"

"Hey!" Jupiter smiled. "I was coming to look for you."

"Sorry. The quick chat took a bit longer than I thought it would." Trev kissed Jupiter. "How's the party?"

"I'm pretty convinced that Rowena is going to tie us up and never let us leave."

"You know, I said almost the same thing to Cold just a minute ago." Trev laughed. "How long is she wanting us to stay? A month? A year?"

Jupiter chuckled. "I told her we might consider staying until Monday, but I had to talk to you first."

"Yeah, I figured." Trev smiled as Jupiter's arm wrapped around his waist.

Music filtered in from Cold's room, something light and jazzy. It was faint, but Trev was pretty sure it was Suzanne singing again.

Jupiter took Trev's hand, slowly swaying them to the beat.

"What are you doing?" Trev laughed.

"What does it look like, baby doll?"

"Like you're dancing with me in the middle of the hallway like a crazy person."

"What's so crazy?" Jupiter smiled. "We got music. We got room to move. You got that beautiful dress on."

Trev squeezed Jupiter's hand and draped his other arm around his shoulders. "Yeah? Keep talking."

"And you look absolutely stunning." Jupiter pressed

their foreheads together as he gently led them around in a lazy circle. "I love you in a dress."

"Oh? Do you?"

"Uh-huh. I've been staring at your legs all night, baby doll."

"Thinking about having them wrapped around you?" Trev teased.

"Over my shoulders," Jupiter replied with a little wink, dipping Trev back.

Trev laughed in delight. "Look at you! You can dance."

"I'm a man of many talents." Jupiter grinned as he swung Trev back into his arms.

"Yeah? I know one of them for sure." Trev wagged his eyebrows playfully.

Jupiter smiled and kissed him. "Plenty more where that came from."

"Later." Trev wrapped his arms around Jupiter's neck.

"Later? Really?" Jupiter laughed. "Has my insatiable baby doll been replaced by a pod person? Did aliens abduct you?"

"Shut up," Trev griped. "I'm just... enjoying this. We don't have to take our clothes off to have a good time, all right? And honestly, after this fucking crazy ass day, this is exactly what I want."

Jupiter chuckled. "No complaints from me."

"Good." Trev leaned his head on Jupiter's shoulder. "Because I wouldn't listen anyway."

Jupiter laughed again, but he didn't say anything else as they danced. It was slow and intimate, and Trev's heart soon thumped with a new emotion he wasn't ready to define yet. The feeling was powerful, overwhelming in a way that stole his breath and made his pulse continue to climb.

But he wasn't afraid.

Not anymore.

"Should we go back downstairs?" Trev murmured. "I'm sure Rowena is gonna be looking for us."

"It's up to you, baby doll." Jupiter pressed a kiss to his brow. "It's your party."

"Mmm, there might be some egg rolls calling my name."

"Well, then you need to answer 'em." Jupiter chuckled and gave Trev's hips a squeeze. "Do you want to get some to go?"

"Go? Go where?"

"Get some plates to go and come upstairs so we can have a little party of our own. Just me and you." Jupiter smiled sweetly. "What do you say?"

"I'd say I think that's the best idea you've ever had."

"Really? I thought it was chaining you to the wall."

"Ha ha." Trev rolled his eyes.

Jupiter gently hooked a finger under Trev's collar, urging him in close. "Pretty sure it's gotta be in my top three at least."

Trev smiled. "Nope. Not even close."

"Oh? Are you making a list?"

"And checking it twice," Trev teased.

"Are you gonna tell me? Or do I have to live in suspense?"

Trev's heart thumped, and he smiled, glancing over Jupiter's lips. "I'll tell you later. When I feel like it." He kissed him.

Jupiter kissed him back passionately, holding him tight.

It was easy to get lost in Jupiter's embrace, and Trev eagerly twisted his fingers around Jupiter's ponytail to give it a playful tug. No one had ever been able to get him worked up with just a kiss, and no other person's arms had felt like home before.

Trev couldn't help but remember what Cold had said the other night about Jupiter's feelings for him. There had been other men in Trev's life who'd claimed to love him in a laughably short amount of time, but Jupiter wasn't like them.

Jupiter respected him like no other partner had, never treated him like a dainty flower, and had gone above and beyond to be with him. He'd proven that he cared about Trev very much, even if he hadn't said those three little words.

There was a part of Trev that almost wished Jupiter would because he was pretty sure he was also starting to fall—

"Hey!" Rowena shouted. "You're missing the *Mean Girls* singalong!"

"Oh, hey." Trev broke away from Jupiter with a laugh. "Sorry. We got a little distracted."

"Come on!" Rowena was already halfway up the stairs to continue scolding them. "You guys can make out later! I just made a fresh pitcher of margaritas with your name on them. Let's go!"

"On our way." Jupiter gave her a dutiful salute. He took Trev's hand to kiss it, smiling warmly. "So, *Mean Girls* singalong, margaritas, and then we grab some dinner to go?"

"Yeah." Trev beamed. "Sounds like a pretty perfect way to wrap up the party."

"I think so." Jupiter kept a hold of Trev's hand as they followed Rowena down the stairs. "Of course, there will be dessert too."

Trev shivered. "Oh?"

"Oh, absolutely." Jupiter glanced over Trev with a hungry little growl. "I love that dress on you, but I'm going to love it even more off of you."

Trev grinned. "All of this is going to look fantastic on the floor."

"Hmm. Even the collar?"

"No. That's definitely staying on."

"God, you're perfect, baby doll."

"Oh, trust me. I know."

CHAPTER Twenty-Five

THE VILLA IN ST. Thomas was just as beautiful as Trev thought it would be and more.

It was right on the beach, with more bedrooms than any sane person could ever need, and the view of Magen's Bay was incredible. The water was clear, the breeze warm, and Trev was totally enchanted by the white sand and lush groves of palm trees. There were several restaurants within walking distance, including a boutique ice cream place Jules and Brick recommended for them to try.

Trev had never tried matcha ice cream before, or any ice cream in a pastry shaped like a fish, but he was instantly a fan.

It was absolute paradise.

And yet, Trev was soon feeling the itch to leave after only a few weeks.

He had no purpose. He had no job. He had nothing to do.

Well, other than Jupiter of course.

Whom he did often and well until they were both exhausted and breathless.

Incredible sex aside though, Trev found that he was restless with nothing to occupy his time. He thought it might be because he'd spent so much of his life struggling and constantly planning his next move that his brain didn't know what to do with a vacation.

His brain clearly did not like it.

Trev kept in touch with Rowena and Jimmy with his new phone, and they chatted and exchanged pictures daily. He messaged Cold too, but the most he ever got in reply was a thumbs-up emoji. Trev called sometimes, and he would get the pleasure of hearing Cold grunt at him in greeting before he'd pass the phone immediately back to Rowena or Jimmy. He'd never pick up if Trev called him directly, but that was all right.

Trev knew Cold cared in his own way and that was enough for him.

He didn't hear another peep about the Luchesi family other than Rowena gossiping that the council had dissolved and the entire family was now crumbling. Trev wondered if that FBI guy had anything to do with it, but he decided it was none of his business. Cold had been right that he didn't want anything to do with the mafia crap.

The real problem was that Trev didn't know *what* he wanted.

He still had his life savings tucked away in the lockbox and no idea what he should spend it on. Cold had said they were welcome to stay at the villa for as long as they'd like, but Trev didn't want to be a mooch. Making his own way was important to him, but he hadn't been able to come up with a new plan yet.

Getting out of Perry City had been his dream, and now that he had done it...

What the crap was he supposed to do next?

Evening was setting in and the sun was dropping, turning the blue sky into a brilliant kaleidoscope of oranges and pinks and reds. Trev watched it from the beach, the waves lapping over his bare feet. He was wearing a glittery hot pink Speedo with a matching sarong tied around his hips, trying to soak up the dwindling rays of sunlight.

With a cold beer in his hand and the lingering warmth of the day on his skin, Trev closed his eyes.

He heard Jupiter approaching, the telltale smack of his flipflops giving him away.

"Hi, babe," Trev said without opening his eyes.

"Hey, baby doll." Jupiter hugged him from behind and kissed his shoulder. "What are you still doing out here? Thought you were coming inside."

"I am." Trev leaned against Jupiter. "Just... thinking."

"Yeah? What about?"

Trev sighed. "Everything."

"Can't get that beautiful brain to turn off, huh?" Jupiter chuckled knowingly.

"Nope. Sure can't. I worked so hard for so fucking long to be able to earn something just like this for myself. A view like this, sand in between my damn toes, and..." Trev shrugged. "I don't know."

"Some people aren't made to sit still, baby doll."

"What about you, hmm?" Trev squeezed Jupiter's forearm.

"Me?"

"Would you be happy if we stayed here forever?"

"I've got everything I could ever want here. But." Jupiter kissed Trev's shoulder again. "If you're not happy, we can go somewhere else. Do something else. Whatever you want."

Trev leaned his head back against Jupiter's chest, frowning. "But what if I don't know?"

"Well, then we just have to figure it out."

"Just like that?"

"Yeah, baby doll." Jupiter kissed Trev's brow. "You could be a dancer. You could open up your own business."

Trev snorted out a laugh. "What kind of fucking business would I even have? You know I never got my GED, right?"

"Good thing we got some time. You can finish that online anywhere."

Trev shrugged. "Okay, but what about after that?"

"We can do anything you want."

"I wanted to be a movie star when I was a kid." Trev snorted. "You think you can make that happen?"

"Might take me a little while, but I'll see what I can do. In the meantime…" Jupiter grabbed Trev and turned him around.

Trev blinked. "What—"

Jupiter slung Trev over his shoulder. "Come here!"

"Hey!" Trev laughed. "What are you doing? Put me down!"

"Nope." Jupiter made a beeline for the house. "I'm planning to write a movie for you. It's gonna be about this really hot guy who gets laid down at the beach…"

"Oh my God, that sounds like a porn! And I'm still *covered* in sand!" Trev kicked his feet. "Come on. At least stop at the shower so I can rinse off."

"If you insist." Jupiter laughed as he carried Trev over to the shower station. It was a small tiled enclosure that pumped in water directly from the ocean. He turned it on, still holding Trev over his shoulder and bending down to rinse him off.

"Hey!" Trev squirmed as the water ran all over him. "What are you doing?"

"Getting rid of the sand!"

"Put me down! Oh my God, you're getting soaked, you idiot!"

Jupiter grinned as he dropped Trev down and pinned him against the tile. "Oh, like this?"

Trev forgot how to breathe, blinking up at Jupiter with a soft groan. "Yeah. Like this is good."

Jupiter smiled and kissed him, firmly holding him in place.

Trev slid his hands up Jupiter's broad chest, dragging his fingers over the wet material of his shirt clinging to his pecs. He squeezed them greedily as they kissed, licking hungrily into Jupiter's mouth.

Jupiter grabbed Trev's sides and tilted forward, connecting their hips.

Trev groaned, rubbing himself shamelessly against Jupiter's hard bulge. He angled his body until his cock slotted alongside Jupiter's, and he reached up to grab a firm handful of Jupiter's long hair. He was so caught up in the moment that he barely noticed the water still streaming over them.

His sarong hit the floor of the shower with a wet smack and then he gasped as Jupiter lifted him up against the tile. He wrapped his legs around Jupiter and hugged his neck tight, kissing him eagerly.

The future wasn't an endless void with Jupiter holding him like this—it held the promise of limitless potential and even hope, and Trev realized then it didn't matter what he chose to do with his life.

Not as long as he had Jupiter by his side.

Trev clawed at Jupiter's shirt and bucked his hips down. "I want you. Right now."

"I'm yours." Jupiter squeezed Trev close. "Bedroom?"

"Yup." Trev grinned as he wiggled out of Jupiter's embrace. He left the sarong where it was and strolled back up to the house, pausing only to slip out of his bathing suit. He knew Jupiter was still turning the water off to the shower because he could hear the squeak of the faucet, so he tossed his bathing suit over his shoulder in that general direction.

"Hey!" There was a pause and Jupiter's voice dropped low to purr, "Mm, baby doll."

Trev continued his leisurely strut, smirking as Jupiter jogged up behind him. "Yes, babe?"

Jupiter growled and grabbed Trev, sweeping him up in his arms.

Trev laughed, absolutely delighted because one, he really did love how Jupiter could haul him around like nothing, and two, Jupiter had also stripped in record time and was totally naked. "Wow, that was fast."

"I was feeling very motivated." Jupiter kissed him sweetly.

Trev laughed as they kissed, soon breathless and panting from the rising passion. He was only aware they had entered the house because the cool air chilled his damp skin. He grunted as Jupiter dropped him into bed and he immediately flailed, pulling the blankets over him. "Fuck! It's cold!"

Jupiter laughed and snuggled on top of him. "Aw, do you need me to warm you back up, baby doll?"

"Yes. Right now. Preferably with your dick."

"I'll see what I can do." Jupiter glanced at the bedside table. "Do you...?"

Trev didn't have to look to know what Jupiter was asking. He smiled. "Yes."

Jupiter reached over to grab Trev's collar.

Trev had several now—including the insane diamond

one that Rowena had insisted he keep because she was nuts—but his favorite was still the first leather one Jupiter had given to him.

Maybe he was a touch sentimental.

Trev closed his eyes as Jupiter gently buckled the collar around his neck. The leather was soft, familiar, and even reassuring somehow. What had once bound him was now liberating, and he smiled up at Jupiter, peering at him through his lashes. "Mm, that's better."

"Do you miss it, baby doll?" Jupiter traced his fingers along the collar.

"No, never." Trev grinned.

"Brat." Jupiter whipped the blankets off Trev in one quick pull.

"Ah! You bastard!" Trev wiggled in protest, his naked body again exposed to the cool air.

"Yes, but also, yes." Jupiter chuckled as he kissed down Trev's chest and flicked his tongue out over Trev's nipple.

Trev shuddered and tried to relax, his breaths catching in his throat as Jupiter sucked his nipple into his mouth. It was a pleasant sensation, warming even, and he dragged his fingers through Jupiter's hair with a soft sigh. "That's better."

Jupiter pulled off with a little pop and then switched to the other nipple to give it the same attention plus a little bite.

Trev's cock stirred back to life, only having briefly wilted from the cold. It was easy to get going again with Jupiter getting him so worked up.

Jupiter's lips teased their way down Trev's stomach and very pointedly avoided his dick. He mouthed along the crease of Trev's groin, his tongue flicking downward to catch the underside of his balls.

Trev inhaled sharply.

"Mm?" Jupiter looked up at him. "You like that, baby doll?"

"I'd like it a lot better if you actually put your tongue where I want it."

Jupiter chuckled. He licked down Trev's taint and then back up to his balls. He sucked each one gently, his hands moving to spread Trev's thighs wide as he swirled his tongue. He pulled off with a little growl and spat on them so he could greedily slurp them back into his mouth.

The extra spit made the slide of Jupiter's lips so slick that Trev moaned, certain that Jupiter was about to suck his entire sack down. He could feel Jupiter's saliva dripping down the crack of his ass as he continued to suck on his balls, and he pulled frantically at Jupiter's hair.

His cock throbbed with its pulse, and precome bubbled up at his slit. He wanted Jupiter's mouth *there* on his dick. He needed more of something, *anything*, and he rolled his hips with a short, impatient whine.

Jupiter pulled off with a wet slurp. He pushed Trev's hips up and forward to spit right on his hole. He used his tongue to spread it and then licked eagerly around his pucker.

"God, yeah," Trev whispered, reaching down to grab behind his knees to keep himself posed. "Fuckin' eat it, baby."

Jupiter pushed around Trev's hole with his thumb, massaging lightly before pressing in the tip.

Trev loved the faint burn, just a tease of the real stretch to come, but he was impatient. He wanted more. "Mmm, come on. Open me up."

Jupiter grunted and continued his slow pace, licking at Trev's hole like they had all the time in the world. He pressed his thumb in a little deeper but offered no other stimulation.

"Come on!" Trev growled, squirming. "Please, baby. I want you to fuck me. Right now." He pulled at Jupiter's hair. "Hey, you. Down there. Let's go."

Jupiter snorted. "Oh, is that how you wanna be?"

"I wanna be fucked into a coma. That's how I wanna be."

Jupiter pushed himself up on his knees and wiped off his mouth. "I think your mouth needs to do something other than complain."

Trev grinned. "Is that so?"

"Yeah. Should really put a leash on that thing."

"A leash, huh?" Trev grinned.

Jupiter raised his brow. "What? Is that a *hey, go grab a leash*?"

"Do we have a leash to grab?"

"I mean..." Jupiter glanced at the door. "Barkie has a leash."

"That is a terrible and wonderful idea." Trev cackled. "He keeps it by the door, so..."

Jupiter smiled wickedly and slid out of bed.

"You know he'll come looking for it," Trev warned.

"Nah, we got time." Jupiter was already on his feet and running out of the bedroom.

"I'll remember you said that!"

Jupiter returned a few moments later with the leash, still grinning away as he shut the door behind him. He slid into bed and kneeled, beckoning Trev over. "Come here, baby doll. Hands and knees for me."

Trev rolled over so he could crawl toward Jupiter. He made a big show of swinging his hips and arching his back, smiling sweetly up at Jupiter. "You mean like this?"

"Just like that." Jupiter cupped his cheek and clicked the leash on. "There. This okay?"

"Fine." Trev nodded. "I promise. It's all good." He lifted

his head to pull the leash taut. "So, you wanted me to do something with my mouth, right? It was keep talking, wasn't it?"

Jupiter chuckled and grabbed the base of his cock, stroking himself toward Trev's mouth. "Nope. Pretty sure it was this."

Trev stuck out his tongue to lick over Jupiter's slit. "Mm, I guess."

Jupiter wound the leash around his hand. "Go on, baby doll. Get yourself some of that."

Trev groaned, the tension in the leash pulling the collar against his neck. It wasn't hard enough to restrict his breathing, but it was thrilling all the same. He let Jupiter direct him down to his dick and he opened his mouth wide.

Jupiter pushed inside. "There you go, baby doll. Suck me good."

Trev ran his tongue up and down the sides of Jupiter's cock to get it wet so when he wrapped his lips around it, he could easily take him deep. He sucked hungrily and licked the underside as he bobbed his head.

He looked up at Jupiter, watching how his lips parted with a soft gasp. He kept sucking until Jupiter hit the back of his throat. He relaxed so he could press farther still, relishing in the breathless groans he could draw out of Jupiter.

More.

God, yes—he wanted more.

Trev was the best there was and he wanted to make sure Jupiter didn't ever forget.

He worked every inch, turning his head this way and that even as spit ran down his chin. He moaned when Jupiter yanked on the leash, urging him to go faster. He sucked in earnest and had to close his eyes to fight the tears welling up in his eyes.

He wouldn't gag.

He was too fucking good for that.

Jupiter had the leash, but Trev still felt in control. He was the one choosing to give Jupiter this pleasure and he could stop whenever he wanted to.

But why would he?

When Jupiter was grunting and moaning so sweetly for him and losing himself in every slam of his cock down Trev's tight throat?

"Fuck." Jupiter hissed, tugging at the leash. "Mm, that's enough, baby doll."

Trev gave one hard suck before popping off. He licked around his mouth to catch some of the spit, trying to catch his breath. "What's wrong, baby? Huh?" He grinned. "You were about to come, weren't you?"

"Your mouth is fucking flawless," Jupiter said. "Nobody can suck a dick like you, baby doll. You're so perfect."

"I know." Trev smiled warmly, even as the praise flushed his cheeks.

"Go on. Turn around." Jupiter slid his thumb over Trev's bottom lip.

Trev sucked on Jupiter's thumb. "Mm?"

"Turn around for me. Let me see that perfect ass of yours."

Trev let go of Jupiter's thumb so he could move as directed. He put his head down into the bed and lifted his ass up. "Gonna eat me out again?"

"Nope. We're gonna open your ass up on my cock, baby doll." Jupiter picked up a bottle of lube from the bedside table. "You're gonna have to go nice and slow."

"Mmm, *bastard*." Trev clenched his fingers in the sheets.

"Think I need to get you a gag next," Jupiter teased as he drizzled the lube directly onto Trev's asshole.

"Hey! Fuck!" Trev grunted. "That's cold!"

"Oh? Is it?" Jupiter smeared the lube against Trev's hole and then dipped a finger inside of him. "How is that?"

"Mm, you... *ass*..." Trev closed his eyes and spread his legs to ease the faint ache. "Please."

Jupiter lightly pulled at the leash. "Please, what?"

"Give me your cock."

"If you want it, you're gonna have to take it yourself, baby doll." Jupiter only leaned close enough for the head of his cock to brush against Trev's ass. "Is this it? Hmm? Is this what you want?"

"Yes." Trev immediately thrust back. "Come on."

"Easy now." Jupiter grabbed Trev's hips to stall him. "Easy before you—"

"You said we're opening me up on your cock, so give it to me," Trev demanded as he tried to spear himself on the head of Jupiter's dick. "Now!"

Jupiter didn't move. "Take what you want, baby doll." He let the leash go slack. "This is your show now. Show me what you can do."

Trev shifted his hands and then rolled his hips, making sure that Jupiter's cock was seated before slamming himself back. The resistance was immediate and he groaned, thrusting with more force to make himself take more. He wanted Jupiter inside of him and he wanted him now.

He tried again to fuck himself on Jupiter's cock and fought against the intense stretch. It burned but he knew he could do it. He gritted his teeth, working back and forth in shorter bursts to get his body to open up.

God...

Fuck.

He kept going, determined as ever, and he sank down a bit farther.

He could do this.

He was the fucking best.

He was...

Fuck, that was a lot of dick.

The leash tightened and Trev couldn't shift forward. "Mmmph, hey," he mumbled in protest. "What?"

"Easy, baby doll," Jupiter said sternly. "Do I need to tie you up to make sure you don't hurt yourself?"

"I've got it," Trev snapped back. "I'm fine."

"Yes, you are," Jupiter said, his tone both soothing and firm. "I'm yours, baby doll. Okay? I'm all yours." Even as the leash wound tight, he still said, "You're such a good boy and I'm yours."

Trev took a deep breath and let himself melt. He stopped clawing at the sheets, unclenching his hands. He wasn't even sure when he'd grabbed them so tightly, and he let Jupiter's voice ease the lingering tension in his body.

Yes, he was good.

He was so *good*.

And Jupiter was all his.

The control was only an illusion because Jupiter didn't own Trev any more than Trev owned him. They were each other's, equally, and that...

That was *everything*.

When Trev moved again, the slide was effortless. He didn't stop until his ass was flush with Jupiter's hips and his insides throbbed from the fullness of Jupiter's cock.

Everything was Jupiter.

Trev breathed in.

The ache, the pulse, the very smell of their sweat mingling.

Trev breathed out.

Jupiter's hands on his hips, the creak of the leash as he pulled it.

Trev tipped his head back and groaned, letting Jupiter's cock move in and out of his body in leisurely thrusts. It was slow, a patient drag that sent shivers cascading from his core to the ends of his fingers and buzzing through his lips. The waves of sensation surged to new heights when Jupiter slammed forward, driving his cock in hard and forcing a cry from the back of Trev's throat.

"There we go, baby doll," Jupiter crooned. "Ready for me now, aren't you? Ready for this cock?"

"Yes, fuck. *Yes.*" Trev surrendered to Jupiter's thrusts, arching up for each one and moaning out his pleasure. The tension on the leash kept his head back and his spine curled, making every connection of their bodies devastatingly hot. He could feel the need for relief, the urge to find release from this sweet torture, but not yet.

No, no, he wasn't done yet.

Trev pushed forward until Jupiter's cock slipped out of him.

"Trev?" Jupiter questioned worriedly.

Trev flipped onto his back and snatched the leash from Jupiter's hand. He used his legs to drag Jupiter within reach, looping the leash around the back of Jupiter's neck. He pulled on the handle to draw him in even closer and press their lips together in a searing kiss.

Jupiter groaned excitedly, tilting his hips forward as he sought to reconnect with Trev once more. He licked into his mouth, sparing a hand to line himself up so he could push back inside, growling low. "*Baby doll.*"

Trev held the leash tight to keep Jupiter's lips against his own, gasping sharply when Jupiter fucked him hard. The new friction was blisteringly hot and the closeness divine. Trev had drawn the leash so taut that when he pulled it, it pulled at his collar too.

His desperation to keep Jupiter close brought Trev's upper body off the bed, and he slung his other arm around Jupiter's shoulders, yowling as Jupiter pounded him even faster. The relentless plowing made Trev moan in delight, his legs falling apart to open himself even wider for Jupiter's cock.

Jupiter grabbed Trev's shoulders to pull him into his thrusts, panting as he glanced down between their bodies to watch his cock as he fucked Trev toward what was sure to be a spectacular end.

"Hey!" Trev gritted his teeth, curling his fingers around the leash. "Eyes on me, baby."

Jupiter looked up and met Trev's gaze, his own gaze lust addled and dark. "Mmm, baby doll."

"I want you looking at me when you come." Trev panted frantically. "Come on. Fuck. Give it to me. Give it to me—"

Jupiter smothered his cries with a deep kiss, keeping up the fantastic rhythm and not stuttering even when he reached down to grab Trev's cock.

Trev bucked into Jupiter's firm grip and he gasped as he was instantly overwhelmed. His pulse thundered in his ears, heat flashed over his neck and face and then throbbed in his balls and his cock as he came. It was a fast and intense pulse that left him sobbing and his eyes fogged over as he jerked against Jupiter, blinking rapidly to get his vision to focus.

Jupiter was coming too, his face pinched in bliss and mouth soft as he groaned. His eyes were glassy, but they never left Trev's—not for a second.

Trev's stomach dipped like he was falling and he gasped desperately, certain he was going to pass out. His skin was tingling, a dazzling buzz to complement the hot throb between his legs, and he gasped for breath, wheezing, "Wow."

"Wow," Jupiter echoed, equally labored.

Trev dragged the leash off Jupiter's neck, rubbing his hand there. "Are you all right? I didn't hurt you, did I?"

"No, promise." Jupiter unhooked the leash from Trev's neck so he could toss it behind them on the bed. He touched Trev's throat and traced the edge of his collar. "You okay, baby doll?"

"Fuck yeah. I am so okay." Trev laughed giddily. "We're gonna have to add that to your list of great ideas."

"Yeah?" Jupiter grinned and kissed him sweetly. "Did that make the top three?"

"It's in a very solid spot at number four." Trev grunted as Jupiter pulled out. "Still didn't win out over growing out that sexy beard or at the party when we took all that Chinese food upstairs."

"That's only two." Jupiter stretched out beside him and grinned. "What's the third one?"

Trev's pulse fluttered. "Falling in love with me."

Jupiter's eyes widened in surprise and then his expression softened. "Yeah? Did I now?"

"Yeah, you sure did." Trev smiled shyly, swallowing hard to push his heart out of his throat. "It was so good I decided to have the same idea and fall in love with you too."

Jupiter kissed him.

And he *kissed* him.

He pressed his lips to Trev's and held him tight, pulling him against his chest. He clung to Trev as if he thought he might evaporate and dragged his hands all over his body, like he wanted to make sure that Trev was really here.

Trev embraced him with equal fervor, and his eyes stung

as warmth boiled over in his chest and made him gasp. "Oh, Jupiter. I love you."

"I love you," Jupiter whispered urgently, an unusual tremble in his voice. "I love you so much, baby doll."

Trev laughed and wiped at his eyes. "Holy shit."

Jupiter smiled. "Yeah. Holy shit."

"Well, I hope you know this fuckin' means you're really never getting rid of me now."

"Wasn't planning to." Jupiter kissed him sweetly.

Trev hugged Jupiter's neck and kissed him back passionately. He moaned softly as Jupiter laid him back down on the bed. He lazily wrapped his legs around Jupiter's hips, enjoying the slow grind of their bodies as the heat between them cranked back up until another round seemed imminent.

The door opened.

"Hi, guys!" Juicy greeted cheerfully.

Jupiter scrambled to cover them up with the blanket, sighing. "Hey."

"Hey there, Juicy," Trev said with a grin, not nearly as bashful as Jupiter. "How are you doing?"

"Great! Just great!" Juicy beamed. "I was going to take Barkie for a walk before my nurse gets here to give me my nighttime meds, but I can't seem to find his leash."

Trev batted his eyes at Jupiter.

"Right. Got it right here." Jupiter groaned as he retrieved the leash from the foot of the bed. "Sorry. We, uh—"

"We borrowed it for weird sex stuff," Trev said, grinning shamelessly.

"Oh, that's all right." Juicy seemed to finally become aware that he might have interrupted something, and he frowned. "I'm sorry. Did I wake you guys up?"

"No, it's okay. We were just hanging out."

Juicy glanced at the leash. "Huh. Oh! Do you guys have a dog too?"

"Yes," Jupiter said immediately. "Yes, we do."

"Did you not hear what I just said about weird sex stuff?" Trev lamented.

"Huh." Juicy's brow furrowed. "That's a weird name for a dog." He smiled again and waved. "See you guys later!" He patted his leg as he left, calling out, "Come here, boy! Aw, there you are, Barkie. That's a good boy! Let's go for a walkie..."

Jupiter flopped back against the bed with a groan. "He didn't shut the door."

"I think he's already seen everything," Trev teased. "Not really a big deal."

Jupiter groaned again. "So says you." He eyed Trev. "You really are shameless, you know that?"

"Hey, it's just one more reason to love me." Trev beamed.

"That it is." Jupiter grinned. "One out of a thousand hundred million."

"Oh? That's all?"

"Give me some time. I'm sure I'll come up with some more."

"Well." Trev pretended to think. "I do intend to be with you forever, so I guess I can allow that."

Jupiter chuckled and grabbed Trev's collar, tugging him into a sweet kiss.

"Mm. I love you, Jupiter."

"And I love you, baby doll."

About the Author

K.L. "Kat" Hiers is an embalmer, restorative artist, and queer writer. Licensed in both funeral directing and funeral service, they worked in the death industry for nearly a decade. Their first love was always telling stories, and they have been writing for over twenty years, penning their very first book at just eight years old. Publishers generally do not accept manuscripts in Hello Kitty notebooks, however, but they never gave up.

Following the success of their first novel, *Cold Hard Cash*, they now enjoy writing professionally, focusing on spinning tales of sultry passion, exotic worlds, and emotional journeys. They love attending horror movie conventions and indulging in cosplay of their favorite characters. They live in Zebulon, NC, with their family, including their children, some of whom have paws and a few that only pretend to because they think it's cute.

Visit Kat's Website

Also by K.L. Hiers

NOVELLAS

Playing For Keeps

Tastes Like Christmas

Shoulda Swiped Left

Here Comes Santer Claus

NOVELS

La Famiglia Mostro

Werewolves Hate Clogs

Cold Hard Cash

Cold Hard Cash

Hard Earned Cash

CHC: The Collection

Strapped For Cash

A Quick Buck

Ready To Cash Out

Sucker For Love Mysteries

Acsquidentally In Love

Kraken My Heart

Head Over Tentacles

Nautilus Than Perfect

Just Calamarried

Our Shellfish Desires

An Inkredible Love

Love You Always, Suckers And All

Ollie's Octrageously Official Omnibus

Days of Monsters

8 Days of Monstrous Pride

13 Days of Monster F#cking: Volume 1

WITH MOZZARUS SCOUT

13 Days of Monster F#cking: Volume 2

13 Days of Monster F#cking: Volume 3

13 Days of Monsters Making Love: Volume 1

13 Days of Monsters Making Love: Volume 2

ALSO BY K.L. HIERS & MOZZARUS SCOUT

Ruthless Daddies: Beast

A Slice For My Demon

Made in the USA
Columbia, SC
23 October 2024

44581486R00246